SCARRED WARRIOR

DARK WARRIOR ALLIANCE, BOOK 7

BRENDA TRIM
TAMI JULKA

During the course of writing this book we experienced many challenges, including great loss, which left permanent scars. This book is for every individual who carries marks from the journey of life. Scars are beautiful so wear them proudly because it means you were stronger than whatever tried to hurt you.

CHAPTER 1

G errick paced another circuit through the warriors milling around, anxious as hell to get the show on the road. "I say we go in guns blazing, right now. And, I know we don't use guns, Mack, so don't go being a smart ass," he snarled at the female who hadn't actually said anything. His muscles twitched in his arms and he reached for his weapons. Adrenaline dumped into his system, making his heart race.

Mack, Prince Kyran's Fated Mate, threw up her hands. "Don't pick on me, Oscar the Grouch. I'm ready to get in there, too. I'm the one who found them, remember?"

Before Mack mated Kyran and became an intricate part of their group, she stumbled upon the archdemon's lair and discovered where he was holding several females prisoner. Gerrick and his fellow warriors had been searching ceaselessly, night and day for the location of the missing females, but were unsuccessful. It had been a source of frustration for him that he hadn't been able to protect the females from harm. It was his duty as a Dark Warrior to protect the innocent from the demons and their minions.

Zander placed his hand on Gerrick's shoulder, stopping him mid-stride. "Patience. We canna go in without setting up the barriers. Pema, Isis and Suvi are doing their part now and you and Jace are up next. Focus on that."

Gerrick took a deep breath, knowing the Vampire King was right, but it was difficult when his blood was calling for him to take action. It was a painful compulsion that was impossible to ignore, but there was no mistaking the command in Zander's tone. Gerrick took several more deep breaths, trying to settle his anxiousness and concentrate on what he needed to do next.

Gerrick paused next to Jace and pulled his staff out of its magical pocket of space in the Goddess' realm. Immediately, he felt the additional power surge through his limbs. The seven-foot, gnarled, basswood pole was given to him by his father when he became an adult and his thumb went unerringly to the small silver pendant wrapped around the leather grip. Sorrow and rage spiked, making it difficult to focus. Not willing to let himself get mired in the past, he checked his surroundings in the dark parking lot.

Gerrick wasn't comfortable with the number of humans in the area. They were about to stir the hornet's nest and he didn't want innocent bystanders harmed because they happened to be in the wrong place at the wrong time. It went against his warrior's oath, but there was nothing they could do about it since Kadir had set up shop in the middle of downtown Seattle.

He glanced around the corner of the brick building and braced himself against the bitter wind and chilling rain. He watched a human male hurry from a shop and make his way in their direction. Gerrick quickly muttered a spell, sending the male into a nearby coffee chop, or at least, Gerrick thought it was a coffee shop. The old-fashioned architecture and brickwork of the businesses in Pioneer Square were all so similar it was hard to tell them apart. He shrugged figuring the human was safe enough.

"This is a much bigger area than we have ever covered before, Zander," Pema piped up a few seconds later. "There are so many exits to consider. I'm not sure we can do this." Gerrick turned around and saw that the witch triplets were holding hands and each of their mates was touching their shoulders. He watched the vibrant pinks and red lights of their magic swirl around their bodies. To his sensitive sorcerer's vision it was bright, almost blinding.

He had faith the witches could manage to spell. After all, the freshly-crowned High Priestesses were by far the most powerful witches in the Tehrex Realm and were the most recent additions to the Dark Alliance Council.

Zander caught his attention as he slid his *sgian dubh* into the sheath around his waist. Zander's presence was vast and it had nothing to do with the fact that he was a king. It was his inherent power and confidence. Gerrick was surrounded by the most powerful men in the realm, but none of them held a candle to Zander. The thing that made him so extraordinary was that he shared this power and confidence with those around him. "I know this is a large area and 'tis going to be impossible to include all possible exits. Cover as many as you can, but leave the ones that lead to the water open. The water will help hem them in. The goal is to keep the demons from fleeing, but, first and foremost, we canna allow feral skirm to get out and attack humans."

Music blared into the night as the door to a bar on Yesler Street opened and several humans stumbled out. Collectively, the group of supernaturals tensed, and no one uttered a word.

"It would be nice if you had the power to order everyone

out of the area, Zander," Gerrick mumbled. He took a deep breath to calm his nerves and took in a lungful of acrid urine with a backdrop of briny sea. It was enough to make him gag and nearly lose his dinner.

"You guys are overthinking this," Mack piped up. "It's two a.m. and any people who are walking around right now are probably drunk and certainly not paying attention to us. Besides, we aren't near a residential area. Just minimize the risk these bastards will pose and let's get in there." Gerrick liked the feisty female and smiled when he saw her latest t-shirt that said 'I love my bloodsucker.' She was always referring to her mate as a bloodsucker, or leech, or some other smartass term and Gerrick had no doubt that Kyran must have given her the tee.

"Make sure to stay by my side, Firecracker. I doona want you running in their thinking you can take on the whole lair. You may be immortal now, but you're no' invincible," Kyran told her, tugging on a strand of her spiky, black hair. The vampire prince had undergone a drastic attitude change when he had been stuck in the dragon realm with his mate, and was no longer the unhappy, distant warrior that he used to be. Gerrick acknowledged the new Kyran was definitely a change for the better.

"Ok, we're done. You guys are up." Pema's voice jolted Gerrick's thoughts, making his pulse leap. They were one step closer to going in and it was none too soon.

"Thanks," Gerrick nodded and checked to make sure Jace was ready. Jace was the healer of their group, but also a kick-ass fighter and the most powerful sorcerer in the realm and Gerrick was glad to have the male fighting by his side. Jace met his gaze and they began chanting in the old language.

Green, blue and purple lights of Jace and Gerrick's

magic were added to the reds and pinks of the witches. Gerrick locked in on the ten-block boundary the witches had cast around Pioneer Square and wove his enchantments with theirs. When the last word of the spell left his lips, he was sweating and breathing hard, but the flash of white light signaled that they had been successful.

Gerrick turned to Zander, "It's done, Liege," he informed. Sorcerers had the ability to see magic whereas the other supernaturals could only feel it. Only the sorcerers had seen the flash of white indicating the spell was completed.

Zander shifted his stance, his authoritative tone grabbing everyone's attention. "Hayden, take your shifters and wait by your entrance. Kyran, take your group to your spot. The rest of you, follow me. Everyone sync the time, we enter in five. Remember, our mission here is to get in and rescue the females and take oot the archdemons if we can."

"Stay alert," Gerrick told the witches and their mates, who would all be remaining behind. "The females may be feral and try to escape. We have to be prepared for the worst case scenarios." He shuddered to think about what horrors they had been suffering at the hands of such evil. It hadn't sat well with him to delay the rescue after Elsie had her premonition, but they all knew better than to dismiss the warning so they had waited.

He adjusted his black leather jacket and returned his staff, wishing he'd chosen a heavier coat since the weather was decidedly cold in December in Seattle, especially so close to the water. But leather offered more protection against knives and teeth, so everyone was dressed in leather from head to toe.

"What do we do if we encounter them?" Suvi asked, pursing her lips and stomping her impossibly high heels on the pavement. How the witch managed to stand, much less run or fight, was a mystery to him, but she didn't seem fazed by them one bit.

"Contain them, but doona harm them unless there is no choice. Jessie is proof that females are no' mindless like male skirm. We are here to help them," Zander replied, echoing Gerrick's thoughts. "Alright, move oot."

Gerrick jumped into motion behind Kyran and Mack. Their group silently made their way to a stairwell that led down to the Underground. The area wasn't ideal to face demons and skirm. They were entering the burned remains of Seattle and Gerrick had no doubt it wasn't the most stable of areas, especially when considering a battle.

Gerrick recalled what Seattle was like before the great Fire of 1889. There were horse-drawn carriages and dirt roads, and there wasn't this sense of urgency to get from one place to the next. It was vastly different from the city today. Then again, life in general back then was very different without modern technology. Gerrick enjoyed the easier way of life, but wouldn't want to give up his cell phone and the Internet. Having information at the tips of his fingers was invaluable to their work.

The group made their way down weathered cement steps and Kyran paused at the bottom when Mack put her hand on his arm. "Don't get dead, bloodsucker," the inked female muttered.

Kyran smiled broadly and stroked her pink cheek with one finger. "Doona do something stupid, like taking on Kadir." Gerrick watched as Mack smiled wryly and nodded. This was their version of 'I love you.' They weren't the mushy type of couple and Gerrick was glad of that. The last thing he needed was to have it rubbed in his face of what he would never have.

Gerrick looked back over his shoulder and took stock of their group. Aside from himself, Mack, and Kyran, there was Rhys and the New Orleans Dark Warriors. Rhys was Gerrick's patrol partner. Like Gerrick, Rhys lived at Zeum with the Seattle Dark Warriors. He was the jokester of their group, always pulling practical jokes on everyone, but Gerrick knew there was more lurking beneath the surface with Rhys.

The sound of metal screeching caught his attention as Kyran forced the door open and made his way into the building. The second the door fully opened the scent of mold and stale air hit him. Underlying it he caught hints of rodents, feces, urine and skirm. As they descended a flight of stairs, weathered cement gave way to newer wooden ones. The human authorities were often replacing rotted sections of the underground and Gerrick wondered why the humans hadn't run into the demons before now. Kadir must be expending a lot of energy to keep his lair hidden.

The next section was very narrow, and they had to go single file. He noted the brick of the previous buildings was wearing away, and in need of repair. They passed several unrecognizable businesses, and had to climb over timber and other debris. What struck him as odd were the many old toilets and it was beyond him that humans left this stuff to rot down here.

Gerrick cocked his ears and heard noise in the distance and pointed in the direction they needed to travel. Aison, one of the New Orleans Dark Warriors, jumped over an old, faded sofa and disturbed a family of rats. Gerrick had to hold back his laugh when the warrior did a little jig to avoid the scurrying rodents.

It was a maze down there and difficult to maneuver at times, which were definitely not ideal fighting conditions.

There was so much flammable material all around them that Gerrick worried they would spark the next devastating Seattle fire when they killed the skirm. Unfortunately, Gerrick didn't see a way around using titanium blades on the skirm since it was the easiest way to kill them.

The scent of brimstone and death heightened, telling him they were close. Kyran held up his hand and they all stopped.

"The females are around the corner and down the hall," Mack whispered.

Gerrick cast a silencing spell over their group and they crept on silent feet around the corner and discovered they were near the old steam baths. It was far less cluttered and it was obvious someone had cleared out most of the rubble, converting the space into living quarters.

Kyran opened the door and flattened against the wall, with the rest of them following suit. Gerrick wanted to laugh at what he imagined was a comical sight with nine large males standing flat against the wall as if pinned there.

Kyran poked his head around and his stance relaxed. They unfolded from the wall and Gerrick noticed that the business they were entering used to be an apothecary, at least according to the chipping paint on the dirt-encrusted window. Several walls had been knocked down to create one large space and the room was empty except for a large circular cage in the middle.

A crash suddenly sounded and Mack took off running, Kyran cursing as he chased after her. The rest of them were in motion a second later and they all came to a sudden halt inside a space that was dark, musty and crowded with cages. These cages were much smaller compared to the last one they saw, and were all full of females. Gerrick stumbled as the stench nearly bowled him over. There were so many different odors competing for dominance it was dizzying. Gerrick detected rotting flesh, feces, urine, and brimstone, as well as, moldy, charred fabric and wood. He glanced around and saw a pile of corpses in the corner in various stages of decomposition and shuddered in revulsion. Those poor beings deserved better than to be tossed aside like garbage.

Gerrick didn't have time to stop and consider anything further as the room was in the midst of a battle between demons and Zander's group. Gerrick recognized the hellhounds from a previous battle at Woodland Park, and bit back a curse. They were vicious beasts and relentless in their pursuit. There were also fury demons and large slimy green demons. He needed to try and put a muzzle on his anger, but the sight before him was infuriating. The last thing he wanted was to feed the fury demons power.

Before he could react, a slavering dog the size of a horse charged into him, knocking him down. He jumped up, weapons in hand and slashed the dog's snout. A high-pitched whine and shake of the head was all the injury earned Gerrick, but it was enough for him to sever the tendon on one of its front paws. Unfortunately, the beast wasn't slowed down on three legs. It glared at him through glowing red eyes, the desire to kill clearly expressed.

Completely focused on his target, Gerrick danced out of the next charge. He cursed when he wasn't fast enough to avoid its canines. When the hound's teeth didn't break through his leather, Gerrick was glad he hadn't gone with the warmer clothing.

Taking the offensive, Gerrick charged the demon and wrapped his arms around its thick neck. He head-butted the beast when it snapped at his face, keeping a firm grip on the animal. Gerrick lifted his weapon, opening himself up to the beast. He brought down his *sgian dubh* and cut into slick, black skin while canines clamped down on his shoulder and gnawed, slowly working their way through the leather.

Grimacing, Gerrick never let up and plunged his knife into the hellhound, trying to hit its heart. He could feel the dog moving them across the floor until metal bars of a cage instead scraped against his back. Finally, after several minutes his weapon hit its mark and the hellhound let out a screech that sounded a lot like tires skidding on asphalt and went still in his embrace. Gerrick gave one last twist of the blade, ensuring the beast was dead. He let go and kicked the hound away.

Gerrick jumped when a hand touched his injured shoulder. Panting and out of breath, Gerrick turned and his heart stopped for several beats when he caught sight of the female in the cage. She was stark naked. Her neck and shoulder had thick scars from obvious bite marks and she was bruised from head to toe. And she was filthy. Her hair was tangled mess and he thought it may be red, but it was hard to tell with how dirty it was. However, it was her eyes that stopped him cold. Their jade green depths were haunted, and, for some reason, very familiar.

They had obviously found the female prisoners and this one couldn't be more of a mess, but she had his body reacting with a ferocity that rocked him. It was the absolute worst time to be turned on and attracted to a female. It was even worse given the trauma this particular female had obviously suffered, but neither common sense nor the life and death fight he was engaged in stopped him from wanting this female beyond reason. He couldn't think straight, he was so enthralled.

"Behind you!" the female shouted, breaking the spell.

SHAE WAS dumb-founded that the Vampire King and his Dark Warriors had come to rescue them. She blinked, wondering if it was a trick of the infrared vision she'd inherited along with the bloodlust. She knew something was happening when countless skirm and demons rushed into the room where she had been held prisoner. Seconds later her prayers were answered with the influx of warriors. She had prayed and begged to be set free or killed and now she couldn't stop the hope and joy that sparked at the sight before her.

Tears brimmed in her eyes when she realized she was finally going to get out of that cage, one way or another.

She stared at the warrior with the gaze that was cold as ice. He had fought the hellhound like a male who had nothing to lose, charging the fiend and wrapping his muscular arms around the beast. It was a bloody and unreal sight, but now that she looked into his eyes, she saw a male lost, broken, and alone. It reflected how she felt inside. She noticed that he was scarred like her, too. The left side of his face had a scar from his temple to his neck, but the sight didn't detract from his good looks. It just made him look dangerous...and delicious.

She caught movement out of the corner of her eye. "Behind you," she warned.

Before she blinked, he swiveled and his blade found purchase in the chest of the approaching skirm. He wasted no time getting right back into the fight. He was a thing of beauty as he killed enemy after enemy, never tiring while blood poured from his shoulder. She smelled his blood and looked down to see it coated her fingers and bloodlust had her close to licking every drop from her skin.

A skirm banged into her cage, distracting her wicked thoughts, and she reached through and grabbed hold of its head. She twisted and pulled and tugged until the body fell at her feet. She lifted her head and glanced into stunned, whiskey eyes. "You came back for us. I thought you were dead," Shae muttered.

"You bet your ass I came back. I'd have been here sooner, but I had a detour in Khoth. We are getting you out of here...just as soon...as we can." The last was said while the female battled a skirm who had come up behind her. She was fierce and fought like the wind. And, Shae noted, she wasn't human anymore. She had mated to one of the vampire royal family as the Tarakesh family mark inked below her left ear caught her eye. Shae hadn't seen the mystical mate mark the last time she had seen the female and wondered if her prompting the search for the King brought her to her Fated Mate.

Shae knew the tales about mate marks, and how and when they appeared. For human mates, the mate mark always appeared below the left ear, and was a mystical mark until the mating was completed. At this point it became inked into the skin, never to be removed. Aside from those of her parents and grandparents, she had never actually seen a mate mark, thanks to a seven-century long mating curse. The curse had been lifted recently and Fated Mates were being blessed once again.

Prince Kyran worked his way next to the female and took care of the fury demon targeting his mate. "I see you've managed to find trouble, Firecracker."

"No more than usual. What the hell are those nasty things?" the female asked. Shae looked over to see several pus demons had joined the fight. Shae recalled fighting one of those bastards in the cage not long ago. The slime they left in their wake made battle challenging as was evidenced when one of the Dark Warriors skidded and slammed into a wall. The brittle boards of the wall rattled, but held up as he pushed into a leap and sliced his knife through the demons throat. Green pus oozed from the wound and the smell it emitted was noxious. It didn't faze Shae like it did the warriors who visibly gagged, but she had to agree it was vile.

Her scarred warrior was embroiled in his own fight with one of the four-armed pus demons. She had no idea why her mind insisted on claiming this stranger, but it did, nonetheless. He was caught by two of the demon's arms while the other two reached for his head. Blue-eyes flashed and he elbowed the demon in the gut in an attempt to free himself. Shae watched as his elbow sunk ineffectively into the fleshy body.

"The groin!" she shouted, trying to get his attention. "Go for the groin."

Ice-cold eyes turned on her and he inclined his head in acknowledgment. A second later, the demon bellowed and her warrior fell to the ground, and without wasting time, proceeded to hack its head off. He was a fearless champion, and made her blood boil hotter than a fresh pot of coffee.

Another warrior cried out as he was caught in four slimy arms. Her warrior leapt through the air and buried his blade in the top of that demon's head as he sailed over it. He landed easily on his feet and swiveled to face a skirm coming up from behind. The first warrior took care of the pus demon while her warrior fought on. Within no time, both males were standing there panting, having vanquished their foes for the time being.

"Thanks, Gerrick." Shae made a mental note that her blue-eyed, scarred warrior was named Gerrick.

"No problem, Caell."

The two warriors turned and raised their weapons, ready to continue, but there were no more enemies in their immediate area. Shae could hear more heading their way. "Get us out, now. Hurry, there are more coming," Shae pleaded with the female who had brought salvation back with her.

"My name is Mack, and it will be my pleasure to finally make good on my promise." Mack lifted her foot to kick the lock while others worked on the remaining cages, but the prince was there before her foot landed.

"I had that, bloodsucker," Mack complained.

"I know you did," he replied as Shae was finally freed. Without thought, she was rushing Mack and enveloping her in a tight hug.

"I'm Shae and I owe you my life." It had been countless weeks, maybe months, of torture, rape and fighting and now she was out of that cage. They may not be in the clear yet, but she wasn't ever going back into that cage. She'd die first. "Saying thank you isn't enough for what you've given us. If you ever need anything don't hesitate to call on me."

"Save that for later. Do you know a fast way out of here? The way we came in is too far from here," Mack said, cutting her off and reached into her backpack.

"I have no idea. I was teleported into this room."

Mack handed her a pile of clothes and Shae shook her head. "Give them to Cami. She needs them more." She glanced over at the human who was shaking from the terror. She wasn't so human anymore. The frail female had been in their midst the shortest amount of time, but was by far the most traumatized.

"We will have to go back the way we came then. Come on, we better get out of here now," Gerrick barked. Even clipped and terse, his voice was a balm to her soul, and damned if her body wasn't responding, as well. It was both reassuring and deeply disturbing that the horrors she had suffered hadn't left her dead inside. Shae turned and started for the entrance, ready to leave this part of her life behind her.

CHAPTER 2

G errick watched Zander lead the way out of the room. His body ached all over from the fight, but he wasn't letting his guard down. He didn't believe for one second that this rescue was going to be that simple. Kadir was a sneaky, ruthless bastard and this fight had been too easy, all things considered.

Cocking his ear, he heard animal snarls and whines coming from the east, away from their path of escape. Perhaps Hayden and his clan of shifters could keep the remaining skirm and demons at bay long enough for them to get the females to the cars. Gerrick examined the frightened females from his position at the rear of the group.

They were all filthy, bruised and bleeding, but none of them attracted him the way Shae did. He was surprised to see the variety of females that had been captured. There was everything from humans to shifters and vampires to Valkyrie and harpies. The sight of the harpy with her wings shackled made him see red. He was shocked she hadn't succumbed to death, being cut off from the connection to everything that made her what she was. No one should be tortured in such a brutal manner. Zander hadn't made any moves to remove the silver chain from the harpy's wings and Gerrick surmised that was for everyone's safety. No one knew how she would react and an out of control harpy was the last thing they needed at the moment.

On a good day, any of these females could be dangerous creatures, but they had been through a great deal and were unpredictable, glancing around nervously and jumpy as hell. When a rat skittered along into their path, the females all crouched down and snarled, brandishing fangs at the harmless rodent. Their eyes roved restlessly from Zander to Kyran to Mack and the rest of them. The wild, crazed look in their eyes told Gerrick that the best course of action was to keep them contained for the time being. A dozen feral females running rampant was the last thing the realm needed.

Gerrick recognized the sign for the steam baths as they passed and was surprised they didn't encounter more enemies. He kept his guard up. This was way too easy and that made him nervous. They crossed through the area that had obviously housed the skirm and demons, finding it empty as well, even though his skin prickled in warning. Sharpening his attention, they continued as quietly as possible.

When the air cleared of the cloying scents of death, his heart raced. Something wasn't right. His first instinct was to bring Shae into his arms and protect her from danger. As a warrior, it was his job to protect both the realm and humans, so this was nothing new, but with Shae, it went beyond mere duty. It came from his soul and the thought scared the shit out of him. He couldn't go there right now because it brought up too much pain and heartache so he shoved it deep down and out of reach of further inspection.

A noise up ahead stopped them in their tracks and he stood on tiptoe to see around their group. "Stay here," he told Aison and Caell as he shouldered his way to the front of the group.

When he reached Mack's side, he saw that Kadir and Azazel were standing in the path of their group. Both demons wore smug grins and stood with their arms crossed over their chests. The difference in size between the Behemoth and the Daeva demon would have been comical if their presence hadn't been stifling. One was over seven feet tall with grey skin and black horns while the other looked like a male model.

Gerrick glanced warily at the Dark magic of black and gray lights that surrounded the two demons. They were gearing up for a spell and Gerrick's gut clenched as he tried to recall what spell he could cast that would effectively protect their group. Unfortunately, there wasn't a spell strong enough to counteract that amount of Dark power.

Gerrick chanced a glance at Shae and saw her frozen in place, glaring at the demons. Her rage poured from her in waves and he saw that she stood there, with her muscles tensed and ready to attack. For the first time, he realized that the normal purple and blue aura that typically surrounded a vampire was sliced by black for Shae. All of the females' auras were shot through with black. Whatever they'd been doing to them was very different from what had been done to Jessie. She exhibited a rainbow of colors, but none of them were black.

"I see you're taking what doesn't belong to you, again, Vampire King," Kadir rumbled in a deep voice that vibrated the walls like the motor of a Harley.

Gerrick felt the females trembling behind him. The snarling, ferocious beings he had just seen were gone and in their place were frightened mice. Gerrick would bet that if Kadir told the females to scurry back to their cages, they would. All but Shae, that was. She wouldn't scurry anywhere. Her rage called out for vengeance.

"We don't belong to you," she snarled and took a step forward. Gerrick put his hand on her arm, halting her progress. She glanced down at his hand and then at his face. He shook his head at her. She lifted her lip, flashing him fang. The sight was more erotic than it should have been.

Zander jumped into the conversation before Shae could speak. Gerrick had no doubt she had plenty she wanted to say to him at that moment. "Och, your plans have once again failed, Kadir. Are you ready to return to your maker, demon?" Zander lunged without hesitation, bent on destruction. Zander was a male possessed on getting revenge for the pain and agony his mate, Elsie, had suffered at Kadir's direction.

"Bring me the amulet and I will let these females go. Well, all but my Shae. Her, I keep," Kadir responded, easily dodging Zander's attack.

Gerrick dropped his hand and gripped his knife tighter, taking several steps forward only to run into a broad back. Kyran had stepped in front of him and was glaring at him over his shoulder.

"Och, but you are dumb as rocks," Bhric taunted the demon. Gerrick wished the other Vampire Prince would unleash his ice and freeze the demon in place. As if his thoughts prompted Bhric, Gerrick saw the lights of Bhric's power flare.

Zander followed his swing and turned quickly to face the archdemons. "You will have no one and I sure as hell am no' giving you the amulet. Lucifer should be used to his accommodations by now, frozen by a lake in hell."

Gerrick saw Kadir's outline waver before he solidified once more. "Like our little spell? That's courtesy of the witch triplets you conspired to eliminate. Know that each of your endeavors will meet failure. It's best if you return to Lucifer with your tail between your legs," Zander promised and swiped at Kadir. Zander's blade managed to nick his arm and black blood trickled from the wound. The scent of brimstone filled the narrow passage.

Kadir bellowed his anger and tossed Zander into the wall. Kyran jumped aside when Zander slammed into the wall next to him, trying to join the fight only to come up against Azazel. Kyran sifted behind the good-looking archdemon and plunged his blade into his shoulder.

"I didn't give the witches my best effort. Perhaps I'll try again," Kadir panted as he danced away from Zander and Kyran. Gerrick bounced on the balls of his feet, wanting to get into the fray, knowing it would only cause more problems. The space was too narrow to allow for freedom of movement and they would be too busy trying to avoid each other to do any damage.

The foursome was a blur as they fought. Kyran slammed into a wall next and dust and debris rained down from the ceiling. Gerrick waved his hand in front of his face to clear the air and Shae took that moment to run past him.

"You took my life from me and now I'm going to take yours!" Shae yelled and threw herself at Azazel. The good-looking demon smiled and caught her mid-air.

"Oh, my pretty, Shae. I didn't take your life. I gave you a new one," he purred into her ear and sank his fangs into the ravaged side of her neck. She screamed and writhed in pain and Gerrick acted on instinct, pulling his staff out of its pocket, chanting a spell. The spell hit Azazel in the arm, making him jerk upright. His fangs tore through Shae's skin as he lifted his head.

She didn't flinch at the injury, but took advantage instead and sunk her nails into one of the demon's eyes. Kyran sifted behind him and went low, swinging his blade. Azazel stumbled and dropped Shae while Kyran cut him again, this time slicing through the injured limb. The severed leg fell to the floor and the demon ripped a beam from the ceiling and hit Kyran with it. Mack joined the fight while Gerrick pulled Shae free of the skirmish. Mack and Kyran fought a weakened Azazel while Kadir faced off with Zander.

Gerrick thought the tides were turning when the rest of their group moved to help those at the front, but a slew of lesser demons and skirm swarmed the tunnels behind them. Gerrick and the others were forced to fight against the newcomers. He kept his staff in hand and cast spells. When the spells were ineffective he resorted to using the staff as a club. With one fury demon he shoved the staff through its neck and forced his magic down the wood, making the demon's head explode from the energy.

Gerrick lost sight of Zander and the archdemons, but heard the shouts. Without warning, black light engulfed the tunnel. When it cleared, the archdemons had disappeared. The only thing that made sense was something must have happened to the witches to allow for the archdemons to teleport.

Breslin came running toward Gerrick and fell over something in her way before she reached him. He thrust the end of his staff into a skirm's chest and muttered an obliteration spell. He relished when the minion blew into a million pieces, while at the same time he ducked as Azazel's severed leg went flying over their heads followed by Breslin's cry of rage. Gerrick was surprised Breslin hadn't used her power to set the limb on fire after it had tripped her.

He found it difficult to track their enemies and the females at the same time with the chaos that had erupted in the small tunnel. One thing that struck him was the ferocity with which the rescued females fought the skirm and demons. Their anger and bloodlust rivaled that of a feral animal, and it concerned him greatly about their state of mind.

As the enemy count dwindled, the warriors' fight mode receded, but the females continued. All signs of the somewhat rational beings had left their eyes. He stepped into the path of the small human they'd called, Cami only to be shoved back as she clawed his arms. Bhric encountered the same when he intercepted Shae. Gerrick saw red when Bhric raised his hand to use his power against Shae and purposely stumbled into his back, making his ice slam into a wall. No one would ever hurt Shae again. He would make sure of it.

The air in the tunnel thickened and Gerrick's body slowed as Zander exerted his power. Gerrick had never felt so much pressure and control from the Vampire King and was stunned he was still standing after such expenditure. Zander's harsh commands blasted through the group, "Enough! Cease!" Zander barked.

Only panting breaths could be heard in the corridor. Gerrick looked around and saw Shae several feet away, leaning against the wall. Her posture seemed nonchalant, but the clench of her jaw and the brackets around her mouth and eyes told a different story. Again, he had the urge to go to her and wrap her in his arms. He shook his head against the bizarre impulse and locked his legs to keep from following through.

"The archdemons willna be back tonight, they suffered too many injuries. We are going to head oot of here and go back to Zeum, and there willna be any more bloodshed this night," Zander told the group before he turned and headed to the exit.

As the groups started to follow Zander, Gerrick realized that all of the females, except for Shae, had been given some type of clothing. Gerrick removed his leather jacket and approached her. He held the jacket open to her and waited while she glared warily at him. "Put it on. It's cold outside." He kept eye contact with her and watched her try to hide the way her body trembled from the cold.

"I can handle a little cold," she protested as she slipped her arms into the sleeves. "That's nothing compared to what I've been through." He saw through her bold words to the core of shame for her current predicament.

She huddled into the jacket and let a small sigh escape. He swore she brought the lapel to her nose and inhaled his scent. He contemplated the small smile playing over her lips as he bent down and removed his shoes as well. The last thing he wanted was for her to walk across the studded boards, broken glass and other debris, not to mention the cold streets above.

She looked from him to the boots dangling from his fingers. "Are you sure your feet can handle being without? I'm used to the discomfort."

His gut twisted hearing the despair behind her words. He'd bet his prized *sgian dubhs* that she wouldn't have taken the jacket if she didn't understand they were about to encounter humans. It was clear to him that she would never break the mandate that no supernatural could reveal the existence of the Tehrex Realm. The way she gazed at Zander and his brothers in awe told him what a dedicated vampire she was.

As for pain, little did she know how much he'd dealt with in his long life. "Physical pain is nothing," he told her honestly and began walking.

"Tell me something I don't know," she muttered wryly before calling out, "I'm Shae, by the way."

He glanced over his shoulder and felt a smile tug at his lips seeing her hop up and down as she tried to put his boots on then hurried after him. Amusement was so foreign it made him scowl. He didn't smile, ever. "Got it."

"You must be the friendly one in the bunch, Gerrick," she snapped sarcastically, making him want to smile again. "Just sayin'."

"Yep, I'm Happy and he's Dopey," he said pointing to Bhric.

"Fuck you. I'm Sexy," Bhric retorted. Gerrick continued with his easy pace until he caught his foot on a board. He wanted to curse when he felt the rusty nail cut the bottom of his heel, but held it back. He didn't want her to give his shoes back. He'd be damned if he allowed her feet to get scraped up.

"Yeah, I can tell you're just a barrel of laughs. Do you always sweat so much when you fight?" she asked, fingering the lapels of his jacket. The movement gave him an enticing glimpse at her breasts, and fuck, if he wasn't rock hard again. He didn't let himself think further about how the sight of her bared flesh affected him, but turned around and continued walking.

"Would you rather have my shirt? It's drenched." He wasn't helping himself forget about her allure, as the image of her wearing his shirt was even more arousing. Sure, he'd had sex with females over the centuries, but he'd never wanted one of them in his clothing. At that moment, he wanted Shae in his shirt and nothing else. He reasoned it had to be because he felt so bad about what this particular female had been through.

"I'm good with the jacket thanks, Sweaty. So, what's the date?" she asked, making her way next to him.

"December first." He wasn't a conversationalist, preferring to listen. And hell, with her sultry voice, he could listen to her talk all day long. Her voice had the barest hint of roughness that set it apart from most females.

"Okay...what year?"

"Twenty fifteen," he responded curiously. How long had she been down here?

"Oh my Goddess," she gasped. He glanced over and saw the devastation on her face. He had the urge to comfort her, but something told him that was the last thing she'd welcome. "It's only been seven months. It feels like I've been down her for decades." At the mention of the time that had passed, the other females began sobbing. It was all the other warriors could do to herd and comfort them. Gerrick expected Shae to break down, as well, but she walked along in silence with her fists balled, her jaw clenched tight and her eyes narrowed. She was pissed, and her reaction spoke volumes about what she'd been through, more so than the tears and hysterics around them.

They'd made it to the stairs and Gerrick paused, allowing the females to ascend before him. Zander and Breslin waited at the top. When their entourage made it to the street, they proceeded to the parking lot as quickly as they could, given the size and injuries of their group. Gerrick cursed as the cold bit into the soles of his feet. He hadn't lied about physical discomfort, but it had been many centuries since he'd been so exposed to the cold. The sting from the nail was an irritant he would just as soon be rid of. Thank the Goddess he healed preternaturally fast.

The sounds of fighting reached their ears before they made it to the parking lot. Gerrick didn't hesitate as he took off running. "Shite, Breslin, stay with the females. You too, Cade, Caell," Zander ordered before Gerrick heard the pounding of his feet.

Rhett, a fire demon and recent addition to their household, came dashing down a side street and joined them as they hit the lot to find the witches and their mates fighting a large group of skirm. Hell, how many skirm were there? Kadir and Azazel had been busy little demons. Now he understood what had interrupted the witches' spell.

A stream of fire left Rhett's palm as he looked over. "Do you guys always have this much fun? When's the next initiation?" Mack laughed at the male. She had a history with the fire demon and he had returned with her and Kyran after their sojourn in the dragon realm of Khoth.

"You thinking of staying awhile, Match? You sure you won't miss your desk job?" Mack teased the male as they fought side by side.

"I wouldn't dream of leaving yet, Sunshine." Rhett grunted when his inattention earned him a punch in the ribs. He ducked the skirm's next blow, laughing. "Besides, I haven't been a big enough pain in your mate's ass. Plus, I like it here. There are so many females and different places I can visit on this planet that promise good times and adventure."

Gerrick bounced on the frozen balls of his feet and slashed out, quickly dusting every skirm within his reach. Two humans chose that moment to cross the street from the ferry dock. Gerrick heard the startled gasps and so did the skirm. Two broke off from their group and headed toward the humans. Without stopping to think, Gerrick was running after them.

The human female began shrieking as the skirm bared bloody fangs at them and lunged for her. Gerrick snarled and cursed as he crouched and sprang at the pair. He landed on the skirm's back, taking him to the ground. Unfortunately, the human female went along with them, screeching the whole way. He hated high-pitched screaming and muttered a spell making the female mute. He sighed in relief when the noise stopped. She looked around wide-eyed in fright, clutching at her throat.

Not giving the female another thought, he thrust his *sgian dubh* into the skirm's chest cavity and felt the satisfying pop as it entered the blackened heart. Never once looking back, he was up and ashing the second skirm. The human male was reaching down to help the female as Gerrick turned and walked away. It wasn't until after he was halfway across the street that he realized he hadn't lifted his spell. He stalked back to the couple, grabbed her shoulders and released his magic. He was ready to be home. It had been a long night.

"Damn, Gerrick, you scared the shit out of those people. Hell, even I didn't know if you were going after them or the skirm. They'll be having nightmares for a while," Mack chastised.

"No they aren't, one of the vampires will erase their memory," Gerrick retorted and rushed back to help finish the rest. It was quick work for their group to eliminate the skirm that had converged on the witches.

He signaled Breslin who then led the females around the corner as the witches were recounting their attack to Zander. They ushered the females to the waiting vans and were loaded up, heading back to Zeum within minutes.

Gerrick laid his head on the seat, wondering what was in store for them now.

SHAE CLOSED her eyes and leaned her head on the window as they drove to the infamous Zeum compound. She was finally free from the archdemons. She had prayed for seven long months for this moment, and now that it was here she had no idea what she was going to do next. Before she'd been kidnapped, she would go home and knit after a long day at work, yet she hadn't had access to her yarn and needles during her captivity. She couldn't help but wonder if the hobby would still bring her any peace after what she'd been through.

She missed her family and wanted to be taken home immediately, but held back. Tears gathered in her eyes as she contemplated her life. No doubt everyone believed she was dead when they hadn't heard from her for so long.

Her parents had to be beside themselves with grief, not to mention her brother. He may have been centuries older than her, but they had been as close as twins. Every one of her memories had him in it. He'd taught her how to play baseball, and later how to drive. On the rare occasion she went out to the clubs with friends, he was always there looking out for her.

Her grandfather's fierce face flashed into her head, making her wonder how many times he'd searched the streets for a sign of her. She'd bet every dime she had that he had used his wolf senses to try and track her, and been frustrated when he had failed. There was no way to track someone when they teleported away from a scene, which was how the demons snatched her that fated night. She loved her grandfather so much and would give anything to feel his big, strong arms wrap around her and make her feel safe again. She didn't think she'd ever feel safe again.

Thoughts of family had her wondering if one of her uncles had turned her bedroom into their office. Like all supernaturals, she lived with her extended family and the space was tight for them. They didn't live in a huge mansion and her small home didn't allow for luxuries like an office. As much as she missed her family she couldn't fathom seeing them right now. She wanted to tell them she was alive, but wasn't sure she'd be able to handle a conversation about what had happened to her.

She was not the same female that had been kidnapped all those months ago. Then, she had been a happy vampire who smiled easily and loved to go out with friends. She enjoyed concerts and wineries and despite the fact that she wasn't an athlete, she played on the bank softball team. Getting a bi-weekly pedi and mani was more her speed. There wasn't anyone special in her life, but she had dated. Now, she couldn't imagine ever letting a male touch her again. Hell, she didn't even know who she was.

And her head was killing her from trying to sort it all out.

She heard someone mention Dante, her boss, and the Cambion Lord. She thought of her job and wondered if she still even had a position at the bank. She recalled the day he'd hired her all those years ago. He'd flirted and told her he'd hire her if she wore short skirts to work. She had told him to fuck off figuring she wasn't going to get the job and had been shocked when he had hired her anyway. Later he told her it was her cockiness that had won him over. She knew Dante was part of the Dark Alliance Council with

Zander and prayed she didn't have to deal with him yet, either.

The van stopped and her eyes shot open in alarm. She gazed around warily and noticed they were parked next to a pair of large, intricately carved black doors. The car trip had gone by far too quickly for her comfort. She wanted to sit there in silence and avoid reality as long as she could.

Without warning, the home's doors flew open and a petite, dark-haired female came rushing out. Heart thundering in her chest, Shae exited the vehicle when prompted and stepped next to the other females who looked just as nervous as she was.

Zander approached the female and kissed her gently before turning her to their group. "Welcome to Zeum. If you haven't figured it out, I'm Zander's mate, Elsie. It's good to finally have you guys here. Come on, let's talk inside. It's way too cold out here," the female said, making eye contact with each of them.

They were herded inside by the warriors, which brought Shae's hackles up. She didn't like the idea going into an unknown situation no matter how many were smiling and trying to set her at ease. When it came down to it, she didn't know these people and had been through enough to know better than to blindly trust anyone. Azazel was a perfect example. He was beautiful on the outside, but the most vicious creature she'd ever met.

She reminded herself this was her King's home, and she had been rescued by the Dark Warriors and they were the most revered supernaturals in the realm. Still, the effort of keeping her reaction in check had her sweating in Gerrick's jacket. She itched to leave again, feeling claustrophobic in the large mansion.

"I need to call my family. They have to be worried about

me," Cami said immediately.

"That's no' going to happen, lass," Zander responded kindly.

Shae was instantly pissed as were the rest of the females. She could feel it. No one was going to hold them against their will again. Her mind began plotting ways to escape the second an opportunity presented itself. It was impossible at the moment, since the warriors and their mates surrounded them, but she would find a way.

"Why not?" Cami snapped.

"Because we doona know enough to contain the fall-oot from this situation. Humans canna know aboot the Tehrex Realm and we need to run tests and learn what effects the demon's venom has had on you," Zander explained.

"I want to go home, now!" Cami yelled.

"She can go home if she wants to," Shae snapped. "We've been prisoners long enough. You don't get to tell us what to do!"

"Calm doon," Princess Breslin cooed, raising her arms in a gesture of peace. Too bad, Shae was good and pissed and wanted to throat punch the female.

"We can't keep them here. It would be barbaric after all they've been through," Gerrick argued. Shae was shocked to hear this warrior coming to their defense. He didn't strike her as the caring type. She'd watched him fight with a cold detachment that made her wonder if he felt anything.

"They are staying, Gerrick. We doona know what we have on our hands or the risk they pose," Zander retorted.

"Zander is right. 'Tis no' safe to have them oot there," Breslin added. Without thinking, Shae threw off Gerrick's jacket and charged the female. Her shoulder hit the princess in the side. A fist smacked into her cheek, making her momentarily see stars. She bared her fangs and remained in her crouch, swiveling around and kicking Breslin in the shin. She heard yelling in the background, but didn't pay any attention to what was being said.

Breslin grabbed her ankle and pulled. Having spent months in the fight cages, Shae was able to maintain her balance while pummeling Breslin. Fighting had become second nature and she never lost. Losing in the cages meant death and she had no intention of dying anytime soon. Breslin hissed and bared her fangs and Shae saw flames of rage flicker in her amber eyes. She wasn't giving in, either. Suddenly strong, warm arms wrapped around her middle and her feet left the ground.

"You alright, sweetheart?" the fire demon asked the princess, crouching beside Breslin. It didn't matter who was holding her, she would make sure Breslin couldn't respond to that question. Shae struggled against her hold and was pinned so tightly against the hot body behind her she couldn't move even an inch.

"I'm no' you're sweetheart," Breslin huffed, storming out of the room.

"I'm getting to her, I can tell," the fire demon quipped at the same time Shae dug her nails into the flesh banding her waist. She used all her strength to twist her head and see who was holding her. It was Gerrick and he had a grim look on his face.

"Put me down. I'm leaving," she spat, throwing her head back. He tried to avoid her strike, but the back of her head hit his chin. She'd been hoping to break his nose and was disappointed at not injuring him in the least.

"You're not leaving, Shae. At least, not right now," Gerrick murmured in her ear, wrangling her into an even tighter hold. Her anger ricocheted through the roof and she fought Gerrick wildly. She refused to be put in another cage.

CHAPTER 3

Gerrick held a wildcat in his arms. Shae had gone off without listening to reason. It wasn't that he agreed with keeping these females locked up, but he understood that they were dealing with an unknown at the moment and there was no way they were going to be able to be released right now.

Crazy thing was that while the other females were upset and had begun yelling, only Shae had lost her shit. The red-head in his arms was out of control.

She threw her head back again and nailed him in the chin. He cursed and snapped, "Stop, dammit. We're trying to help you. This isn't helping your cause any." He could have been talking to a wall for all she listened. He glanced at Jessie, shock written across her features.

Jessie, Cailyn's friend, had joined them a few months ago after she had been bitten and infected by the same archdemon. It was through her that the realm became aware of the difference in the reaction of a male and a female when they were bitten by an archdemon. Before Jessie, a female had never been infected by an archdemon, so everyone assumed being bitten by an archdemon meant you would become a mindless skrim.

He focused his magic and muttered, "*Codlata.*" Blue light flared under his fingertips and he felt the familiar tingle as his enchantment took hold. Moments later Shae slumped in his hold, her eyes slipping closed.

"What did you do to her?" Cami asked.

Gerrick met her gaze and saw her flinch. She was obviously not ready to take him on as Shae had done. He knew many saw him as a cold, uncaring and ruthless warrior. He never corrected them because he preferred it this way. He believed it was better that he was feared, rather than approachable. "I didn't kill her if that's what you're worried about. I merely placed her under a sleep spell. She was bound to get hurt."

He swung Shae up into his arms and cradled her against his chest, immediately aware of her soft flesh against his. He gazed down at her and was drawn to the sight of her head falling over his arm. Her hair was a dirty, matted mess, but it was the longest hair he'd seen in centuries. He'd guess when it was clean and brushed it would nearly reach her pert ass. Females in modern times didn't keep their hair as long as they used to, making this female even more of an enigma.

The knotted locks slid off her shoulder, diverting his attention to the fact that her bare breasts were right in front of his face. Her skin was filthy, yet through the dirt he could see that her nipples were a rosy pink. He'd bet they would turn red and pearl to hard points under his attention.

He took a deep breath and started for the basement stairs. For the first time, he caught a hint of her natural jasmine scent through the stench that clung to her skin. She smelled divine and he couldn't stop the erection that once again sprang to life. He willed it away, but his stupid cock wasn't listening. It wanted what it wanted and didn't give a shit that it wasn't the right time.

He was appalled by his body's reaction. Here he was carrying the female to their dungeons to once again be imprisoned, yet he was hard as stone for her. The last thing he needed was for Rhys or Orlando to catch sight. They would never let him live it down. He made sure to lead the way down the stairs focusing on anything but the female in his arms.

It was impossible as her soft breaths and tiny mewl caught his attention. Awake she was a snarling, furious ball of fire, but like this she was a fragile female he wanted to bury inside his chest and keep safe. And fuck did he hate this female for making him react to her. He hadn't felt this attracted to anyone since his Evanna. This place of his heart and soul belonged solely to his lost mate.

He had met Evanna four hundred years ago and it had been love at first sight. He had been a young sorcerer of only fifty at the time, but she had enchanted him from the beginning. He recalled her blonde hair and jade green eyes and how easily she laughed and smiled. Come to think of it, he did, too, at that time.

They'd discovered they were Fated Mates the first time they had sex and their mate marks appeared. He had lost her shortly thereafter, taken from him by an archdemon and its skirm. Nothing could bring her back to him, not even his ability as a Time Tracer. He had nearly destroyed his ability after repeatedly trying to save Evanna that fateful day, and learned there is always a cost associated with using his power. The scar on his face was the cost the Goddess required for trying to reverse fate. He would have accepted scars all over his body if he could have saved Evanna. He scowled as he stomped down the steps, banishing the painful memories from his mind.

He heard Zander and the others leading the remaining females down the stairs behind him. He heard Zander's mate, Elsie, trying to reassure the frightened females. Gerrick didn't know why she bothered. He might not like the situation either, but there was no changing it. It was pointless to offer reassurance, and frankly, a waste of breath if you asked him.

He wasn't as cold and callous as many believed; he just didn't see the point in telling these women that everything would be okay. They were being locked up again mere hours after having been rescued. No one knew if it was going to turn out well for these females or if they were going to need to be eliminated because they were too dangerous. He looked down at Shae's peaceful face and vowed he would never allow her to be harmed, no matter what they learned.

Gerrick continued past the basement level where they had a medical clinic, weapons room, training facility, and additional rooms for visitors. The next level down, the brick and mortar gave way to stone and dirt. It was a challenge to have a basement, let alone a dungeon in Seattle, but with the use of pumps and magic they had managed. He remembered digging the holes and then using stone to reinforce the walls of the dungeon.

He shivered from the chill in the air and looked down to see goose bumps raised on Shae's skin. He made a note to make sure she had warm clothes and plenty of blankets. He stopped at the first cell and used his foot to wedge the door open.

"Grab a blanket and sheets. I don't want to place her on the mattress like this," Gerrick called out. Unlike some of his fellow warriors, he had never been locked in their dungeons, but he was glad they'd upgraded to actual beds. Shae shouldn't sleep on the dirt floor or a flimsy cot.

"I'd have had them all ready," Nate answered rushing through the door with a pile of fabric in his hand, "but no one told me that you were locking them up. Would it kill you people to actually tell me what's going on? How hard is it to send a text? Well, hello there," Nate purred, dropping his bundle as he caught sight of Shae.

Gerrick shook his head. He had no idea why Angus, the dragon shifter who'd previously been their majordomo, wanted to leave Nate as his replacement. Anyone would be more capable and focused than Nate. Nate spent more time drooling over females than he did running the house.

"These females have been through unspeakable horrors and don't need you being a jackass. Get the sheet on the bed so I can lay Shae down," Gerrick snapped, wanting to gouge the male's eyes for looking at Shae's naked body. He snatched up the blanket and draped it over her. Nate turned from the bars and the pink that tinged his cheeks, as well as, his silence told Gerrick that he understood his timing couldn't have been worse.

Once the sheet was on the mattress, Gerrick laid Shae down. Technically, his job was done here, but he realized he really didn't want to leave her side. "Shae is going to be out for a while yet and needs to be cleaned up. Send down some of the staff to take care of it," Gerrick requested as he glanced around Shae's new home. Bars lined the front wall while stone made up the remaining three. She'd have more privacy than she had before, and Gerrick would venture to guess that having a working toilet and shower were going to be welcome, but he guessed she wouldn't be thrilled at her new living arrangement.

He looked at the sleeping female. She seemed peaceful

in her respite, but Gerrick couldn't forget the feral rage that had poured off her not moments ago. He ran a hand over the top of her head, wondering again what she'd look like once she was clean. He imagined her hair was a vibrant red and maybe she'd have freckles across the bridge of her nose.

"Och, Nate," Zander called out. Gerrick snatched his hand back before someone caught him caressing Shae's head. He had no idea what was up with him, but he needed to get a grip. "Have linens and toiletries brought to each of the females. Get their sizes and have clothing delivered to them ASAP. You will need to make sure to have extra food delivered as well as bagged blood to feed our additional guests."

Gerrick left the cell when several servants entered carrying towels and other items. Jace entered right behind them. "Let me draw some blood before you clean her up so we can start running the tests." Gerrick's instincts reacted automatically and he snapped his teeth at the male. He didn't know why he was being so protective of her, he knew they needed to get the samples, and agreed that the sooner the better.

Jace narrowed his eyes at Gerrick. "What's your problem? I'm not going to harm her. She won't even know I've taken her blood."

That was a very good question, Gerrick thought, ignoring the healer as he walked out of the cell. He stood in the hall and watched the flurry of activity unable to make his feet carry him upstairs. He had no business there anymore, yet he couldn't take his eyes off the female.

Their dungeon was small, and nearly all of the cells were occupied once the females were settled. As Jace finished up and the rest of the warriors left, Gerrick lingered outside Shae's cell. Two female shifters brought buckets of warm water from the shower and began cleaning Shae.

He was utterly captivated by the sight of her. As the dirt washed away from her arms, he realized how pale she was, not that it detracted from her beauty. Hell, the filth and grime didn't even detract from that. She was stunning no matter what she looked like and he suddenly felt like a voyeur.

Finally, he forced himself to walk away and made his way up the stairs. Not wanting to be alone just yet, he followed the conversation to the kitchen. The aroma of garlic and onions wafted from the room, making him wonder what Elsie was cooking this time, his mouth watering in anticipation.

In his opinion, Elsie was the best cook on the planet. There wasn't anything she couldn't turn into a masterpiece. Whether it was a grilled cheese sandwich or crawfish etouffee, it was always delicious. He pushed the door open and wasn't surprised to find most of the warriors and their mates present. Since Elsie's arrival on the scene, the kitchen had become a frequent gathering place, although you entered at your own risk. Zander and Elsie were known to do more than just cook in the kitchen. Not that Gerrick begrudged them their happiness. In fact, he couldn't be happier for the vampire who had waited seven centuries to find his other half.

"How are they?" Zander asked him when he entered the room.

"Shae is still asleep and the others are still upset, but I'm sure they're grateful to be out of that shit hole," he replied and took a stance against one of the counters. He crossed one boot over the other and folded his arms across his chest.

"That's an understatement," Hayden, the Omega of the

shifters, said as he took a sip of his drink. "What do we do now?"

"We do everything we can to help them get better. They don't deserve to go from Kadir's clutches to our dungeons," Elsie said, tossing the vegetables she'd been dicing into a large pot. He hoped she was making her stew. It had been a cold and long night and that would hit the spot.

"We will, *a ghra*, no one wants to see them doon there longer than necessary. Jace has already given their blood samples to the scientists, and has assured me they are already hard at work in the lab downstairs," Zander replied, kissing the top of Elsie's head.

"It looks like they targeted supernaturals of nearly every species. We will need to hold a council meeting and invite the harpies and Valkyrie. We can't make decisions for those outside of our leadership," Hayden pointed out. Gerrick watched the big, burly Omega cross the room to peek into the pot.

"Och, the question is whether the archdemons have control over them. 'Tis clear they are no' the same as Jessie. We canna be blinded by the fact that they are female," Zander added.

"They are completely different than I was. I was never filled with rage like that. I was confused by the changes my body went through, but I was always in control. There was minor pressure in my head. Jace explained it was likely Azazel was trying to reach me, but it was easy to ignore. The biggest thing was adjusting to the changes... oh, wait... the tracker. Do you think they could have placed them in these women, too?" Jessie asked, giving Elsie the bowl of potatoes she'd diced. Definitely stew, Gerrick thought as his stomach growled. He was hungrier than he realized. He'd bet Shae was starving. Her ribs had been showing as if she was malnourished. He made a mental note to make sure Shae got a big bowl as soon as she woke.

Jessie's comments about her predicament had Gerrick recalling when they had rescued her and Cailyn from a car accident several months ago. Azazel and a Fae named Aquiel, along with the archdemon's skirm, had driven Cailyn off the road before they had attacked the females. Azazel placed Cailyn, Jace's mate and Elsie's sister, under a deadly Fae spell and Jessie had been envenomated.

The only way to cure Cailyn had been for Gerrick and several others to embark on a dangerous mission to New Orleans to retrieve an antidote. Jessie had been writhing in pain from an archdemon bite when they'd reached her. It had been in the days after that they'd discovered she had been turned from human to something else, something no one in the realm had ever seen before. She had dubbed herself a dhampir.

"I doubt it," Gerrick interjected. "They had no idea we were coming. There is no way they would have stayed put and allowed us to free these females if they had any inkling we were coming. It was clear they had no intention of giving up their play things."

"Aye, I agree," Zander interjected, setting his drink down. "The archdemons were confident their lair couldna be found. Still, it couldna hurt to check the females. The protections at Zeum disable the devices so there is no worry they can locate us, but that is no' the case when they leave here. The real concern and focus must be on their attitudes and behavior. Such overt aggression canna be allowed to roam freely. I only hope their blood tests hold the answers we need. The difference between them and Jessie is obvious and I want to know more. Kadir seemed to target Shae specifically. I want to talk to her and see if she knows anything aboot his plans."

"I can't imagine the torture these women have been through," Jessie shuddered and wrapped her arms around her middle. "Did you see their necks? It looked like some of them have been the demons' chew toys? I remember how bad it hurt when Azazel bit me. It burned like the fires of hell. I hate the thought that they suffered that more than once. For once, I wish I *was* the only dhampir in the world."

Gerrick clenched his fists where they rested under his arms. The left side of Shae's neck had been riddled with thick, raised scars. Zander was right, it was clear she was a frequent target of the demons and it made Gerrick want blood. He didn't know anything about the female, but he couldn't believe she had done anything to deserve that kind of treatment.

"I doona know what we have on our hands, Jessie, but you have never been alone," Zander assured the female. "What strikes me is how the repeated exposure to archdemon venom still hasna turned them into a skirm."

Gerrick was grateful for that fact. Skirm lost all their identity and became a mindless minion to the demon. And, despite the rage that had boiled out of her, he didn't sense that another controlled Shae. Her obstinate refusal to give in and her determination to hold onto every bit of self that she could was proof of that.

Zander continued, "If the injuries and her feral response is any indication, I'd guess that Shae has gone through the worst. She may hold more answers than the others. At a minimum, we need to develop a way to get her rage under control. She is one of mine and I refuse to lose her to those bastards." There was no way in hell Gerrick was allowing that to happen, either.

"Zander, how do you want me to handle the families of the humans? I can't inform them that their loved ones have been rescued from captivity only to be imprisoned in our dungeons," Orlando interjected. Orlando, a fellow Dark Warrior, was their link to the human world through the Seattle Police Department, and often performed the task of keeping families informed of current details.

"We doona tell them anything until we have answers for them. We doona even know if they are safe to be around their families. Protecting the realm comes first. The last thing we need is panicked humans and irate harpies out for revenge. Orlando, you and Santiago gather all the available information on the families that you can. Speaking of, where is Santiago?" Zander asked, glancing around the crowded kitchen.

Gerrick wondered the same thing. The warrior had been gone more and more lately. He wrote it off to the fact that the shifter's wolf seemed to be more restless lately and he figured the male needed to release his beast.

"I don't know. He took off without a word when we left the underground," Orlando answered. Gerrick noticed the way Hayden bristled at the interchange and wondered if the old power-dynamic was back in play. There had been a point that Hayden had been pissed and nearly pulled his shifters from the Dark Warriors because they demonstrated allegiance to Zander over their Omega.

"Don't worry about him, Zander. His wolf was keyed up after the battle and needed to go for a run," Hayden interjected, confirming Gerrick's suspicion. There was definitely more going on there than Gerrick was privy to, but he didn't waste any energy trying to figure it out. As infuriating as it was, his thought kept going downstairs to the redhead who should be waking from his sleep spell any minute.

CHAPTER 4

S hae woke feeling sluggish and her mind was fuzzier than a newborn kitten. It had been far too long since the demons had given her blood and she needed to feed soon. They denied her sustenance to the point she was ravenous and by the time they brought donors to her she attacked viciously, draining her victims dry. The demons and their minions enjoyed her torment over her actions.

There was nothing she could do to change her control over her appetite, either. Anytime she backed off and got control of her hunger she felt Azazel's pull in her head, urging her on. She had never killed so much as a fly before she was kidnapped, and now she had killed countless innocent humans.

Rolling over, she immediately realized something was different. It was nice not to be shivering from the cold and felt fantastic to be wearing clothes again. Gone was the cement floor and in its place was a mattress that felt like a cloud. Hell, she swore it was the softest thing she'd ever laid on. Had the Goddess finally answered her prayers and taken her to *Annwyn*?

She opened her eyes and saw a stone ceiling. Not *Annwyn*, but not her cell, either. The stench of brimstone and death was non-existent, and there wasn't a trace of the mold, dust and decay anywhere in the air. She ran a hand through her hair and was shocked to find that her fingers glided easily through the silky strands.

She jolted upright and tugged a handful over her shoulder, seeing that the snarls and filth was gone. She ran her fingers along her arms and realized she was clean. She had no idea who had cleaned her and it was unsettling that someone performed such an intimate task when she was asleep, but she was too thankful about being clean to get angry. Bringing the locks to her nose, she inhaled the fresh scent, noting the sweet floral scent was close to her favorite shampoo.

Goddess, she had missed the simple luxury of taking a shower. After all the torture and torment she'd suffered over the past seven months of her captivity, she had forgotten the pleasure that could be found in something as simple as bathing. She had never been the type of female who enjoyed long, hot bubble baths, but right now she would happily soak in one for a week.

That bath would have to wait until she figured out where the hell she was and who she was going to kill now for daring to lock her up again. She looked around her cell and saw a half wall. She stood on shaky legs and crossed the room. The ground and floor was smooth grey stone and was far cleaner than the hellhole she'd come from. She found a shower and toilet, as well as, a sink behind the wall. There was also soap and a toothbrush and toothpaste. She hurried over and grabbed the toothpaste and spread it over the toothbrush, scrubbing her teeth. Whoever had cleaned her earlier hadn't bothered with her teeth and fangs and damn did it feel good to clean them. Another luxury that had been denied her.

As she brushed, images came flooding back to her about her King and his Dark Warriors rescuing her and the other females. The subsequent flight and fight as they escaped her prison brought tears to her eyes. It hadn't been another dream. She really was free of the demon's clutches. She'd given up on believing she would ever get out of that cage alive. The relief she experienced over her freedom from the demons was the sweetest thing she'd ever experienced.

She wanted to bury her head in her hands when she recalled why she was in another cell, albeit a much nicer cell. She had attacked the princess, Breslin. Shae didn't know what had come over her. When they said they were going to have to be locked up again she had exploded and gone off. It was as if a switch had been flipped.

Even now, that anger was still there. If she were being honest, it hadn't left her for months. Not to mention the vibration in her veins that never ceased. Like fingernails on a chalkboard, it was enough to drive her crazy. There was no relief from the torment. She had tried everything to stop or escape it. She'd even scraped furrows into her arms trying to rid herself of the sensation. And, that was the tip of the iceberg of what she'd been put through.

Distracting herself from those disturbing thoughts, she wondered about the other females. She spit and rinsed then rushed back to the bars. She shoved her face through and called out. She could hear what sounded like others sleeping, and noted the king had designed his dungeon well because she couldn't see into the other cells.

With a start, she realized it would help ground her if she could see them. During her time in the cage, she had refused to form any lasting connection to the others in the event she was forced to fight and kill one of them. Clearly, she hadn't been successful because, now, more than anything, she needed to know that they were okay. Looking out for them had been her primary focus. She had placed herself in the demon's path time and time again to prevent another's torture. Better her than someone else, she thought.

When no one responded to her, she tried again. "Cami, Crystal, are you guys there?"

Rustling of sheets sounded before a relieved cry. "Shae. Oh my God," Cami called out. "I thought that guy killed you."

Ice-blue eyes flashed in her mind, making her stomach clench with awareness. Gerrick. The sorcerer who had been part of rescuing her had placed her under a spell when she attacked Breslin. That fact had rage bubbling even as she thought about what an undoubtedly sexy male he was. To her utter surprise, her body reacted with interest when she thought of his strength pressed up against her back. "He used his magic to knock me out. I'm fine. How are you guys?"

"Everyone is here and they gave us clothes and food." At the mention of food, Shae's stomach rumbled loudly. She hadn't eaten real food in over six months and was famished. "We're frightened. Well, I am, but they haven't hurt us. I keep waiting for someone to come in." Shae could hear the uncertainty in Cami's voice.

"Zander is a good leader and won't hurt us unless we pose a risk to the safety of others. You will be safe here. And, don't worry. Zander isn't going to leave us here indefinitely. He will use every resource he has available to help us."

"You really believe that? I was thinking they would just kill us." Shae understood Cami's doubt, but the human didn't understand supernaturals. They didn't think like humans.

Humans were a throwaway society with a high divorce rate. There was no such thing as divorce in the Tehrex Realm. You were born carrying a portion of your Fated Mate's soul and once you found that one being made just for you, you didn't betray that in any way. The fertility rate amongst the Tehrex Realm was extremely low, thus supernaturals treasured children and families in general. They invented the term 'family first.'

Shae believed there was a deeper appreciation and devotion amongst supernaturals, and as the Vampire King, Zander would do everything to save them. That was the one thing Shae didn't doubt. What she did question was whether or not they could be saved. They were no longer decent members of society. They were unpredictable, ruthless killers.

As she stood there, her hunger morphed to a lust for blood she'd only ever experienced during her captivity. As a vampire, she had always had control over her fangs, but now they were ever-present and had a mind of their own. With the thought of feeding, they descended even further, filling her mouth. She felt more like a saber-tooth tiger than a vampire.

One thing was certain, she couldn't feed from anyone until she curbed her appetite; otherwise, she would kill the next person she fed from. The sound of boots on stone had her turning her head to the stairs and she cringed that one of the warriors would be witness to her struggle. She didn't want anyone to see her like that, especially Gerrick.

She took a few steps back and stood with her arms crossed over her chest. Within seconds, Zander and another female came into view. They weren't there to kill them. Zander would have sent the warriors to do that task. And, Shae had no doubt, this female wasn't a warrior. Not only had she been absent during their rescue, she didn't carry the mark of a Dark Warrior on her forearm.

"Liege," she murmured, genuflecting in respect.

"Shae. 'Tis good to see you awake. How are you feeling?"

"Much better than I was when you found me, but not like my old self. When can I go home? I miss my family and I know my mom is worried about me."

"Your *mamai* and the rest of your family have been hounding my warriors for months. I'm positive they would love to see you, as well. But, I canna allow you to go home yet. Your earlier outburst is only part of the reason. We took blood samples to help us understand what we are dealing with. But, I promise you will have anything you need to make you comfortable."

She gritted her teeth and bit back her angry retort. She would never be comfortable in a prison cell. The urge to gouge his eye-sockets was overwhelming. Chanting herself that it wouldn't be prudent to piss off her king didn't do shit to defuse her increasing rage. What did was the knowledge that Zander had enough power to kill her without blinking and she very much wanted to live now that she'd been freed. "I can't stay locked up like this. I have to get out of this cage or I will go nuts."

"I understand, but I have a duty to the entire realm, as well as, the humans. This is my final ruling on the matter and I'd like your cooperation. From all of you," he said, addressing the other females.

"I'm the one that acted out. Let the others go. They don't need to be in here."

"You know that wouldna be wise, Shae. Each of you has been through a hell I canna comprehend, but trust me when I say that you will be released as soon as it is safe. And, I have the scientists and Jace working on this as we speak. No one wants to see you locked in these cells," Zander assured, confirming Shae's suspicion. He wanted to release them. Question was, would that be possible?

"You have to understand that I was caught off guard and the thought of being confined again made me lose my head. I won't do it again," she promised, doubting her own words. As much as she hoped she would be able to reign in her temper, she couldn't swear it.

"Och, Shae, you're playing a dangerous game pushing this matter. I have already given my final ruling. There are too many unknowns, end of story. That was only one reason I came doon here. The demon venom has changed many things and one of them is that I canna read your thoughts. The only other time I have experienced this is with Jessie, here," he said motioning to the female next to him, "who just so happens to be like you."

Shae's jaw dropped and she took an unconscious step toward the bars, looking from Zander to the female next to him. She had been so busy fighting her anger and talking to Zander to notice before, but now that she concentrated something in her recognized something in Jessie. And, if what Zander was saying was true, she's bet it was the demon venom.

She took in the beautiful blonde before her with her large, brown, doe eyes. There was nothing as obvious as scars on her body to indicate Zander was telling the truth, but there was something familiar about her.

"It's true," Jessie offered, answering Shae's unspoken question. "Azazel bit me and placed an electronic tracker in my side several months ago. I will never forget the feel of those teeth cutting into my neck and the pain that came after," she related as she pulled her shirt down and revealed the two small scars Shae could barely even see. Calling them scars was a vast exaggeration. They were more like mosquito bites, Shae thought bitterly.

Shae touched her own scars and indignation bubbled over the texture of her ruined skin. She had always been a confident female free of insecurities, but now she was riddled with them. She felt ugly and used and she didn't know how to live in her own body anymore. Her mind wasn't entirely her own and, without warning, her anger spiked out of control. Not to mention she now saw the world in reds and oranges. Her appetite had changed and her fangs had a mind of their own. The visible disfigurement was a minor part of the deeper pain Shae suffered.

Yeah, this female didn't know pain. She was bitten once and never again had to feel the searing burn of the venom again. Nor was she raped or tortured or forced to kill countless demons, humans and fellow inmates. Sure, Shae had relished killing every last demon she'd faced in the ring, but the innocent ones left a stain on her soul that could never be removed.

"But you weren't brought to suffer in the cages with us and you're standing out there while we're in here."

"Jessie was in that verra cell before she proved to us that she was no' a danger. You will get there," Zander added, crossing his arms over his chest, standing with his legs braced apart. Shae wanted to believe that with all her heart, but hope was a fragile thing she didn't dare cling to too tightly.

"You're right," Jessie chimed in, surprising Shae, "I wasn't taken with him when he disappeared and for that I am grateful. I'm sorry about what you and the others went through, but we are more alike than you think. Have you mastered the infrared vision? That took me forever to learn how to turn it off."

Shae raised an eyebrow at that. "You can turn it off?" With further contemplation, jealousy burned through Shae that this female had it so easy. On top of everything else, she didn't even have to deal with the blinding headaches the new eyesight caused.

"Yeah. I can teach you," Jessie offered, with a warm smile. Shae sensed every one of the other females were listening intently and knew this was something they all would want. She had to be careful in how she responded because the other females would follow her lead and benefit, or not, based on what she said.

"I'd like that, we all would. It's been giving me headaches for months. It would be a huge relief to get rid of them. Can I ask you something? How do you feed?" she asked tenuously. She didn't want to reveal her uncontrollable bloodlust, figuring it would help her cause, but at the same time she needed help getting control of it.

"I recall the headaches, although the scientists believed it was the archdemon trying to control me, not the change in my vision. I eat food like I used to, but I don't think that's what you're asking. I drink blood about every other day or so. And, can I say that for a human to go from not knowing anything about the supernatural to craving blood was enough to make me believe I had lost my mind. In my world, this wasn't real, so, at first, I thought I had really gone insane. Thankfully, Zander and the other Dark Warriors helped me cope and get through the transition."

Shae considered Jessie's words and wondered if she was right. The thought of either of those assholes trying to influence her had her ready to tear through the walls to get to them. She didn't want to continue living if they were able to manipulate her mind.

The other part of the female's statement sunk in. "I haven't eaten actual food in so long. I miss shrimp and scallops," she said wistfully. "What happens to your victim when you feed?"

Jessie looked at Zander then back at her and Shae realized she'd given away more than she'd intended. She tensed, ready for whatever may come next. "We doona consider our donors victims. You know this, Shae. And, Jessie most often consumes the bagged blood that Jace brings back from the hospital."

"But, the times I did feed from a person, I wasn't overcome with bloodlust. It was easy to control my hunger and take only what was needed." The other female held her gaze, but there was no censure there. Only, understanding. "I may not have gone through everything that you guys did, but I do understand the changes you've gone through. In fact, they didn't even have a name for me and I refused to be associated with skirm, so I decided to be called a dhampir. And, Zander has taken me in as one of his own."

"Dhampir," Shae tried it out. "I like it." She had been torn up over where she belonged now. She was no longer a vampire, but she agreed with the female, she wasn't a skirm. Titles were important in their society. She had been a female vampire, a loan officer, a daughter and sister. It was comforting to have a way to talk about her new identity. She hated being left in limbo.

"Can you tell me anything aboot Kadir's plans? You may no' know this, but he used a vampire to kidnap my mate and

I need to know if she, or any others, are in immediate danger." Zander asked, changing the subject. Shae reared back in shock. They must have kept this a secret from the realm because she'd had no idea that the same scumbags had kidnapped his mate. That was, after all, her Queen and her heart went out to the female. She knew all too well what being tortured was like.

"I can't tell you much. He never hid how pissed he was at you for foiling every one of his plans. It gave me hope each time you beat him even if his retaliation was to throw one of us in the fight cage."

"Shae, I'm—" Zander began.

"No," she cut him off, not wanting his apology. "We were glad you stopped him. The last thing the realm needs is for him to become more powerful. As for his plans, I'm not sure beyond the obvious desire to steal the Triskele Amulet from you." Shae thought about the Goddess-blessed amulet and how it bestowed certain powers on the bearer, which currently was Zander. She didn't envy Zander having to be the protector of the Godly artifact. It placed a target on, not only his back, but of those he loved, as well. That couldn't sit well with the Alpha male before her.

The sound of footsteps stopped the King's reply. All three of them turned their heads as someone descended the stairs. Black leather boots became visible, making Shae tense with anticipation, hoping it was the scarred warrior.

"Jace. Do you have news?" Zander asked the male that came to a halt a few feet from him. Disappointment was a crushing weight and she wondered if Gerrick was avoiding her. Not that she could blame him after the way she had acted. Mentally shaking her head, she focused on her bigger concern at the moment, getting the hell out of the dungeon.

"I do actually," he replied, glancing at Shae as he did.

"Preliminary results are in from the blood tests on the females." Shae's heart thrummed in her chest and she had trouble breathing as her nerves got the best of her. Could they have a way to help them already? What if it was bad news? She wasn't sure if she wanted to hear what the healer had to say. She wrapped her arms around her waist and waited.

"What have you learned?" Zander questioned.

"Not surprising, the venom levels in the recovered females are far higher than what we found in Jessie. In fact, in the case of one female, the levels were one hundred times higher." He didn't have to say her name, Shae knew it was her. She'd purposefully provoked the demons so they'd bite and rape her, leaving the other females alone. "The scientists theorize the venom has multiplied of its own accord. I don't believe that explains it. I think it's linked not only to the number of times they were bitten, but also to the spikes in their anger. We haven't seen that phenomenon with Jessie. Her levels have declined steadily since she was turned and she hasn't displayed the emotions these females have, so this is all conjecture at this point."

"Take another sample from them now that they are calmer. That's the only way to determine if there is merit to your theory," Zander ordered. Shae didn't care for being a lab rat. In fact, the idea had violence churning below her skin. Only her desire for answers outweighed the thought of any discomfort from being poked and prodded.

"Are we any closer to finding a cure?" Zander asked the healer as he approached Shae's cell.

Jace glanced back over his shoulder at the Vampire King. "We have actually taken the cure we've been working on and adapted it to the structure of the venom we see in their blood. We have an antidote that we can test. Unfortunately, we can't do anything more in the lab without empirical data. Problem is I have no idea what side effects this will have in a live trial." Hope beat wings in Shae's chest. There may be a way to go back to who she'd been before this nightmare. She didn't give a rat's ass about side effects. She wanted that cure.

CHAPTER 5

"I didna know you were that close," Zander replied, excitement in his tone.

Jace approached the bars of her cell and responded to Zander as he set his kit on the ground. He stood with several items in his hand.

"Here, let me help with that," Zander murmured, walking to the warrior's side.

"We have had many different antidotes over the centuries that we thought would work. It hasn't been until after Jessie that we came up with something that may be viable. Would you place your arm between the bars so I can take a sample?" Jace asked Shae.

"What makes you think it can work with these females?" Zander asked.

"Because something happened that has never happened before. The serum we added to the blood samples neutralized the venom that contaminated it."

Shae listened raptly as she pushed her arm through the metal caging her. "Do you really believe it's possible?" she asked, wanting to believe more than anything it was. She would always have the scars and the memories, but if she could get rid of the uncontrollable bloodlust, she'd really be a free female.

"Like I said," the healer responded as he tied a strip of plastic around her arm before swiping an area with alcohol, meeting her eyes. "We have no way of knowing if this will be effective, but the initial tests are promising."

"Och, this is the best fucking news we've had all day," Zander exclaimed, handing Jace a needle and tube. The needle slid into her arm without discomfort. "I know you didna mention this to us without being prepared to move forward."

"Yes, I have an injection with me." Shae's heart skipped a beat at the healer's words and her palms began to sweat with her excitement. Suddenly, she didn't mind being their guinea pig. "The scientists," Jace continued, "and I agree that we need to use it on one of the females with lower venom levels." Excitement was instantly replaced by disappointment, making her heart drop to her feet, knowing it wasn't going to be her.

Jace removed the tourniquet and needle then swiped her arm. "I'm sorry, Shae. I can tell you want to volunteer, but your levels are too high."

Shae didn't bother hiding her anger and disappointment. "I figured as much. But, promise me you'll do everything in your power to heal the others."

"I don't plan on leaving any of you like this," Jace assured her before he and Zander moved on to the next cell.

Shae tried to push her head through the bars so she could see what they were doing. She growled in frustration, unable to see a thing, so she focused on what was being said. She heard them asking one of the females if she'd be willing to allow them to inject her with the antidote. It didn't surprise Shae to hear that they had chosen the last female the demons had captured. This one had only been with them for a few days before their rescue and Shae didn't even know her name.

She heard metal clanging and low murmurs as Jace explained what he was going to do. It all sounded very clinical, nothing to give away the importance of what was about to happen. She hated not being able to see what was happening. It seemed as if everyone in the dungeon held his or her breath, waiting for her reaction. All of a sudden, chaos erupted. She heard screaming and shouts and then Jessie was taking off in the direction of the cell.

"What's going on?" Shae yelled, but no one answered her. She heard Jace bark out orders to hold the female down and a chill crept up her spine, telling her this wasn't going as the healer had hoped.

After an agonizing wait, Jessie walked down the corridor. "Jessie, what happened? Talk to me," Shae pleaded, but the female continued without responding or even making eye contact. Several minutes later, Zander and Jace passed her and what Shae saw had bile rising in her throat. She screamed her denial and rattled the bars. There was nothing recognizable in the body they carried.

She was bleeding from her eyes, nose, and ears. And blood trickled out of what used to be her mouth. The flesh covering her body had begun to blacken and rot and only a few patches of her caramel skin were left. Shae wanted to gag when the stench reached her. It was obvious that the female was decaying from the inside out. Cracked black flesh exposed the tendons in her neck as her head hung back and her limbs looked as if they'd tear free of their sockets. Shae gagged when a chunk of black skin sloughed off her little finger and landed with a wet splat on the stone floor. Tears sprang to Shae's eyes knowing that the female had died for no good reason. In a flash, Shae's fury boiled out of control, leaving her seething.

"You killed her. How could you do that?" Jace glanced over at her accusation and she saw the remorse in his amethyst depths. He hadn't intentionally hurt the female and he was obviously torn up over what had happened. Shae had known her whole life that these warriors were good males, deserving of her faith and respect, and despite her current anger, that hadn't changed.

"I had no idea," Jace replied and they left the dungeon, taking the body with them. Shae stared at the stairs for long moments before she crossed to the bed and sank down, ignoring the cries and questions of the other females. She had always been the one to reassure them, tell them that they would be rescued, but she had nothing left. The one ray of hope she'd had in seven months had been yanked out from underneath her. There was no way out and it made her want to tear through the walls and run until she dropped. She was never going to be the female she had once been and neither would the rest of them, so why tell them point-less lies?

She lay down on the pillow and contemplated what this meant for her future. She had prayed for death countless times over the months and had been denied. She silently cursed the Goddess for dangling the carrot in front of her, only to take it away. She hadn't calmed down from her earlier rage and her current line of thinking only added fuel to the fire.

As she spiraled, she swore someone was whispering in her ear to take her revenge, like having a proverbial devil on her shoulder. She told herself she was being ridiculous and tried to calm down. She tried deep breathing like Jessie had mentioned, yet her finger nails cut through the sheet and dug into the mattress.

A tap on the bars of her cell had her head snapping up. She'd been so preoccupied that she hadn't heard anyone approaching. Initially, she saw a bright red-orange image standing there and then the male's scent registered, telling her who it was. She had to blink several times before she could see Gerrick's scarred visage. It still had the infrared overlay, but she could see the grim set of his mouth, as well as, his ice-blue eyes clearly. Oddly enough, her anger bled away like dust in the wind. His presence alone calmed her and she allowed it to wash over her.

"I brought you food. The other females ate while you were asleep," he informed her, holding up a metal tray. Her stomach rumbled as the scent of the food reached her. She wanted to snatch the tray and inhale the food before she sought a neck to sate all of her hunger. Feeding had become a nightmarish event for her and the intensity of her current need frightened her.

For the past six months, her hunger and any desire for blood had been honed by the demons into a weapon of violence and death. She hated her lack of control, and just when she thought she'd gained the upper hand, it would spin away from her grasp. As she stood staring at Gerrick, enjoying the delish aroma of actual food, her gaze was drawn to his pulse. She had to have his blood. Nothing mattered but getting his blood and drinking every last drop.

"You okay, Red?" His deep rumble broke through the killing haze that had clouded her thinking. Harming this male would destroy what good was left in her heart and soul.

"No, I'm not. It's like there is this thing living inside me and all it wants to do is kill. I hate it," she admitted, hanging her head in her hands. She hadn't meant to tell him the truth, but her mouth opened and the words had poured out. Now that it was out there, she didn't want to even try to take them back. She wanted this male to know everything about her. The good, the bad and the ugly.

"So, you're giving up? You're going to allow them to win?" He cocked his head to the side and looked at her through the bars.

His ice-blue eyes appeared cold and distant at first glance, but she saw the heat and drive living deep inside. "Must be nice to sit there and judge me while you're the one standing on the other side of this cage. You have no idea what I've been through or how much I've fought," she snapped.

"Now there's the fire I saw in you earlier. You're going to need to hold onto that to make it through. Now, would you like this food? I'm not on the menu." Pity, she thought, wanting his blood more than anything else. She almost smiled when she saw the corner of his mouth tilt the slightest bit. His half-smile made her stomach knot and her core weep with need. "Don't worry, they will be bringing you blood soon."

"As if I'd bite you. Give me the food." Her mouth watered for a taste of his life's-blood, belying her harsh words.

"You're going to need to come closer," he challenged with what she swore was lust in his eyes. She wondered if she saw correctly and hesitated, but got up and walked toward him. She didn't miss how his eyes flared as he watched her. Anxiety had her heart racing. After everything she'd been through, she had sworn off males, but he was making her question that decision.

"That smells delicious," she murmured, focusing on her immediate need for food.

"It's Elsie's homemade beef stew and it's the best. One taste and I'm sure you'll agree." He paused next to the pass-through.

"I haven't eaten since I had a ham sandwich the day I was kidnapped. All we were ever given were frightened humans to drain." She didn't know why she was opening up to him. He had to have cast some kind of spell to make her spill her beans to him because she couldn't seem to keep her mouth shut. "They tortured and raped us if we didn't kill them when we fed. And, worst of all, was that part of me liked the killing." The way she figured it, if she wanted him to know her she had to put it all out there. She met his gaze, expecting to see revulsion, but saw understanding.

Gerrick shouldn't have any concept of what it was like for a female to be violated in the most horrendous way imaginable. Nor should he understand what it was like to have your choice in sparing an innocent victim stripped from you. Hell, having all choice robbed from you as you are subjected to pain and torment. But there was no mistaking his compassion.

"The blood of every life you took is on Kadir and Azazel's heads, not yours, and I won't rest until theirs is on mine." She blinked at the vehemence in his tone, touched by his protectiveness. Sure, it was the nature of a Dark Warrior to protect civilians, as well as, humans, but this felt like something more. "Let's not talk about them anymore. You need to eat." He held her gaze as he pushed the tray through the slot.

She reached out and grasped the wood platter, their hands touching in the process. Immediately, she was propelled to another world. Disoriented, she had no idea if she had actually traveled somewhere or if she was in a memory. What she did know was that she was now standing in a meadow she was certain she'd never been to before.

The scenery was breathtaking, full of purple heather as far as the eye could see. There was a chill in the air and she glanced down to see that she was wearing a coarse cotton dress unlike any she'd ever seen.

The material was thick and rough against her palms and extremely heavy. The blue and green tartan fabric of the skirt went to her ankles and billowed about her body. Her top was white and had so many layers she didn't know how to move. She felt the restriction of a corset underneath. The device smashed her ribcage and made it difficult to breathe. Her breasts were practically overflowing the low neckline and there was a black vest tied over the outside of her blouse. The whole outfit reminded her of clothes from centuries earlier.

"Goddess, where the hell am I?" she whispered. She took several steps and a rock bit into the bottom of her foot. Cursing, she lifted her foot and saw that she wore thin, silk slippers that provided no protection. They had to be the worst excuse for footwear she'd ever seen.

"Evanna," a low, husky voice murmured into her ear. She whipped her head around and nearly fell over. Gerrick was standing before her, but didn't look anything like the warrior she'd met.

He had a huge smile on a handsome face that was free of the scar. His blonde hair was long and tied in a tail at the nape of his neck rather than the short cut she was familiar with. His ice-blue eyes sparkled with warmth and invited her into their depths. There was nothing remotely cold or distant in his expression. This was not the warrior who had fought like he had nothing to lose.

His dress wasn't as foreign to her as her own. She recognized the kilt and billowy top as was common to the Scottish. He even wore knee-high socks and black shoes, as well as, the small pouch tied around his waist. He was gorgeous and she couldn't help but wonder what he wore under the kilt.

He pulled her into his arms, kissing her on the mouth and she knew his embrace, his taste. She melted into him, playing her lips across his. A gasp escaped as he pulled her tight against his broad chest and enveloped her in his strong arms. Gone was the pain and disgust that she had felt when she was touched. To have a male evoke passion and desire rocked her.

She ran her hands over his biceps and wrapped them around his neck, tunneling her fingers into the silky strands of his hair. He made sounds of pleasure against her mouth while she pulled the leather tie free. Gripping his hair, she nipped his lower lip, preparing herself for her fangs to descend but she didn't feel her fangs at all. She also didn't feel any bloodlust.

She opened her mouth to ask him what was going on, but he took advantage and slid his tongue inside. He was aggressive and took charge, taking what he wanted from her. All thought but of this male and his kiss fled her mind. He was everywhere at once. Tugging at the strings of her blouse, he loosened it before he broke the kiss. Lifting her head, she sucked in a breath. "Gerrick," she intoned.

"Mmmm," he murmured against her neck as he caressed her side, making his way to her breast. "You feel so good, Evanna." Two things should have intruded into the intimacy of the moment, but there wasn't enough room in her brain. One, he was speaking with an accent she hadn't noticed before, and two, he'd called her Evanna. Who the hell was

Evanna? What was going on? Her name was Shae...wasn't it?

She opened her mouth to ask a question, only to shut it when he chanted a spell that caused the fabric draped over his shoulder to float to the ground, acting as a blanket. He kissed his way back to her lips, coaxing her to the ground. He fisted the length of her hair and brought it over her shoulder before she lay down.

The strands were blonde. Startled, she looked up into his eyes. He laid his palm over her cheek and the vision ended as quickly as it began.

Between one blink and the next, she was back in the dungeon and Gerrick was standing in front of her with his hand against her cheek. She jerked back and nearly spilled the contents on her tray.

"Where'd you go? You froze up for several minutes," he commented.

She must be losing her mind. "Do I know you?"

"Yeah. We met a few hours ago when we rescued you from Kadir." He stepped back and leaned against the wall behind him, crossing his ankles, confusion clear on his face.

"No, I mean before that. I could swear..." she trailed off not sure what to say to him. No way was she going to admit to him that she imagined making out with him in a field of flowers, dressed in clothes from centuries ago.

"We've never met before that. I wouldn't forget you," he admitted. He may have been standing there with his arms relaxed at his sides as if he didn't have a care in the world, but his eyes told another story. He was attracted to her, as well, but it was obvious he didn't like it. "Eat," he ordered.

She sat on the bed and crossed her legs, picking up the bowl. Groaning as she took a bite, the rich, warm broth tasted like heaven. "Thanks for bringing this to me. I figured I wasn't going to get food," she remarked.

He scowled at her. "Did you think we would let you starve? We aren't savages, Shae."

She chewed and swallowed the bite in her mouth and narrowed her eyes at him. "I know Zander would never torture one of his subjects like that. I just figured that with the failed experiment, feeding me wouldn't be a priority tonight."

"You don't know the Dark Warriors very well, then. None of you are experiments," he practically snarled, he was so angry. "Jace told me what you said. He never meant to harm her."

"I know that. He mentioned that he didn't know what affect the antidote would have on us. I could see how upset he was by what happened. I don't know what came over me...I just reacted. But, Goddess, I've never seen anything like that and trust me, I saw plenty while I was held prisoner."

"I can only imagine what you saw in that lair. I know all too well what they are capable of. Death and destruction follow in their wake, but thankfully, we put a wrench in their plans when we freed you guys."

She looked down at her bowl and realized she'd devoured the meal in record time, belatedly thinking she should have eaten slower. Her stomach wasn't used to food and it was cramping, but she had to admit that Gerrick had been right. It was the best stew she'd ever eaten. It was beyond her comprehension that her Queen had done something as menial as cook this meal. She couldn't wait to tell her mom that the Vampire Queen had cooked for her. Her mom would be as shocked as Shae. In Shae's mind, the royal family was above such tasks, especially knowing they had servants to do it for them. They had a far more important job of leading the vampires.

Thoughts of the royal family and her mom built urgency about getting out of that cell. "I thought I was going to die in those cages. I had given up hope of ever escaping and seeing my family again. I may be out of their clutches, but I'm not free. Let me go, Gerrick," she pleaded, hoping to play on his emotions. Looking at his stoic face, she told herself she may have made a mistake. Rumors may be true about him not having a sentimental bone in his body.

Still, she persisted, "I need to return to my family. My poor parents don't need to believe I'm dead any longer," she whispered, making sure to look as pitiful as possible. It wasn't too difficult, she was battered and bruised and was certain she looked pathetic. Getting angry and demanding to be released hadn't worked. Perhaps, this approach would do the trick.

His stuffed his hands into the front pockets of his leather pants and didn't appear to be moved by her plea. "Nice try, but not gonna happen. Can you guarantee me that you won't turn on one of your family members? Do you really want to take that chance?" He pushed off the wall and approached the bars.

She stood up and scowled at him, clenching her fists. He may be sexy, but he was infuriating. Having been strong for so many months, she wanted to bury her head in the sand and pretend everything was normal again. She wanted to feel safe, secure and loved. Home had always provided that for her. There was no way the demons were taking that from her, too. Pain in her hand made her look down to see that she had crushed the spoon in her hand. Shit.

"I've done unspeakable things...I never want to hurt another living soul, especially my family. But, I can't be behind these bars a moment longer," she screamed at him, not able to control the rage.

The walls were closing in on her and she struggled to breathe. She dropped the spoon and grabbed the tray and threw it at the bars. Unfortunately, it didn't hit the male like she wanted. Chest heaving, claws extended from the ends of her fingers, she turned the bed over, shredding the sheets in the process. When there was nothing left to destroy, she stood there glaring at the impossibly gorgeous male.

"Done?" he asked with his implacable calm. Afraid of what she'd say she nodded, looking into his eyes. Without warning, she crashed hard and fast, tears blurring her vision. This male woke something in her that she didn't understand and she didn't know if she wanted to. She was too raw and for once since Gerrick had entered the dungeon, she kept her mouth shut.

Gerrick reached through the slats and gripped her hands. "I won't rest until we get you home to your family. If it takes me becoming a scientist, I will."

The sincerity in his gaze was undeniable and warmed her cold heart. She had no doubt the male would do exactly as he said. She wrapped her fingers around his and squeezed. The heat burned all the way up her arm, breathing new life in its wake.

CHAPTER 6

It seemed as if the tension in the house had been at level red since Zander met Elsie, Gerrick thought a couple hours later. As one of the Dark Warriors, Gerrick was accustomed to a certain amount of stress and chaos, but lately, it had been worse than ever. And, it didn't help that he couldn't get Shae off his mind. Something had happened when he'd taken her dinner. He had felt a rush of power and recognition the moment their skin touched. Then she had gone somewhere in her head and despite her denial, he had the feeling that whatever had happened was important, but given everything she had been through, he was ignoring it...for now.

Continuing down the hall, he entered the media room. He'd tried sleeping, but gave up and was searching for something to do. What he really wanted to do was head back to the dungeon. He'd started that way numerous times only to stop in his tracks. There was no reason for him to go to the dungeon and he hadn't been able to manufacture a reason.

"Are we really going to have the Winter Solstice this year?" Gerrick heard Rhys ask. He entered the room and saw it was filled with Rhys and the females of the house.

"Aye, we are really going to have the celebration," Breslin informed him. "This family has been through enough this year and we need to reconnect." Gerrick couldn't deny she was right, but wasn't sure he was up for a celebration.

"You're just looking for an excuse to buy a new dress," Mack teased the vampire princess.

"I doona need an excuse to buy a new dress, but when else am I going to get to dress you up?" Breslin threw a smile over her shoulder as she typed into her laptop. Gerrick had heard Mack rebuff the princess many times and deny her attempts to change her style. It had become a comical sight in the house.

"What exactly is the purpose of this celebration anyway?" Jessie asked.

"It has evolved over the centuries. The original purpose was to link with our ancestors, but the Tarakeshes have always used it as a way to bond with one another and strengthen ties. In recent years, we have expanded the celebration to invite select others to join us," Breslin answered.

"This is a first for me, too. What happens during one of these parties? And, what do I need to know as the Vampire Queen? I'm sure there is something important I'm supposed to do." Elsie inquired.

She wasn't your typical queen with her long, curly, brown hair pulled into a ponytail and most days she had on jeans and a sweatshirt. Not that it diminished her inherent power. The small female was ferocious, strong and commanding and took to her leadership role naturally. She cooked for them, set them straight when needed, and could take on any enemy in battle. Elsie might not look like your average queen, but she more than filled the shoes.

Breslin rolled her eyes at Elsie. "We hold a candlelight circle and then you will stand with Zander to give the offering to the Goddess. Aside from that, *puithar*, we eat, dance and drink."

"A candlelight circle doesn't sound so bad, but what kind of offering do we provide the Goddess? We aren't talking sacrificial or anything, are we? I've had enough of those to last a lifetime," Mack interjected, narrowing her whiskey eyes.

Rhys laughed with Breslin. These females may be fully immersed in the supernatural world, but they still thought like humans, Gerrick thought. "Nay, we doona have to sacrifice anything. We leave wine and gemstones for the Goddess."

"Yeah, we like to get her drunk and leave her bling," Rhys joked.

"Fucking Rhys," Breslin chided with the familiar sentiment.

"What are you going to wear, Jessie?" Rhys asked with a purr. "A barely there dress, I hope."

"I'm thinking a sexy, red number. How big is this thing anyway?"

"Och, last year we had a couple hundred. Though, I imagine Zander will cut that number doon this year. Things have been verra unpredictable lately. Besides, we doona know what will happen with the females in the dungeons."

They wouldn't be locked up if Gerrick had anything to say about it. He couldn't stomach Shae remaining locked up until solstice. Her need to be free plucked his every nerve until he felt raw. She was rapidly becoming his obsession and it was nearly impossible for him to stay away from her. Maybe she would go to the party with him. Cursing himself, he liked that idea more than was good for him. Of course, if she was out of the dungeon she would want to go home to her family. That thought opened another can of worms. He didn't know what he'd do when she left the compound.

"Hopefully they will be out of here by then. We know they're ready to get back and join their families. What do their leaders think of them being here?" Mack asked, popping a handful of nuts into her mouth.

"Their leaders agreed with Zander and the council about keeping them here until the scientists have had a chance to gather the information they need," Elsie answered, curling her leg under her body.

Cringing at the thought of what happened the last time they tested an antidote, Gerrick wondered how they were ever going to get the answers they needed. Neither Jace nor the scientists would be too keen on taking the chance again. Shae tried to volunteer before and she'd try again. That protective instinct reared its head with that thought and Gerrick vowed to do everything in his power to stop her. His chest constricted at the idea of her being injured, or worse, killed.

"I, for one, would like to see the dungeons with fewer occupants," Gerrick added. "I assume Zander used this as an opportunity to open talks with the Harpies. How did that go? Are they willing to come to the table with the alliance?"

"Och, they are being bluidy stubborn. Even with me there, the females refused to join our forces," Breslin added. "Regardless, if they become alliance members, we will have the Harpies loyalty after this which is a win. I have to believe these females will be oot of the dungeons by the time of solstice. I canna fathom keeping them much longer. On another note, we need to get the final details to Nate for the layout. He needs to familiarize himself with how the ballroom is going to be designed because this is his first celebration since becoming the majordomo. How big should we make the dance floor?" Breslin asked the room at large.

"Ugh, please tell me I don't have to dance at this thing. I don't dance for a reason. It's not pretty," Mack complained, throwing her body dramatically into her chair.

Rhys smiled. "Just wait until you have some of my *hey juice*. It's guaranteed to make you think you can dance."

"I thought you said it was guaranteed to make women rub on you and say *hey baby*, while begging to experience your...magnificence," Elsie teased.

Rhys walked over to Elsie and wrapped his arm around her shoulders. "That's how most females will react, but Mack is mated. It's a shame that you had to go and get mated before you got to try me, but I promise my juice will help you shake your thang. That's what the super-secret blend is designed to do."

Gerrick narrowed his eyes at the playboy warrior. The lecherous comments couldn't hide the longing Gerrick could see within his friend. The male was far more caring than he let on and was deeply connected to everyone in the house. He may tease and carry on as was expected of a cambion, but he would never disrespect any of the females in the compound. Hell, Gerrick had spent enough time around the warrior to see that he respected all females.

"Getting mated was the best decision I ever made. And, like I said, I don't dance. So, are you going with Thane?" Mack asked, turning to Jessie and trying to act casual.

"I like him and I'm sure we will dance, but we aren't going together," Jessie admitted, shrugging her shoulder.

Mack leaned back against the cushion and crossed her legs. "I'm surprised he didn't ask you."

The Tehrex Realm had different rules and expectations and their expectations had undergone a major change after the mating curse had been lifted. These females didn't really understand the depth of what that meant. "He's a Dark Warrior. Honor is our middle name. He won't get too close because he doesn't want to give you the pretense of a relationship. One day, he will find his Fated Mate and you will be left on the sidelines. When he finds his female, nothing and no one else will matter." Gerrick knew all too well what that felt like and his loss was still a knife in his gut. That he was drawn to Shae in a way he had only felt with Evanna was salt in the wound.

Jessie sighed. "I wish I knew if I was going to get a mate. There is still so much we don't know about my kind. Do you think the females downstairs, the ones that are supernaturals, still carry their Fated Mate's soul?"

Jessie's question made Gerrick's blood ice over as he considered her words. The Goddess Morrigan created most of the beings in the Tehrex Realm and had designed them to be part of a pair with each of them born carrying a portion of their Fated Mate's soul. It was theirs to guard and protect and no one was truly complete until they found their other half. To lose the soul you carried was tantamount to experiencing a death. He should know, he'd felt exactly that when Evanna had been killed. It had been devastating.

"Aye, the Goddess protects her creations as much as she can. Lucifer is the only one who can steal a soul and he is too weak where he is trapped in hell. No matter what his lackeys do, they canna take that from them," Breslin answered. Gerrick knew that everything Breslin said was true and was relieved that Shae's soul was safe.

"That's good news. Zander is taking that female's death hard enough. It's bad enough that he feels responsible because he ordered the testing and development of the antidote." Elsie rubbed her stomach and grimaced, looking a little green around the gills.

"You feeling alright, sweetcakes?" Rhys asked her.

"I'm just a little under the weather. I'll be fine."

"Ah, I hate to tell you this El, but you're a vampire now and shouldn't feel sick," Rhys stated the obvious.

"That's true, but I'm not exactly your average vampire," Elsie countered, raising one of her eyebrows in the same way Zander always did.

"Elsie's right. She's anything but average. Besides, she's an immortal vampire now. She's not dying, but I might," Nate complained, walking into the media room and joining the conversation. "What do I have to do for this damn party? And, why can't Angus do everything before he leaves."

"If you had lived for a thousand years without the female you had chosen for your mate and just found out she was alive, you'd be leaving, too. Suck it up and deal. It's a party, not an army you have to battle," Gerrick countered, happy to see Angus going. He understood what it cost Angus to keep his promise to help rescue the females. Gerrick had always thought himself an honorable male, but he doubted he would've been able to wait and fulfill a commitment before seeking Evanna out, had it been him.

"I'd rather fight. I'm a Máahes on Khoth, not a party planner or babysitter," Nate complained.

Gerrick understood where the male was coming from, but also knew that was exactly why Angus wanted him to stay. He wouldn't want to leave his family without a dragon for extra protection. And, Gerrick didn't doubt that Angus saw every one of them as family. "You're a dragon shifter and as soon as we find Kadir's new lair, we will be putting you to use. That bastard will pay for what he has done."

Jessie grimaced and sat forward. "I'd like to see them both become dragon barbeque. I can feel Azazel trying to control those females."

Gerrick stood straight. The thought of those bastards trying to manipulate Shae had him clenching his fists. "What do you mean," he barked.

"It's not like he can influence me or anything. More like I feel a buzz in my blood and find myself getting worked up for no reason," Jessie relayed.

"This buzz, do you think you can follow it to the demons?" he asked, hoping they could end both demons once and for all. Not that it would stop the war, but Gerrick wanted these archdemons gone, now.

Jessie closed her eyes and the room was silent for a couple seconds before they popped open. "No, it's too weak. Sorry."

"Well, it was worth a shot. No matter, we need to go back and see if the skirm left anything behind," Gerrick suggested, needing to be doing something.

Gerrick stood up and turned to drag Rhys with him when he noticed Elsie. Her eyes had gone vacant and she sat perfectly still, not moving a muscle. He glanced around noting that everyone waited with the same bated breath he did to see what she would say this time. Gerrick was coming to despise her particular gift. Each time she had a premonition it meant more trouble for them. "Take Mack with you," she said, coming out of it.

"Kyran isn't going to like that" Mack interjected. "Can you tell me anything more before I go toe to toe with my mate?"

Elsie met the female's gaze. "All I know is that you need

to be there. I couldn't get much more than that, sorry. It's like there is static or something interfering with the images."

"Your gift couldn't have crapped out at a worse time. Let's grab Kyran and head out. It's almost dark," Gerrick muttered, cutting off any further discussion.

KYRAN PULLED into the same parking lot they'd parked in the night before and Gerrick marveled at the difference. It was just past sunset and they had to circle the full lot a couple times before they found an empty spot. Humans milled about huddled in their winter jackets under umbrellas. It astounded Gerrick how oblivious humans were to everything. He agreed that the realm needed to be kept secret, but he doubted humans would notice if Orlando stood in the middle of Pike Place Market and shifted into his leopard. Sure, the animal would be talked about, but the fact of the transformation from male to cat would be overlooked or explained as new-age technology at play.

Gerrick climbed out of the car and shivered in the cold air, wishing it would stop raining at least for a little while. But, in Seattle, that was like wishing the sun didn't rise each day. Mack got out and walked around the car to Kyran's side. "I doona like this. When Elsie has her visions, they always involve death. I doona care what she said, you're staying with the car. I willna lose you," he promised.

Mack stood on her tiptoes and kissed her mate on the mouth. Kyran readily melted into her embrace, making Gerrick glance away from the easy display of affection. He never would have guessed that there was a perfect fit for Kyran or the change finding her would have on the male.

"Thanks to you, I'm not that easy to kill, bloodsucker. I can see that you're afraid. Stay behind me and I'll protect you," Mack quipped.

"Och, this isna the place for foreplay, Mate. But, later I plan to show you what I think of your statement," Kyran husked. Gerrick had pegged Kyran for a more submissive female and had to laugh at the Goddess' choice, but damn if Mack didn't make Kyran smile.

"Promises, promises. Let's get the hell out of this rain. It's making my hair fall," she said, shielding her spiky black hair.

"Nothing could make that hair fall. It's held up with concrete," Gerrick teased as he headed to the underground entrance.

Mack flipped him off as they splashed through puddles and made their way down the old steps. The second he opened the door, the scent of death hit him. The first time he'd passed through he had smelled mold and dust, but now brimstone and death overpowered all else. Darkness surrounded them as soon as the door closed behind Kyran. After they waited a few seconds for their eyes to adjust, they quickly progressed along the walkway. Gerrick was shocked at the difference this time around. Where there was rotting timber and debris, there was now black blood and carnage. He hadn't been aware that the fighting had reached this end of the tunnels.

Gerrick shuddered at the sight of a pus demon carcass in one of the old buildings. Fuck, the stench was overwhelming. "We're going to need to clean this shit up before the human authorities find it."

"I wish everything disappeared like skirm," Mack declared, pinching her nose.

"If only it worked that way, Firecracker," Kyran agreed, swatting her ass.

Mack squealed and laughed. "So who gets the shitty job of cleaning this up? And, what the hell do you do with the bodies anyway? It's not like you can parade them through Pioneer Square to a truck."

"Yeah, that would be a sight. Shit, I guess we're going to have to open a portal to our Whidbey Island property where we can have a bonfire. What we really need is to create a cleaning crew with all of these new lesser demons finding their way through," Gerrick relayed. "Looks like I'll have to be in charge of this project since Jace is working on the antidote. Maybe Killian can help me."

"Thank God I won't have to be part of it," Mack muttered.

Gerrick grinned evilly. "I didn't say that. You haven't been properly hazed into our ranks. You will definitely be part of the cleanup."

Kyran laughed and leaned down to whisper in Mack's ear. "Gerrick is right. And, if you're lucky I'll wash your back after."

"There is no way anything will convince me to help with this. The smell alone is enough to kill me. And, I am not touching that thing," she said pointing to the dead pus demon that was a heap of smelly, green meat.

"I can portal them right to your room, if that's easier."

"Oh, no you wouldn't," she said, waving her finger through the air. "How many of these things do you think escaped anyway? Could they be stalking humans in the city?" This female cared about her race and had made it her life's mission to give victims a voice. Gerrick admired that about her and wondered what was going to come of her vigilante organization. She'd taught the SOVA members to hate vampires, but things were different for her now that she was mated to one.

"I doona believe many of them escaped. Hayden and his shifters patrolled the area after we left and would have tracked as many as they could," Kyran assured her.

Gerrick knew when they were nearing the area where the females had been held because he caught a faint hint of Shae's jasmine scent lingering in the air. It immediately caused his body to harden with desire. Swearing under his breath, he called himself all kinds a fool.

"None of them will survive for long," Gerrick promised, excitement building. This was what he lived for, killing skirm and hunting the archdemons who made them, not a female with jade green eyes.

They made it to the room where the females had been held and Gerrick stopped cold. The sight had his gut in knots, making him want to kill something. The conditions they had been held in were deplorable. There was so much he had missed before. He'd seen the dead bodies, but hadn't realized how large the pile was. It appalled him that Shae had lived for months with a decaying mass of flesh and bones a few feet from where she slept.

To lie in your own filth staring into the vacant eyes of a dead human, one that you'd drained and killed had to be a special kind of hell. Not to mention, having to go to the bathroom in a bucket and not being able to clean yourself. He gritted his teeth at the icing on this particular sundae which was she had also been brutalized beyond comprehension.

He prayed to the Goddess that the cowards appeared before him so he could avenge Shae. The fervency of his need rocked him, making him question his reaction. For a split second, he wondered if Shae could be his Fated Mate and then reality sank in. There was no way she could be his. You were only given one mate in a lifetime and he'd already been given his...and lost her days later. He would never have what the others like Mack and Kyran had.

CHAPTER 7

Gerrick shook off his maudlin thoughts and completed his investigation of the room. After several minutes, it became obvious they were going to find nothing but macabre reminders of what innocents had suffered. He turned to Mack and Kyran, "There's nothing here. Let's move to another section. I'd say we should split up and cover more ground, but there's no telling what we may encounter."

Kyran grabbed Mack's hand and twined their fingers together. "Shite, this could be a futile effort. I hope the skirm were too stupid to stick around and cover their master's tracks. Those bastards would have been too weak from injuries to come back and do it themselves."

"Skirm are dumb as rocks. All those fuckers do is feed and kill," Mack blurted, walking back out to the hallway.

"Och, what have I told you, Firecracker?" Kyran asked, tugging on her short hair.

"I know, I know. The big thing that looks like a devil controls them and they do what he says. They were innocent victims once, too. Blah, blah, blah. Try telling that to the people they attack."

"It doesn't matter what they once were. The only thing that matters now is how fast I can kill them," Gerrick added from behind them.

Mack glanced at him over her shoulder. "Sounds like you hate them as much as I do."

He grunted and looked away. He hadn't told anyone about how he'd lost Evanna for four hundred years. Not until after the mate blessings had resumed. "Yup," he said, not elaborating.

"Okaaay," Mack muttered, turning back around. "I see someone is still as talkative as ever. You know you'll need to warm up a little if you ever hope to have more with Shae."

"What the hell are you talking about?" he snapped, mouth hanging open in disbelief.

"Gimme a break, Gerrick. I've been on patrols with you several times and not once did you give a victim your jacket, let alone your shoes. Normally, you wouldn't care if she paraded around town naked. Don't even try and deny it. And hey, who could blame you? Shae is beautiful."

Kyran laughed and leaned down to kiss the top of her head. Gerrick couldn't stop the jealousy he felt watching them. Shame followed on its heels. He was truly happy for Kyran and the others who'd been lucky enough to find their Fated Mates, but that didn't stop him from yearning for what he'd lost. He didn't know how long he could stay at Zeum once everyone was mated. It might be time to ask Zander for a transfer.

Zeum had been his home for two centuries. Hell, he'd help build the place. It would be difficult to leave the camaraderie and family they had developed. But, he refused to be a black spot in the happiness of their lives. There were countless other Dark Warrior compounds where there weren't any mates.

"You're right, she is beautiful. I feel bad about what happened to her and want to help. End of story." That's all it ever could be, he thought to himself. One day, she would be blessed with her mate and live happily ever after, as it should be.

"You keep telling yourself that," Mack chided.

Thankfully, they were all distracted from their discussion when they came to a large section with a television and couches, likely used as a main gathering area. He walked over to the sofas and tossed cushions before throwing the whole damned thing across the room.

Together, the three of them had ransacked the entire room within minutes. Looking as frustrated as Gerrick felt, Kyran crossed his arms and rubbed at his chin, deep in thought. "Shite, there's nothing here, either."

"Let's try that store over there with the creepy window," Mack suggested. Gerrick glanced over and saw she was pointing to a stained glass window depicting various demons. "How the hell did they get that made and then placed in the frame? No way would I have guessed demons had skills working with glass. It goes against the hulk-smash image I have of them."

Kyran laughed at that and Gerrick felt his answering smile. "I don't think it's a stretch to say they used dark magic on the previous plate-glass," Gerrick replied as he picked up a chair and threw it at the image. The sound of shattering glass was music to his ears.

They hadn't gone very far into the room when he felt the magic of a portal opening. He went still and ducked behind a half-wall, Kyran and Mack following suit without hesitation. They remained hidden, quietly listening for a hint as to what was happening. The hair on the back of Gerrick's neck stood on end. There was a malignant quality to the power that had him snarling.

Instinctively, he knew it had to be a portal from the hell realm. He stretched his senses and detected traces of skirm, too strong to be remnants of the previous battle, but not strong enough to indicate a large contingency. Adrenaline dumped into his system, escalating his heart rate and readying him for battle. He signaled Kyran, letting him know what he sensed. Kyran whispered in Mack's ear and Gerrick pointed in the direction they needed to head.

On Kyran's signal Gerrick headed out on silent feet followed by Mack. The clunk of her combat boots was too loud for his liking and he worried it would give them away. Muttering a quick silence spell, her shoes absorbed the purple-blue lights of his magic and the three of them continued on their path.

Gerrick held up his hand outside an empty storefront. They plastered themselves in a line outside the door and he poked his head around to see what they were facing. There were at least a dozen skirm guarding a portal. They may have been outnumbered, but he could take out skirm in his sleep. It was the hellhounds and fury demons pouring through the portal that concerned him. He called his staff to him and cast a blocking spell so no new immigrants could come through. *Seattle is now closed, motherfuckers*, Gerrick thought.

As soon as the portal was blocked, chaos erupted and Gerrick rushed in followed by Mack and Kyran. He encountered a hellhound and drove his staff through its skull without pause. His white magic clashed with the dark of the beast and brain matter splattered across his leather pants.

Distracted by the disgusting mess, a fury demon caught his right shoulder and bit down.

Twisting, he swung his staff in a wide-arc, catching the fury in the side. It went flying into the wall and crumpled to the floor. The second he turned, he noticed the determination on Mack's face as she made a bee-line for a particular skirm with Kyran hot on her heels. When Kyran went to shove her behind his back, Mack yelled at him.

"This is my fight! *That* is the bastard that stole my life and now he's gonna pay. You can't take my vengeance from me, Kyran." Gerrick could see what it cost Kyran to accede to his mate's wishes, but there was no way anyone would have denied Mack's command. The fortitude it took to hold her ground against the protectiveness of her mate was astounding. It shouldn't surprise Gerrick; she'd proven time and again that she was a fierce warrior, and, if anyone deserved revenge, it was Mack.

Gerrick would love nothing better than to have his own revenge on the demon responsible for Evanna's death. He had tried for years, but never discovered a name. Every time he fought, Gerrick wondered if this one had been responsible. It burned his gut that he had failed Evanna. Now he added the bastards responsible for keeping Shae locked up to his list and allowed his wrath free rein, knowing his eyes had turned black with his anger.

Gerrick put his staff back in its pocket of space and had his weapons out in the next heartbeat. The Dark energy was an annoying distraction against his shield as more demons tried to pour through the portal. Releasing his frustration, he kicked the skirm running at him, knocking it into a hellhound. The demon didn't care for the interruption and tore into the skirm. Taking advantage of the preoccupation, Gerrick thrust his knife into the dog's thick neck, cursing as he had to put more force behind his weapon before penetrating the tough black skin.

A fury demon took hold of one of his arms, yanking on Gerrick. Letting his body go, he used his momentum, holding the knife in the hellhound's neck. Skin separated, revealing muscle and tendon and black blood sprayed his face, burning him. Fuck, he really hated fighting these demons. Not only were they a pain in the ass to dispose of, their skin was like acid.

Tugging the knife free of the hellhound, he proceeded to lodge it into the eye socket of the fury. A loud piercing shriek rattled the walls, causing dust to float to the ground. Waving away the cloud of dust, Gerrick was suddenly surrounded by three fury demons hissing their anger. He wondered if Shae had ever been forced to fight so many at once. Demons were vile creatures that crossed to the mortal plane for the pleasure and strength in torturing their victims. Generally speaking, only the lower ranking demons could cross the veil between worlds because it took too much of Lucifer's power to send his more powerful demons to earth.

Recalling what Shae had gone through in this lair had his rage spiraling out of control. It burned hot despite the fact that he knew it was fueling the demons. His vampire should have never gone through these horrors. He kicked, hit and slashed like a madman until his energy was gone.

Out of breath, he stopped to focus his attack and took the opportunity to look in the direction where Mack had been fighting. She was battling the skirm she'd targeted and was kicking its ass. Kyran remained close to her keeping the remaining demons in the room at bay.

Refocused, Gerrick kicked out and tried to launch himself over the head on one fury. The creature was smarter than he gave credit and grabbed hold of his foot. He went down like a stone and his head hit the hard floor. Stars winked in his vision and fangs sank into his thigh. Not his best fighting due to the mixed emotions churning in his gut. It was a distraction he wasn't used to. No, he was used to going in balls to the wall until there was nothing left standing.

Fire erupted in his shoulder and he realized one of the others had bitten into his flesh. He bucked and tried to kick, but the demon didn't budge. Snarling, Gerrick surged upward, tearing his shoulder in the process as he head-butted the fury holding his ankle. The moment he was free, he thrust both blades into its skull. The crunch of bone was followed by the release of his leg. Able to move freely, he managed to get one in a headlock before another barreled into the two of them.

Maintaining his hold as they went sailing across the room was a challenge, but Gerrick would have to be dead before he gave up. Suddenly their momentum stopped as they hit something. The Gaelic curse told him it was Kyran. The warrior joined the fight and the four of them fell to the floor in a ball of tangled, bloody limbs.

"I'm going to sift, Gerrick," Kyran warned a millisecond before he disappeared. The confusion gave them the distraction they needed. Both demons looked around wide-eyed in fear for where Kyran had gone. That little disappearing trick had likely confused them and it was almost too easy at that point for Gerrick to tighten his hold and squeeze until he was left holding a severed head.

Breathing heavily, Gerrick tossed the head through the portal and watched it disappear. The other fury snapped out of his stupor and grabbed Gerrick's arm. Tired of playing games, Gerrick held onto the demon and turned until the portal was at its back then pulled his arm away and kicked with all his might. The fury went sailing through the portal and disappeared.

Going to his knees, Gerrick watched as Mack jumped into Kyran's arms and lowered her head to his shoulder. "It's finally over," she murmured.

There was a slight tremor in the arms she'd wrapped around Kyran's neck. It was obvious the female was overcome with emotion. Gerrick could only imagine the gratification and sense of closure she had to be feeling. Gerrick had heard the stories about her brutal attack and subsequent mission to eradicate the world of skirm. To have finally vanquished the skirm who had started her nightmare had to be a sweet victory for the female. He would never have that where Evanna was concerned, but he would move *Annwyn* or hell to ensure Shae had her chance at vengeance.

"Does this mean you'll stop patrolling and stay home with the females, Firecracker?" Kyran was playing with a live grenade, Gerrick thought. But, if the smile that spread over his face was any indication, he was anticipating the explosion.

"Not on your life, bloodsucker. What's with you men wanting simpering females sitting at home knitting while the big-bad mates go hunting? You just hate that I kill more efficiently than you," she boasted. It was impossible to miss the buoyancy and spirit in her voice.

"Will you show me the error of my ways when we get home?" Kyran asked, caressing her back.

"We're not going anywhere until we drag these bodies through the portal before it collapses. It'll be far easier to dispose of them this way. No vile smelling bonfire," Gerrick interrupted as he tossed a body through the wall of shimmer.

"Shite, I'd rather take my mate home. Stupid fucking demons," Kyran muttered, releasing his hold on Mack, letting her slip to the ground.

"You owe me a bubble bath and a thorough scrub later," Mack grumbled as she kicked her way through body parts.

It was going to be a long night and Gerrick hurt all over. And the thought of Shae giving him a hot bath and scrub had his blood rushing south and making matters worse.

A BLOOD-SOAKED GERRICK, Mack and Kyran limped into the entryway at Zeum several hours later. The bleeding in Gerrick's thigh and shoulder had finally stopped, but was congealing and making his leathers stick to his leg. It was rubbing his skin raw every time he took a step. The first item on his agenda was to take a shower and then have Jace stitch up his wounds. All that went to hell as soon as he entered the compound and caught the faintest hint of jasmine in the air. The urge to forgo everything and make a beeline to Shae in the dungeon was a compulsion he couldn't ignore.

Zander's voice stopped him on his way to the stairs. "Och, apparently this wasna a simple reconnaissance mission. Looks like you guys have been in a war, for fucks sake," the Vampire King observed, coming out of the war room when they entered the house.

"It wasn't my idea of a fun night. That Goddess-damned archdemon had his minions opening a portal from hell. If I hadn't contained it, the thing would have blown up all of Pioneer Square," Gerrick grumbled, holding his shoulder.

"I didna know that was possible. How the hell can he give his minions that power?" Zander asked, following him as he proceeded down the stairs. Gerrick heard Kyran and

Mack following in his wake. With everyone following him he'd have to settle for getting patched up before he sought out Shae.

"We don't really know everything an archdemon of his caliber is capable of performing. I would have told you it wasn't possible, but I watched it with my own eyes. I should have suspected after we discovered he'd imbued Lady Angelica and Cele with his Dark power," Gerrick cursed, recalling the ugly displays of that power by the evil females. "The problem was that the skirm had no idea how to contain the energy."

"Shite, how many escaped? Bhric, you take Orlando and Santiago and get over there, now," Zander snapped over his shoulder.

"Doona bother," Kyran added. "We killed them all, of course."

"Gerrick was the man, he kept the portal stable long enough for us to throw all the remains through," Mack added with a wince as they entered the medical room.

When the door shut, Jace looked up from his micro-scope and shook his head. "You should see the other guys," Gerrick joked at the grim look on the healer's face.

Jace chuckled as he opened several cabinets. "With you in the fight, I can only imagine."

"Anymore headway?" Zander asked, changing the subject.

Jace paused and placed his palms on the table. "Not on the antidote. But, we have seen the level of venom drop since they've been here. In fact, the females we released a couple hours ago had shown an even further decrease in their levels. Some of them are even close to Jessie's levels now."

Who the fuck had made the decision to take such a risk?

Anxiety had Gerrick's heart galloping in his chest when he heard the females had been released. "Where's Shae? She wasn't safe to go home to her family," he blurted before he could stop the words. Normally the quiet one of the group, he received several shocked stares from the group. All except Mack. She had a smug grin that said I-told-you-so that he wouldn't be living down anytime soon. Setting his mouth in a grim line, he clamped it shut. Defending his question would only look more suspicious. What happened to the deliberate, careful male? Since he'd met Shae he felt as if all of his actions were out of character.

Zander raised one black eyebrow and glanced at him. "Shae is one of mine and will remain here under our supervision until she is safe." Gerrick bit back his challenge. He didn't like hearing Zander claim she was one of his. Of course she was one of Zander's; she was a vampire, after all, but that didn't mean Gerrick liked it. No, his mind was shouting *mine* when it came to Shae.

"Take your shirt off and sit on the table," Jace instructed, startling Gerrick. "I have a feeling it will be awhile for Shae to stabilize. Her levels were easily five times what any of the other females were," the healer continued.

Nate entered the room carrying an armful of towels. Gerrick was shocked to see the male quietly go about putting his burden away before he went to Zander's side with a clean towel and peroxide. He remained silent as he assisted Zander in treating Kyran. There was hope for the male yet, Gerrick thought. Although, if he were honest, the irreverent dragon was growing on him.

"Why do you think hers were so much higher when she wasn't even held the longest?" Zander asked as he cleaned the injuries on Kyran's back. Gerrick watched the brothers, contemplating the question when his gaze snagged on the mate mark on Kyran's chest. An ache bloomed in his heart when he thought of the mating brand that he'd lost when Evanna had died. He'd lived for a few glorious weeks with the pain of the mark before it disappeared when she was killed. That had been another blow as far as Gerrick was concerned. Would it have killed the Goddess to leave him with some small connection to Evanna? All he'd been left with was bitterness and a sense of profound loss.

"From what the others have told me, anytime the demons approached their cages, Shae egged them on, making herself their target," Jace explained as he patted Gerrick's shoulder. "I can't heal these wounds, there's too much venom."

Gerrick shrugged, taking in the gaping wound. The five-inch gash had started to turn gray around the edges and blood still trickled from it. Not the worst injury he'd ever had. "Just stitch me up."

"It's too deep for regular stitches. I'll need to do several layers and use the staple gun to get it closed."

"I figured as much. Just do it," Gerrick told his friend. Jace nodded and picked up the needle.

"Aren't you going to numb him before you do that?" Mack asked abruptly.

Gerrick glanced over where she was washing her face with a wet cloth. "Why bother? It's a waste of time and medication. With our metabolism nothing lasts that long anyway."

"Your physicians haven't formulated serums that are more effective for your kind?" Nate asked.

Jace cocked his head at the dragon who had been silent since he'd entered the room. "No, we haven't. We don't need them all that often and when we do it's usually with the warriors who are a resistant bunch."

"I'd rather your efforts be spent developing a counter to the venom. The rest is bearable," Gerrick said through gritted teeth.

"Don't let your daddy eat your dawg," their new major-domo quipped, shaking his head in disbelief. Gerrick glanced at the male sideways, his pain forgotten. What the hell did that mean? Half the time he didn't understand what the male was saying. "For the record, I want drugs. I'll have Lorne bring some back for my kind."

Jace's eyes lit like he was a stripling seeing his first naked female. "That'd be great. I can analyze the chemical make-up and see if I can adapt the formulation to suit our races."

"So how many females are still in the dungeon?" Gerrick changed the subject, wanting to know what to expect when he went to see Shae.

"Only two, thank the Goddess. Shae and the human, Cami," Zander explained. "Breslin mentioned you'd asked aboot talks with the harpies. Oot of gratitude for our actions on her subject's behalf, their Queen, Tania, is going to join the next council meeting. Now, if only we can convince her to join us." This was great news and the furthest they had gotten with Tania in the past hundred years.

"Okay, all done. I'm going to take another sample from Shae, see if her levels have dropped again," Jace announced, taping gauze over Gerrick's shoulder. Suddenly, the harpies were long-forgotten and his complete attention shifted to Shae.

"Let me grab a shower and I'll go with you," Gerrick called over his shoulder, heading to the locker room attached to the training room. The pain suddenly fled his body in the wake of his anticipation at seeing Shae again.

CHAPTER 8

Gerrick gave up trying to contain his attraction to Shae and focused on building shields around his heart and soul so she couldn't reach him there anymore. He stomped down the stairs as irritated as he was aroused. He'd always had control of his cock, until Shae. She grabbed him by the balls and shattered all his reservations.

"Hello," Jace said, waving his hand in front of Gerrick's face. "You okay, buddy?"

"What? Oh, yeah."

"Could've fooled me. I've been asking if you wanted me to grab Bhric instead. You aren't in the best shape right now."

Gerrick scowled. He knew Jace wanted somebody there in case Shae flew off the handle again, but there was no way another male was going to be there in his place. "Don't fucking insult me."

Jace held up his hands in defense and continued down. "I wasn't insulting you, but you nearly lost an arm a few hours ago."

"Your point?" Gerrick snapped, close to losing his patience.

"No point at all" was his only response before they both fell silent. They reached the basement floor and rounded the corner to see Shae sitting on her bed with various balls of yarn surrounding her crossed legs. She looked up and smiled at them and Gerrick's heart leapt in his chest. She was the most breathtaking creature he'd ever seen.

"Hey, Shae. I see you got your knitting supplies," Jace said, walking closer to her cell. Gerrick wanted to grab Jace by the throat and shove him against the wall for giving Shae anything. His possessiveness was off the charts. Or, was it the fact that he wished he was the one who'd provided for her. Either way, he needed to get a grip.

"Yes. Thank you, Jace. Hi, Gerrick." He felt the caress in her intonation all the way to his toes. She claimed to be a vampire, but he was convinced she was a siren using her spells to ensnare him.

"Shae," Gerrick tilted his head, trying to mask his attraction. "Are we in a better mood?" She had cleaned the cell, her mattress had been replaced and she was threading black yarn into Goddess only knew what. He shook his head, disgusted with himself at the desire to wear whatever she was making just to have a piece of her close to his skin.

He saw a spark of anger flash in her eyes as she opened her mouth then quickly shut it. "If I tell you to fuck off does that answer your question?" He smiled at the steel in her spine. She was sexy when she was annoyed.

"As interesting as this battle of the sexes is," Jace interrupted, "I have other things to do and need to take another blood sample, Shae."

Gerrick leaned against the wall. His posture may have look relaxed, but he was strung as taught as a bow. He silently watched as she set her yarn down and stood up. The hairs stood on the back on Gerrick's neck as Jace spoke about the reasons he believed the antidote failed and how he was going to isolate the remaining venom in her system and try again.

Shae held her head high and confronted reality head on. The defiant tilt to her chin spoke volumes for what she thought about all the blood samples, yet she willingly submitted. There was no doubting the importance she placed on the wellbeing of others. He'd never met a more selfless person. Gerrick wanted to shake her and force her not to sacrifice any more than she already had because he knew she'd give her life if it would save these females.

However, underlying it all, Gerrick saw the wounded spirit at her core. He wanted to wrap her in his arms and tell her it was going to be okay. He wanted to lie down on that mattress and talk all night with her. Protect her, caress her, take care of her... where the fuck that urge came from he had no idea. He wasn't a touchy-feely male. He was known as a ruthless warrior who had no heart.

Others took one look at him and avoided him at all costs. He had been convinced it was his obvious disfigurement until he heard the rumors about him being merciless and coldblooded and they weren't wrong. No one since Evanna had touched the softer part of him, not even Zander when he gave Gerrick's life new purpose.

Jace packed up his supplies, drawing Gerrick's attention away from Shae. "You coming?"

"I'll be right behind you, go ahead," he replied, turning back to Shae.

"Was my fuck off not clear enough?" Shae asked sweetly.

"It was crystal clear. You look much better than last time

I saw you." Pushing off the wall, he winced at the pain it caused.

"Much better than you. What happened?" He could see the concern bracketing her delectable mouth. And damn, he wanted to kiss those full lips. They had been dry and cracked the last time he'd seen her, but had healed and looked soft and moist and delectable.

"We went back to Kadir's lair," he said, pausing at her indrawn breath. Horror and fear played across her face.

"Were they there?" He couldn't help but see the vulnerability she tried to hide. The urge to stand in front of her and protect her from further harm nearly consumed him. In fact, he felt like he'd failed her. He had known they shouldn't have waited so long to go after the females, but they'd listened to Elsie after her premonition. No one had questioned following her advice, especially when her gift came from the Goddess herself, but as Gerrick stood there contemplating everything Shae had been through he had to stifle his anger. He could have saved her from at least some of the pain and torment.

"We encountered a handful of skirm and lesser demons. Those bastards didn't show up," he replied, moving closer to the bars.

"Good. I plan to hunt them down and tear them apart with my bare hands," she vowed. He appreciated her need for vengeance and knew she needed it to regain some of her lost innocence. Problem was that it went against his nature to allow her to place herself in danger.

"That's not going to happen as long as you're in here." Distracted by her jasmine scent, he accidentally leaned his injured shoulder against the bars and cursed, "Shit."

She walked closer to the bars. "You were hurt. Take off

your shirt, let me see." The thought of her hands caressing his skin had his shaft hardening and his eyes glowing.

There was no hesitation to comply. Watching her carefully, he pulled the fabric over his head. "It's nothing really. Just a scrape."

She reached her hand through the bars and lifted one edge of the bandage then snorted. "If you call that a scrape, I'd hate to see what you think of as bad. How did this happen?"

"I was surrounded by fury demons and didn't act fast enough. Bastards used my emotions against me before I realized my mistake," he huffed, leaning into her touch. The heat of her fingers on his skin made him forget everything else. He wanted nothing more than to feel them travel all over his body.

"The key to beating a fury is to let your rage loose in a sudden burst. It acts like a drug in their system, intoxicating them to the point of delirium for just a few seconds, but it's long enough to remove their heads."

Shock had his eyes widening. "You've fought them," he said without thinking.

"Yeah, many times, until they realized it was no challenge for me. I learned quickly that half the fun for them was to watch me suffer, as well as, to watch me agonize over having to kill someone. I denied them that by shutting down and donning a mask before I entered the cage. Once there, I did what I needed to survive. Worst part was they didn't want me dead. They enjoyed watching me die on the inside," she whispered the last, having lowered her hand from his shoulder.

"If you think you're dead inside, you're crazy. I've never seen anyone more alive." They stared at each other for several heated moments and the connection he'd felt to her the moment he laid eyes on her strengthened. The sudden appearance of Mack's pet, Pip, broke the moment.

"What is that?" Shae asked, causing Pip to stop and look up. The furry animal began chittering and grabbed onto the bars. He pulled himself up and perched on the middle brace watching her.

"That's a kippie from the Khoth Realm. Kyran and Mack brought him back with them."

Shae held out her hands and the fuzz-ball jumped into them, immediately purring. She laughed and rubbed the top of its head, holding it next to her bosom. Gerrick glared daggers at the animal, jealous of the attention she was doting on it. He wanted his head resting on her breasts. Of course, he wouldn't really rest there. He'd lick and nip and suck her until she begged him to fuck her.

"This is possibly the cutest thing I've ever seen. It's like a tiny koala bear. I've never heard of Khoth. I take it's a separate dimension," her voice interrupted his fantasy.

Using every excuse he could to be close to her, he shoved his hand through the bars and rubbed Pip's back. Their fingers kept brushing and it sent electricity arching through him each time. His blood zinged in his veins, awakening every nerve ending in his body. It was a struggle to focus on their conversation. "Yes, Khoth is another dimension, ruled primarily by the Cuelebre dragons."

"Pip, are you down here?" Nate called out, coming into view.

"He's here," Gerrick answered.

"Oh hey. Didn't know you were down here, too," the male told him. "Hey Shae. I see you've found the little trouble-maker."

"He's not a trouble-maker. He's adorable...look at that face. I don't think he likes you very much, though. He's shaking." The little animal knew how to work the females, Gerrick thought. Pip knew better than anyone that Nate wouldn't hurt him, but he sure played it up. He swore the fuzz-ball smiled when Shae held him closer.

"I left the door open and I thought I'd lost him. I'm babysitting him tonight while Mack and Kyran are out, but she'd have my head if he got away. Come on, let's get you a treat," Nate coaxed. At the mention of treat, Pip jumped to the floor and scampered away. Laughing, Nate followed. "See you guys later."

"Nate feels different to me, but I can't figure him out. He feels closest to shifters, but he's not a species I recognize." She shook her head and met his gaze again. "One thing is certain, Zeum is nothing like I imagined," Shae sighed, with a bemused expression that softened her face.

"It's never a dull moment, that's for sure. And Nate is one of the dragon shifters from Khoth. Now, can I get you anything?"

"I'd really love to get out of here. I'm trying to hold on, but it's difficult to be in these dungeons. I'm still locked up and it's not helping calm me down. It's completely counter-productive. Hell, I don't even know if its day or night." She wrapped her hands around the bars in front of her.

"It's night," he murmured. He stood there and glared at her, not caring for the way she so easily manipulated his emotions. He wondered if he could take a chance on her. Confusion crossed her features and he let out a sigh of defeat. "If you promise to remain by my side, I can take you out of here, but only for a few minutes." He was going out on a limb, but he couldn't stand to see the agony in her eyes. He never wanted to see that look in her eyes again.

Her eyes went impossibly wide and giddiness washed over her face. "Seriously? You'll take me out? Zander said no earlier..." Hope was a fragile thing and he refused to crush what he'd extended to her, but hearing Zander didn't want her out told him they'd need to be covert in their departure. The last thing he wanted was to piss off his liege. He shouldn't be doing it at all, but found there was no way he could leave her in that cell a minute longer.

"I will. As long as you understand that you aren't going home and I have to put you back in here."

"I know. I won't fight you...much," she winked at him. He found himself returning her smile as he placed his palm over the mystical lock and it immediately unlocked. Luckily, all of the cells in the dungeon were programmed to the warriors' handprints.

"Oh, I don't know. I think I'll enjoy holding you down, Red," he husked as the door swung open.

"I'm too much female for you. Just sayin'," she returned. He didn't miss the blush that stained her cheeks or the light that entered her gaze. Challenge accepted, he thought.

SHAE FOLLOWED Gerrick down the corridor, reeling from the flirtation between them. Her initial reaction had been revulsion when he mentioned holding her down, but that quickly burned away and was replaced by the heat of arousal. She hadn't reacted to him like she did every other male she'd come into contact with since her rescue. She couldn't get far enough away from males, except Gerrick. She had been attracted to him from the beginning and that had only increased over time. She shook her head and focused on the fact that she was going to have a few minutes of freedom.

They traveled past Cami who watched them with wary eyes, but she kept her mouth shut. Shae expected her to beg to be let out, as well, and was glad when she didn't say a word. It was selfish of Shae not to ask for Cami to be included in their little outing, but she wanted to be alone with Gerrick. He made her angry, aroused her to a fever pitch and made her feel things she hadn't known she was capable of and she couldn't help but want more.

"This goes on further than I would've guessed," she commented as they continued walking down the corridor.

"We added these tunnels as an easy escape in the event of emergencies. They lead to the trees lining our property. We couldn't risk full-sun exposure with Zander and his siblings."

"You guys dug these tunnels?" she asked, surprised once again that the Vampire King and his Dark Warriors had done such a menial, time-consuming task.

"Don't sound so surprised, Red," he said as he opened a large, heavy door. "Stick close to me. You won't like it if you make me chase you down. I bite." He grinned at her and she noticed he had perfectly straight white teeth that accented his crooked and oh-so-sexy smile.

The scent of pine trees was heavy as they stepped outside and the forest floor was covered in greenery that was soft under her bare feet. He grabbed her hand, tugging her along. "Come on. The lake is right over there," he said pointing to the right. "There's an area that is out of sight of the house and you can see the water."

She shivered in the cool air, realizing she only had on a thin cotton t-shirt and sweats. "It seems like forever since I've seen the lake. I can smell...ouch, crap," she blurted when she stepped on a large, jagged rock that was hidden in the foliage.

His grip tightened and he stopped walking. "What happened?"

"I stepped on a rock, I'm fine," she quickly relayed, not wanting to complain because she didn't want to go back inside. Before she knew what was happening, he had scooped her into his arms and was carrying her. She stiffened automatically, but resisted pushing out of his arms. She had to admit it was exhilarating to be enfolded in the strong sorcerer's arms.

"I'm not giving up my boots this time," he informed her with the half-smile that made her insides melt.

"Thank you for not taking me back yet." She didn't bother arguing she could walk, not wanting to separate from him. Her heart raced and her chest constricted at their closeness.

Despite her heightened responses, she relaxed into his hold and watched where they were going, seeing everything through new eyes. They cleared the trees and the water gleamed large and dark before them. There wasn't a beach area here, but she noticed one in the distance. That was rare for this area. Most people didn't have land that would support a beach and used docks to enter the water. She felt the tingle of spells, telling her they had strong magic shielding their property. They had clearly spent a lot of time creating their little oasis.

"I'd say that your setup rivals Bill Gates'. Not that I've ever been there, but I've seen pictures."

He chuckled and set her down. He kept one arm wrapped around her back so she slid against his body in a sensuous glide as she found her feet. "Is this better?"

"Well, let me think. Standing here in one of the most beautiful settings I've ever seen or staring at those stone walls? Yeah, I'll go out on a limb and say this is better."

He tugged her hair and made her meet his heated gaze. "Don't push your luck, Red. You make me crazy...and all I can think about is kissing you," he admitted, his breath skating across her face as he leaned close.

The ice-blue glow of his eyes mesmerized her. "Now who's pushing..." His lips crashed down on hers before she could finish.

She was surprised at how soft they were given how hard everything else on his body was. She laid her palms on his shoulders and felt his muscle twitch in response. Liquid heat rolled through her body, leaving her tingling in its wake. The male could kiss like no male she'd ever been with.

He licked her bottom lip, making her shiver. A moan escaped her throat and he responded with fervor. His hands wrapped around her hips and held her close to his body. He slid his tongue into her mouth and tangled with hers. His fingers tightened their grip as he devoured her mouth, making her core clench. She hadn't expected that response, but before she could think any further, he was sliding his hands up her back and pulling her closer. The erection she could feel pressed against his jeans was impressive in size and pulsed against her stomach as he dominated her with his tongue.

He broke the kiss and nibbled his way across her cheek and along her jaw. Both of their panted breaths filled the night air. With each indrawn breath, her breasts rubbed against his chest, making them tingle and furthering her ache. "Gerrick." It was a warning and a plea. She wasn't sure how much more she could take.

He returned to her mouth and she sucked in air right before he sealed his lips over hers. He once again kissed her into submission. No other male attracted her the way he did. Her hand slid up his scarred cheek to tangle in his hair. She gripped the short strands. This time when he broke away, he kissed down the left side of her neck. She wanted to pull away, but he refused to let her.

A hundred objections filled her mind, but each flew away in the wind before they left her lips. His nose brushed the side of her throat before he tenderly kissed every one of her scars, making her eyes fill with tears she refused to let flow. His message was clear, he accepted her for who and what she had become. If anyone understood what that meant, he did.

"You're the sexiest female I've ever met," he murmured. His breath caressed her skin, giving her chills with every word he spoke. His hot mouth returned to hers and the jolt as his tongue touched hers was just as powerful as the first time. The heat of his palm branded her through her shirt before it slid under the fabric. Her heart raced frantically in her chest.

One big hand braced the small of her back, pressing her lower body close to him and he continued his masterful domination. Her hands returned to his shoulders at the same time his other hand slipped to her breast. The second his palm closed around her enlarged globe, her fingernails dug into his shoulders and she panicked. This was what the demons had done to her initially. The beautiful one, Azazel, had seduced her while she was under the influence of some spell.

She pushed slightly against him, but he misunderstood and he pinched her nipple, sending her over the edge. She recalled the way sharp claws sliced into the sides of her flesh while fangs sank into her neck. She was back in that underground lair with gray flesh covering her naked body. There was never any kissing, but they bit her neck and fed from her while they pinched and cut into her flesh. Rage took over and she thrashed against his hold, kicking and biting.

She braced herself for the painful surge of his body into hers, but it didn't come.

Strong arms wrapped around her body. "Shae. Shae. Come back to me. What the fuck?" Gerrick breathed bringing her back to her senses until she realized where she was. "Are you okay?"

She nodded while she attempted to get control of her heartbeat and breathing. "What happened?" he asked, confusion in his voice.

"Nothing, can you please take me back to my cell?" she asked, refusing to meet his eyes. She didn't want anyone to know her shame, especially this male. What had happened to her was bad enough, but she didn't think she could ever share the ugly details with anyone. She could barely face them herself.

CHAPTER 9

Gerrick sat next to Shae at the large table while Angus argued with Nate. He hadn't had the heart to return her to her cell when she'd asked. He hadn't understood her reaction to his kiss by the lake, but in hindsight he was grateful. While he hated to see her embroiled in a struggle to survive, he understood. He may be the callous warrior, but he'd seen enough in his life to understand that something during their interlude had triggered a memory about what she had suffered at the hands of the demons.

If she hadn't begun fighting him, he would have taken her and instinct told him it wouldn't simply have been sex, but he didn't have room for anything else right now. There was no doubt that he would have lost a piece of his heart to her, but it wasn't his to give. His heart and soul belonged to his lost mate, Evanna. His draw to Shae both pissed him off and worried him. Before he met Shae he had belonged completely to Evanna, but now he was questioning his love and loyalty. To make matters worse, every passing second pulled him closer to Shae and he hated her for that. His entire world was off kilter now and he didn't understand any of it.

He passed her the hummus and felt the same electricity when their skin touched. "Thank you," she murmured, finally meeting his gaze. The tension that had been ready to snap since their encounter unfurled when he saw her unspoken appreciation for the fact that he had gone to Zander and argued to have her and Cami released from the dungeon. He sat taller in his chair when he noted the way she looked at him. She was looking at him like he was a hero. Many in the realm saw him and the other Dark Warriors as heroes, but this was different. More intimate and meaningful.

It mattered more than it should that she saw what he had done for her. And he had done it for her and her alone. There wasn't another soul he would have stood up to Zander about. As it was, it had been tough for Gerrick to challenge his liege and request freedom for Shae and Cami. Zander was a fair leader and they knew better than to question his edicts. He didn't respond well to having his authority questioned.

Hell, he was known to throw them in the dungeon for a month without food if he saw fit. As supernaturals, they wouldn't starve to death, but the experience was excruciating and a brutal punishment. Gerrick could handle that better than most, especially a warrior like Rhys, who couldn't go that long without sex.

Having stuck his neck out for the females, Gerrick knew that should anything go wrong it was his neck on the line. Shae could flip out at any second and attack again, but even that didn't cause Gerrick one ounce of regret. He would do everything in his power to ensure she was never locked up again. Besides, the way he figured it, with only Shae and

Cami in the house, it was much easier to ensure containment. It helped that both females agreed to around the clock supervision for the time being. Of course, Gerrick assumed responsibility of keeping track of them. The idea of anyone else watching Shae that closely didn't sit well with him and he wasn't about to allow anyone else such an intimate glimpse into the female. That was for him and him alone.

He shut off that train of thought before it got him in trouble and focused on the conversation at the table. Their majordomo, Angus, was leaving them after two centuries and the mood was less than jovial. He was astonished when he learned recently that Angus was the king of dragons in his home realm of Khoth. The male had become such an integral part of their household that his absence was going to leave a huge gap in their group.

It would be quite some time before things felt even remotely normal again, but Gerrick wouldn't deny him the opportunity to embark on an expedition to find his lost love, Keira. Given Gerrick's history with Evanna, he felt a kinship with Angus after learning that he had lost Keira before they could be mated. That kind of experience scarred a male. Because of that, Gerrick was exceedingly happy for the dragon when he had discovered that she was alive somewhere on earth. Still, Gerrick was insanely jealous of the second chance Angus had been given. He wanted to feel that light of hope and anticipation again.

"Why can't Lorne stay here with the Dark Warriors and I go with you? He's much better suited to be the new majordomo," Nate interrupted for the millionth time, sounding like a broken record.

Angus pinned him with a glare that Gerrick had never seen from the male. "Och, I have explained this to you many times. I know I've been gone for millennia, but the fact that you believe it acceptable to argue with your king is answer enough. You need to learn discipline."

Nate turned scarlet and lowered his head. "Sorry, Sire. I meant no disrespect. I'm just out of my depths here and I don't understand how this realm works. It seems crazy that supernaturals live secretly beside humans. I don't want to mess this up and be stuck here longer than necessary. I promise to do my best while I'm here, but I'm not a glitz and glam dragon. For starters, I don't know anything about planning parties. The last party I attended was the mating ceremony for Kyran and Mack and the females were in charge." Gerrick heard the desperate, pained tone to Nate's voice. He'd bet the dragon would rather shove hot pokers through his eyes. Gerrick was grateful that Angus felt a loyalty to their household and refused to leave them without an appropriate replacement, but he had a hard time imagining that Nate was going to be able to fill his shoes.

"Stop whining, Nate," Breslin teased. "I'm no' about to leave this event to you. 'Tis too important for our people and as you said, you doona have a clue." Gerrick saw the relief cross Nate's face before Breslin continued talking. "But, that doesna mean you willna be heavily involved. Nay, rest assured, you will work your arse off, doing everything I tell you."

"I'll happily work my *arse* off for you, Flame. Tell me where you want me," Rhett interjected, openly flirting with Breslin. The fire demon was playing with fire, literally, and Gerrick scooted his chair away from the male, not wanting to be in the line of flames that might be shot his way. The move made his arm and thigh brush against Shae and sent arousal, hot and potent, coursing through his body.

He glanced at the Princess who had the power to control

fire and noticed she looked murderous at that moment. Rhett had come from Khoth with Kyran and the others and had proven an ally in fights, but, like Nate, he was a little too friendly with the females. Breslin was a warrior forged in the flames of hell and Rhett needed to rethink his approach if he hoped to have a chance with the female.

"I want you to return to the volcano you crawled oot of. What makes you think you're qualified to plan this event? Tupping females doesna give you anything but a limp dick," Breslin countered, anger causing her eyes to darken.

"My mind hadn't gone to tupping, but I'm glad yours did. And, trust me, there isn't anything I can't do. I spent a thousand years on Khoth doing every job there was. There is no job, too large, or intimate," he purred," that I don't have knowledge of." The fire demon's orange eyes glittered with interest as he spoke to Breslin.

Breslin snorted and turned to Angus, dismissing and ignoring Rhett. Gerrick knew Breslin well enough to see that she was covering the fact that she was deeply affected by the male's attention. "We are going to miss you, Angus. Please promise you'll come back with your mate. I want to meet the female who has captured your heart."

Angus set his drink down and folded his hands on the table. The male didn't show emotions often, but it was clear he was struggling with the goodbye. "I happily make that promise, lass. I want my Keira to meet the people who have become my family, but you have to agree to visit me in Khoth. That goes for all of you."

Everyone readily agreed and then the stories began. Gerrick laughed as Elsie and her sister told the story about the time Angus took them to a battle on his back. He hadn't heard the entire story about that night and had to work hard not to laugh given that Zander was still pissed off at his mate defying him and leaving the compound. What was even more interesting than the silent interaction between Zander and Elsie was Shae's fascination by it all.

Her heat was a hot brand at his side and it was impossible for him to think of anything but how soft and supple and close she was. He told himself to put space between them, but his body refused to comply. The smart thing to do would have been to choose a chair across the room, not lean into her further. It seemed he was destined to do the wrong thing as he inched even closer so that more of their bodies were touching and his soul sighed in relief. He was well and truly fucked!

SHAE COULD HARDLY CONTAIN her excitement at being out in the 'real world' again. Her nerves were on a razor's edge and she wasn't entirely certain it was a good idea, but she couldn't refuse when the females of Zeum had asked if she wanted to join them on their hunt for dresses.

She was finally free and ready to resume her life. Besides, she reasoned, she was surrounded by strong, competent females who would make sure she didn't hurt anyone. What was the worst that could happen? With renewed excitement, she followed the females into a shop off Pike. A blast of warm air engulfed her, making her skin burn and her body sigh in relief. The night was cold and rainy and it felt good to get out of it.

Stomping her feet, she glanced around the opulent shop. They'd entered a realm boutique that she'd never been to and she knew the moment she stepped into the place that it was way out of her price range. It always amazed her how a shop like this could be located in a busy shopping district with humans milling about right outside the door, yet they were unaware it even existed thanks to magical cloaking spells.

Some realm shops catered to both humans and supernaturals, but most didn't because it was difficult to hide books that shelved themselves or sprites fluttering about keeping the shop clean and stocked. This particular store carried one-of-a-kind realm creations. Picking up the edge of a Fae-made masterpiece, Shae smiled when it changed from red to a shiny green material. Green was her favorite color and she was instantly in love with the softer-than-silk gown. It appeared see-through, but when she placed her hand inside the bodice, she realized it was an illusion of the fabric. She let it slide over her hand enjoying the luxurious feel.

"That would be stunning on you with your hair and eyes. Every female must own at least one Fae gown in her life," Breslin enthused, walking over.

Shae looked up from the dress and saw that the princess had several hung over her arm. A tall, slender witch walked over at that moment and addressed Breslin, "Can I take those to a room for you, Highness?"

Breslin handed the garments over. "Aye, thank you, Nique. She's the store owner," Breslin explained after the female walked away. "Now, I think that dress would be perfect for you, but if you don't like it, Nique has a wide variety of designers in stock." Shae could swear that the Princess was genuinely excited to help pick her dress and she couldn't help but be excited, too.

Shae looked at the dress again and her enthusiasm deflated when reality struck. "I could never afford anything like this. Hell, I don't even know if my account is still open."

"Your accounts are still there. I asked Zander," Elsie

replied as she walked up holding her own selection, clearly having heard their conversation. At least one thing in her life had remained, but even so, there was no way Shae was spending that much money on a dress. She had no idea when she would be working again and she refused to mooch off her parents for everything.

"What do you think of this dress?" The Queen continued, holding up a blue gown. Shae could see how close the Queen was with her sister-in-law because she wasn't asking her sister or the other females. Speaking of, where were Cailyn, Jessie and Mack? She glanced around the store and saw them huddled around a rack on the other side of the store.

When Shae turned back, she saw that Breslin had taken the dress from Elsie's hands and was holding it up in the light. The blue was the same color as Zander's eyes, Shae realized, which was probably why the queen had picked it. "The color is perfect for your skin tone, but I think you should look for something strapless."

Elsie rolled her eyes. "I've told you before that I can't wear stuff like that. My boobs aren't big enough."

Breslin chuckled. "And, I've told you that you have to pick clothes that enhance your natural attributes, which are your long slender neck and your flawless skin." Shae brought her hand up to her neck to cover her scars. These females must think she was hideously disfigured. One thing was certain, Shae's days of wearing a strapless dress were long gone, as were the days of wearing her hair up.

More days than not, she would pull her long hair into a ponytail, but that was the last thing she wanted to do. She was glad her hair was so long she could bring it around the front and hide her neck. Anger spiked at the thought of never getting past what the demons had done to her. She would always wear the scars, the interior ones more grotesque than the exterior.

Breslin continued talking, momentarily diffusing Shae's anger and diverting her attention. "Besides, you are no' that small. In fact, I believe my *brathair* signed a proclamation that your breasts are perfect." At that comment, they started to laugh, and Shae suddenly felt uncomfortable and out of place. She may have had more in common with these females at one time, but not anymore. She was no longer a simple vampire and it was becoming increasingly difficult to be around them and maintain her composure.

She glanced away and noticed Mack walking toward them. The dresses on the display rack she passed automatically changed to a style that would look fantastic with her hairstyle and inked arm. "That would look good on you," Shae told Mack honestly.

Mack grimaced. "Do I really have to wear one of these?" she asked, holding up the black dress with an empire waist and cap sleeves. It was a sharp contrast to the t-shirt, jeans and combat boots she'd seen the female wear. Today's shirt said 'Please Cancel My Subscription to Your Issues.' Shae admitted that the snarky slogans and casual attire fit the female's personality much better than a fancy dress.

"If you're going to the party you do. You're a Vampire Princess now, it's expected. Trust me, it would be the talk of the realm and blasted all over TRex if you wore jeans and a t-shirt. Besides, I think that one was made for you," Shae told the female. Mack met her eyes and then her gaze slid to where Shae's hand was covering her neck.

"Don't hide who you are, Shae. And, never be ashamed or feel less than because you carry scars," Mack stated matter-of-factly. Shae flushed with embarrassment. The room had gone quiet and everyone was listening to their conversation.

"That's easy to say. I can't hide these with tattoos. The sight is disgusting and I don't want them anymore." Shae's hands clenched at her sides, anger rising again.

"You aren't defined by your scars, Shae. Carry them with pride. They are a symbol of your strength and fortitude. You stood in the storm and didn't blow away. You managed to adjust your sails and make it to safe harbor. You are a survivor, stand tall and proud," Mack told her wrapping one arm around her shoulders.

Mack was right. Shae swallowed hard around the lump in her throat. "Can you read minds?" she teased, trying to lighten the suddenly somber mood.

"No, that's my power," Cailyn interjected, startling Shae. She hadn't really spoken to Elsie's sister before and was surprised by the vehemence in her tone. "And you, my friend, need to stop beating yourself up. You sacrificed yourself for those females, saving them from a worse fate. That took more courage than you can imagine." Elsie's sister might be quieter than Elsie was, but she had a heart of gold. One thing the demons hadn't been able to take from Shae was her judge of character and she would bet that Cailyn was the type of friend that always had your back.

"You can read my thoughts?" she asked, distraught by the idea of them knowing what she'd gone through. Or, even worse, how she fantasized about Gerrick. These females lived with him and knew him better than Shae. It would be beyond embarrassing if Cailyn knew how Shae was drooling over the hunky warrior.

"I don't peek into people's minds without cause. I believe that's a violation, but there are some things you project so loud that I can't ignore them. You deserve that dress and so much more. Now, get in that dressing room and show us how stunning you'll look."

"I don't know," she hedged.

"I do," Breslin said. "Doona fash aboot the cost, either. Gerrick gave me his credit card and instructed me to buy you what you wanted. And, I've picked the perfect shoes to go with it, too." She gaped at Breslin. The Princess had to be joking. Shae hadn't been able to determine how the stoic warrior felt about her. He was so hot and cold that it made her head spin. One minute she was convinced he was into her and the next he was placing a wall of ice between them. His actions didn't make any sense.

"Don't let *her* pick your shoes unless you like six-inch stilettos," Elsie warned, making Shae laugh. "I'm serious."

"I'm not wearing heels that high," Mack protested. "You bitches may get me into a dress, but wearing those walking-death-traps is sooo not happening."

"What about these?" Jessie asked holding up a pair of black, studded, low heels.

"Oh my God! Those are perfect. They're like witch boots on steroids, I love the black spikes on the back. Those have my name all over them," Mack gushed, grabbing the shoes and darting for the dressing room. Shoes always made the outfit, Shae thought. Suddenly excited by the explosive energy of these females and buying a gorgeous dress, she followed Mack. Before she knew it, Shae found herself standing in a fitting room staring into a mirror.

She shrugged and tugged her shirt off, wanting to see what she would look like in the gown. Quickly, she undressed and slipped the fabric over her head. It settled over her body, but she was unable to lift her eyes and see her reflection, not ready to be disappointed. She took several deep breaths and finally glanced into the mirror.

The first thought she had was that even the mirrors in the shop were enchanted because the female looking back at her wasn't the hideously scarred creature she had seen in the mirror that morning. She smoothed her hands down the silky fabric. She'd never looked more beautiful.

She jumped when there was a knock on the door. "Come on, Shae. We want to see you. And, I want your opinion on this ridiculous contraption they have me in," Mack called out.

She opened the door and exited the stall. "Och, I knew it would be perfect," Breslin boasted, but was cut off when the door to the shop opened. They all looked up to see several males enter the establishment.

The air around them shimmered like asphalt on a hot day. The second the door closed the air thickened to a dense fog and the vibrations of strong, evil magic filled the room. The pressure built, nearly suffocating Shae and when it released its grip, Azazel came into view, as well as, a dozen various demons and skirm. He smiled and met her gaze. "Shae, my pet. You look spectacular. That dress is absolutely perfect for you. I just can't decide if it would look better on, or off. But, I can see now how remiss I was in my care of you."

Sweat beaded on her spine and her heart beat a frantic rhythm in her chest. Somewhere deep inside, she had known they would come back for her. It was too much to hope that she be allowed to live a free life. Azazel and Kadir had marked her as theirs and they were never going to let her go. She'd rather fight to the death than be taken again, she thought, clenching her jaw. She tensed to attack, but when she tried to move, discovered she was rooted to the spot by an unseen force. She cursed, fighting against its hold.

Mack and Breslin didn't have any such problem as they were the first to jump into action. Mack sprung toward a pus demon, reaching under the skirt of her dress. Her hands came up shining as she slashed out. Her weapon sliced into green, gooey flesh, releasing the horrific odor she'd hoped to never smell again.

Breslin snarled something to the demon and bursts of fire left her palm as she surged forward. A couple skirm caught fire on her way and fell to the floor, writhing in agony. The owner began chanting spells to protect her merchandise from the flames Breslin continued to throw. Shae tried to move her legs again, but was still rooted to the spot. She focused all her energy on her body and located the magic that had once again made her a prisoner. All she could do was stand and watch.

Elsie darted into a dressing room and came out with two weapons. She bared her fangs as she handed one to her sister. "Stay next to Shae," she ordered. Shae's toes twitched, but she was still unable to move. Her gaze jumped to Azazel when she felt him enter her mind. She screamed into the melee of the invasion. To her, it was another form of rape to have him trying to manipulate and steal her freewill.

Jessie jumped into the fray next with weapons in her hands. Where in the hell did these females keep all these weapons? It didn't surprise her that they were armed to the teeth, they lived with and were mated to Dark Warriors, but for the life of her, she couldn't imagine where the weapons had been hidden. Shae gaped at the obvious skill Jessie had as she managed to ash two skirm in rapid succession. She hadn't pegged her for a fighter, but she could hold her own in any battle.

All of the females were fierce fighters as they compe-tently battled the demons. She'd known Breslin was a warrior, but the three human females were a pleasant surprise. Sure, they were all now immortal, but their origins were in the human world and she hadn't expected them to be so ferocious. Even Cailyn, who was undoubtedly the weakest of their group, joined the fight.

Shae's heart leapt as Breslin threw fire at the archdemon. Perhaps this would be the distraction she needed to get free of his control. Unfortunately, he dodged the first volley and a rack of clothing went up in flames. It felt as if Shae's veins were on fire with her rage and frustration. She was once again helpless before the demon and this time was worse. The females she had just begun to form a friendship with were in the line of fire and she was forced to watch instead of joining them. Elsie cried out as she went sailing across the room. Cailyn was bleeding from a cut on her chin and Jessie had a vicious wound to her left arm. Mack was uninjured, but the new dress had seen better days.

A steady stream of fire left Breslin's palm and finally hit their mark. Shae felt Azazel's connection snap and she began moving. In the next moment, all fighting ceased.

"You can't fight back, demons!" Nique yelled as quietness and calm blanketed the entire. "I've enacted a nonviolence spell. Now get out of my store!" the witch bellowed. The burning flames dissipated along with the smoke and stench in the air. Nique was a witch with some powerful magic of her own. No wonder Breslin shopped here.

"You've won a brief reprieve, Shae. I'll be back for you," Azazel purred before he disappeared, taking the two remaining pus demons with him.

These females had fought to protect her instead of running away. It was an unfamiliar feeling to have someone care for her rather than being left to her own devices. Problem was, she wasn't sure if she liked it or not. When you've come to depend on only yourself, it was hard to trust anyone would be there for you in the future.

"Fucking demons. I got pus and blood on these shoes, dammit," Mack cursed. "I couldn't care less about the dress, but these badass shoes are ruined."

Shae's adrenaline evaporated and her muscles began to tremble. Azazel had taken control of her body without breaking a sweat. Right before Breslin had attacked Azazel, she thought she'd identified his signature in her mind and had been battering at it while erecting a shield. The next time, and she had no doubt there would be a next time, she wasn't going to lose her chance to destroy one of the creatures that had stolen her life. They would pay for taking her from her family and turning her into a being she no longer recognized.

"Don't worry, Mack. I will make sure you have a new pair of those boots by morning," Nique promised. "It was worth the loss to send those scoundrels scurrying away like the rodents they are."

"We need to let Zander and the others know what happened," Elsie said, picking goo out of her hair.

"Aye, and he'll send a crew to help clean this mess. And, we'll pay for all the damages," Breslin reassured the witch. Shae braced herself for anger and accusation. She expected them to start pointing the finger at her and blame her for the attack, but no one did. Instead, Elsie called her mate and while they waited for the warriors to arrive, they worked together to pile the bodies in a corner as Nique made arrangements to temporarily close the shop.

Breslin came up to Shae's side and put her hand on her shoulder. This was it, Shae thought. She was going to kill her and end the threat she posed. "Doona fash, Shae. Those bastards will never get their hands on you again. We doona leave our own," she promised.

Shae nodded, speechless. She hadn't felt like one of anything for a long time and the sentiment touched her battered soul. She wanted more than anything to belong again, but didn't know if that was possible. The demons had taken so much from her she didn't know if she'd ever feel accepted again. One thing was certain, until the demons were dead, she would never be free.

CHAPTER 10

Shae sat on the leather couch wondering how she managed to be talked into attending the party. She didn't trust her erratic emotions, but the females had begged and Gerrick had insisted. He had taken one look at her standing in the dress shop and instructed Nique to have a replacement gown sent to Zeum for her. Now, she had make-up on and her hair was styled to cover the left side of her neck and she was wearing the ridiculously expensive gown. She'd never felt more beautiful or more ugly all at the same time. She felt like a ping-pong ball bouncing across a table as she switched from happy and exhilarated to angry and resentful.

"Och, doona look like we killed your dog, Shae. 'Tis a party. The most important party of the year," Breslin said, coming to sit by her side.

"I know. Just like I know the real reason you want me there is because you don't want to leave me alone tonight. I don't blame you. I am a wildcard," Shae countered, smoothing her skirt nervously.

"If that is what you think then you doona know much

aboot us," Breslin countered, not a trace of upset in her tone. "You are one of us and we will be behind you no matter what. We will protect you with our lives, as well as, try to give you your shot at vengeance. Believe it or not, we care aboot you. You've worked your way into our hearts verra quickly. Everyone worked night and day to find you and the others. And, no one worked more than Gerrick, he was like a male possessed."

Shae was choked up at the raw honesty in the Princess' voice. The only people who had ever cared about her were her family and to hear that Gerrick had searched for her sent butterflies winging through her stomach. She didn't understand her draw to the sorcerer. In a matter of days and one scorching kiss he had become her obsession.

Her best friend, Rebecca would laugh her ass off at the absurdity. Rebecca had always been the voice of reason between the two of them, pointing out the reality of any situation. Shae could imagine Rebecca telling her that she was gaga over the male because he had played a major role in rescuing her, but he had done it because he was a Dark Warrior and that Shae didn't mean anything special to him. Even as the thought formed in her mind, Shae's soul rejected it and refused to banish thoughts of him.

"Speaking of the sorcerer," Shae hedged, hoping to gain a little insight into the enigmatic male without tipping her hat. "He's a hard one to figure out. What's his story? I mean it's not every day that a male puts so much effort into finding lost females and then goes out of his way to ensure they are adjusting to their new lives."

Breslin chuckled knowingly, making Shae wonder if she had she been that transparent. "Gerrick has always been a ruthlessly focused warrior who places duty above all else. But, he is haunted by shadows that we only recently began to understand. He came to us with demons behind his eyes and it took centuries and Zander finding Elsie for him to open up."

Somehow that didn't surprise Shae. If she hadn't had that strange vision of Gerrick, she'd say he'd been born merciless. It didn't take much to see that he wasn't a warrior who laughed, or even smiled, for that matter. "So, what made him the way he is?" she asked, suspicious about his personal demons.

Breslin turned to Shae and held her gaze. Shae had to swallow hard at the look in the Princess' eyes. Somehow she didn't think she was going to like what she was about to say. "Normally, I wouldna tell his story, but I can see your interest is heartfelt and genuine. He is no' for you, Shae. Pursuing him will only lead to heartache. You see, he has already lost everything a male has to lose. He found his Fated Mate four centuries ago and she was killed by an archdemon and his skirm."

Shae gasped and put her fingers to her mouth, "Evanna," she whispered, knowing it had been her in the vision. How had she had a vision of Evanna with Gerrick? What did it mean? Worse, could the demons have altered her so much that they gave her the sight? An evil version of the sight? She contemplated what she had seen and immediately her heart ached at how deeply the incident had scarred Gerrick. His heart had been ripped to shreds by the experience and he had never recovered. The remembered pain had tears brimming in Shae's eyes for him.

There shouldn't be a connection between the two of them, yet it was there and growing stronger by the minute. A sharp ache pierced her heart. She had wondered if he could be her mate, but that hope was dashed with Breslin's revelation. No, he couldn't be because you were only given one in a lifetime and he had lost his. Despite the pain that caused her, she wanted to hold him, tell him she was sorry and make the shadows she saw in his eyes disappear.

"What?" Breslin asked, looking at her sideways.

"I had no idea his mate had been killed. How has he gone on living after such a loss? I've never heard of a male surviving four centuries after losing his mate. He's got to be the strongest male in the history of the realm."

"Aye. He is verra strong. He vowed to enact revenge and ensure no other mate suffered the same loss. 'Tis that mission that kept him going. 'Tis what drove him so hard these past months. Knowing each of you was a mate, he refused to rest until you were found. He played a big role in ensuring you will one day meet your mate. Now, enough with the melancholy, we have a party to attend. Do you hear that? The band has started, time for us to get downstairs," Breslin stood, motioning Shae to the door.

Shae banished her grief to a corner and followed Breslin. "You're right. Thank you for insisting I attend the celebration. For the first time since I was taken, I feel like I'm getting my life back. And you're right about the gown complimenting my eyes, even if I feel like my boobs are going to pop out of it. By the way, thanks for the tip on using tape to hold the dress in place. I've never worn a dress where that was an issue."

"Doona fash, you're boobs are no' going to pop oot. That tape is like glue. Although, I think there is at least one warrior who wouldn't mind if you did." They burst into laughter as they walked down the stairs and it felt to Shae that they had become friends. She was still in awe that she was in the royal family's house, let alone, becoming friends with the Princess. Moments like that reinforced her feeling that she'd fallen down the rabbit hole.

She sobered the second they entered the ballroom and she saw the crowd. Heart pounding from panic, she worried she didn't have enough control to be around so many. There had to be a hundred people, if not more, and if she lost it, she would harm an innocent. Not that attacking Breslin had been wise, but the Princess could more than hold her own and wasn't seriously injured. Shae could kill any one of these people in a fit of rage before anyone knew what was happening.

The thought had sweat breaking out on her spine. She wished to go back to her normal life more in that moment than she ever had. Being with the royal family and Gerrick was certainly exciting, but she would trade it in a second to be with Rebecca at their office Solstice party, laughing at the males try to convince the females they needed to spend the night with them.

Breslin bounded to Elsie and the others while Shae made a beeline for the corner. She'd be safest there if the archdemon decided to take over her mind. It would give the Dark Warriors time to neutralize her before she reached anyone.

She recalled Nate complaining about not knowing anything about party planning, but it seemed as if he'd rallied. Of course, the females in the house had likely whipped him into shape. Each of them had their own talents and strengths and they worked well as a unit.

Glancing around, she noticed the trees that dotted the walls. They weren't in planters, but appeared to grow right out of the wood floor. Someone had used magic to add lighted spheres that floated along the ceiling, providing a romantic atmosphere. It made her wish that Gerrick would pull her into the corner for another heated kiss. Sighing at her folly, she admired the red and silver decorations that adorned the tables and walls. They were classical and bright spots of color amidst the white of the linens. The King and his household knew how to throw a party, Shae thought as the liquor flowed and laughter echoed all around her.

Her stomach chose that moment to rumble and she cursed herself for taking up position away from the food. She was starving for more than just food. It was dangerous to allow her hunger to build, but she wasn't willing to brave the crowded dance floor to reach the tables lined with assorted foods. Perhaps Nate would bring her a plate. She scanned the room for the dragon shifter and her heart stopped when she spotted Gerrick.

He was lounging against the wall near the entrance and watching her with a hooded gaze. He gave her that smile of his when their eyes met and her insides melted. Goddess, he was mouth-watering and she couldn't take her hungry gaze off of him. Food, she reminded herself, not Gerrick's talented tongue dancing in her mouth as his large hands perused her body, driving it to a fever pitch. She scanned the room and smiled when she saw Nate trying to convince a nymph to dance with him. She wasn't getting food anytime soon unless she got it herself.

"You look beautiful, Red." She jumped and turned at the sound of the masculine voice whispering down her neck. He was nothing short of spectacular in his black tuxedo that was tailored to perfection. She was a half foot shorter that his six feet and had to stand on tip toe when she'd kissed him before, but now her heels placed her in perfect position to nibble on his jaw and neck. She could feel his pulse beat a steady rhythm that was in sharp contrast to her racing heart. Her eyes went to the dangerous looking scar on his face. He was a ruggedly-handsome male and the scar only enhanced his appeal. She couldn't deny the desire to kiss and lick that scar before losing herself in a night of passion she'd never forget.

She took in a deep breath and lowered her gaze in an effort to stifle her undeniable attraction. Unfortunately, that wasn't helpful as the sight of his wide shoulders and strong arms captivated her even more. Her core spasmed with need. She wanted the male more than freedom at the moment. He cleared his throat, drawing her attention. Her breath caught at the desire she saw in his ice-blue eyes. There was no doubt he was perfectly aware of the affect he had on her. "You don't look too bad, yourself."

He grunted and lifted the object in his hand. "I brought you some food."

Her stomach rumbled in appreciation and she accepted the offering, smiling when she noticed his eyes never left her cleavage. "I used to love parties," she commented, needing a distraction or she was going to take advantage of the corner they were in. Several seconds of silence had her fidgeting until she popped a bacon wrapped shrimp into her mouth. He finally lifted his gaze and met her eyes. She swore he could see straight to her battered soul and she wanted to drown in his mirrored pain.

"Why do you let them have so much power over you?"

"As if you don't?" she countered. His brows lowered in obvious confusion. Of course, he had no idea what she was talking about. He didn't know she was aware of his mate, just like he had no idea she was aware that he'd been a different male before his loss.

He narrowed his eyes. "Nice try. You can't deflect the bull, Shae. Or haven't you caught on by now? I'm like a wolf on a hunt when I catch a scent. Now answer the question."

She sighed as if put upon to cover her jitters. This male had a way of breaking through her barriers with his mere presence. He made her feel truly alive and made it easier to fight the darkness inside, but there was no way she was going to allow him in any deeper. It wouldn't be difficult for her to fall for this male, but he had already loved and lost and that meant she could never own any piece of his heart. It belonged to a female that had been dead for four hundred years. And, for some unknown reason, she wanted to own his heart, and, if she were honest...his soul.

"I have no idea how to get my life back. I can't go back to the life I once had. I'm not the same female. Besides, I feel them inside me. It's best if I keep my distance."

She watched him digest what she said as she threw a crab filled tartlet into her mouth. Mmmm, that was delicious she thought, wanting an entire platter of them. "I'm not surprised that you feel them. But, fight them, Red. Refuse to give them anymore of yourself."

"You make it sound so easy. They've been inside me, Gerrick. They turned me into a vicious creature," she hissed quietly.

He suddenly grabbed hold of her arms, making her flinch and stiffen. "You think I'd hurt you?" he asked, releasing her as if he'd been burned.

"I think you'd do anything to protect your friends," she pushed.

"Yes, I would." No apology in that unwavering gaze. "Is this fear why you haven't called your family yet?"

"Yes. They would be horrified to see me, let alone the mood swings I'm having. Trust me, it's better this way."

"Better for you maybe," he challenged, reaching up to sweep her hair from her shoulder. He cupped her cheek then ran his hand down her neck and trailed his finger along the edge of the dress, brushing across her cleavage.

Heat suffused her body and a blush crept up her bosom. She wanted this man with a desperation that frightened her.

"I'm protecting them," she shivered, praying the tape held everything in place. The last thing she needed to do was embarrass herself further in front of a crowded room.

"Bull-shit. You're scared. You're afraid that they will reject the female you've become and you can't face that right now," he said, laying her bare.

"You don't know anything about me," she countered, hoping he didn't detect the lie, even as she knew it was futile. Somehow, this male knew her better than anyone else.

"I know your eyes," he leaned in and whispered in her ear, "dance with me." His husky voice made her putty in his hands.

Not wanting to appear too eager, she paused before responding. He held that infuriatingly sexy smile in place until she finally placed her hand into one of his. "One dance." He pulled his hand free and placed his palms onto her hips. She'd expected him to lead her to the dance floor, but he wasn't budging.

"Right here?"

"Why not right here?" He tugged her flush against the hard length of his body. She recalled the heat and passion that had consumed them the last time they'd been this close. It was dangerous to allow such close contact, but she didn't dare move away.

"There's nothing wrong with right here," she lied. "But, do try to keep your hands in place. You got carried away the last time and I don't have any extra tape on me," she teased, needing to lighten the mood.

He chuckled and the ice in his eyes turned liquid. "You don't need tape, Red. My hands will cover you just fine."

She melted at the intent in his lascivious words. Body thrumming, he seemed to surround her. "We'll see about that," she hedged, biting her lip nervously.

He was intimidating as hell and scared her, yet he also inflamed her and called to the wild, wanton female inside. He reached up and tugged her lip out of her mouth. His head lowered, but he caught himself scant inches from her face. His hot breath seemed to brand her mouth as his as his eyes told her of the battle he was waging.

He ran his finger across her jaw then wrapped his hand possessively around the back of her neck. She waited to see if he would let his beast loose and found herself wishing he would. It would be a feral thing, devouring her whole. Her body tingled with anticipation. And, she desperately wanted him to kiss her.

He had scorched her with his kiss, but this moment was by far the most erotic one of her life.

Just when she thought he was going to give her what she wanted, he snapped upright and swiveled to face the room. She peered around his shoulder to see what had drawn his attention, but saw nothing. In the next instant, Gerrick was walking toward Jace, pulling her along with him.

GERRICK CALLED his staff to him as he strode across the crowded room. The silver charm vibrated beneath his thumb, centering him. He sensed Dark magic, which should have been impossible. Jace was already headed in his direction. "You felt it, too?"

Jace nodded. "Do you know what it is?"

Gerrick flared his senses and focused his vision on the colors of the magic in the room. "I don't see anything that doesn't belong," he said, frustrated he couldn't detect what the source was. He met Zander's gaze over the heads of their guests and nodded. He did a quick scan and noted that Elsie was surrounded by several Dark Warriors and was in a more defensible position. Unfortunately, they couldn't clear the room without causing a major panic.

Thick black smoke suddenly filled the room, causing screams and shouts. Gerrick cursed, unable to see anything around him. He squeezed Shae's hand and pulled her to his side. His pride grew when he felt her tense in readiness. She was definitely a warrior and he loved that about her.

"It's Angelica," Jace snarled from next to him. The warrior would know that better than anyone given what he'd suffered at the female's hands. She had tortured him for centuries and Gerrick could feel the fury seeping out of every pore on the male's body.

Together they muttered a reveal spell that cleared the smoke and removed her advantage of surprise. The vile sorceress was slinking toward the exit, clearly hoping to get free reign on their compound. No doubt she was creating an opportunity to search for the Mystik Grimoire, a magical tome that held ancient spells, lore and prophecy. The book had the power to disappear and reappear of its own accord and had only surfaced a couple months ago. The book was tied to Jace's lineage and Angelica wanted control over Jace in hopes of connecting to the grimoire.

Gerrick wasn't surprised to see that she'd come prepared with several of her goons by her side. Although, how any self-respecting sorcerer bowed to her like a sycophant was beyond him. Likely, because she was beautiful, powerful and manipulative. She had proven herself to be a cunning and wily enemy with a penchant for making powerful allies.

"You're not going anywhere," Zander declared. Without

hesitation, Jace and Gerrick cast an invisible barrier across the entryway. It was a risk trapping all the guests in the room, but they had no choice. They couldn't allow her to leave. With her sorcery she could place hidden spells that would give her future access to the compound. This way, at least they contained that problem.

"Jace, my pet. I've missed you," the words oozed like tainted oil from the female's lips.

"I'm not your pet," Jace snarled. "What do you want?"

"I want what is mine. You didn't think I would forget about you, or the Grimoire, did you? We will be so beautiful together. Come, share my power." Angelica lifted her hand and reached for Jace. The female was insane, Gerrick thought. Jace was not only a mated male whose allegiance would always be to Cailyn, he loathed her for the torture he suffered at her hands.

"You can give up the pretense, Angelica. Your ploy failed. You will never have the Grimoire and I will never stand by your side," Jace vowed.

"You will see the error in your ways soon enough," Angelica said as she turned rapidly and pointed in the opposite direction, chanting a spell. Anticipating her move, Jace jumped towards Angelica and Zander dove and knocked Cailyn to the ground. The spell missed Cailyn and slammed into Shannon, a Zeum staff member, who was serving food. Shannon flew backwards and crashed into the wall before slumping to the ground. Gerrick hoped she was okay and a quick glance told him that the rest of the females were unharmed.

Jace slammed into Angelica, taking her to the floor while her toadies surged toward the warriors. Gerrick let go of Shae's hand and whispered *duck* which she did without hesitation. He swung his staff around, putting all his strength into the blow. The wood slammed into one of her sycophant's gut. Unfortunately, it didn't have the impact he'd hoped. Rather than falling to the ground in two pieces, he flew back a few feet, but rebounded quickly.

Shae followed his hit by chasing the male, Gerrick two steps behind her. He didn't bother with another spell because it would take too much time and concentration that he couldn't afford right now. That was the reason they typically fought with weapons rather than magic during combat.

Putting on a burst of speed, Gerrick overran Shae and reached the male first. The one thing he appreciated about supernaturals was that violence was familiar in their realm and the guests hadn't panicked. After a brief uproar, the crowd settled and made way to the edges of the room to stay out of the way as much as possible.

The lighted spheres the Rowan triplets had added to the ceiling began to burst as wild spells left the lips of Angelica's goons. The dark-tinged lights of their enchantments told him they'd siphoned Angelica's tainted power. Dumb-fucks, Gerrick thought. Not only was someone was going to get killed by their wild spells, but they were playing with forces they didn't understand. Dark magic corroded you from the inside out and landed your soul in hell. Gerrick was left with no choice except to kill them.

These enemies were far tougher to fight than the skirm and lesser demons because of their Dark magic. He dodged spells every other second as he pummeled the male he fought which left him continuously off balance. Everything suddenly stilled as the ballroom was filled with blinding light and mist. When the light dissipated, a large slate dragon with blue eyes stood in their midst. Nate roared and his tail swished, taking down several guests in the process. It was beyond impossible to be careful when you were the size of an airplane stuffed into a room, albeit a ballroom.

Zander was yelling something to Nate and suddenly the dragon curled his body around Elsie and the other females. A weight lifted off Gerrick's shoulders at seeing the mates protected and he had to admit it was nice to have a dragon on their side. "Go, get behind Nate," Gerrick ordered Shae.

She chuckled and smiled at him, "Not a chance. Looks like you need my help," she replied, kicking the male in the side of the head. Gerrick shook his head as he watched the male fall to the ground. Gerrick stabbed his staff through the male's neck and sent a burst of power through the wood causing the head to explode. Brain matter splattered his pants and the hem of Shae's dress.

"Dammit, I liked that dress on you. I'll have to buy you another," he remarked, running his finger down the slope of her cleavage. That quick, even in the midst of chaos and bloodshed, he wanted her to the point of madness. He didn't know how much longer he'd be able to hold himself back.

"Even you can't beat a dragon, Angelica," Jace taunted, bringing Gerrick back to the battle.

Angelica fluttered her fingers by her side and smiled wryly, "Oh, but little do you know, I've already won." With that she disappeared in a puff of black smoke, leaving her remaining goons behind. The warriors made quick work of dispatching them and Nate chomped those who tried to make a run for it.

Gerrick and Shae joined the group in the middle of the room and stood next to Nate as he stood guard. Mack reached up and patted his snout. "It's okay, they're gone. You can shift back now."

A quick snort and another flash of light and mist and a naked Nate stood among their group. The mated males growled at the sight, and Gerrick was startled to realize that his growl was the loudest. Mack laughed, "You'd better get dressed Nate, the males are staking claims. By the way, is your magic different here because I noticed your dragon eyes weren't jewels just now like they were on Khoth."

Nate accepted the pants from a servant and slid them on. "I feel different here. I can't tell if I have less power, or not, but it's definitely different."

"What's this?" Shae asked picking up an obelisk from the ground where Angelica had been standing.

"Don't touch that?" Gerrick warned, detecting the power emanating from it. "It has power of some kind."

"I don't know about that, but it has a timer that's counting down," she replied.

"Can you contain it?" Zander asked Gerrick.

"I'm not sure," Gerrick responded.

"Well, you better do something fast because we don't have much time," Shae added, making his blood turn to ice.

CHAPTER 11

Gerrick was about to take the object from Shae's hand when his fellow warriors surrounded them. The room was quiet while they all took in the scene Angelica left behind until Mack broke the silence, "Let me see that. And, someone get the guests out of the house." Seeing that as permission, the guests didn't wait for an escort before they headed for the exit without looking back.

"No' happening, Sunshine," Kyran told her.

"Look here, bloodsucker, I feel the power coming off the thing. Give it to me," she countered.

"I may allow you to patrol and fight, but I willna allow you to place yourself in unknown danger," Kyran replied, his tone resolute.

Mack rolled her eyes and sighed, "Sometimes you men are blinded by your arrogance and need to protect us women. You are forgetting my ability to nullify magic. I haven't been able to sense any magic since we got home so I thought it was limited to Khoth, but I feel this, so let me try." She reached up and cradled Kyran's face in her hands.

"Argue about this latter," Shae interrupted. "I'm afraid I started the countdown when I picked it up and I can't be responsible for it going off." Gerrick's instinct had him snarling like Kyran and just as unhappy about the danger.

Gerrick took the object from Shae, noting its warmth, and held it out towards Mack who approached him with Kyran glued to her back.

"I doona like this," the Vampire Prince complained, but didn't stop his mate from touching the smooth, black stone. Gerrick admired the male's restraint. Hell, he didn't think he would be able to stand by so calmly. Symbols floated to the surface when Mack touched it and she ran her fingers over it. She paused and looked over her shoulder at Kyran.

"I have no idea what will happen, I don't understand the first thing about my ability. There is an oily feeling when I touch it so I know the intent behind this thing is evil, but I know I can diffuse it. And, before you freak out on me, allow me to follow my gut," she expressed and waited for Kyran to nod his head before she turned back and pressed one symbol after another.

Gerrick hadn't realized until then the amount of mutual respect the couple had for one another. They weren't as demonstrative with their love as the other couples in the house. In fact, he'd never heard either one of them tell the other that they loved each other, but it was clear their love ran very deep.

Mack paused and closed her eyes as she felt around the obelisk, pressing symbols here and there. Several minutes later the numbers stopped and the stone dimmed.

Gerrick looked up in astonishment. "Holy shit, you did it."

"Don't look so surprised, Gerrick. I do have my talents," Mack teased, kissing Kyran on the cheek and sliding her hand up his chest. Gerrick could see the feral light leave Kyran's eyes as his mate soothed him with her touch.

Gerrick looked around the ballroom. "This didn't turn out like we planned. Goddess, we didn't even get to the candlelight circle."

"Is that a problem with your Goddess?" Nate asked.

"Nay, the ceremony is more an acknowledgement than anything," Zander explained.

"Good. I'm too tired to run for my life should she strike you down. This place is a disaster," Nate complained. Gerrick laughed at that as he once again glanced at the destruction around them.

"Most of this damage was caused by you when you shifted, so get to it," Gerrick said, punching the dragon on the arm.

A piercing scream brought everyone's head around. Sheila, another staff member, was crouching beside a body on the opposite side of the room. Zander and Elsie were running in that direction before Gerrick blinked.

"She's dead," Sheila cried, kicking Gerrick into gear and he grabbed Shae's hand and headed across the wood floor. "They killed her," Sheila continued, "They killed my sister." Gerrick saw something shatter in the female's eyes as she looked at Zander. The utter devastation on her face caused a responding echo in Gerrick's chest.

"Bluidy hell. How the fuck did this happen in my house?" Zander cursed as Elsie took Sheila in her arms, offering comfort. Shae trembled by Gerrick's side and he realized seeing the dead body must remind her of the horrors she'd gone through. He wanted to wrap her up in his arms and shield her from the pain. Once again his desire to protect this female was all-consuming and he didn't understand a bit of it. He shouldn't feel this way about anyone, yet he couldn't deny the impulses, making him question if she was his Fated Mate, even though he knew that was impossible.

"Gerrick and I felt the moment Angelica broke through our shields, but we couldn't act fast enough to stop her," Jace said. Gerrick knew this issue needed to be solved immediately, but he couldn't ignore the trauma emanating off Shae. Before he could take care of her though, he needed to ensure her safety within the compound.

"Let's recast the protections before anything else gets through. This time add an extra impervious layer designed against Angelica's signature. She made a mistake coming into the compound because now we have her magical signature," Gerrick told Jace. A satisfied gleam entered the healer's eyes as he nodded. Gerrick smiled back and together they chanted, quickly replacing the barriers. The room filled with colored lights that swirled and morphed as they rose to the ceiling and outside their home. As soon as he felt the spell snap into place, Gerrick turned to Shae.

"Come on," he whispered in her ear, diverting her attention from the sight of Sheila crying over Shannon.

"I'm taking her outside. We'll be back," Gerrick told Zander and headed for the door the second Zander nodded his acknowledgment.

Shae walked next to him and edged closer the further they went from the house. When they came closer to the boat house, she slid shaky fingers into his hand. He twined them together without question and led her into the deserted boat house. The structure wasn't heated, but offered a break from the cold night of winter in Seattle.

"Please tell me we're not going swimming," Shae said, breaking the silence between them.

He punched in the code for the door and smiled,

bringing her hand to his mouth for a kiss. "No. We have an indoor heated pool for that. I had something else in mind."

She quirked one eyebrow, but didn't object. Instead, curiosity and interest became silent shadows in her expression. He held back a groan at the obvious direction of her thinking. He was more than happy to ignore his better judgment and oblige. Beeping cut that train of thought off before it got out of hand and he hurried to disarm the alarm.

"Are we going on the boat?" she asked.

"Yeah. I thought you'd like to get away for a short while." In truth, he thought she would enjoy an exhilarating ride. To him there was nothing like going balls to the wall, either in a fast car, on a motorcycle, or in a boat. He particularly enjoyed his Harley, but didn't want to take the chance of the demons finding them on the streets.

"That sounds fabulous to me," she murmured as he lowered the boat. He made quick work of getting the craft into the water, hopped in and helped her to a seat before he took the wheel. She laughed as they headed out of their cove and into Lake Washington.

"Faster," she shouted against the wind, a huge smile breaking across her face. Her red hair was flying around her eyes and her cheeks were pink from the cold wind and she was absolutely breathtaking.

He smiled as she tied her hair in a knot. He always wondered how females managed to get their hair to stay without any kind of a fastener. Not that she wasn't beautiful with it restrained, but he missed the wildness from a moment ago. She was definitely a spirit he didn't want to tame. He knew she saw herself as different now, but he imagined, in part, that she had always been what he was now seeing. Her spine of steel may have been tempered in the fires of hell, but that didn't change who she was inside.

That only made her more attractive. Watching her, he admitted that he wanted to know everything about this female.

The lake was dark and deserted this late at night and they didn't encounter another boat. The cool spray of the water was refreshing and he inhaled deeply, taking in the scents around him. Shae's jasmine overwhelmed the damp of the lake, making his erection pound in the confines of his pants. It was a nice diversion from the chaos of the evening and the violence that typically consumed his nights. He had never resented his duty, but he hadn't realized what he was missing, either. Many supernaturals had developed committed and lasting relationships with others, despite the fact, they weren't Fated Mates, but he had never allowed himself to contemplate that option. Not until Shae.

He'd been fighting his instincts towards her for days and couldn't get their kiss out of his mind. He wanted to do it again. Remembering her previous reaction, he'd have to be careful with how he approached her. Shae's piercing scream had him pulling into a cove and he cursed himself all kinds a fool for being so distracted.

SHAE'S HEAD was going to split. The pain was beyond horrible and she was convinced that her brain was being torn apart by the demon. She'd be lucky if she had enough brain cells left to recall her own name. "No," she protested, refusing to give an inch. She threw up every kind of barrier she could think of in hopes of keeping Azazel out. She slumped to the floor of the boat and curled into a ball, holding her hands protectively around her head.

"Shae. What is it? Where's the danger?" Gerrick asked,

worry obvious in his tense voice. That was who he was, she thought. A warrior to his core, always ready to slay the demons. The hand he placed on her shoulder provided a bit of relief from the pressure.

She reached up to him. "Make them go away,please. Kiss me now," she pleaded, wanting him to slay her demons.

Without hesitation, he pulled her up and into his arms. Her stomach twisted in a vicious wave of need. She luxuriated in his strength and lifted her chin, more than ready to force the demon out. "Tell me what's wrong first," he demanded.

"I don't want to talk right now. I want to forget," she pleaded, running her hands up the planes of his hard chest. He'd removed his suit jacket at some point and was in shirt sleeves. She ripped the fabric open and buttons flew in every direction. She didn't stop there and extended her claws, shredding his undershirt.

He growled and gripped her head pulling her so close they were scant millimeters apart. Her hair came loose from its knot and the tape gave up the task of holding the dress over her breasts. The globes were free to rub against the silk of his heated skin with every indrawn breath. The sensation was tantalizing and revved her need even higher.

"Fuck, Shae. I'm trying to be good here and you aren't making that easy," Gerrick said through gritted teeth, his hand tightening in her hair.

She lifted one leg, wrapping it around his hip, bringing her core in contact with hardness his pants didn't have a hope of hiding. "I don't want you good, Gerrick. I just want you. Now," she demanded.

A white-hot whip of electricity shot between them, making her forget the reason she'd asked for the kiss in the first place. Without warning, he took her mouth in a claiming and a concession, and at the moment, she didn't have one complaint.

Snaking her hands into his hair, she kissed him back with every ounce of passion she was reclaiming. She was a butterfly emerging from a cocoon of pain to discover a world of pleasure she'd never known existed. She slid her tongue against his, deliberately provoking him. She wanted more. She wanted him raw and unleashed.

He hesitated, slowing the kiss and she worried she was losing this moment. Through her connection to him, she felt him going cold and wondered if he was thinking of Evanna at that moment. The thought pissed her off enough to break the kiss and bite his neck hard enough to draw blood. He should be thinking of her and no one else. A low, masculine sound of arousal rumbled in his throat and he wrenched her head back. She had been careful not to draw his blood into her mouth, but she knew it coated her lips.

"Are you sure you want this because once I start I'm not stopping until you scream my fucking name." She swallowed hard and tipped her lips in a half-smile.

"You sure you're ready for me, warrior? Just sayin'," she countered then squealed when he gripped her ass and hitched her up his body. Instinctively, she wrapped her legs around his waist.

She tried to insinuate a hand between them to cup his erection, but he refused to allow her any freedom of movement. This was the ruthless warrior she'd heard legends about. She loved him like this. His dominance had wet heat dampening her core. She'd never tangled with a male this dangerous and she'd never wanted anyone more.

It was exhilarating. Lethal as he was, he was hers and she knew him, down to his soul. He'd never hurt her.

Anyone else he'd shred without a second thought, but never her.

She hissed in a breath, and suddenly, he was taking that breath from her in a primal kiss while he ripped her dress from her body, tossing it over the side of the boat. She sank her claws into his back, anchoring herself.

"I've been waiting centuries for you, Red," he murmured and closed long, strong fingers over her breast in blatant possession. He owned her in a way no one ever had. His talented fingers pinched and pulled at her nipples, effectively pulling her completely out of the abyss that had threatened to tear her apart from the inside.

Squeezing her thighs around him, she maneuvered her body, positioning him exactly where she wanted him. "You're overdressed, warrior. Take off the pants."

"Or what? You'll shred them?" he asked, ripping the panties from her body before she could blink.

A moan escaped her throat as she luxuriated in the feel of her naked flesh rubbing against the soft fabric of his dress pants. He snaked his fingers from the flesh of her ass to the wet opening of her body. One long finger teased her with feather light touches. "Give me more. I need more," she begged, not stilling her movements.

He stilled his finger and met her gaze. The ice in his eyes had melted completely and turned to a molten pool, glowing brightly. She wanted to bath in their warmth until the acid in her veins burned away. "So needy," he murmured, unbuttoning his pants and letting them drop to his ankles. Mmmm, commando. It was such a turn on knowing he hadn't had on underwear beneath his pants.

She felt a cool breeze before hot, hard steel was pushing inside her robbing her of reason. He was so big and thick that he stretched her tight and awakened every nerve ending in her body. It was a delicious sting and exactly what she needed. This was the pain she wanted.

Unable to wait, she began lifting herself up and slamming back down on him. His rhythm went from zero to sixty in a second flat and she was meeting his every thrust. He gripped her back and wrapped one hand in her long hair, pulling her close for kiss. His tongue danced in her mouth as his cock shuttled in and out of her core. She moaned into his mouth and took everything he had to give. She was panting when he broke the kiss and so close to orgasm she thought she'd die.

"Is this what you wanted?" he asked, his breath falling like knives against her lips, his hips never stopping. His primal nature was awake and he took her with a force that should have scared her, but instead set her afire.

"Yes, don't stop," she demanded. His answer was to wrap his arms up her back and pull her shoulders down with each of his upward strokes. The violence with which he took her told her he was exercising demons of his own. She had a fleeting thought that he didn't want to want her as much as he did and hated her for it.

Those thoughts scattered as her body clenched around his hard length. He lowered his head and took a nipple into his mouth and bit down. She detonated in his arms and stars bursting behind her eyes, silencing the archdemon trying to take control.

He released her nipple and took her mouth in a kiss as his climax barreled through him. Rather than diminishing, her pleasure increased until a sudden excruciating pain had her crying out. At the same moment a deep groan left Gerrick's lips and he dropped her to the deck of the boat. He lost his footing and fell next to her.

She grabbed her right leg and rocked back and forth as

fire spread through her leg. She had experienced pain over the past few months, but nothing like this agony. Tears blurred her vision as she prayed it would end soon. It seemed like an eternity before the worst of it stopped and she was able to sit up. He was sitting before her with his knees bent, his pants pooled at his ankles and his shoes on his feet. It was a comical sight, but there was nothing funny about the look on his face. He was furious.

"What did you do to me?" he growled.

"I didn't do anything. Azazel left my head a few minutes ago. He couldn't stand up to the affect you had on me," she said, unsure why she was defending herself.

"What spell did he teach you?"

"None. I can't do magic, jackass." She had no idea what he was talking about, but she wasn't about to tolerate being accused of something she didn't do.

"Then how do you explain this?" he asked, standing up to give her a view of the back of his right calf. There was a red brand in the shape of lightning surrounded by barbed vines.

"Is that what I think it is?" It couldn't be a mating mark. He'd already been given and lost his Fated Mate and you didn't get two in a lifetime. She had to be careful with what she said or he would distrust her even more. She turned her leg and the moon shone down on an identical mark on her right calf.

"It's a mate mark," he said confirming her suspicions. "And, what I want to know is how this happened."

"You're my Fated Mate," she whispered, awed by the knowledge and completely flabbergasted.

"No, I'm not," he denied, walking away from her. She watched him walk below deck and wanted to rip out his throat. Tears suddenly blinded her as reality sank in. Her mate had just rejected her. Her vision that had been stuck on infrared since her captivity suddenly turned black as night. She wasn't sure what was worse at that moment, her pain or her anger. She ripped a seat from its mooring and threw it overboard. Several life preservers and seat cushions followed. She wasn't going to be a victim ever again.

CHAPTER 12

Gerrick stalked into the house pissed, and yet, hungry for more of Shae. He hadn't intended on having sex with her, but hadn't been able to resist her. What had started out a joyride on the lake took an unsurprising turn and had given him the most powerful orgasm of his life. Sorcerers didn't ejaculate during climax until they had sex with their Fated Mate. When he'd been with Evanna those centuries ago, he'd experienced the sensation for the first time. It had been indescribable for him, but his memory paled in comparison now that it had happened again.

He'd cherished the few times he'd had with Evanna because after her death that pleasure disappeared along with his mating brand. Now, both were back with a vengeance. The gratification he'd felt with Shae had turned him inside out and was the reason he'd dropped her, not the pain from the brand reemerging. He wasn't prepared for the buildup of pressure in his balls so his shields were completely down and the orgasm had blown through him before he could stop it. In fact, it nearly caused him to black out.

The entire experience made him want to hunt down the Goddess and tear her a new one. Piece by small piece he was losing the only thing he had of Evanna. The mating and ejaculation was something he'd only had with her. Every aspect of their mating had been his most treasured memories and now they were being impinged upon.

And now, the mating brand that had disappeared after her death was back and he'd ejaculated for the first time in four hundred years. To add insult to injury, the orgasm had been unlike anything that had come before. As was his connection to Shae. He was desperate for another taste of her, and, at the same time, he hated the sight of her. None of this should be happening and he wasn't convinced it was Goddess-driven. Not after the hell she'd been put through. Not to mention the fact that no one knew what Dark magic was capable of replicating. His life hadn't made any sense since he'd rescued Shae.

He needed answers and headed straight for the stairs as soon as he entered the house. He heard her following him, although they hadn't spoken since he'd retrieved clothing for her on the boat.

"Are you just going to ignore me? I think we need to talk," she finally said to him, breaking the silence. Her voice slid over him like a caress, making him hard as stone in his pants.

"I have a meeting in fifteen minutes," he replied, opening his door. He shouldn't leave her alone, but if he didn't get away from her he would have her on her back, or all fours, in the next heartbeat. He hurried to the bathroom and went to shut the door, only to find his way blocked by her body.

She looked too damn sexy for words standing there in the huge t-shirt that he kept on the boat. She was naked beneath the clothing, making it hard to think of anything but tearing it off and tasting her more fully. That had been a quickie, just enough to take off the barest edge of his need.

"That's not going to work for me. You don't get to have sex with me, learn we are mates and then shut me out," she challenged.

"I'm not the mate you want, Shae. Undo the spell and save yourself the trouble of it backfiring later." He pushed her back and shut the door in her shocked face. He was all kinds of a bastard, but his control hung by a thread and was looking for any reason to snap. If he took her when he was so angry, he was afraid he'd inadvertently hurt her. He needed to learn more about what was happening first.

He took his cell phone from his pocket and sent a text to Zander and Evzen requesting a meeting then turned on the water. He took an ice cold shower, hoping it would diminish his arousal, but that was impossible with tendrils of Shae's scent reaching him through the closed door. It was mixed with his the way it should be and the only dampener was the acrid scent of her hurt and anger.

He saw the shadow of her feet as they paced a circuit on the other side of the door. He dried off and slung a towel around his waist, unable to hide the erection tenting the terry cloth. She opened her mouth to scathe him, no doubt, but her words died as her eyes settled on his groin. He smiled, understanding exactly how she felt. She had him in knots and so aroused he thought he could pound nails with his cock. He sauntered slowly to his closet, teasing her.

Dropping the towel from his waist at the door, he relished her indrawn breath. Grabbing a black tee, he realized how much he enjoyed teasing, even when he was livid.

She challenged him and he reveled in how much fun she brought to his life. His chest constricted and his soul cried out that she was his and his cock hardened in agreement.

Suddenly, he broke out in a cold sweat as he dressed. How could Dark magic replicate that type of reaction? He shoved his erection into his pants, refusing to think about the anguish he knew his behavior was causing her. There was a possibility this was Dark magic.

"I don't know what you think I've become, but I don't have any kind of power and those vile creatures left me with nothing but pain and suffering," she told him when he walked out of the closet. He saw the torment in her familiar green eyes and knew he had wounded a part of her he hadn't meant to. She had trusted him with part of herself that had been deeply violated and here he was twisting the knife.

He continued and paused at the door with his back to her. "You'll be safe in here," he promised, having no other words to make the situation better, before leaving and locking her inside. He expected to hear evidence of her anger, either her throwing things or hitting the door. The fact that he heard only silence made a boulder settle in his gut. There was nothing worse than silence. It was easier to deal with yelling, screaming and even hitting, but you couldn't battle silence. There was nothing there.

Even as he denied that Shae was his mate, he prayed he hadn't ruined his chances. His heavy boots pounded down the stairs and he went straight to the war room. Zander was there with Evzen. Neither looked over as he entered, but continued their discussion over Angelica's actions. Gerrick understood Zander's anger over her breach of his home, as well as, his demand that Evzen get control of her. As a sorceress, she fell under the Guild Master's purview, but

Evzen wasn't ever going to be capable of governing Angelica.

Gerrick went to the bar and poured himself four fingers of Bhric's favorite scotch. He took a healthy swallow, appreciating the smooth texture as he turned around. Zander was watching him with that raised eyebrow of his. "Tough night with Shae?"

"You have no idea," Gerrick muttered, feeling the weight of the situation on his shoulders.

"Och, that doesna sound good. I assume that's why you called us here, so what happened? Is she still alive?" Zander sat back in his chair and folded his arms across his chest.

Gerrick fell into a chair and scowled. "Of course she's alive. What do you think I am?"

Zander looked straight at him. "I think you will do whatever is necessary to uphold your vow. You wouldna hesitate to eliminate any threat to humans and the Tehrex Realm and Shae is unpredictable."

"You're right. She's a wild card. One that I think may be capable of doing Dark magic." That grabbed the males' attention as they sat up and leaned forward.

"Explain," Zander barked at the same time Evzen said, "Vampires aren't capable of performing magic."

He gave them a rundown of what occurred on the boat as he stood and lifted his pant leg, showing them the brand on his leg.

"Is that what I think it is?" Evzen murmured as he touched the edge of the mark. Gerrick gritted his teeth against the pain and sat down.

"How did this happen?" Zander asked, echoing Gerrick's thoughts.

"That's why I called you two. This can't be possible. I was given Evanna and then she was taken from me. We are only given one mate in our lifetime. Have you ever heard of it being any different?"

"Are you certain Evanna was yours?" Evzen asked, and Gerrick had to remind himself that he couldn't punch his Guild Master in the face.

"Of course she was mine. You might not understand this, but you will never forget the feeling of being branded by your mate. Not to mention the sexual pleasure. I have no doubt that she was mine," he bit out.

"Aye, he is right," Zander added. "There was nothing like being branded by my Elsie. Was it the same with Shae as it was with Evanna?"

Gerrick took another drink then blew out a breath. "Fuck, that's the problem. It was so much better than I remember which makes it so much worse. Nothing can be better than Evanna." He heard the distress in his voice.

"What happened to cause her pain before this happened?" Evzen asked, placing his palms on the table before a large leather tome appeared.

"Shit. She never told me, just insisted that I kiss her and then I was so angry at her for trying to force this mating that I forgot to ask. Goddess, I'm a fucking idiot," he cursed. The sinking feeling in his gut intensified, telling him he had fucked up more than he realized.

"Bluidy hell. Understand one thing, Gerrick. 'Tis no' possible for the archdemons to affect something created by the Goddess. Nor can they replicate a mating. Evil canna understand the reasons for, or the mechanics, that are necessary." Gerrick shifted under Zander's reprisal and scrutiny.

Evzen looked up from the book with a why-didn't-I-think-of-that expression on his face. "Stand up again, Gerrick," the Guild Master instructed. Gerrick obliged and the other male knelt next to him. He muttered the same spell they used to follow the trail of skirm. Gerrick wasn't sure if the spell would reveal anything, but had to admit it was a clever way to try and detect any subterfuge. Designed to follow skirm, it should be able to detect any Dark magic created by archdemons. Holding his breath, he watched his leg for a reaction.

A yellow glow would outline the brand if Dark magic was used. When nothing happened after several minutes, Evzen sat back down, relief written all over his face. "I had to be sure Zander was correct. It wouldn't due to ignore due diligence and assume that our most precious gifts can't be altered. It seems Zeum has another reason to celebrate. Shae is your Fated Mate, Gerrick."

"Aye, she is. And, if you want my opinion, you willna tell her of your doubts. That'll just piss off a female," Zander said, smiling. Too late for that, Gerrick thought. "That answers one question, but doesna tell us how this happened."

"I lost Evanna and no one should be sent to replace her. That's why I doubted it," Gerrick said in defense, despite the fact that Shae wasn't there to hear him. He needed to be saying that to Shae, but didn't know if he ever could. Evanna was his Fated Mate, her soul was part of him. How could he carry two different souls? Shae carried his soul, but what if he didn't have a part of hers?

"Tell me about your mating to Evanna," Evzen muttered as he continued to turn pages in the ancient book. "Perhaps, there are answers in the grimoire."

"There's not much to tell. It was a short story of love at first sight. We discovered we were mates soon after meeting, but she was killed two weeks later. We hadn't even told anyone that we were mates," he explained, going back four centuries in his memory.

"So you didn't complete the mating then," Evzen observed.

Gerrick snapped to attention. He'd sat back down and was now sitting so stiffly it felt as if a rod of steel were in his back. "Are you saying this happened because Evanna and I didn't complete the ceremony?"

"Aye, that has to be it," Zander added. "The mating ceremony is detailed for a reason. Once everything is completed there is nothing on this world or any other that can dissolve that bond. That bond wasna cemented between you and Evanna, leaving room for another to fill that void."

That was the problem, Gerrick mused. He didn't want anyone or anything filling that void, yet he couldn't stop thinking about Shae. She'd drawn him in from the moment he'd seen her. A connection snapped into place and had been growing stronger ever since. He admired her strength and courage, as well as her grace under pressure. She was a true treasure. And now, he'd treated her like shit before locking her into another cage. He could imagine her pacing and plotting his death, and, like it or not, he was going to have to face the music at some point.

"There is nothing here that can shed more light on this situation. Your explanation makes sense, Zander, but I don't want this information being leaked into the population. We don't want those that have lost their mate thinking there is hope of them finding another," Evzen commented, closing the Mystik Grimoire.

"Shite, the last thing we need is to shatter existing families. Not to mention the heartbreak that false hope would bring to the individual. The Goddess, it seems, is breaking the mold all over the place," Zander said, no doubt talking about how his Fated Mate, Elsie, had become the first human-turned-vampire.

"I can't believe I've been given another Fated Mate. I'm not ready to accept it yet, but I know what you're saying is true. This is supposed to be a blessing, so why does it feel like a punishment?" With that, he stalked out of the room.

SHAE UNDERSTOOD GERRICK'S DOUBT, but that didn't make his actions hurt any less. She had been floundering to find her footing since her rescue and instead of being the steadying force a mate should be, Gerrick made her so angry she feared she would snap and hurt someone. Like most of the realm, she had grown up not giving much thought to having a Fated Mate because it seemed the centuries-long mating curse would never be broken. The curse had been broken shortly before she'd been kidnapped so she really never gave the idea much thought. What consideration she had given it had been fleeting, but she had never imagined it would be like this.

No one had prepared her for any aspect of the mating and not knowing what to expect made her edgy. She wasn't a virgin, but she hadn't really dated much, either. No one had sparked enough interest. Relationships were complicated. She was all about going to work and spending time with her family and friends. She and Rebecca may have frequented Club Confetti, but Shae hadn't been involved with very many males. It was easier keeping interactions with males uncomplicated, enjoy each other's company for however long it lasted and then part on friendly terms. In fact, Shae and Rebecca joked about the three-month limit on relationships with males.

She missed Rebecca greatly and wished she had the courage to call her up. To be able to meet up at Confetti for a drink so she could tell her the colossal mistake she had made in falling for Gerrick. She choked back a sob when she recalled that Confetti had been destroyed by the archdemons who had stolen her from her safe, sheltered life. Acknowledging one more loss to the demons always had rage spiking the surface.

As if thinking about him opened a door, Azazel chose that moment to resume his efforts at mentally battering her and trying to command her to do his bidding. She squinted and tried to force him out. It wasn't so bad at the moment and she prayed her experience during the boat ride didn't repeat itself. The demand to steal the Triskele Amulet and kill the Dark Warriors had sent searing pain to her brain and it'd felt like a white-hot poker in her frontal cortex. Gerrick had been the key to breaking the connection Azazel had established, ending the compulsion and pain. She had to assume that being at Zeum lessened his reach because the pain wasn't nearly as intense as it had been.

She tensed at the sound of the lock turning and shifted her stance. The door swung open and she lunged at the sexy sorcerer. He caught her mid-air and pinned her against the wall, kicking the door shut. The action had her melting against him and sighing in relief when the demon's presence in her mind disappeared. A muttered spell left his lips and they were locked in the room together. His chest kept her in place while his hands gripped her wrists. He turned his head and surveyed the room.

"I see we've been busy redecorating," he murmured when he glanced around and saw the destruction. She braced herself against the deep masculine voice, but he still made her insides turn to lava. "I like the change," he teased.

"You'll get my bill in the mail. Now that I'm finished with all of this," she told him, not wanting to put herself through anymore, "I'd like Nate to take me to my room."

She needed to get away from Gerrick. His presence was killing her. The bond, that was apparently one-sided on her part, grew stronger with every second, but the disdain was clear on his face. Besides, she felt like a ticking time-bomb.

"That's not happening, Red. This is your room now."

"Then get out. I don't want you here." She swallowed at the narrow-eyed look he gave her as if what she said pissed him off. Well, too damn bad.

"Look, I've not handled things very well, but this situation isn't exactly typical."

"Yeah, I get it. You don't need to remind me that I'm damaged. Now, get out," she demanded, breathing heavily with her agitation. This male made her head spin. One second she was melting for him and wanting another kiss and the next she wanted to rip out his intestines.

"I don't think you do," he said, his lips so close to hers they brushed hers when he talked. "You aren't damaged. You're perfect." It would have been more believable if he weren't scowling when he said the latter.

"This mark says that you're mine. Neither of us is going anywhere until we figure this out," he finished.

"I don't need pity or lies. And, I won't allow you to deny me one second then come back here and act like you own me." She refused to allow her inner beast to claim him and barely held the words back. Only the knowledge that he didn't want her, but another female, kept the words from escaping anyway.

"I'm sorry, Red. I fucked up, but it's been a long day and we're both tired. We will talk more after we get some rest."

She hadn't realized how tired she was until that

moment. She had been fighting to keep the demon out since the boat ride, and, between that and the mating, she was exhausted. "You get the sofa. Well, what's left of it and I'll take the bed."

His smile had her toes curling in anticipation. "I don't think so. We're sharing the bed."

She started to object when he swung her up into his arms. She had every intention of fighting his dominance, but she was tired. She had been fighting for months. He dropped her onto the bed and stripped his shirt and boots off in record time. He left his jeans on and slid into bed next to her.

"This would have been easier if you hadn't destroyed the room," he murmured as he reached over and picked up the blanket and pillows. He pulled her into his arms and held her close.

"Don't piss me off again, Gerrick," she said with a yawn. She heard his chuckle and fell asleep with his strong, steady heartbeat in her ear.

GERRICK WOKE to the kiss of steel at his jugular. He had been sleeping with Shae next to his side and was shocked by how content he was to remain that way. He had never in his four hundred fifty years slept next to a female. He couldn't erase the doubts about the mating, but neither could he deny how good it felt to have her by his side. She was lush and soft and her feminine scent wrapped around him, fuzzing his brain.

"Shae? What's going on?" he asked, looking around the room for a threat that he knew wasn't there. She was the best Trojan horse the archdemons could have devised. They knew Zander and the warriors would care for the females rather than killing them outright.

"You need to unlock the door, Gerrick," she said, her face a mask of cold determination. There were no remnants of the female who'd set him in his place last night.

He opened his mouth to deny her but saw something flicker in the back of her eyes. She was locked in an internal battle and he could only guess what it was about. He wanted to keep her there and protect her, but ultimately he conceded to her wishes and it had nothing to do with the knife at his throat. The truth of the matter was that he could take the weapon from her in a heartbeat, but he refused to contribute to her suffering. What he wanted to do was shelter and care for her. Erase the reasons for the fine lines around her eyes.

When she heard the door unlock, she jumped from the bed and sprinted out of the room, dressed in a pair of his sweat pants and her heels from the night before. Her hair flew behind her as she fled. The sight of her running from him when she should be running toward him caused a sharp, twisting pain in his chest.

CHAPTER 13

Shae's heart was going a million miles a minute as she sped away from Zeum. She couldn't believe her luck when she ran out the front door and a Mustang was sitting there. Without hesitation, she'd jumped in and fist pumped the air and shouted her excitement when she saw the keys in the ignition. Of course, the warriors wouldn't have bothered with locking their cars in front of their compound. The engine's loud roar made her jump and she worried someone would hear and come running. Quick as a whip, she'd punched the accelerator and whipped the car around and drove like a bat out of hell off the property.

She was still driving too fast through the slick, silent streets, but she was afraid she was going to be located any second. Nervously, she kept checking the rear view mirror, expecting to see Gerrick or one of the other warriors speeding up behind her, but she had to get out of there.

She'd been having the first peaceful night's sleep in months when Azazel's coercion had begun again. The blinding pain was accompanied by the urge to slit Gerrick's throat and find the amulet. The last thing she wanted to do was hurt him so she had to get out of that house. She'd taken for granted that Gerrick's presence would keep the demons at bay and had relaxed her vigilance when Azazel once again exerted his influence on her.

When she reached Queen Anne she decided to leave the car in a parking lot far away from her destination and walk the rest of the way. There was no way she was going to lead the Dark Warriors any closer to her home. It was probably a mistake to go there, but she had no money and nowhere else to go.

She traveled the streets on foot and paused when she passed a gas station that still had a payphone out front. It had been years since she'd seen a payphone. Hands on her knees, she caught her breath as she contemplated calling Rebecca. Her best friend would be there in a heartbeat, no questions asked, and it would keep her family out of it, but she would never place Rebecca in the line of fire like that. No doubt, Gerrick would rake Rebecca over the coals for aiding Shae. He was insanely possessive and had slept with his arms wrapped so tightly around her that it had been a challenge for Shae to extricate herself. That was the way it should be between mates, Shae's soul screamed.

Then there was Shae's stability to consider. She could harm Rebecca if she lost it again. No, she couldn't place Rebecca at risk. Decision made, she ducked behind a store and crossed a few neighborhoods in the blink of an eye. She was far faster now than she'd been before her abduction. She was trying to see that as a good thing when she found herself in her parent's front yard moments later.

Sudden nerves stopped her and she crouched outside one of the side windows. She wasn't sure how they'd react and didn't know what she would do if they rejected her, too.

Never before would she have questioned her parents or grandparents, but she was an unpredictable monster now.

She stepped back under the canopy of a large maple tree in the front yard and glanced back at the Victorian. The gingerbread detail of the eaves and the bright, colorful trim was highlighted in the early morning sunrise. The dark blue of the wraparound porch matched the trim around the windows and still bore the marks from Austin's claws. Her brother had been running from their mother after one on his shenanigans. The sight of her family home was so familiar and comforting, and, vastly different from Zeum.

Zeum was a large grey mansion with Goddess only knew how many bedrooms. Shae figured it could easily house a hundred with how big it was. Their kitchen alone was almost as big as her home. Yet, there was a sense of intimacy when you walked in the door. The connections shared by those living there were as powerful as those between her family. It made sense, Shae thought, given their missions and how closely they fought together.

Rising above the windowsill, she peeked through the clear glass and saw part of her family gathered in the living room. She was lucky that they hadn't yet pulled the heavy drapes that offered protection from the sun's lethal rays. Her mother was playing a card game with her Aunt Shelly and Uncle Keith. A sharp pang in her chest brought tears to her eyes because normally, she would have been playing with them. She loved the time she spent with her family, but deep down, she didn't feel like she fit here anymore.

She heard her brother, Austin calling out to her mom from the back of the large house about a lost shoe or something. She smiled. Austin was always losing his stuff. More than likely, her father was whipping up something delicious for their last meal of the day while her grandmother sat in the kitchen talking to him. It was a normal scene in her house and she couldn't stop one of her tears from escaping.

She wondered if her grandfather was home from work yet. She had imagined their lives had stopped while they searched for her. But, here they were as if she wasn't missing at all. Wild and crazy thought raced through her mind and suddenly she wasn't so sure this had been a good idea. Hell, they may have given her room to her aunt for her office. They might not want her back at all.

Pale rays of sun hit the ground beside her, freezing her breath in her lungs. She hadn't survived the past seven months of hell to be burned to death by the sun. The imminent sunrise made her decision for her and she ran to the porch, ringing the doorbell.

Her mother answered the door and screamed. Before she knew what was happening, she had been pulled into a hug and was surrounded by her mother's familiar rose scent. She gripped her mom tightly and let the tears fall. She heard the others in the house run to see what the ruckus was about, but didn't pull away from her mom.

"Kay, you need to back up before the sun reaches the both of you," her dad said trying to tug her from her mother's grip, but her mother refused to let her go. Shae felt them being led into the house as her dad cried and grabbed them both. "Oh, Goddess. I can't believe you're finally here. Where have you been? What happened? Are you okay?"

"That's a long story. I missed you dad."

"What is it, Matthew?" her grandmother, Philomena, asked coming into the room. "Goddess, child," her grandmother cried out and rushed towards them. The familiar mint scent of her grandmother joined the menagerie of her parents as her small arms worked their way into the embrace. "We have missed you."

She sobbed harder hearing that and they stood in their huddle for several minutes. She felt her brother and aunt and uncle hovering near the edges and knew they wanted to join the group. When she lifted her head, she met Austin's gaze. Silent tears streamed down his cheeks and she nodded her head to him. She understood what he wasn't saying. They may irritate each other, but they loved each other more than words could say.

"Let's sit down," her dad said, crossing to take a seat on the sofa. Shae's mom didn't let her go and Shae didn't try to extricate herself. It felt too wonderful to be home and in her arms. Her aunt and uncle each gave her a hug where she stood in her mother's arms and told her they loved her and then her brother nearly squeezed the life out of her, bringing more tears to her eyes. Finally, she and her mother sat together on the other sofa and her grandmother sat on her other side and grabbed Shae's hand.

"You have no idea how good it is to see you and be home. I can't believe it's all the same, even the throws on the couch," she said, looking around. They had the same faded, mismatched furniture they'd had for several decades. The stuff needed to be replaced, but it was nice to see the red chair and green couches as well as the purple recliners.

It was all ridiculous, especially after seeing the lush leather furniture in the King's home, but it was perfect for them. Her eclectic grandmother had chosen every piece and hadn't seen anything she liked to replace it, no matter how hard they looked. She took a deep breath of the familiar scent. This was home. And, they hadn't rejected her.

"You look so tired," her mother observed. Shae knew she was fishing for information, but she wasn't ready to tell them. She didn't want to see looks of disgust on their faces when they looked so happy to see her. She wouldn't ever tell them everything she'd been through, but what little she could tell them would be enough to ruin this happy mood.

"I'm not that tired, but I could use a shower. And a change of clothes. Are my things still here?" she asked hesitantly.

"Don't be ridiculous. Of course they are and your room is just as you left it," her grandmother said, smoothing Shae's hair back from her face in a tender caress. Unable to stop herself, Shae flinched at the contact and jumped up. She didn't want anyone to see her scars.

"I'm going to clean up. I'll be out in a bit," she told her family.

"We never gave up hope," her mother said, tears now slipping from her dark green eyes. Her father stood up and wrapped an arm around her mom. "Food will be ready when you're done," he added. She nodded and headed down the hall, emotion a hard lump in her throat.

Her brother was the only one who refused to let her be. He followed her down the hall and up the stairs. Thankfully, he kept silent. Not that she wasn't blazingly aware of his wariness. It was obvious to her that he didn't trust her sudden reappearance and she was glad. She didn't really trust herself. Gerrick and the Dark Warriors had one thing right. It was best to have someone close by.

"I'm glad you're back, sis. We have all been out of our minds with worry and mom hasn't slept. You know her. They may ignore this and not push the issue right now, but something is different about you," he challenged, leaning against the wall, crossing his feet at the ankles. It was a typical Austin pose, all insouciance and vigilance. She welcomed the smile that spread across her face.

"I know you guys have questions and I will answer what I can. You're right to be suspicious. I'd be disappointed if you weren't. But, please, know that I'm just as overwhelmed as you are," she admitted, asking for his understanding.

He held her gaze for several seconds then nodded. She touched his shoulder before she entered her room. She immediately closed the indoor shutters and curtains, noting that no one had touched a thing, and yet, it was dust-free and fresh. No doubt it killed her mom to enter every day and clean without making the bed or picking up her pajamas off the floor, but this was her way of believing Shae would return.

She grabbed some jeans and her UW sweatshirt then headed to the bathroom. Austin hadn't moved a muscle, but did stick his tongue out at her like he had when they were kids. She reciprocated and they laughed as she crossed the hall into the bathroom. Goddess, she had missed her family.

She sat down on the edge of the tub and put her head in her hands. Her heart hadn't yet settled and she felt the demon probing her brain. She checked her mental barriers and found them intact, not that it was keeping him out. No, he was at the back of her brain like a pounding headache and it was infuriating. She wanted to know how he was able to influence her and wished she could shut him out without Gerrick's presence.

Just the hint of his name and her mind immediately diverted to her Fated Mate. She missed his scowl and wanted him there by her side to face her family. He had provided her strength at every turn since her rescue and she needed him now more than ever, but he wasn't with her. And, it was because she'd run away.

She had been blessed with her mate and yet he loved another. He didn't have to tell her, she felt it through their bond. She also felt his confusion and worry. It mollified her somewhat to know he was worried about her. Perhaps there was hope for them yet.

She took of his clothes and brought them to her nose, inhaling deeply. There were minimal traces of his scent left on the fabric, but it was enough to wreak havoc with her. The mark on the back of her calf had been a constant throb since it had appeared, but right then a stab of agony shot through it.

Ignoring what she couldn't change, she turned the faucet to hot, grabbed a spare toothbrush her mom always kept in the cabinet, and brushed her teeth. Once that was done she stepped into the tub and took a long shower. The familiar scent of her favorite shampoo was another balm to her battered soul. She picked up the bar of her grandmother's homemade soap and brought it to her nose. Vampires were highly sensitive to scents and she had missed the honey and rosemary that would always remind her of her grandmother. She had forgotten how good the soap made her skin feel. It felt as if it washed away the remnants of her captivity. Unfortunately, it also washed away all hints of Gerrick.

She cut the water off and stepped out of the tub and grabbed a big fluffy towel. Wrapping her body in the terry cloth, she wiped the mirror clean and glanced at her reflection. Somehow she'd hoped she'd look like her old self in her own bathroom, but the same disfigured monster looked back at her. She dried off and dressed quickly then opened the door. She stopped short when she saw Austin in the same spot. He was on his phone, but he stuffed it in his pocket when she came out.

The smell of her dad's famous blueberry waffles greeted her as they descended the stairs. That wasn't a typical last meal for them, but it was her favorite and no doubt the reason her dad had made it and it warmed her heart. Austin laughed when her stomach rumbled loudly. "He still makes the best chicken and waffles in the world," her brother teased, ruffling her hair.

His body went stiff and she looked up. His eyes were riveted to the side of her neck. She lifted her hand and covered the scars, turning her head away. He wrapped his arm around her shoulders. "Come on before Grandpa and Uncle Keith eat all the food," his voice was thick with emotion. He didn't say what he was thinking, but she could see the pity and disgust in his eyes. She couldn't blame him. It was horrific and would be a reminder everyday of her life. If she could cut the flesh away and live she would, but the damage was too extensive.

As she brought the long length of her hair forward to cover her scars, she was grateful it hadn't been cut. For whatever reason, the demons left their hair alone and she'd often wondered why. She walked into the kitchen and hugged her dad from behind. "This smells delicious. I missed this more than you know."

"Does your Papa get a kiss?" came the husky request from behind her. She swirled around to see her grandfather, Theodore, had come home while she was in the shower. Her grandfather had always been a larger-than-life figure to her. He was a wolf shifter and was Killian's head of security. She had prayed countless times that he would come barreling in and save her from the demon's lair. Now, after her imprisonment, he paled in the face of Kadir's strength and she was glad he had not made that attempt.

She tried to hide the anger over being taken from her life as she crossed the kitchen and was gathered into her grandfather's big arms, but didn't quite manage it. No matter what she did her anger was always there bubbling below the surface and she had prayed that being home would make it go away. No such luck. There was nowhere she could go to escape it and the futility ate at her.

"Your father has made blueberry waffles everyday hoping you'd come home. We are all sick of them, but today we gladly eat them," her grandmother teased, winking at her. The female had been a cornerstone in their family for as long as Shae had been alive and her familiar candor dampened her rapidly rising anger. Shae pulled back from her grandfather and smiled at her grandmother.

"I love you, too, Nana," she said, kissing her cheek. She chuckled to herself when she remembered the last time she was in a store and the humans had given her odd looks when she called her Nana. Philomena didn't look a day older than thirty and had a body most females would die for. The humans would have dropped dead on sight if they knew her Nana was over a thousand years old and a vampire.

"Let's eat," her dad instructed, taking the platter of chicken to the table. Shae lingered by her mother's side and grabbed a waffle off the platter she carried.

Nibbling on the golden, fluffy piece of heaven, she worked up the nerve to open the can of worms she'd been avoiding. She set her fork down and took a few deep breaths, clasping her hands in her lap. "I know you all have questions about where I've been and I'm going to tell you, but please don't ask me anything until I'm done. I need to get through this."

Her grandmother grabbed her hand and squeezed it. "No one will say a thing until you're ready." The scowl and tone of her voice told everyone at the table that they'd have to deal with her wrath if they opened their mouths.

It was either now or never, Shae thought, and proceeded

to tell them about her capture and imprisonment, leaving out the gruesome details and the extent of her torture. It was considerably harder to tell them what had happened and she found it impossible to make eye contact with anyone and found herself focusing on the untouched platter of chicken on the table instead. "They kept me locked up like that in a cage for months in their lair with several other females and that's why I couldn't escape or find a way to contact you sooner," she finished. An anvil of silence descended over the room, making her squirm in her seat. What were they thinking? Did they see the monster she had become?

After what felt like an eternity of silence, she finally lifted her gaze and glanced around the table. Her grandfather sat forward, his face partially shifted to his wolf. "Where the hell is this lair? I will tear every demon and skirm limb from limb." His voice was laden with his need for retaliation and the ferocity frightened even her. Although scary, she was filled with pride to see this male that she'd looked up to her whole life coming to her defense.

"Add me to that list, Papa," Austin growled, his wolf at the surface, as well.

"No one will be safe from our wrath," her father vowed.

"You guys will have to get in line behind me," her mother hissed, flashing her fangs.

"We will all get a piece of these demons. I'm just glad you got away, sweetheart. By the way, how did you escape?" Nana asked.

Everyone had stopped eating the moment she began talking and Shae picked up her fork, eating again as she answered her grandmother. "Zander and his Dark Warriors rescued me and the rest of the females. I have been at Zeum for the past few days, healing from my injuries."

"Are you certain you're completely healed?" Her grandmother swept her hair over her shoulder in a gesture meant to soothe her, but it exposed her scars. Nana's gasp drew everyone's attention. Her mother was sitting on her other side and had to stand up to get a look at the physical evidence of how damaged she was.

"Where. Is. That. Lair?" Papa gritted out, his claws digging grooves into the wood table.

"I could tell you, but trust me, there isn't anything there. Zander and the warriors killed everything when they rescued us and then sent Gerrick and Kyran back the next night to make sure." Her chest ached at the mention of Gerrick. She wasn't going to mention her mating to her family yet. That was one too many issues to dump on them at once. Besides, she wasn't sure how she felt about Gerrick, but she wanted him alive for the time being. Her family needed blood for what she'd been through and would gladly take it out of Gerrick's hide if they discovered that he'd denied her. She glanced at her grandfather, noting he had yet to calm down. Yeah, Gerrick would be in pieces before lunch.

"I had heard something from Killian about a raid, but had no idea it involved you. I'll skin that sorcerer alive for not telling me that you were involved," Papa seethed. "For the first time in my life, I regret not joining Zander's forces. I could have been doing something to stop the demons." Shae recalled the stories of how he had been sought after because of how ferociously he had fought during the Great War.

"You're where you're meant to be, Ted. She was taken from a parking lot. You couldn't have prevented this," Nana replied at the same time she wrapped an arm around Shae's middle.

"No, but I would have rescued her," he said, holding eye contact with Shae. He blamed himself for not being there for her. His guilt was a punch in the stomach and more than she could deal with at the moment. Averting her gaze, she caught her father and then her brother's eyes and cringed when she saw the same remorse reflected there.

She reached across her grandmother's arm and patted her grandfather's thick arm. The muscle jumped under her palm, reminding her of the animal that was barely leashed. "Don't blame yourselves. I can't stand to see you beating yourselves up. There was nothing you could have done. Hell, the King wouldn't have found us if Prince Kyran's mate hadn't stumbled upon us. Like you've always told me, the Goddess never abandons her subjects. I admit that I questioned her more than once during those months, but she was there for me when it came down to it," she admitted, thinking of how she'd placed Gerrick in her path, "I'm here with you now and that's what matters."

"How do we properly thank the Vampire King for giving us our Shae back? You could cook for them, Matt. Would it be appropriate to ask them over for a meal?" her mother inquired of no one in particular.

She laughed at that. Her mom was the first one to take meals to sick neighbors or help friends in need and to her food was always the answer, which was probably why the meals the Queen had cooked for Shae had meant so much. "He doesn't expect anything, Mom. And, not that you aren't the best cook in the world, Dad, but the King's mate is no slouch in the kitchen. She actually cooked every meal I ate at the compound."

Her grandmother sat up. "Don't they have servants?

That's preposterous that the Queen would be making the household meals. Surely, the Tarakeshes aren't struggling for money."

Shae shook her head. Her Nana had prescribed roles and expectations for the royal family and it had rubbed off on Shae without her realizing it. "No, Nana, they aren't hurting for money, and yes, they have plenty of servants. But, the rumors we heard are true. The Queen was a human before she was turned into a vampire and because of that she has a unique way of doing things. One of them is that she loves to cook."

"I can't believe you stayed at Zeum," her brother murmured, awe in his tone. "What were the warriors like? After you were taken, I considered enlisting in the training program, but I couldn't give up the hours searching for you."

"Sorry to have cut into your free-time," she teased, sticking out her tongue at him. He chuckled and threw a piece of waffle at her. She laughed and pondered what he'd said. Her brother would make a great warrior. He was built like Papa, tall with muscles on his muscles and a relentless drive. Yeah, the more she thought about it, the more she realized Austin's strength and dedication would make him a great warrior. Not to mention, females were always drooling over him, swooning over his green eyes and long, black hair, so he was a shoe-in.

"The warriors are a lot like you. Always eating, teasing each other and drinking. And, the unmated ones are just as friendly with the females. You should enlist, you would fit right in."

"Don't feed his ego, child. We don't need him any cockier," her Nana joked as they all resumed eating. The rest of the meal passed with laughter and them catching her up on what she had missed.

Gerrick was going to be pissed at her for taking off, but she had needed to leave and was glad she'd come home. It had been a few hours and so far she was fine. She loved her family more than anything and would never hurt them. Besides, her mate didn't get to tell her what to do and it was best that he learn that now.

CHAPTER 14

Shae woke just before sunset after a fitful day's sleep. Agitated, she sat on the edge of her soft bed and twisted her hair into a knot at the back of her head. Several times throughout the day, she had been forced to beat Azazel or Kadir from her mind and the ordeal had been exhausting, pushing her to her limit. She recalled how Jessie had talked about the archdemons not having the ability to sway Jessie. How the hell she had gotten away from her encounter with Azazel with nothing more than mild buzzing and irritation was beyond Shae. The female was so well-adjusted Shae could throat-punch her.

Frustrated at the lack of answers, Shae stood up and threw on her favorite skinny jeans and a sweater that she had knitted for herself. It was the first one she'd ever made and had been her way of practicing before she made her mom and nana one. She smiled as she recalled the way her brother had teased while she was making it and then ate his words when she was done. He'd loved the final product so much he'd begged her to make him one.

Shoving her feet into knee-high black boots, she made

her way downstairs. Sweat dripped down her spine and her heart raced. She wiped her brow and looked around anxiously, for what, she had no idea. All she knew was that the walls were closing in on her and she couldn't breathe.

"Hey, Fly Girl. What's up?" Uncle Keith asked, coming down behind her.

"Nothing," she eyed the stairs and then the door. "Did Papa leave?"

"Yeah, he wanted to talk to Killian before his shift started and your dad is at the store. I was just heading to grab some coffee. Want some?"

"No, I..." She trailed off, rubbing her arms. Her veins were thrumming and her skin felt like it was vibrating.

"You're scaring me, sit down." He grabbed onto her arm and tried to lead her to the couch.

"No!" she screamed, breaking away from him. She immediately went into a crouch, ready to take him out if necessary.

"Shae," her mother called out, rushing into the room. Panicked, Shae headed to the front door, but was tackled on her way there.

"Don't ever fucking touch me," she snarled and kicked her uncle in the face.

He flew back and knocked the couch over, but was up the next instant. Blood trickled out of a cut on his cheek. "I don't want to hurt you, Shae."

"I just want to leave," she said, grabbing a fireplace poker as she circled to get to the door.

"Where is it you want to go?" he asked, refusing to move out of her way. She bared her fangs at him and he tricked her by lunging to the right only to dart left when she tried to slip past him. She clawed his arms and he retaliated by punching her in the side, causing her weapon to fly across the room and embed itself in the wall. Traitor, she thought, swinging. Her blow grazed his cheek before she lunged at him where he stood in front of the door, blocking her way.

"Anywhere but here," she countered and ducked as he threw a fist her way. She may be faster than she used to be, but she wasn't fast enough and his fist smashed into her left temple. Stars winked in her vision. Damn, the male hit like a rhino and was twice as big as her.

"I can't let you do that to that to this family again. It nearly destroyed us when you disappeared." Without letting up, he hit one of her ears, making her momentarily dizzy.

"You don't know anything about being destroyed," she yelled as she darted to the poker. She yanked it out of the wall and swung out with all her might. Her weapon connected with his side, ripping across his clothing and flesh. Blood sprayed and he collapsed to the floor.

Shae took advantage and fled when her mother cried out and ran to his side. The sun had not set completely and her eyes watered and her skin burned as she dashed across the front lawn. Familiar with the area, she darted behind businesses that offered cover from the sun. She kept to the shadows as she made her way across town. She hadn't planned on attacking her uncle or fleeing, so she had no idea where she was going. She was back where she had been that morning with no money and no phone.

She couldn't believe what she had done to her uncle. It had been like a switch had flipped inside. Once the rage had taken hold, she hadn't stopped to think about anything but hurting him and getting away. She may have killed him in a stupid fit of anger.

She didn't even know why she had been angry. He was only trying to help her and she had lost it completely. As much as she hated to admit it, Gerrick had been right. She wasn't safe. Hastening her steps, she rushed through downtown traffic.

Abomination, her mind whispered. She truly was a monster. She picked up her pace even more, wanting to outrun the reality of who she was. She put on a burst of speed as tears built in her eyes. She wasn't even safe to be around the humans that were happily on their way home. The tears fell in a stream down her face as she ran past the aquarium. Unnoticed by the tourists, she quickly passed the busy piers.

How had her life gotten to this point? It wasn't fair, she'd always been a good vampire, and that only fed her incoherent rage. She channeled that into her legs as she raced on. Where she was headed she had no idea, she only wished she could outrun her misery.

An hour later she found herself near Alkai beach watching a winter storm roll in. Dark grey clouds filled the sky, obscuring the moon. A few moments later, lightning danced overhead, illuminating the area around her. The clap of thunder competed with the sound of the waves lapping at the rocks on the shore and the howling wind. The sight was eerily beautiful, even as she shivered from the cold and cursed herself for not having grabbed a jacket. Her hair blew around her face, as she breathed in the briny, sea air, trying to figure out what she was going to do.

She couldn't go home. She had run from her Fated Mate and had stolen a car from the Vampire King. She'd be lucky if they weren't hunting her down to kill her. Unable to control her rage, she had attacked her uncle and ruined things at home with her family. She'd thought her life was over before, but now it was spinning out of control to the point where she didn't even know which way was up anymore.

Despondent, she hung her head when warmth exploded in her chest as Gerrick's soul wrapped around her, trying to center her. Before she had a chance to appreciate how her mate was able to pull her back from the edge, two of the last creatures she ever wanted to see again, materialized fifteen feet from her. Azazel and Aquiel.

Scanning the area, she searched for anything that could be used as a weapon. Swooping a long piece of driftwood that would serve her purpose, she prayed for protection against the Fae magic. If Aquiel unleashed his power on her she would be helpless. She contemplated turning the wood on herself so she couldn't be used as a weapon against her family or Gerrick ever again when her mate's soul blasted her for even considering it. On second thought, kicking their ass sounded so much better. Quickly breaking extra limbs from the wood, she made a makeshift spear.

"Shae, my pet. You have become a very difficult female to track down. Let's have a chat," Azazel purred as if they were best friends. He was so smug, believing he had her under his thumb. She couldn't wait to teach the asshole a lesson or two.

"I'd rather tear out your throat," she countered, then cursed. Azazel would enjoy that.

"We can play first then," Azazel coaxed. "I've missed the taste of you." The pair sauntered closer to her without a care in the world. Every instinct in her body shouted this was her chance, spurring her into action. She sprang at Azazel, making him falter and unable to deflect the wood aimed at his face. Keeping a death grip on the wood, she only managed to rake it across his cheek. Black blood bloomed and bone was revealed through the gaping wound. She'd been hoping to hit the artery in his neck, but would take what she got.

Shae continued running and veered toward the Fae, startling him and shoving the wood into his mouth. She took the male down and plunged the implement deep into the sand, leaving it lodged in his mouth.

She wasn't surprised when Azazel took his time slowly walking to her rather teleporting. It was psychological warfare meant to unnerve her, but too bad for him that shit didn't faze her anymore. The way she saw it, he couldn't do anything worse to her than he already had. And, wasn't that liberating. She had been at her lowest in his cage and was never going back there.

She stooped and grabbed up some sharp rocks, holding them in tight fists. She threw a punch and Azazel caught her hand, crushing it. Bones snapped, but didn't distract her because she'd fought under far worse conditions.

Instantly, warmth spread from her chest down her arm. Part of her was in awe over the strength of the mating bond trying to heal her wound while the other part was focused on the demon and enacting her vengeance. With the mating bond supporting her, she felt as if she could do anything, even beat an archdemon. "Surely, you can do better than that. Just sayin'," she taunted.

"A little time with the Vampire King has made you an over-confident bitch," Azazel spat, brushing blood from his cheek. Shae was glad to see the wound hadn't yet fully healed.

"It had nothing to do with Zander. I was honed in the fires of hell, you should know that," she challenged. He would hate being the one who'd made her such a formidable fighter.

He caught her off-guard, slicing his razor-sharp claws across her shoulder blade. She danced out of his reach, but that meant she couldn't retaliate. He dodged her steps, but unfortunately, didn't give her time to regroup. She needed to do something he wouldn't expect. Problem was that he was intimately familiar with her fighting style.

Determined that this wasn't going to end with her dying at the hands of this male, she refused to allow him to use her again and her mate mark twanged in agreement. She was going to see Gerrick again. She had plans to beat some sense into him about belonging to her, not some long-dead female.

With her blood leaving a trail on the sand, she ran towards Azazel and at the last second slid across the sand, sliding between his legs. She lifted her arm and cut through pants, skin and muscle. The archdemon's howl of pain was satisfying as she castrated the motherfucker. Too bad his balls would grow back.

Black lightning shot from his hands as he blindly tried to hit her. Rocks exploded, sand and water shot into the air and Shae raced back toward him. He reached out and grabbed her, sinking his teeth into her abused neck. For a split second, she was back in that cage completely at his mercy, but this time when she felt his magic build in her blood, the mating bond gave her the strength to break away just in time. A second later, he teleported away.

She bent over with her hands on her knees, trying to catch her breath. Movement out of the corner of her eye made her turn. She expected to see Azazel again, but thankfully, it was only Aquiel and he was still pinned to the sand. His hand was flopping around, no doubt searching for the stick. Unwilling to allow him to get free and possibly use a spell against her, she walked over.

Placing his head between her hands, careful to keep the driftwood in place, and twisted with all her might, she pulled the Fae's head from his shoulders. Slumping to the ground as the heavens opened up, she stared into wide, empty eyes. Shouting, she threw Aquiel's head out to sea as rain pelted her body, cleaning her cuts and washing away the gore. She stood up with her arms out at her sides, allowing the rain to purge the violence.

Hating what she had become, but unwilling to give up the fight, she realized she only had one choice and took off running.

≈

GERRICK WAS STANDING in the open doorway, scowling at the last person he'd expected to see. Shae had stolen Orlando's car and taken off before dawn. He had searched the city from one end to the other, but all he found was the abandoned car. Shortly before dusk, Jace had called him to her family's house.

She had done the unexpected and gone to her family. He had been convinced that she would never return there for fear she'd harm them and figured she was hunting the demons.

"You look like hell," he said, his anger melting when he saw she was injured.

"It hasn't been my best night. Can I come in?" she asked, clearly unsure of her reception. He wanted to pull her into his arms and reassure her that he would always welcome her, but he refused, stuffing his hands in his pockets to avoid acting on his impulses.

He stepped aside and shut the door behind her. "You need stitches on that shoulder. And you were bit again," he growled, wanting revenge when he saw the fresh bite mark. That bastard was going to die a slow, painful death for harming what was his.

"You're a genius," Shae quipped. "Is Jace here?" Jealousy hit him in the gut. His mate was asking for another male when she should be reaching out to him. But, he'd given her no reason to believe she could depend on him, had he?

He crowded her space and wrapped his fingers around her wrist and immediately the spark of chemistry was back. "Yeah, Jace just got back from treating your uncle."

He twined their fingers together and led her to the war room. He stuck his head in, seeing Rhys and Bhric. "Hey, can one of you tell Jace to meet us in the clinic. Shae needs treatment."

"You've finally found her. Maybe you should try chaining her to the bed," Rhys responded then shifted his gaze to Shae. "Damn, sweetcheeks, you look like hell. Head down, I think Jace is already down there with Cami."

"Thanks," Gerrick muttered and continued to the basement stairs in silence. He was still so angry at her for taking off that he didn't trust himself not to yell at her or strip her bare and remind himself that she was alive and well in the most primal way possible. Her scowl told him that if he tried to touch her he'd be losing his balls.

"So, you know what I did," Shae finally whispered. Beneath those words, he heard her unspoken plea. She was clearly worried about being welcomed. "What's going to happen to me now?"

"First, you'll change out of those wet clothes and then Jace is going to heal you and stitch your neck. After that, we'll grab some dinner. I can feel how hungry you are."

"Am I going back down to the dungeons?" The uncertainty in her voice broke his heart.

"Of course not. Your things are in our room and you'll be lucky if I let you out ever again. I hope you learned something. Never, ever run from me again, Shae."

She flushed and lowered her head. "I made a mistake. Goddess, Gerrick, I know that now. I'm not right and I want to change that. Those demons can't win." That fast, her steel spine and determination was back and sexier than hell.

"Wait a minute." She stopped in the middle of the hall and tugged his hand. "You said my things are in *your* room. Why am I going to be in *your* room and what *things* are you talking about? I don't have anything here."

He couldn't help the smile that lifted one corner of his lips. "You're in *our* room because you're mine, Shae. And, your mom was nice enough to give me some of your clothes while I was there."

Her eyes went wide then narrowed. "What did you tell my parents?"

"Only what they needed to know." He twirled a lock of her fiery red hair around his finger.

"I do hope you replaced the furniture in *our* room. Especially since it's your fault it was ruined in the first place. I'd like dark wood and pale blue for our colors." She let go of his hand and resumed her trek. Gerrick caught up with her and once again claimed her hand.

The medical clinic was in the basement near the training facility. Gerrick was shocked at the transformation since he'd been there last. The two exam tables were shoved to one side of the room and various machines and instruments were strewn about the space with several scientists bent over microscopes.

"Jace, Shae needs to be treated. Should I take her upstairs?" he asked his fellow warrior.

"No, let me set this program to run and I'll be right over," he replied, pointing to the empty beds.

"Stay here," he instructed his mate before he headed to the closet to get her some clothes. They were often injured while out fighting and this was a frequently visited room so there was always spare clothing. He grabbed a t-shirt and some sweats.

Jace was already at Shae's side when Gerrick returned. "...need to cut some of the damaged tissue away in order to place the stitches you need."

Shae met his eyes and he saw the shame in her depths. A sudden thought struck him. He took a deep breath and caught the faint scents of Fae and demon blood, as well as, Shae's blood, but nothing to indicate the archdemon had sexually violated her again. He unclenched his fists and laid the clothing next to her.

"Do what you have to. It's just too bad you can't cut all of it away," she muttered.

Gerrick gripped her chin between his thumb and forefinger, refusing to allow her to look away. "Scars don't matter. You fought and you survived, again, that's what matters."

"No, scars don't matter," she agreed, tracing the scar that bisected his face with a feather-light touch. He looked into those familiar green eyes and his heart opened a bit more to Shae. Emotion traveled along the bond that existed between them, leaving no room for doubt that this female was his. The question was whether it was Goddess blessed or created in hell.

And, did he even fucking care?

CHAPTER 15

Shae sat in a room surrounded by daunting warriors who were waiting for answers, but she had no idea where to start. And, to make matters worse, the demon's compulsion was beginning to once again outweigh the mating compulsion. Exasperation at the fact that they were managing to take even this from her was a bitter pill to swallow. This one aspect of her life should be sacrosanct, untouchable by any entity, and yet, the evil bastards were trying to overtake it.

Clenching her hands until her nails cut into her palm, she took deep breaths. Gerrick reached over and stroked her arm, causing her to shiver. The contact was enough for the mating bond to take front seat. Grateful, she glanced at Gerrick and was caught in his penetrating stare until Zander broke the silence. "I need to know what happened, Shae. Doona leave oot any detail because even the smallest piece of information can be useful."

She turned her head and nodded before she proceeded to tell them what had happened from the time she'd left Zeum until the fight by the water. "I have no idea how they found me. It was nothing like Jessie described with the tracking device. There was no humming and I haven't seen or felt anything to indicate there is an implant anywhere on my body. Oh...I should have told you this first, but I got side-tracked...I left Aquiel's body on the shore in the Alkai Beach area."

"Shite," Zander cursed, "Bhric, you and Rhys go clean up the scene. And, be quick aboot it. He's been there far too long already. We'll be lucky if the humans haven't already found him. I'm glad you came back where you belong, Shae. You willna leave here until we get to the bottom of this," Zander warned, raking his hand through his jet-black hair.

"I understand," she murmured and watched as Rhys and Bhric jumped up to carry out their orders. Zeum was a well-oiled machine and Zander's power over the Dark Warriors was readily apparent. It was the kind of power so many sought to obtain for nefarious purposes, yet Zander didn't abuse one ounce of it. His restraint was admirable and she could see why the Dark Warriors had such a close bond and would die for him.

"How are your symptoms after another bite? I need to get another blood sample. No doubt, your venom levels are up after this attack." Jace's voice snapped her back to atten-tion. Next to her, Gerrick leaned forward, a snarl on his face. She clasped his hand and brought it to her lap, hoping to calm his anger. He seemed to relax a little and she was relieved to have the same effect on him that he had on her.

"Unfortunately, they are much worse now. Since the first bite, I have felt some measure of coercion from the archdemons, but in the days after my rescue it seemed to lessen. Now..." she trailed off, unwilling to admit that even the most powerful force in the realm couldn't keep it out.

"That makes sense. Your venom levels had decreased,

but I have a theory that each bite amplifies the effects ten-fold," Jace explained.

"That explains why it's so much worse this time. I have to put all my efforts into blocking him. And, that's not even including my fits of rage." She didn't know if she could say anymore, but needed to if she was going to get help with this. Gerrick's presence by her side gave her the support she needed to continue. "You know how I attacked my uncle. I'm afraid of doing worse. I don't know how to shut him out. Even now, he is in my head telling me to unleash my beast and do whatever is necessary to get to the amulet."

"He's in your head?" Gerrick leaned into her line of vision, taking up her entire focus.

"Yes, he is. It's like he's screaming at me to hurt you."

"I know you're afraid you're going to hurt me, but I don't think you will. You could have cut my head off and you didn't. You're stronger than he is," Gerrick surmised, offering the reassurance she needed. The last thing she wanted to do was hurt him or anyone else who had come to mean so much to her. Taking back control was going to be done one painful step at a time. She hoped she'd just taken the first one in asking for help and leaning on someone other than herself. There was no turning back now.

"Gerrick is right, Shae, and, now we know what they hope to get from you and the others. It didn't really make sense before because Jessie is so different," Jace said, clearly thinking out loud.

"You actually hear them in your head?" Jessie asked, the disbelief clear in her voice.

"Yes, I do," Shae admitted, unable to hide her relentless pain. Her head felt as if it was going to split open. "And, it causes one hell of a headache. You don't hear him?"

"No, but like I said, I was only bit once. It's only ever

been minor tendrils of a pressure, but nothing specific," Jessie shared.

"Yeah, I'm the lucky one," Shae murmured, unable to hide the acid in her tone. Shae should feel a kinship to this female, but she couldn't get over her bitterness. It wasn't fair that Jessie hadn't been forced to suffer. No, the female barely had a scar and was beautiful, confident and loved by everyone. And, she didn't have to worry about flying off the handle and killing someone she loved without thinking.

"No, I was taken from the only life I've ever known and lost my job and home and I haven't even seen my family since I was turned," Jessie countered. Shae instantly felt guilty. She hadn't considered how Jessie's life may have been affected.

Gerrick squeezed Shae's thigh and rubbed his palm over her tense muscles. She met his gaze and smiled at his attempt to soothe and comfort. The male may infuriate her most of the time, but he had his moments that showed how much he cared.

"Let's not focus on blaming each other or who was hurt the most. You were both victimized. Right now we need to consider the ramifications of this for Shae. Neither of the demons planned on one of the females being a Fated Mate," Zander postulated, grabbing an apple from the large platter of fruit on the table. "He has no way of knowing you were Gerrick's mate, Shae. Just like he clearly doesna understand the connection of mates. 'Tis one bond that will always be stronger." Shae hated to tell him that with the venom fresh in her veins, the demon was very close to overtaking the mating bond.

"Before I forget, welcome to the family, Shae," Elsie said, giving her a bright welcoming smile across the table. Apparently, Gerrick had informed them that she was his mate while she was gone. That both surprised and pleased her. If she were a betting female, she'd have said he would keep their mating a secret. She only wished his acknowledgement erased the dark shadow Evanna had over them. Even now, through their bond, she could sense his torn loyalties and love for the dead female.

"Things might seem really dark right now, but it's going to work out and I'm so excited to have another new sister join our home. You've already fit right in so stop worrying about that. You're one of us now. Back to the issue of Kadir, I wouldn't say that he wasn't aware of Shae's status," Elsie countered. "Remember what happened with the Rowan triplets and their mates?"

Shae had no idea what the queen was talking about. As far as she knew the Rowan sisters enjoyed the nightclubs and were a fun, lively part of the party scene. Something big had to have happened to the triplets if they were now mated. She hadn't been super close friends with them, but had hung out with them on occasion and worked with them when they came in the bank.

Zander's eyes went wide. "Shite, you're right. Kadir managed to give Cele the identity of Isis and Suvi's mates so she could torture them. But, why keep Shae and the others locked up in their lair? It still doesna make sense."

"It does if your aim is psychological warfare. To incite mates against one another," Elsie explained, making Shae's blood turn to ice in her veins. Those evil bastards were using her as a pawn. She would kill herself before giving them the satisfaction of harming Gerrick.

"I see where you're going with that, *a ghra*. But, it doesna explain why he kept them so long. I doona think his only aim is to pit mates against each other. I guarantee he is taking advantage of our distraction and is planning something bigger. I think that's the only reason he took the risk and attacked Shae again." Zander sat forward, leaning his arms on the large conference table, deep in thought.

"That sounds like the fucker." She felt Gerrick's anger and how much effort he was putting into keeping a lid on it. "Problem is we have no clues as to what else he may have planned. Do you think he's working with Angelica?"

"I have no doubt he added to Angelica's darkness, but she has her own agenda. Kadir may expect certain things from her in return, but she is too much of a narcissist, after her own power to ever really meet his demands. She plays by her own rules and always has," Jace added with a heaviness that spoke from experience. Cailyn, Jace's mate and Elsie's sister, slid her arm around his back offering him respite from his inner turmoil. Shae found she was immeasurably jealous of their closeness and affection. She hadn't known she wanted that, but at that moment she wanted nothing more. Problem was that a gulf stood between her and Gerrick and the gulf's name was Evanna.

Sighing, Shae glanced at Gerrick and watched him pick up a piece of garlic-sausage pizza and take a huge bite. His powerful jaw worked, drawing Shae's eye to the pulse pounding in his neck. She was suddenly ravenous and grabbed a piece of pizza, hoping to curb her bloodlust.

"I agree with Jace. Angelica represents a host of other dangers. Whether or not this is his plan, we can't ignore what's right in front of us. Our priorities should be to discover a way to decrease the amount of venom in Shae's system. There is no way I will tolerate my mate suffering for a minute longer." Shae swallowed hard at Gerrick's declaration. She'd never been anyone's anything and now she was Gerrick's Fated Mate and Elsie's new sister. She only wished the demon wasn't a huge black cloud on what should be the happiest time in her life.

"The last thing I want to be is a pawn in Kadir's game, but I can't even go back to my family's home until I get a handle on my rage. As much as I hated being thrown in those cages to fight, it was the one thing that centered me and allowed for coherent thinking, at least until they bit me again. And, I can't stomach the thought of hurting anyone else, especially, someone I love. That's why I came back here. I need help," she admitted, feeling more vulnerable than she ever had in her life.

Much like her mother and grandmother, she'd always been a capable, self-sufficient female who solved her own problems with ease. It didn't sit well with her that she couldn't solve this one on her own.

She understood enough about the mating compulsion now to understand that it had caused Gerrick to say and act the way he had. It hadn't come from a place of love for her, but she trusted that he would do anything to keep her from being locked in a cell and forgotten about.

"You came to the right place, Shae. If there is anyone that can help you, it's Zander and the others. I wouldn't have survived the transition without them. And, don't forget that you belong here more than I do," Jessie told her. The honesty of the female's words shocked her. The female truly didn't feel as if she belonged, but saw the way Shae fit as Gerrick's mate. With that remark, Shae finally found that elusive commonality with Jessie. They'd both been torn from their lives and were struggling to find their place in the realm.

"While I can't feel anything more than an annoying buzz, you actually hear them speaking. Have you considered that you are the clearest link directly to them?" Jessie finished, tucking her blonde hair behind an ear.

"I never thought of it that way, but what good does that do us? I want to cut the link." Hunger for blood was making her cranky and she grabbed a second piece of pizza.

"Maybe we should play reverse psychology and use his tactic against him," Zander suggested. "He wants to maintain a direct link to you then we turn that on him. We reverse that connection and use it to find their new lair." Shae sat up straight with the excitement in Zander's voice. She could be useful again, rather than a burden and she liked the sound of that.

Gerrick bristled with annoyance and snapped, "No! We aren't using her, it's too risky."

"Och, Gerrick you are no' thinking clearly. You're too close to the situation to see this objectively. I can see how much the mating compulsion is affecting you. Before, you would have been the first one to agree to this proposal. I understand your objections. Shite, I doona want the lass hurt, but this is the closest we've ever come to ending the bastard."

"Would you place Elsie in the same position?" Gerrick countered, trying hard to keep the bitterness out of his voice. Through their bond, Shae felt the amount of respect Gerrick had for Zander and how difficult it was for him to resist ripping off the king's head.

Suddenly, Zander's power surged in an invisible explosion that felt like razors against Shae's skin. The Vampire King was well and truly pissed, she thought. "Leave my mate oot of this. Need I remind you of your oath, warrior?"

"Why? You aren't leaving mine out of it. And, that's a low blow, Liege. I'm the most dedicated warrior you have and you know it," Gerrick countered, coming precariously close to insubordination. Unsure what she could do, Shae placed her hand on his thigh and gripped the muscle. Gerrick shuddered under her palm before some of the tension left his body.

Elsie stood and placed her hands on Zander's shoulders. Knowing the touch of a mate calms, she realized it was the most effective way of holding the king back at that moment. "Stop. Don't you see what's happening? He's coming between us and now we aren't even focusing on helping the females anymore. We cannot afford to have an internal war right now. Save your pissing match for another time."

For the first time since she'd met the petite female, Shae understood why the Goddess had chosen her for queen. Elsie took command of the entire room with ease and everyone listened to her immediately. It was amazing to see a group of the strongest males in the realm sit to attention as if they were striplings who had been scolded by their mother.

Shae turned to Gerrick and captured his gaze. "I know you're worried for me, but I have to do this. Trust me," she said, placing her fingers over his lips when he went to argue. "I feel like the only way I'll be normal again is to have a hand in bringing him down. I'd like to face him and be the one to eliminate him, but I'll settle for being involved in his demise."

She could see the struggle in his ice-blue eyes. He grabbed her hand and placed a gentle kiss to her fingertips before he brought it to his chest. The chemistry between them was explosive and had her melting in her chair. She needed to be careful or the entire room would know how badly she wanted her mate. "If you do this, don't think you're going alone. And, if you get hurt, I'll never forgive you," Gerrick promised and she felt like she'd just won a huge battle with his concession.

"If I get hurt I'll never forgive you, warrior. Aren't you my personal bodyguard now?" she teased, hoping to lighten the mood. The slight uptick at the corner of his mouth felt like another victory and made her core clench with need. It was easy to forget that sorcerers had a predatory nature, but Gerrick was also a Dark Warrior. They didn't bend or compromise, especially with the task of protecting others and he was protecting what was his.

"I'm going to enjoy guarding your body, Red," Gerrick husked, tugging her into the line of his body. She was awkwardly, half-sitting on her chair, but wouldn't have moved if the building was on fire. She needed the closeness of her mate. Not only did he ignite every nerve ending in her body until she was on the razor's edge of arousal, but he quieted the demon's voice in her head.

"Before the two of you start tearing off your clothes, can we get back on track and figure oot how we are going to locate the demons through Shae?" Zander said, humor lacing his tone.

Shae half-listened as the warriors threw around ideas and made plans. She was too focused on the way Gerrick played with her hair, wrapping it around his finger. And, she lost complete focus when he ran his hand over her thigh. The thin cotton fabric wasn't enough of a barrier and she moistened under his caress. He was either an amazing actor or he wasn't aware of how he was ramping up her desire. He not only followed what was being said, but participated in the discussion. She couldn't have repeated anything that had been said in the past five minutes.

He turned his head slightly and gave her that smile of his that drove her insane with lust. The fiend knew exactly what he was doing to her. Two could play at that game, she thought, and her hand traveled across his abdomen, feeling the quiver of his muscles, before she stopped right above the waistband of his leathers. The last time they had been together had been a fast and furious experience and she wanted more of him. The discomfort in her mate mark heightened with each passing day, especially, when she was aroused. Right now, it was a blazing inferno.

He grabbed her hand and placed it on the table. She smiled as she thought about how she got to him as much as he did her. He may carry the ghost of a female, but Shae would be damned if she played second. Whatever the Goddess did to make it so, Shae was Gerrick's Fated Mate now and he needed to accept that fully. There was no other way forward for them. Remaining mired in the past would only taint their future.

Determination set, Shae tuned into the conversation. "...I'm not sure I can help, but maybe between the two of us, we can pinpoint the direction, kinda like a compass," Jessie added, looking directly at Shae.

She had no idea what had been said, but she was grateful not to be the sole focus of the conversation. "That's a great idea. If we add Cami, that's three of us," Shae suggested, guessing at the direction the conversation had taken.

"Aye, 'tis worth a try. Shae, Jessie and Cami will guide us in what I hope is no' a wild goose chase. We leave at dusk," Zander said in dismissal.

Everyone left the war room in a flurry of conversations. Shae proceeded to the exit when Zander waylaid Gerrick. A Dark Warrior she had only met once on the night of her recuse stopped her in the large entryway. Santiago Reyes was a wolf shifter and Orlando's partner at the Seattle Police Department.

Sweat beaded on her spine from nervousness. What did the Dark Warrior want? What if Bhric and Rhys hadn't gotten to the Fae fast enough and the humans found the body? To cause information about the Tehrex Realm to leak to the human population was a death sentence. Surely, she hadn't survived thus far only to be killed now.

"I just need a quick minute with you. Don't worry, you're not in trouble," he hastened to reassure her.

"I'm not sure what more I can tell you than I haven't already said, but okay." She crossed her arms over her chest and waited to hear what he had to say.

"It's not really what you can do for me, but what I can do for you."

"That sounds ominous," she quipped.

He chuckled. "Look, I heard what you said about your temper and the outlet that the fighting cages gave you. Be at this location in two nights at midnight if you want to find another channel for that anger. I know you don't want to hurt anyone, but rage has a way of making those decisions for you."

"You sound like you're speaking from experience," she said, accepting the business card from him. One side was printed with his SPD information and the other had a hand-written address that she recognized. It was way out in the boondocks beyond the suburbs of the east-side. This area was well known as being a great place for shifters to run safely because it was heavily wooded and sparsely populated.

"Be there if you want to learn more," he instructed, ignoring her statement. He tipped his head to her and walked off before she said another word. She tucked the card into the pocket of the borrowed sweats as Gerrick came up behind her.

"What was that all about?" he asked, eyeing his fellow warrior as he climbed the stairs with an animal's grace.

"Honestly, I have no idea. He didn't really say much," she prevaricated, following him up the stairs. She didn't think Gerrick would agree with her going to the middle of nowhere on a vague recommendation from another male. It didn't matter that they'd fought side by side for centuries, the mating compulsion made males insanely protective of their female. Gerrick wouldn't want her in any risk whatsoever. The sentiment should have given her hope, but it didn't. She understood he was helpless against the impulses. The reality was that he had closed himself off to love long ago and she wanted the fairytale...his body, heart and soul.

"We've both had a rough couple days and you need to get to bed before you fall asleep standing up," he muttered.

"I'm not tired," she whispered on a yawn, but fatigue had her drooping. He picked her up and carried her up the stairs. Electricity zinged through her the second they touched and had her surging awake between one heartbeat and the next.

CHAPTER 16

Rhys O'Morda, cambion and Dark Warrior, stopped sprinting and braced his hands on his knees, catching his breath. The presence was back and it was beginning to annoy the hell out of him. He'd begun feeling as if he was being watched about six months prior, but had never been able to find anything. It was as if he had an invisible stalker, a shy one at that.

He stood up and wiped the sweat from his brow and glanced around the park. It was early morning and numerous humans had started their day by getting in a run, as well. Even though experience as of late told him he wouldn't see anyone there, he was still disappointed when he detected nothing. Stretching his legs and back, he considered going for another ten miles. The twenty he'd already run hadn't been enough to take the edge off his sexual needs. He should have gone to Confetti Too and hooked up with a willing female, but he was tired of that same old game.

His fellow warriors teased him incessantly about his sexual exploits and Rhys knew they saw him as little more than a sex demon, but there was so much more to him. He didn't blame them for their preconceptions and honestly hadn't tried very hard to dispel them. He lived his life to the fullest, loved to have a good time and loved flirting with the females. Still, he'd tired of the same old pursuit over a century ago. The others would have scoffed at him if he'd admitted how jealous he was of everyone finding their Fated Mates. Truth was, Rhys longed to find his other half. Typically, he would seek female companionship when his sexual need could no longer be curtailed by physical exercise, but he was never truly satisfied.

Rhys was twisting his torso when the air around him shimmered. He went on instant alert and glanced around the clearing. What the hell was going on? Could the demons have found him? And, if so, what would they want with him? The morning sun was cresting the horizon which told him it was unlikely a demon. Thank the Goddess neither the archdemons, nor their skirm, were able to go out in the sunlight, but he didn't relax his vigilance.

An opaque veil surrounded him, muting the world around him. Three red-winged figures appeared inside the veil and stood shoulder-to-shoulder facing him. What the fuck? He'd heard stories about angels, but had never faced any, let alone three male angels. Pissed off angels, if their facial expressions were anything to go by.

"I didn't know there was going to be a party in the park this morning. I'd have brought some of my *hey juice* had I known," he quipped, hoping against hope that they had a sense of humor.

"I told you he's an imbecile. We should behead him now and look elsewhere for Illianna," snarled a male with black hair and even blacker eyes. Okay, so no sense of humor.

Rhys inched his hand to the side of the veil and when electricity zapped his fingertips, he knew he was in trouble.

"Don't bother, mongrel. There is no way out of our net until we get our answers," declared another male with brown hair and green eyes.

"Well then, I guess I'll need those questions." Rhys worried the humans were going to notice this little scene. It was hard to miss three massive angels with red wings, but no one seemed to pay them any attention.

"Where is our sister Illianna?" spat the last male who had blond hair and brown eyes.

Rhys' eyebrows lowered in confusion. "I have no idea who you are talking about. I don't know any Illianna and I don't think I've ever slept with one. What does she look like? I assume she's an angel," he replied wracking his brain. Surely, he hadn't fucked an angel and not known it. He didn't think they could hide their wings.

"She's nothing like us. Her wings are gold to befit her station and her hair is nearly the same shade. Her silver eyes reflect the world to you and she has the sweetest heart of any living being. She went missing over a century ago and we haven't been able to get hints of her location until tonight when our searches led us to you. What have you done with Illianna?" With that, the angel with black hair took a step forward and grabbed Rhys by the throat. Rhys wasn't a small male, but these angels towered over his six-foot-two-inch height. And their wings made them seem more massive than even Bhric. Rhys gulped, suddenly more worried about being trapped by three pissed off angels. Whoever started the rumor that angels were sweet and loving creatures hadn't met this bunch.

"Whoa," Rhys croaked, "I admit I don't recall all the females I've slept with, but I remember names and I've never heard that name before, I swear. I don't have your sister. Hell, I would never harm another living being, unless they were demons or their minions."

"He's lying. Let's kill him and move on," snapped the brown-haired angel.

"No!" Rhys croaked past the hand constricting his throat. The angel that had hold of him rolled his broad shoulders and his massive red feathers ruffled, sending the smell of a thunderstorm into the air. At first glance, he'd thought their wings were all one shade of red, but up close, he noticed there were multiple layers and they were various shades of red. He knew a little about angels, but couldn't recall what the color red signified. Somehow, he doubted they were angels of happiness.

"Fuck you. I'm not lying. I've taken an oath with the Goddess Morrigan to act as one of her Dark Warriors and it is my sworn mission to protect the Tehrex Realm and the humans of earth from demons and their skirm. We can help you find this Illianna, but I swear to you that I do not have her and I don't know where she is."

"Stop, brother. He's telling the truth. If you backed off and used your truth-sense you'd see that," the blond angel murmured, taking the atmosphere from immanent-death to might-survive.

The black-haired angel snatched his hand away from his neck with a growl. "Where the fuck do we go from here? And, why the hell did my cloud send us to this male?"

Rhys felt for these males. They obviously loved their sister and something inside his soul reacted to them. He'd meant what he said when he offered to help locate Illianna. In fact, his entire being strained to join that hunt, surprising him given that they had come at him with hostility and threatened his life. "I'm not surprised your cloud sent you to me. I am made of pure awesomeness," he joked as he rubbed his neck, cursing that he was going to carry bruises for the next few hours. That was going to be difficult to explain when he returned to Zeum. The last thing any warrior wanted was to appear weak.

Shaking his head, he refocused on the group. "We have a bit of a crisis in the realm right now, but I promise you that I will do what I can to search for her. Do you have a calling card? Or, will you magically appear if I think of you?" They visibly bristled at his comment. Yeah, red-wings definitely didn't have a sense of humor.

"If you find our sister, we will know," the brown-haired angel promised and they launched into the air, disappearing in the next moment. If Rhys never saw them again, it would be too soon, but something told him that this was far from over.

GERRICK KICKED the door closed and murmured a spell to lock it. He had plans and didn't want to be interrupted. He almost felt guilty about rousing Shae from her sleepy state, but the second their skin touched he'd sizzled with a need so great it was unbearable.

"What do you plan on doing with me?" she asked demurely as they passed through the living room.

He paused after entering the bedroom and muttered a spell to start a fire in the fireplace. The room filled with the amber glow from the flames, providing the perfect lighting for what he had in mind. "I'm going to fuck you, Red. I wanted this time to be more leisurely, but my need is too high right now. One day soon I plan on taking my time with you."

He threw her to the mattress so hard that all four corners lifted full of air then hissed slowly in release as he rose on his knees to join her. He prowled up the bed and lay down next to her. He pulled her top over her head and tossed it in the corner. Her sweats and shoes followed. He propped himself up on one elbow and glanced down at his mate.

She lay on the bed in a lacy bra and matching boy shorts of emerald green. The sight of her shyly trying to cover her body had blood trying to fill flesh that was already heavily engorged. Shit, he could have broken cinderblocks with his cock at that point.

"You have too many clothes on," she murmured.

"If I get naked right now then this will end sooner than I want," he countered and reached behind her to unclasp her bra. She wiggled her arms and the fabric fell to the bed forgotten as her breasts mesmerized him. The first time they had been together had been hurried and frantic and he hadn't gotten a good look at her.

Leaning down, he captured her mouth in a kiss. Lips sliding overs hers, he relished the zing of contact. She quickly tried to take over, licking and nipping wanting him to open his mouth. Grinning, he gave in and her tongue slid inside immediately to tangle with his.

He hovered over her and slid his hand up and down the side of her body, luxuriating in the feel of her silky skin. Unable to resist the taught globes, he cupped her breast and squeezed. She moaned into his mouth, pouring more passion into her kiss.

He pulled and tweaked her nipple and his mouth watered for a taste. Breaking away from her lips, he kissed his way down her throat and to her pearled nipples. By the time he'd taken one into his mouth, she was squirming in impatience and need. She was so hot it nearly robbed him of his seed. Goddess, she was lush and delicious.

His free hand pushed her panties down and she helped kick them off her legs, his mouth never leaving her breasts. His hand traveled to the new center of his universe and ran through her slick folds. "Gerrick. I need more." He opened his eyes and smiled down at his mate, allowing her to see the molten lust simmering there.

Uncomfortable with the scrutiny, she tried to hide from his gaze. He saw when she steeled her nerves and opened to him fully, laying herself bare. She was amazingly beautiful in that moment. It was breathtaking to see an imperfect female become stunning just because she willed it from the inside out. "You have nothing to hide. Everything about you, even your scars, is so damn sexy, it makes my head spin. I'm going to lick and nibble them because everything about you turns me on. There is nothing about you that is less than perfect to me."

Her hand lifted to her neck. "The mating compulsion is making you say that," she protested. He saw the vulnerability and insecurity, as well as, her deep desire for him to truly mean what he'd said. She wanted to be loved and accepted.

"The mating compulsion does a lot of things to me, most of them involve my cock and snarling at any male who looks your way, but it doesn't have control of my eyes or my words. And, I never say what I don't mean." He used his magic to remove his clothing and take away the objection he knew she was planning on voicing.

Her mouth opened and closed and then her small hand crawled across the comforter to his aching shaft. It leapt into her touch and she licked her lips. His little devil wanted a taste. He closed his eyes and took a deep breath. He wanted that more than anything, but that was going to have to wait, he needed to be inside her.

His eyes snapped open when she twisted her wrist and did something with her hand that stole his reasoning. "Goddess, you have no idea how good that feels," he ejected on a gust of breath, hips moving against her grasp. Her smile turned into a sly little expression that touched her eyes so wickedly Gerrick's soul shuddered in anticipation and delight.

She pushed on his shoulder and he rolled to his back, curious what she had in mind. She kept hold of him and straddled his thighs, stroking his erection with sure, heated ministrations. His hips lifted of their own accord and she laughed openly, clearly pleased with the power she had over him.

"I'm on a razors edge, Shae. You're killing me," he groaned. She ran her thumb over the tip of his shaft and he snapped.

He sat up and lifted her from under her arms and settled her onto his cock in the blink of an eye. She yelped in surprise then cursed as he filled her in one swift thrust. "I had planned on teasing you, but this is so much better," she admitted and began a swift pace of riding him.

Gerrick fell to the bed and lifted his hips, meeting her thrusts, punctuating his rapidly rising need with sharp jabs into her welcoming body. Her core clenched around his shaft, bringing him even closer to the edge. He chastised himself for his lack of discipline. He wanted to hold off and make this last a little longer.

He needed to bring her to orgasm before he came so hard he blacked out. He refused to leave an unsatisfied mate in his bed. He placed his finger between their bodies and sought the bundle of nerves that would send her over the edge. Pressing into the rigid nub, he released his magic in rapid waves that he knew created a subtle vibration.

Shae was a vision as she surged above him, sweating and panting, lifting and lowering on his shaft. "That's it, Red. Take your pleasure and cum for me." Her glowing jade green eyes flared and her core squeezed him painfully. His body was on fire from the charged effect she had on him. The sensation of his cock filling with seed was intense and still foreign to him and enough that it threatened to rob him of all control. Sex had never felt this good for him and it was enough to steal his breath.

With fervent thrusts, he claimed her like an explorer stabbing a flag into uncharted territory. Shae was his and he settled deeply inside his mate, holding her to him, electrified by the dominance of it. The most exquisite female in the universe belonged to *him*.

She panted and screamed and moaned as she came and it gave him a feeling of satisfaction he'd never forget. He pushed deeper into her, determined she'd never forget the moment, either. His release rushed up on him and unable to hold back his orgasm, he cried out frantically and came just as wildly.

Shae collapsed on top of him, gasping for breath along with him. His hot semen overflowed their meshed bodies and ran down his thighs. He would never get enough of this sensation. Everything about ejaculating was exhilarating to him. To be able to release after four centuries was a revelation. He'd only experienced the phenomenon most males took for granted a handful of times in his life, but he could easily say it had never been as intense as it was with Shae.

"That was unbelievable. I'm just sayin'" Shae murmured, kissing his chest. He couldn't help but laugh at the connotation he was becoming very fond of as he rubbed her back, her body relaxing on top of his.

"It was indescribable, Red," he replied, kissing her as she drifted off into a sated sleep. It felt right to have her sleep like this, with him still inside her. Everything with her felt right. Yeah, he was in big fucking trouble with this female.

CHAPTER 17

errick inhaled the crisp winter air, clearing his lungs. He'd laid awake watching Shae sleep while her intoxicating jasmine scent enveloped him. He hadn't been able to totally let his guard down around her given the knife to the throat he awoke to last time. She's been so peaceful, free of the incessant fury he felt pulsing through her when she was awake. It gave him an enticing glimpse of what she would be like when she was free of the archdemons.

At some point while she was gone, he had accepted that Shae was his Fated Mate. He only wished it had silenced the echo of Evanna in the back of his mind. It was impossible to ignore the pain of losing Evanna or the bond that they had shared. It may have been in its infancy and not completely cemented, but it had existed.

How was he ever going to fully embrace Shae and be the mate she deserved? He'd given his heart to Evanna a long time ago and it had shattered into a million pieces when she died. He simply didn't have it to give Shae, even if he wanted to. A sudden stab of pain shot through his mate mark in objection.

He opened the passenger door to the SUV he and Shae would be riding in and turned to the female who consumed him. "You ready for this?" he asked, unable to resist tracing the fine lines of stress bracketing her pursed mouth.

"Ready as I'll ever be. How do we connect to each other?" she asked Jessie, wrapping her arms around her torso protectively. Gerrick didn't even stop to think, but enveloped her in his embrace. Rather than melting into him, she stiffened and stood still when his arms came around her.

"I've never done anything like this so I have no ideas," Jessie answered. The female had her hand on the door of the car and turned her head slightly. "Any ideas, Zander?"

Zander paused by the driver's door of the SUV parked next to theirs. "I called Pema and we're meeting them at Black Moon. They've had firsthand experience with the Dark magic, and if anyone can help channel the energy, it's them."

Gerrick nodded his assent. That idea made sense and he had to admit that the young witches had come to be an invaluable asset. Sorcerers were creatures of instinct, magic, and the power of the moon, whereas, witches were creatures of potions, circles and the four elements. The two types of magic were different, yet both stemmed from the Goddess.

He ushered Shae into the vehicle and by the time he climbed behind the wheel, Jessie and Rhys were already in the backseat. Rhys had returned from his run that morning in an odd mood. Looking in the mirror at the scowl on the warrior's face, he wondered what was going on with his friend. He'd been partnered with Rhys for the past century, and over time, had learned he used humor to cover deeper emotions. Rhys was an enigma, preferring to show what they expected to see from a cambion, a sex-crazed male, rather than someone who actually cared. Gerrick made a note to talk to the warrior later as he followed Zander across town to the witches shop.

Gerrick parked at the curb and jumped out. Zipping his jacket against the cold night air, he went around to Shae's door. It made his heart jump with joy when she placed her delicate fingers into his hand. He helped her out of the car and then fastened her parka. The sight of her standing there all bundled up was a marked difference from the female who had stood in nothing but his leather jacket and boots a week ago.

Stepping up onto the curb, he pulled the door open to the shop and held it for Shae and Jessie to enter. Zander entered after Gerrick and quickly crossed to the witches, "Thanks for agreeing to meet with us."

Gerrick glanced around at the changes to the establishment. The last time he'd been there was after an explosion. The triplets had clashed with the former High Priestess, Cele, and the ensuing magical battle resulted in mayhem and destruction. The old wood shelving had been replaced with new polished mahogany, ornate wooden bookshelves stood in place of glass display cases and the floor was overlaid with rich bamboo flooring. The one thing that remained the same was the various magical accouterments that filled the space.

As a sorcerer, he didn't have a use for potions or raw ingredients like eye of newt, troll snot or rainbow seeds. In fact, aside from using candles for ambiance, he wouldn't use anything the Rowan's sold. It always amused him that humans assumed all creatures performed magic in the same way.

"Pema, Isis, Suvi, this is my mate, Shae," Gerrick introduced when Shae shied back and tried to melt into the shadows.

"Nice to meet you," Suvi said, holding her hand out to Shae. For the first time, Gerrick saw the emerald mating stone embedded in her palm up close. Normally, the mating stone wasn't set in flesh like it was with Suvi and her sisters, but the witch triplets were unique. They were the subjects of a long-standing prophecy and their stones were intricately tied to their combined powers. An ache set up residence in his chest. He'd been denied everything about the mating process with Evanna and for four centuries he'd wanted to go back so they could finish the mating. He'd been given a second chance with Shae and wanted it more than anything.

"You guys were there the night I was rescued," Shae shared freely, surprising Gerrick. She cocked her head to the side, considering Suvi. "I'll never forget watching you fight in those high-heeled boots. Do you always wear such high heels?"

Her question eased the tension in the room as everyone laughed. "Sure do. If you ask me, the higher, the better. Not only do they make me look good, they can be used as weapons, as well. For instance, the boots I wore that night were retrofitted with titanium heels, just in case. I can hook you up if you want," the youngest triplet offered.

"That's nice, but I think I'll stick to mine."

Suvi laughed, "Suit yourself. Now, I hear you guys need our help tracking the archdemons."

"Aye, we do," Zander broke in. "As you know, Jessie only minimally experiences the influences of Azazel, whereas Shae hears him giving her commands."

Isis pulled a wood bowl from a cabinet and placed it on

the counter. "I'd love to get my hands on the bastard. He and his cohort gave Cele the ability to find our mates and hurt my son." The lights flickered and Pema and Suvi immediately went to her side. The three joined hands and the flickering stopped. Isis was known for absorbing emotions and had a very short fuse. Her sisters were able to diffuse her anger and channel the energy in a more positive form.

Shae stepped away from them and at first he thought she was wary, but then noticed she was drawn to a display of jewelry. She picked up a pair of silver earrings that had a dragonfly hanging from them. "That sounds like something the two of them would do. And, you'll have to get in line because they are mine," Shae declared.

"Those would look great on you," Suvi said, referring to the earrings. Gerrick looked at her askance. Surely, the witch wasn't focusing on accessories at a time like this.

"You think? They seem too long, but I do love dragonflies." Gerrick would never understand females. How could they stand here talking about earrings at the same time they were discussing something as dangerous as tracking an archdemon?

"Suvi's right. And, they aren't too long," Pema pointed out, before continuing, "I think it's best that we use Shae as a conduit to trace the demon's location. Their connection to her isn't like that of the mating bond so it will be the best bet of getting a location," Pema suggested as Suvi put the earrings into Shae's ears.

"And then we slaughter the fuckers," Isis snarked. Shae's hair was a deeper shade of red than Isis', but they shared a fiery temper. Gerrick wondered what Shae had been like before her abduction. Was she always so quick to anger?

"Sounds good to me. Then I can move on with my life." Shae fingered the delicate silver and went to take them out.

"Keep them. Suvi's right, they look fantastic," Gerrick told her honestly. "What do they need to do to help with your spell?"

"Remain open to us. We need to cast a spell to enter your mind and follow the dark path backwards to them," Pema explained, turning to gather the supplies they would need.

Gerrick didn't miss the way Shae tensed in alarm and he could feel her fear along their bond. He wanted to tell them to call it off, that she'd been through enough, but he knew her well enough by now to know that she wanted to see this to the end.

All he could do was show his support. He stood at her back and placed his palms on her hips. The contact of his fingers on a strip of her flesh seared him to the bone. She shivered in response, robbing him of rational thought and making him want to strip her bare and place kisses all over her body. And, he'd chastised the females for focusing on earrings at a time like this when he was far worse. All he could think of was fucking her senseless.

Putting his libido on lockdown, he focused on anything but the feel of the soft skin beneath his fingers. "This won't hurt her, will it?"

"It shouldn't. We plan to obscure her location in a circle and follow the link. Think of it as giving us a piggy-back ride. From what you're describing, your link to them is always open. We will camouflage our presence and then cast a tracker spell," Pema explained, adding salt and dried lavender to the bowl that Isis had placed on the counter.

Shocked jade green eyes took in the large picture window that consumed the entire front of the store. "Are you doing this here? Now?" Gerrick smiled, Shae was always considering others before herself and it wasn't surprising to hear her worry about the witches and the risk to the realm with humans in such close proximity.

Three heads bobbed up and down. "It's going to be here, unless you want to travel across the bridge to our house. Besides," Pema opened a drawer and pulled out a small remote control, "this baby will turn the windows opaque to hide our activity from prying eyes."

Suvi placed a silver chalice of water in the middle of the room while Isis led Shae and Jessie to kneel beside it.

"I'm assuming they are bulletproof given how many times they've been blown out in the past couple months." Gerrick added as he watched Pema take the salt mixture and walk deosil in a perfect circle. After she had completed her first circuit, white light projected from the salt. Aside from the witches, he and Jace were the only ones in the room who would be able to see the manifestation of the magic. While the others could feel it, no other supernaturals were able to see magic.

On her second turn, she began chanting, "I cast this circle to keep us free of all energies that are not of The Light." Gerrick and Zander had been left outside the circle and it made him edgy. Patience eluded him. Sorcery didn't use ceremony, candles and athames. He got immediate results when he chanted spells, but he wasn't able to perform magic like this, either. Still, it was damn near impossible to stand by and give the witches a chance to do their work.

Pema continued, "I allow within this circle only the energies that are of The Light. So Mote It Be." White light flared to the ceiling and the circle was set. If this situation with his mate went to shit, he wouldn't be able to get to her until the circle was broken.

Isis picked up a white piece of chalk and knelt to call the

quarters. As she scribed the pentacle, she invoked the element in each direction as she went. "Hear me, Sentinels of the East, I summon the powers of Air! Hear me, Sentinels of the South, I summon the powers of Fire! Hear me, Sentinels of the West, I summon the powers of Water! Hear me, Sentinels of the North, I summon the powers of Earth! As above, so below. As within, so without. Four stars in this place be, combined to call the fifth to me! So mote it be."

Gerrick was impressed how seamlessly the triplets worked together. They were extremely young supernaturals and it took most centuries to master their craft like they had. "Live and learn, learn and live. I endeavor to receive what life can give. Bring to me the lessons true. And knowledge of what to do. Amid the mess and chaos fierce. Shine a light to darkness pierce. Show the way to knowledge deep. Which to let go and which to keep. Clear the way so I might heed. The lessons that I truly need. Show me what I need to learn. As life's pages I do turn. So mote it be," Suvi called out. The sisters clasped hands and closed their eyes.

Gerrick watched as Shae stiffened as if in pain while Jessie sat, seemingly unaffected. Shae lifted one shaking hand and touched the edge of the bowl. Sparks exited her fingertips and connected with the water and Shae went to her knees. Instinctually, he surged towards her, but was stopped short by the invisible barrier of the circle. She had suffered alone for months and he didn't want her to be alone in this. Between one heartbeat and the next, fog swirled in the water and cleared to reveal an old, boarded up house near the human juvenile detention center. They'd done it. The witches had actually traced the location.

Pacing outside the circle, anxious to get to Shae's side, he watched as Jessie helped Shae up. The witches thanked the Goddess and Pema cut a path in the circle with the athame, dispersing the energy safely. He rushed to Shae's side and pulled her into his arms. She looked up at him and he saw the unspoken emotion in her jade green eyes. He was just as grateful for her at that moment.

"We finally have a location," he told Zander who was standing behind them. The Vampire King's eyes turned black and his smile spoke of retribution, but he was going to have to get in line behind Gerrick.

SHAE GLANCED out the windshield at the house across the street. The run-down two-story home had peeling yellow paint and all of the windows were boarded up. It appeared as if it was abandoned. She cocked her head to the side at the symbols decorating the plywood. It looked like human graffiti, but she wouldn't put it past the demons for it to be imbued with Dark magic. She opened her mind and cursed. "Don't tell me that this was nothing but a waste of time." Her irritation at the fact that the archdemons weren't present quickly escalated to a killing rage.

"Don't worry, Red. There are plenty of skirm to kill in there. They won't get away." She heard the undertones in Gerrick's promise. He wasn't going to allow the archdemons to get away with what they'd done to her. She hoped she didn't have to fight his male ego for her chance to see to her own revenge because there wasn't a force on this earth that would stand in her way.

"Take one of my blades," Rhys told Jessie, handing her a small titanium *sgian dubh*.

Jessie took the weapon and gripped it tightly. "I'm so glad I'm leaving to visit my parents after this. I really need a break from all this chaos."

Shae opened her door and shook her head. "I hope your visit goes better than mine did."

Jessie squeezed her shoulder. "Me, too. My parents don't know about what happened to me, yet."

"They'll love you no matter what," Shae reassured. That was the one thing her family had made clear to her during her visit home. They still loved her. Still, Jessie's was going to be one hell of a visit, Shae thought, climbing out.

They were met by the rest of the Dark Warriors seconds later on the sidewalk. Zander sent her and Gerrick along with a small contingent to the back of the house while Zander and several others entered through the front.

They paused at the sagging back door and waited for Zander to distract the skirm. If there was one thing Shae had learned it was that skirm were dumb as rocks and wouldn't expect to be ambushed from both sides. Loud shouts echoed through the gaps in the wood right before Gerrick kicked his way into a kitchen.

Two startled skirm looked up and bared their fangs. Gerrick and Bhric had their blades out and attacked without hesitation before anyone else moved. Her heart raced like a jackhammer in her chest as she watched her mate attack the skirm. She didn't like seeing him face danger, but had to admit that he was a thing of beauty in action. She envied his confident, fearless demeanor. She was a wild card, either frightened or furious and it remained to be seen whether she would be able to act when the time came.

Shae took a deep breath, ignoring the scent of brimstone and rot and entered a kitchen that had seen better days. The cabinets were hanging off the walls and covered in a century of grime. She wondered how humans could allow a home to go into such disrepair.

As she went further into the room she smelled rodents

and saw a nest in the corner. She couldn't help the shiver of revulsion. She'd had enough of rats during her months of captivity and quickly shut out those horrific memories.

She walked to the sagging linoleum counter and noticed used needles and other drug paraphernalia. Like all creatures, supernaturals had their share of drug or alcohol addicts. The difference was the incidence rate was far lower in supernaturals. It was harder to become an addict when you had the support of your entire family, generations at that, living with you.

"We're missing all the fun oot there," Bhric quipped and ran toward the front of the house. "Feel the freeze, bitches!"

Gerrick gave her that smile that never failed to have her in a puddle at his feet. "How 'bout it, Red? Think you can kill more than me?" He handed her his knife.

She took the offering and shuddered at the spark that seared her when their fingers inadvertently met. "With my arms tied behind my back, baby," she teased, enjoying how he was playing with her.

His ice-blue eyes glowed brightly and his blonde hair fell over one corner of his forehead. "I've never been into that kind of thing, but I think I'll make an exception for you." He leaned forward and kissed her deeply.

She was panting and in a sensual daze by the time be broke the kiss. He spanked her bottom and murmured against her lips, "See if you can keep up."

She flew into action right behind him and took a play out of his book, rushing headlong into the fight without pause. In her flight across the main room, she noted the holes in the floor, the location of the other warriors, as well as, several skrim frozen in blocks of ice. Apparently, Bhric had meant that literally and not figuratively.

She had her weapon in hand and slashed out at the

chest of the nearest skirm. He kicked her knee and her leg gave out. She went to the trash-strewn ground and he stabbed her in the upper arm, pissing her off. She screamed and wrapped her arm around the skirm's neck with one arm while she thrust her blade into his back.

She jumped back into action before the flash seared her flesh. The cloud of ash covered her in the next moment. This was ridiculously easy compared to what she'd faced in the fighting cages. She had wondered why she hadn't fought more skirm, but now understood. It wouldn't have been difficult to eliminate them, physically or emotionally, and Kadir and Azazel liked to see her suffer. The fact that skirm held the faces of young humans didn't stop her from taking their lives, because she'd seen the vile creatures they became after being infected by the archdemons. Hell, even she was living proof of the archdemon taint.

In rapid succession she ashed two skirm and turned to watch the rest of the group. Her infrared vision flared back to life and the Dark Warriors were vibrant images, whereas the skirm hardly had a glow at all. She concentrated and shut the infrared off again. Now that she'd gotten control of it, it was too difficult to fight like that. Gerrick's gorgeous face was the first that came back into full color.

Her distraction hadn't cost her, and thankfully, the fight was nearly over, but in the next heartbeat, a skirm pulled out a gun, pointing it at Zander and firing. Bhric jumped in front of his brother, taking the bullet and immediately collapsed to the floor. Zander's eyes went black and Bhric's chuckle broke off in a groan, "You assed out, mother fucker. Now you're gonna get it. Shite! How the hell is it that I always end up with the worst injuries?"

Zander ripped the gun from the skirm's hand and turned it back on him. He fired a shot directly into his face, finishing with a thrust of his knife to his heart. The ash blew away in Zander's wake as he rushed to Bhric's side. "Och, you're a mess again, *brathair*."

"But still handsome as ever. Fuck, be careful." Bhric hissed as Zander helped him to his feet.

"What the hell were the archdemons doing in a place like this?" Shae asked.

"This was a complete waste of time," Gerrick cursed. "If they were here it was in passing. They haven't set up a lair in this dump."

"No' a total waste. We eliminated at least fifteen skirm," Zander replied, helping Bhric out the front door.

Shae's adrenaline was still high as Gerrick came up to her side. He wrapped his arm around her waist. "Don't worry, we're going to get them," he promised, kissing her temple. The intimate gestures were coming automatically to him now and she didn't think he was even aware of it half the time. She felt their bond strengthening and her mate mark shot pain through her leg in agreement. The more time that passed the more intense the pain became. She knew the phenomenon was normal and would escalate until they completed the mating, but she refused to bond fully to him while she was still so intimately connected to the archdemons. She didn't want her mating tainted by their evil. Not to mention that he was still holding pieces of himself back.

More than anything, she wanted to believe his affection was genuine, but the voices in her head told her a different story.

CHAPTER 18

Gerrick placed the tray of food on the coffee table as Shae shut the door behind them. Smiling, he ran a hand over the dark wood. He'd done just as she requested and replaced every destroyed piece of furniture in the room with dark alder wood. The bedding was a blue and chocolate paisley. Elsie assured him Shae would love it when he'd shown it to her. He'd wanted Shae's opinion, but had wanted to surprise her more. And from the look on Shae's face, he'd done a good job.

"You remembered. I can't believe you did all this for me..." he pulled her easily into his arms and silenced her with a kiss. Where he expected her to be hesitant, she was molten fire instead. He wrapped his hand around the back of her neck and splayed his fingers into the mass of her curling, red hair.

Gerrick broke the kiss and trailed his lips to her jaw, breathing in her jasmine scent. Like an addict, he couldn't get enough. It was like he was main-lining her, she went straight to his blood, intoxicating him within seconds. He had gone too long without allowing himself to really indulge in a female. It had been eons since he'd had any desire to.

Shae was his drug of choice and he willingly indulged. He unzipped her winter coat and flung it across the room. Her sweater was a soft accent to her silky skin.

He was lost to her and it wasn't just her beauty, sharp intelligence and fiery demeanor. She challenged him at every turn. Her unexpected openness was as engaging as her secrets and the horrors of her past. He ran his hand down her back and gripped her hip, wanting her naked and writhing beneath him. His blood pounded with the force of his craving for her.

He'd never before felt such intense arousal. His beating heart was a staccato rhythm in his chest, reverberating throughout his body. She slipped her hands under his shirt and around his back. He shuddered with the pleasure. Her touch was an electrocution and fever exploded to his bones, branding him as sure as the mark on his leg.

His shaft surged painfully in his pants, threatening to break the metal tabs of the zipper. He wanted to take this slow, but as always with her, his need was rapidly over-coming all of his willpower. He returned to her lips and relished the ambrosia of her taste. He plunged her depths with abandon, inciting her arousal. She arched toward him while she lifted the hem of his shirt.

He wasn't able to pull himself from tangling his lips with hers and she ripped his shirt down the front. Caught up in the frenzy, he poured his demand into his kiss and relished the fact that she didn't shy away, but met him and took more. She sucked his tongue into her mouth, making him think of what else she could suck into that warm, wet cavern.

Groaning, he broke the kiss and traced his mouth down

to the hollow of her throat. Shae moaned softly as she dropped her head back, offering him free reign. She hadn't allowed such freedom with her ravaged skin and his chest ached with the trust she was extending. He licked and nipped her scarred flesh, making her tremble in his arms.

"Shae," he murmured, outlining the shell of her ear. He pulled her impossibly closer so that she was smashed against his chest. It was impossible not to feel the pressure of her breasts with every shallow breath she took, despite the fabric separating their flesh. It was the sweetest of temptations.

He kept his hand wrapped possessively around her neck and lowered the other one until he was cupping her ass in his palm. She placed open-mouthed kisses on his neck and he squeezed the firm globe in his hand. The pleasure threatened to kill him, but what a way to go.

She lifted her head and he saw the pink flush that rode high on her cheeks, her lips were red and kiss-swollen and her eyes were glowing pools of green. She was a stunning vision who had on far too many clothes at the moment.

Her abdomen felt like fire where he gripped her sweater. She gasped as he whipped it over her head in the next breath. He took her silence as consent to continue and slid his hands up her bare back. He was astonished that touching her so intimately could feel so indescribably good.

He didn't recall feeling this with Evanna and was grateful. Shae was an altogether different female and engendered volatile emotions. He needed Shae like he had never needed Evanna, with a fierce, raw passion that wasn't sweet and gentle. He'd always thought he wanted a female like Evanna, but after a taste of Shae, he realized he wouldn't have been happy living a life without the fiery female in his arms.

He paused over the clasp of her bra and traced over it lightly. Her full-body shiver betrayed the heat licking beneath her skin. "What kind of spell have you cast over me?"

"I'm not the one casting spells, Red. You have me in your thrall," he admitted, kissing her neck as he twisted the closure with one hand. She lowered her arms and wiggled slightly. He heard the soft thud as her bra fell to the floor.

Wanting to take in the sight of her, he set her away from him. She wrapped her arms around her chest, hiding her pert breasts from his view. He tugged her hands and forced her to lower them, keeping his gaze on her face. "I wasn't done looking at you."

She huffed her annoyance, but allowed him a few more seconds. "Take your shirt off. I want to see the rest of what the Goddess gave me," she ordered. One corner of his mouth lifted at her imperious tone as he shrugged out of the torn fabric. Her eyes dilated and goose pimples rose along her skin.

Clearly liking what she saw, she toed off her shoes and kicked them aside. He stopped her when her hands went to the waistband of her jeans. "Why in such a rush, Red? We have all night."

"I've never been very patient, especially when it comes to something I want. You have the body of a God. No female would be patient with you standing there half-naked. Mmmm, just sayin'." Her claws slashed out and his leathers gaped open. He didn't have time to react before she was shoving the fabric down.

He chuckled and his shoes were gone followed by his pants. He stood there in his black, boxer briefs, trying to regain control of the moment. He wasn't sure how she had managed to take over, but damn, if it wasn't a huge turn-on.

She was next to him an instant later and kissing him, keeping him off-balance. All he could think of was getting her naked and in the bedroom. He picked her up and she wrapped her legs around his waist.

He pulled her head down and claimed her lips, kissing her deeply as he walked them to the bedroom. She fisted his hair and her claws scraped his scalp. Setting her down, she arched into him. Her softness melded with his rigidity and he lifted one hand and palmed a breast while his other hand freed the button to her low-ride jeans.

His fingers brushed the thatch of hair between her legs as he unzipped her pants. The minx wasn't wearing any panties and she moaned at the contact, writhing to get closer to him. He put his thumbs on the sides of her undone jeans and pushed them down, his body following along until he knelt before her.

She lifted her legs and stepped out of the fabric, but his attention remained on the glistening flesh inches from his hungry mouth. His hands ran up the backs of her legs, luxuriating in the feel of her.

He paused at her inner thighs and Shae arched her back ever so slightly, begging for deeper contact. Wordlessly, she twisted and moved her lithe body, guiding his questing fingers to the place that he so eagerly wanted to be. His finger parted her flossy curls and her sweet, moist scent registered in the primal part of him that knew only lust and want and need.

The call was fierce, intoxicating. He remained on his knees before her and his palm spanned across her stomach. He pushed until she was sitting on the bed. "Put your legs over my shoulders," he ordered. She complied and he turned his head to kiss her thigh, tracing his tongue along her flesh.

He paused, inhaling her jasmine sweetness into his lungs. Using his thumbs, he parted her lips and ran his tongue along the seam of her body. "Goddess," she husked and dropped her upper body onto the bed. He found the bud of her desire, licked and sucked it, already addicted to her taste.

He lifted his eyes and they landed on the erotic sight of her clutching and squeezing her breasts. She pinched one ruby nipple between her fingers and he nearly came right then and there.

He traced the wetness seeping from her core and inserted one finger into her tight sheath. Her muscles clamped on the digit in response. His cock pulsed with every frantic heartbeat and his mate mark burned like the fires of hell, but he wouldn't change one thing about this moment. He had been given a gift he thought he'd never have again. It didn't matter that he no longer had a heart to give her. She was his.

Her body was drawn taut as he continued his intimate kiss. He pressed his slick tongue flat against her clit and sent waves of sorcery along his tongue, causing a high frequency vibration. Within seconds, she was crying his name in climax. He gave her one last lick and surged to his feet.

PANTING FROM AN INTENSE ORGASM, she watched Gerrick stand before her, a towering golden warrior...and that fast she was desperate for more. He was strength and seductive splendor rolled into one glorious package that she wanted to unwrap. She caught the elastic of his waistband in her fingers and toyed with him. She teased his abdomen and watched his arousal leap beneath the cotton.

"Shae," he growled and she heard the desperation. She shoved them to his knees and her mouth went dry when his erection sprang free. Her wanton gaze couldn't waver from that part of him that was all steel and silk. He toed off his boxers as she palmed his shaft. He was large, much larger than anyone she'd ever been with. She had a moment of fear until she realized they'd done this dance very successfully before. It had been so frantic the first couple times that she hadn't gotten a good look at him.

Her fingers didn't fit all the way around him. She pumped her hand up and down his length as she leaned forward and placed an open-mouthed kiss on the flat disc of his nipple and bit down. Suddenly, he gripped her hips and tossed her to the bed.

A million butterflies took flight in her stomach as she anticipated the raw pleasure his look promised. She watched his chest heave up and down as he prowled up her body. He was a vision of male perfection with his close-cropped blonde hair and glowing ice-blue eyes. His broad shoulders obliterated the overhead light, reminding her of just how strong he was. She trailed her eyes over his bronzed chest to that perfect V that only males like him possessed. Goddess, he made her weak at the knees.

A drop of moisture beaded on the blunt crown of his thick, large sex. She licked her lips, wanting a taste. He was watching her with an intensity that made her clench with need. His jaw was clenched tightly as he gripped his shaft and ran the tip through her slick center. She arched, wanting skin on skin contact.

His nostrils flared and the scar that lined the left side of his face stood out in contrast as proof of his feral nature. It wasn't the scar that frightened her, but the look in his eyes that was heated and raw, promising a night that would change her forever. Half-afraid this was all a dream...she ran her hands up his chest and wrapped them over his shoulders.

He continued to run his shaft through her folds of flesh and he leaned down on his other arm, bringing his body flush with hers. The feel of him chased away the darkness of the demons, leaving no room for anything but him. He twined their fingers above her head on the mattress and pressed his hard length to her entrance. He claimed her mouth in another searing kiss as he entered her in a rush.

Once he was seated fully within her body, he broke the kiss and exhaled in a sigh that carried the depth of his desire for her. His free hand traveled up her side to cup her swollen breast. He played with her nipple as he pulled out then thrust back in. Apparently, he was going to make love to her slowly, killing her in the process.

She dug her heels into his backside, urging him to go faster. He bit her bottom lip in reprisal then licked the wound. "Gerrick, I need..." she trailed away, not able to vocalize her demands.

"So wet," he husked against her lips, placing kisses along her jaw and to the scarred curve where her neck met her shoulder. "So tight."

Gerrick released her breast and grabbed her knee, bending it to take her deeper. He began a rhythm of thrusting and withdrawing that left her incapable of anything but the rapt indulgence of this spell he wove over her. She felt the blunt head of his cock pressing against the mouth of her womb, a sensation she craved like nothing else ever before.

Everything in her focused on the primal, wild force of him pounding in and out of her body. His muscles bunched and flexed over her, drawing her eye. He draped her leg over his elbow and reached between their bodies. His thumb gathered her wetness before he pressed it against the throbbing bundle of nerves. He bent his head and sucked one nipple into his mouth. With that she began bucking wildly, seeking her release.

His steely strength surrounded her and stars burst behind her eyes as she detonated in million pieces. She felt the sheen of sweat cover his body as he chased his own climax, never letting up the pressure on her clit. He gave a coarse shout as his body constricted. The muscles in his chest and the tendons in his neck stood out in stark relief. Gerrick snarled like a wild animal and threw his head back, roaring his pleasure. She felt each pulse of his hot semen as it shot into her body.

Her arms fell to her sides. She was on a euphoric high and he was nothing short of exquisite. At that moment, he glanced down at her and smiled a smile that spoke of pure, male satisfaction. "I can't get enough of you, Red. You have ruined me. You'll be lucky if we ever leave this room again."

She didn't hear what he said next as she was catapulted into another memory. She was lying in tall grass and Gerrick was leaning over her with that same smile on his unscarred face.

He lovingly cupped her cheek and leaned down, kissing her gently. She had no idea where they were, but they were naked on a blanket and she couldn't hear anything for miles around. She'd never seen him without the scar except in these odd visions and he had never kissed her with such tender care.

"That was even better than the last time, my Evanna. You will spoil me yet," he confessed in that odd accent she'd only heard one other time.

He withdrew from her body and lay on his side next to

her and traced a pattern across her ribs. "When will we tell our parents, love?" She heard the words, but wasn't sure who had spoken. Shae would have sworn she heard the words in her head as if she'd spoke, but it wasn't her voice. She concentrated, trying to move her head to look around, but she wasn't able to move.

He tucked his longer hair behind his ear and his look turned solemn. "Let me have you for a short time more. Once we announce our news, we won't be left alone. The mating curse has been a blight on the realm for centuries. We are the first miracle."

"You're right," that voice again. A feminine laugh echoed and suddenly Shae was running through the grass, glancing back over her shoulder at Gerrick who was running after her. Even in the confusion of the memory, she couldn't help but admire Gerrick's flawless masculine body.

He caught her and tackled her to the ground, claiming her lips. Shae closed her eyes and gave herself over to the passion between them. She opened her eyes when he broke the kiss and they were back in the bedroom and he was hovering over her. Rather than lust, his gaze was full of fear and concern.

"What the hell just happened? One minute you were with me and the next you wouldn't respond." He was in her face and looked terrified.

She pushed against his chest, trying to get space between them. He refused to move an inch. "I should never have trusted you," she yelled and pushed.

Shocked, he fell back on his heels. She scooted to the headboard and sat with her back against it. She pulled a pillow into her lap to cover herself and twisted it in her hands.

"What does that mean? Was I too rough? I would never

hurt you," he sounded contrite and concerned about her wellbeing.

With the confusion from the vision and her rage at the fact that he would never talk to her the way he had Evanna, she had lashed out. She had no idea whether the memory was a manifestation of her greatest fears, or what it was, but it disturbed her deeply.

"Nothing. Forget I said anything. I need to get out of here," she replied, surging to her feet.

"Oh, no you don't. You aren't running from me this time."

"Let me go. I need to go meet Santiago."

He had her pinned against the wall by her shoulders and his eyes had gone black with his fury. "You are *mine*, Shae. You will not meet another male, ever! Is that what he told you? To meet him? I'll kill that motherfucker."

She latched onto his arm in desperation to stop him as he headed for the door. "No, he didn't say that. He told me that he has a way for me to get some of my anger out," she said in a rush to keep him from seeking Santiago.

He stopped and looked over his shoulder, a crease marring his brow between his eyes. "Explain."

She slumped to the floor and clutched her head as pain nearly split it in two. Gentle hands stroked over her hair and shoulders. "Shae, I'm sorry. I can't help how the mating compulsion makes me possessive."

"I can hear them again. The archdemons are louder. I'll explain more on the way, but I need to see Santiago, now. He said he could help me. Will you go with me?" she asked, meeting his gaze. She'd never changed emotions so rapidly in her life and was beyond disoriented. To go from the happiest moment of her life after making love to Gerrick to being angry when she had a vision of Gerrick's past to being full of rage and in pain as the archdemons forced their commands into her mind. She questioned if it really was too late for her, if she had completely lost her mind.

He softened his expression and picked her up, carrying her to the bed. He ran his hand up and down her back in calming circles. "I wouldn't let you go without me. I don't know what the hell Santiago is up to, but we're about to find out."

She prayed Santiago had some answer because she couldn't take much more of this.

CHAPTER 19

Gerrick gripped the steering wheel so tightly his knuckles were white. The female sitting next to him drove him up a fucking wall. One minute they were having the best sex of his life and the next her eyes went blank and she started screaming about the Goddess-damned archdemon in her head. Now, a few hours later they were driving down a deserted road on the eastside searching for Santiago.

He was going to pummel the male for giving his mate hope of some relief. He felt the pain and anguish Shae experienced at the hands of Kadir and Azazel and knew how badly she wanted it to stop. All he wanted was to find the bastards and make them pay for what they'd done, not chase after Santiago.

He glanced over at Shae, unable to miss the lines of strain around her mouth. He imagined the demon whispering commands in her mind and it had him itching to spill demon blood. She had been through enough and deserved a break, and, that was the only reason he had agreed to this wild goose chase. If there was even a fraction of a chance that whatever Santiago had in mind could work, Gerrick was taking it.

He couldn't do anything less. From the moment he'd seen Shae in that house of horrors in Kadir's lair, his life had been turned upside down. That was how it was when you found your Fated Mate, he thought. He'd watched it happen to three of his closest friends now and knew it was part of the process. Evanna's soul wrapped around his heart in a familiar embrace, adding a layer of complication he didn't want or need.

His blood ran cold as it occurred to him that it might not be Evanna's soul he felt. If Shae was his Fated Mate then it must be her soul he carried now. It seemed extra cruel to take that last piece from him, but he had no way of knowing for sure. His thoughts automatically traveled down the road that the demons had used Dark magic to replicate a mating, but he immediately shut down that line of thinking.

There was no denying the connection he shared with Shae. Nor could he deny that it was touched by the Goddess. Shae was his and he was hers. He might not be able to give her what he'd already given to Evanna, but he was a bastard who wanted it all from Shae.

Shae reached over and laid her hand on his thigh, squeezing. The mating compulsion turned his blood to lava the instant they touched. Material was no barrier to the desire that flowed between them. It hadn't been like this with Evanna. Sure, he had been drawn to Evanna and had wanted her, but with Shae it was a painful ache that threatened to consume him whole.

"Thank you for doing this with me. I know you don't want to be here and it means the world to me that you are." She returned her hand to her lap, and without stopping to contemplate his actions, he pulled it back to his lap.

She looked over at him and he knew there was something more going on in that brilliant mind of hers. She was sad about something, and for whatever reason, didn't want to share it with him. He wanted to pummel something at the idea of his mate keeping secrets from him. Then shake her and make her tell him. He wasn't known for his patience. "What's wrong? And, don't give me any bullshit about it being the demons."

She yanked her hand back and narrowed her eyes. "You're one to talk. You've got more secrets than I've got fingers and toes." She turned her body and glanced out the window.

Her words cut like razors. "My life is an open book," he replied. He was a Dark Warrior and made it his life's mission to protect humans and supernaturals alike. End of story. There was nothing more to him. In his anger, he almost missed the hidden dirt road and turned at the last second in a squeal of tires. "Do you want to tell me what's really going on?"

She fisted her hands on her thighs and her only response was, "Humph."

After several tense seconds, she leaned forward and a patch of moonlight fell on her face. It illuminated her vibrant skin and full lips, making him want to kiss her senseless. "Are those lights up ahead?" she asked, grabbing his attention.

It was difficult to see with all the trees, but he caught sight of lights in the open door of a large barn. As they continued down the dirt road, more details became clear. There were countless vehicles parked around the barn, which was situated in a clearing. Shadows passed in front of the doorway, but it was impossible to see what was going on.

He parked his SUV and went around to her side. She

was out and heading to the barn before he reached her. The stiff set to her spine told him she was pissed at him and it wasn't the irrational rage the demons incited. This was personal and he had no idea what he'd done.

He heard the shouting from inside the building as he hurried to her side. The crowd was large and boisterous. When he reached her, he placed his palm around the back of her neck, in a possessive move. There would be no doubt that she belonged to him. He expected her to melt into him, but she remained stiff and distant and he didn't like that one bit. Too bad he was at a loss for how to fix it. He would never fucking understand females.

The barn appeared rundown on the outside as they approached and he noticed the two huge males guarding the doors. They were bear shifters if he wasn't mistaken. The one closest stepped into their path. "What is your business here, warrior?" he asked, glancing at the tattoo on Gerrick's forearm that clearly marked him as a Dark Warrior.

"Santiago invited us," Gerrick responded. "Is he here?"

The male nodded to the interior of the barn. "Yeah. He's fighting in ring three."

"Thanks." Gerrick was shocked as he entered the infamous fight club. What the hell was Santi doing here, of all places? Gerrick pushed his way through the crowd and pulled Shae close to his side. He wasn't letting her go far.

No one paid any attention as they made their way to the inner circle. The outside may have appeared rundown, but the inside was anything but. Where he expected a dirt floor he found it was concrete. In the center of the open space were four rings that you would typically see at a boxing match with the padded floor and ropes. And, there were fighters in each one.

The crowd roared as one of the males in the closest ring flew into the ropes. Blood flew from his mouth and he shifted into a leopard before he landed on the mat. The other male bared his fangs and crouched ready to catch the rapidly approaching animal.

Gerrick glanced at Shae and noticed that the sight of the leopard sinking its teeth into the vampire's side transfixed her as it shook its huge head back and forth. He lifted his head and a chunk of flesh was dangling from its jaw. "I knew this place existed, but we didn't know of its location. Zander is going to be pissed," he observed absently.

The copper scent of blood overwhelmed the air, but the injury didn't stop the vampire. Gerrick scanned the other rings for Santiago and tugged Shae with him when he found him a couple rings over.

The fervor of the crowd agitated Gerrick. These people were slavering for bloodshed. They were drinking and egging on the fights. He noticed several males walking around exchanging money with some of the spectators. They were betting on this shit, he thought, incredulous. And, the females were just as involved as the males.

He stopped a few feet away from where Santiago fought. Santi was vicious as he double-tapped his opponent's face, making blood spurt from his nose. They danced around one another, landing blows every now and then. Santi looked like he was barely breaking a sweat as he danced around the ring. Where he had a small cut to his lower lip, the other male was beat to shit, wounded and bleeding.

Gerrick felt Shae lean forward and he glanced over. She was perched on her tiptoes, her eyes lit with excitement. She was glued to the sight. In fact, he sensed her anticipation through their bond, as well as, the relief. She believed this was the answer she was looking for. She wanted to beat the shit out of an innocent in hopes of ridding her demons. Over his dead fucking body was he going to allow that to happen. He knew her well enough to know that she may want that now, but she would never forgive herself if she hurt someone.

He glanced back to Santiago and watched as Santi half-shifted into his wolf, claws extended from his fingertips and sliced through the male's stomach. He fell to his knees and a referee jumped into the middle of the ring, lifting Santi's hand into the air and proclaiming him the winner. Gerrick wondered how far his friend would have gone if there hadn't been a referee.

As a Dark Warrior, Gerrick was no stranger to fighting and violence. Hell, his life was filled with death and destruction. Difference was he didn't go out and beat on someone for no reason. He eliminated evil in an attempt to protect humans and the realm. What he was witnessing bordered on slaughter. Being a Dark Warrior and human cop, Santi had an unfair advantage. This wasn't what they were about. In fact, it went against the oath they had taken.

Gerrick didn't see the appeal of any of it. It reminded him of human cock-fighting. The illegal activity pit animals against one another and what his fellow warrior was engaging in was no better. Worst of all, it was activities like this that placed the realm in the most danger of being discovered.

Gerrick turned and began walking to the exit, but Shae didn't budge. Snarling, he had her arm in his grip a second later. "We're leaving, now."

"Go ahead. I'm not leaving. I need to talk to Santiago and ask him to get me in the next fight."

Gerrick stepped into Shae's space and got right in her face. "You aren't fighting here, Red."

Tears brimmed her eyes and she recoiled as if he'd slapped her. "I knew you wouldn't understand. You want me to be something I'm not, someone I will never be!"

It was his turn to wince against the sudden pain. He opened his mouth to deny her words when she interrupted. "Don't you dare deny it! If you hope to have any future with me, don't stand here and lie to me. I deserve that much respect, at least."

"I've never asked you to be something you're not. I brought you here, didn't I? This isn't your answer, Shae." He understood for the first time that whatever was bothering her hadn't begun in the car.

"How do you know what will help me? You don't know anything about me." She wasn't holding back any longer and her strength only attracted him to her even more.

"I know more than you think. You're in my soul, Red. This place is filled with nothing but animals. Is that what you want to become?" He refused to allow her to sink to this level.

"I am an animal!" she spat in his face. Her chest heaved with every indrawn breath and her eyes were black with fury. "Sorry to disappoint you, but I'm not your perfect little mate."

He cupped her face between his palms and forced her to look at him. "I don't know what is really going through that pretty little head of yours, but all I'm trying to do is save you from doing something you will regret. If you climb into that ring, you will seriously injure an innocent female and you will never forgive yourself. Not to mention that doing so will be giving into the demons. They want you out of control and wild in your rages, that's why they threw you into a cage to fight. I don't know exactly what, but they get something out of it when you do, and I refuse to have you in that situation again."

"This isn't the same," she protested, but he saw some of the fire was dying.

"No, it's so much worse. Before you killed demons." He turned her in his arms and wrapped one around her waist, pointing to a female across the way. "What do you think it would do to you to unleash your beast on her?"

He felt her body shake and knew she understood his point. "You will never come back from something like that Shae and I'll be damned if those bastards take anything else from you."

She turned in the cage of his arms and he hated how she'd gone pale. "I hate having their voices in my head and just want them to stop. I understand the term insanity because I feel like that's what I am."

"If fighting helps, then I will spar with you, but you aren't doing it here."

She quirked a corner of her mouth. "Think you can take me?" she challenged.

His answering smile came easier now. "No, but I'll take my beating as long as you promise to play nurse afterwards."

She ran her hands up his chest and wrapped them around his neck. Just like that, the chaos of the arena disappeared and it was only the two of them. His hands landed on her lower back and pulled her flush against the erection pounding in his pants. "I like a male who can admit defeat. I'll kiss all your boo-boos."

Her eyes shone with mischief and he couldn't help but imagine her teasing him as she kissed and licked her way across his chest and down his abdomen before she sucked his shaft into her mouth. "Can we spar naked?"

She threw her head back and laughed at him. "There's

good naked and bad naked. Jumping around fighting would be bad naked."

His hands slid south and latched onto her ass. "There is no such thing as bad naked where you're concerned. I have never in all my life seen a sexier female." He leaned down and meshed his lips with hers. She tasted of ambrosia and he loved how she responded. He stroked his tongue across her lips, seeking entrance. She toyed with him until he shook the ass he held firmly.

The way he rubbed her against the steel of his cock made her gasp and he took full advantage. He thrust his tongue in and out of her mouth demonstrating what he planned to do to her when they got home. She fisted his hair and pulled it, making his scalp tingle. He broke the kiss and ran kisses along her slender jaw. Reverently, he placed his lips over her scars, wanting to show her he loved every inch of her.

"You say the sweetest things. Let's get out of here and test that theory," she panted, pulling him to the exit.

They couldn't get home fast enough, he thought.

CHAPTER 20

S hae's body was humming after her session with Gerrick. He had stuck to his promise and taken her down to the training room when they'd returned to Zeum. They had barely stopped kissing long enough to get into the house and she'd enjoyed teasing him and running from him once they hit the mats.

She hadn't imagined him quite so playful as he had been during his pursuit of her. She'd leapt onto the middle of a climbing rope and he had used his magic to snap the rope above her head, catching her as she fell. He'd kissed her like crazy while managing to get her shirt off. She discovered a new love for magic that she hadn't had before meeting Gerrick.

It had been fun to wiggle out of his arms and jog backwards as she removed her bra. When he'd finally caught her, he loved her so thoroughly that she had passed out from the pleasure. And, for those all too brief minutes there had been nothing but bliss. No archdemons trying to exert control over her mind and no dead mate haunting her. It had given her a taste of what she wanted.

"Thank the Gods you two are done in there," Nate called out as he descended the stairs above them. She blushed furiously and Gerrick growled at the male.

"My job description does not involve cleaning up after you two." She didn't miss the sarcasm in Nate's comment.

"From the looks of it, your job description doesn't involve cleaning at all." She stifled her laugh against Gerrick's shoulder.

"Ouch, Scarface, that hurts. I thought I was doing a bang-up job around here."

She couldn't help but laugh at that. "Nate, there is a difference between banging the staff and doing your job," she quipped, making Gerrick chuckle and kiss her temple.

"She's got your number, dragon-breath."

"What can I say? I'm a lover not a cleaner. Zander is looking for you two. He's in the war room," Nate replied, continuing down the hall.

Gerrick paused and looked over his shoulder. "Oh and Nate, you need to restock the training room with clean towels." Nate didn't disappoint when a second later he responded by giving Gerrick the middle finger.

"What do you think he wants?" Shae asked, hoping she wasn't causing more problems for Gerrick because she had no doubt that the request had to do with her. It seemed she was the cause of all the troubles since she'd come Zeum. She chanced a glance Gerrick's way and noticed his easy, sated lope hadn't changed. He clearly wasn't bothered in the least.

She wouldn't have guessed that they had spent the past couple hours making love the way her hormones reacted to the sight of her mate. He cocked his head to the side and gave her that half-smile of his. "We could always ignore him and go to our room."

She gasped and smacked his shoulder. "Gerrick, I can't believe you'd ignore an order from the King."

"He knows what it's like to be in the middle of the mating dance, Red. You should have seen him when he was all twisted over Elsie. He was impossible to be around and they were constantly found in compromising positions in the kitchen." She laughed at the way he scrunched his face in disgust. "Still are, actually. They don't seem to get that our food is prepared in that room."

"What was it like here before the mating curse was lifted?" She couldn't imagine Zeum without the females.

"We spent all of our time patrolling and fighting skirm. There wasn't a lot of down time and there wasn't nearly as much laughter in the house. Looking back, we were stuck in the status quo with very little spontaneity. I wouldn't want to go back to how things were before the mates came along. They challenge the way we think and offer much needed perspective."

He held the door open and stood aside for her to pass. "I never imagined life was like this here. The Vampire King and his Dark Warriors were untouchable for us normal civilians so I always saw you guys as larger than life."

"And now?" They continued down the hall, past the ballroom that was busy being repaired after the damage during Winter Solstice.

She glanced meaningfully at his groin and raised one eyebrow. "You're still larger than life." She squealed and twisted away from him as he tried to tickle her.

They came to a halt as Jace and Zander stared at them when they practically fell into the war room. "Nate said you wanted to see us," Gerrick said, oblivious to the tension.

She didn't understand what was going on, but the pressure in her head was suddenly unbearable as if a switch had been flipped. The archdemons seemed to sense when she was close to Zander and were always more active when she was in his presence.

"Aye, Jace was just updating me aboot the progress on the serum." Gerrick went still and took a step to the side, placing himself between her and the others. She tried to step around him, but he refused to allow it.

Finally, she tilted her head and looked around his arm, meeting her King's gaze. "What did he learn, Liege?"

"I thought we were stopping that line of research. We can't risk another female's death," Gerrick added before anyone responded.

"Sit doon, both of you. Jace, tell them what you've told me." Zander sat back in his chair with his palms crossed over his stomach and was the picture of ease that did nothing but make her nervous. Gerrick led her to a chair opposite the two males.

Jace leaned his elbows on the table and blew out a breath, running his fingers over a silver cuff he always wore on his wrist. "The scientists and I isolated the element we believe was responsible for the death and eliminated it from the serum. Shae still has the highest concentration of venom in her system and when we injected a sample of her blood with the serum that number was cut in half."

Gerrick surged to his feet, causing his chair to fall over. "You are not using my mate as an experiment. I don't give a shit what results you get. I will never place her in that danger."

Shae scented the blood before she saw it dripping from his clenched fingers. She stood next to him and wrapped her arm around his waist. "Let's just hear them out, Gerrick. I need to hear what they have to say."

"Don't do this to me. Don't make me go through this

again," he told her, turning haunted eyes her direction. She held her breath, praying he was finally going to tell her about Evanna and how he'd lost her.

Jace broke the silence after several seconds. "I don't want to be responsible for another death, either, Gerrick. We don't have to try this on her right now, but I will tell you that her numbers are the only ones that have increased since she's been here."

"Gerrick. Listen to him. I can't continue to live like this. He has access to my mind whenever he wants. He knows when I'm in Zander's presence and I want him out of my head. I refuse to be his pawn any longer."

"Jace tested this thoroughly and then retested it a hundred times. And, he has a theory that he can hold her to us." Zander ran his hand through his shoulder length black hair. "I willna force you to do this. It is your choice, Shae."

"No. She's mine. It's my choice, too. You want to take her from me?" Shae felt the fear and rage through her bond to Gerrick and wanted to save him from this, but she couldn't live like this anymore. In fact, she'd rather end her own life than become a weapon that destroyed him or anyone else.

"I have to do this, Gerrick. I wish you would understand," she pleaded with him.

He wrenched from her embrace and was across the room before she blinked. "I will not stand by and watch you play Russian roulette. This is not only your life you play with, Red, but mine, too. Have you considered what losing you will do to me? I will never forgive you for this." She'd never seen him so angry and it was directed at her.

"I'm sorry..." her voice trailed away as he stalked from the room. Moments later, she heard the slam of the front door. She stood there stunned that he'd left her.

"We doona have to do this, Shae." She turned and met

Zander's concerned gaze.

"No, we do." There had been no other answer and instinct told her this was the closest she was going to come to a cure. "What do we do next?"

Jace stood up and crossed to her side. "Sit down and Zander is going to give you the injection while I connect with you. I am going to hold you to me with my healing powers before the serum hits your system so that I can pull you back from the edge should things go wrong. I wasn't prepared before and it acted too quickly."

She suddenly reconsidered going through with this. Everything Gerrick had said was true, but the fact still remained that she needed to try. "Okay," she responded, sitting down and holding her arm out to Zander who had come to her side, as well.

Jace placed his warm palms over her head and she felt a tingling sensation as he entered her mind. She knew when he grabbed hold of her consciousness because it jolted her. She closed her eyes and felt the sting of a needle. At first she felt nothing, but Jace and distantly Gerrick. He was trying to fuse their souls together by chanting a spell, aware that they were going forward with the plan. He would never let her go, even if she never earned his love, she had his loyalty.

Pain suddenly scalded her from the inside out. It was ten times worse than when the archdemon bit her. Unable to hold back, she cried out in pain, worried she'd made the biggest mistake of her life.

Her back arched and she went into convulsions. Her connection to Jace snapped and she heard snarling next to her ear. If that was Kadir or Azazel, they had a firm hold on her now.

"You aren't leaving me, Red. You hear me? Fight this." It was Gerrick's husky voice and she wanted to open her eyes and reassure him, but she felt the battle for possession of her mind. She clung to the bright, gold beacon that linked her to Gerrick.

"Jace, heal her, you bastard," Gerrick cursed.

She couldn't tell if Jace responded, but after what felt like an eternity, the wracking pain ended and her shaking stopped. Her muscles relaxed and she felt Gerrick's strength at her back. He'd come back for her and was the only reason she wasn't lost to the demons at that very moment.

"Gerrick," she croaked, opening her eyes.

"I'm here, Shae. I'm here." He was holding her and they were on the floor several feet from where she'd been sitting. Relief swamped his features and he brushed the hair from her eyes. "You will never volunteer for another shot. I know you want your freedom from those bastards, but you're stronger than them."

"The mating bond is," she explained.

"What?" he asked, placing a tender kiss to her lips.

"I felt you, even before you came back. Jace was there, holding me and Kadir threw him out, but he couldn't touch our connection. It was because of you that I didn't lose my mind to him completely."

The loving way Gerrick cupped her cheek belied the ferocious expression on his face. "I told you before that you belong to me. No one will ever take you."

"Yes, I'm yours. But this bond is a two way street, Gerrick. You belong to me, too. Heart and soul," she hedged, needing him to share that part with her. She was fragile and felt as if she'd break if he rejected her.

He pressed his forehead against hers. "You've carried part of my soul for centuries, Shae. Of course, I'm yours." She didn't miss the way he danced around the issue.

"Did the serum work at all?" Zander asked, interrupting

the moment.

"If you count giving Kadir open access to my mind working, then yeah it worked like a charm."

"That shouldn't have happened," Jace muttered, pacing around the room.

"There is so much we doona understand aboot Dark magic and archdemon abilities. We canna continue this research. 'Tis too unpredictable," Zander proclaimed, standing from his crouching position next to them.

Gerrick ran his fingers over the scarred side of her neck, making her shiver. She sat up suddenly and reached up to feel the area. It was still marred with thick, ruined flesh, but the new wounds were completely healed. "The new bite is gone."

"What?" Zander was next to her in a flash and Gerrick was lifting her hand. "Goddess. She's right. 'Tis no' there anymore."

"We weren't trying to heal the wound. We were trying to eliminate the venom in her blood stream." Jace crossed to the bar and poured a glass full with amber liquid.

"That's good though, right? Have you ever been able to heal wounds from venom before?" she asked.

Gerrick kissed the top of her head and ran his hands down her arms. "No we haven't. They have been working on that one for centuries, but have never been successful."

"At least you know the work you've done is good for something. I just wish it had cut my tie to them."

"We will find a way to live with this, Red," Gerrick promised. Shae nodded her agreement, but deep down inside she didn't think she could live without having her freedom.

Everything that had been good in her life had been stolen from her and now her future was being taken, too.

CHAPTER 21

S hae's strength never ceased to amaze Gerrick. He'd
been so pissed at her for putting herself at risk that
he'd taken off. He couldn't stand by and watch her
die even if leaving had felt like a fist had been punched
through his chest. As he stood on the porch, struggling to
breathe he felt the demon sink its claws into her mind. He'd
taken off and ran like Lucifer had been chasing him to get
back to her side, cursing the entire way. When he'd seen her
writhing on the floor with Jace struggling to keep hold of
her, panic had set in. It had been the power of the mate-
bond that had saved her life and he'd said a silent prayer of
thanks to the Goddess for bringing them together.

And now, scant minutes later, she insisted they join the
others in the library for their search. Elsie and the rest of the
Dark Warriors were combing through their shelves for any
information they could find about archdemons and the
sharing of Dark magic. They'd rebuilt the protections
around Zeum, but if Angelica had gotten through once, she
could do it again.

"Don't give me the cold shoulder, Gerrick. I had to try." She'd leaned into him to whisper the words, but all he felt were her breasts pressing into his shoulder. His distraction worsened when he realized that the action turned her on, as well. Her nipples hardened beneath her thin top, brushed against his arm, adding to the erotic torture.

"Let's go to our room instead," he husked. She kissed him lightly, ignoring his cajoling and tugged him to a table at the side of the room.

He groaned when he saw the piles of books laid across its surface. Glancing around, he saw that the desk in the corner was just as laden as the table. Their library was two stories high with countless shelves lining the walls, all filled with books. There was everything from the history of the Valkyrie, to books of witchcraft spells and incantations, to ledgers documenting various demons encountered during the course of the war. This task was like looking for a needle in a haystack.

Gerrick searched for a comfortable chair for Shae. She'd just been through an ordeal and if she insisted on helping, then he was going to make sure she was as comfortable as possible. Aside from the leather chair in front of the desk, there were several groupings of leather couches set in different places throughout the room. Some of the new trainees were at the desk, which left the sofas near the fire.

Elsie sat in front of the fireplace with her head bent over a book, eating a sandwich. As they approached, she lifted her head and smiled. "Hey, you two, grab a book and have a seat. I assume Jace and Zander explained what we're doing," she murmured around a mouthful of food.

Shae screwed up her face in distaste and shook her head. "What exactly are you eating?"

Elsie covered her mouth, laughing. "It's pastrami and peanut butter with bananas."

Zander knelt in front of Elsie and ran a finger across her cheek. "Are you in need of more blood from me, *a ghra*?"

Elsie leaned into his touch and closed her eyes. "Hmmm. I think I am. I can't seem to get enough." Zander grabbed her up in a bear hug, making her squeal.

"If this isn't a mandatory task then we're leaving, too." Gerrick went to turn around, but Shae stayed rooted in place.

"Are you pregnant?" Shae asked the Vampire Queen. Gerrick gaped at his mate's bold question. Glancing back at Elsie, he realized Shae might be onto something. Elsie had been different lately.

Jace was next to them in the next second. "How much extra blood have you needed?"

Elsie went pale as she clutched Zander's neck. "Um, I'm not sure. It's like all my appetites are on super-drive. And, I do mean *all* of them." Zander smiled at her and Gerrick didn't miss the insinuation there.

"Could it be? I didna expect it to happen this soon." Zander glanced down at his mate's stomach, shock clear on his face. "Supernaturals are no' as fertile as humans. Most are lucky to have two *bairns* in a lifetime."

"After everything I went through, I just assumed I couldn't get pregnant. How do we find out? Do I do pee on a stick?" She wiggled in Zander's arms and he carefully set her down. The petite female bounced on her feet in front of Jace, clearly eager to find out.

Jace laughed, "No, but I will need to take a blood sample."

Cailyn grabbed Elsie's hand, beaming from ear to ear.

"This is so exciting. Can you imagine a baby running around here?"

Breslin jumped into the conversation. "Aye, and we'd get to decorate a nursery. Maybe you'll have twins. It runs in our family, after all."

Elsie threw up her free hand. "Okay, slow down, one step at a time. We don't even know if I'm pregnant yet."

Gerrick glanced at Shae and saw the unfiltered joy on her face. She wanted children, he thought, and as her mate, he could give them to her. He had never once contemplated having children. He'd given up on that dream after Evanna died. Sorcerers could only ejaculate with their Fated Mates so it was impossible for them to get anyone else pregnant.

He imagined Shae round with his child and smiled. He liked that idea. He maneuvered himself behind her and wrapped his arms around her waist, settling his palms over his stomach. She looked up at him and stood on tiptoe, placing a kiss to his lips.

"Come down with me to the lab and we will have the results within minutes," Jace told Elsie and Zander, making Shae turn in his arms.

His mate's eyes were bright with hope and enthusiasm and the sight was contagious. "How exciting will that be if she is pregnant?"

"Who?" Mack asked from the doorway, Kyran standing behind her.

"The Queen. She's been having symptoms and they've gone to do a test," Shae gushed.

"Uh-oh, let the baby proofing begin. If you thought Zander was protective of Elsie, can you imagine him with fang junior?" Mack quipped, making Kyran laugh. Kyran's mate had a unique way with words that could rub some the wrong way, but Gerrick thought her dry sarcasm rounded out the household perfectly.

"I have news of my own. Look what I can do." Mack vanished and reappeared at the top of the ladder, laughing and then was back at their side a second later.

Gerrick glanced at Shae and saw the question there. "Kyran can sift, and, as you know, mates share their abilities with one another. Mack hadn't yet developed that skill. There's no stopping her now, Kyran."

"Shite. Doona I know it. She's been sifting around the room stabbing our furniture yelling *booyah motherfucker*. I need to get *her* pregnant so she has to stay home." Kyran heaved a huge sigh, but had a huge smile on his face and his eyes were dancing as he watched his mate.

Gerrick chuckled and stepped back, pulling Shae with him, right before Kyran went flying. He landed hard on the floor and before he could jump to his feet, Mack had sifted to crouch over him. "You'll be the one staying home with the baby, bloodsucker." She offered a hand and helped him up.

Breslin chuckled. "You asked for that one, *brathair*."

"He's a protective ass most days, but he's all mine. It helps that he buys me kickass shirts like this." Mack lifted the corners of her black t-shirt, displaying it for everyone to read. This one said, *Why drive when you can sift?*

All of a sudden Gerrick heard squeals down the hallway, no doubt broadcasting what the results of the test were. In the next second, Elsie came tearing into the room, vibrating with delight. Gerrick couldn't help but smile with her, she was beyond happy.

"We're pregnant!" she shouted. Zander had Elsie in his arms in the next instant with his head buried in her neck.

Bhric, Rhys, Orlando and Santiago followed Cailyn and Jace into the room. Nate and Rhett pulled up the rear carrying a tray of champagne glasses. Gerrick glanced around at his friends and silently thanked the Goddess for all she had given them. This is what they fought to protect, their friends and family. This was what life was really all about.

Breslin lifted her glass to the air. "A stripling is a blessing, a gift from the Goddess above, a precious little angel to cherish and to love."

"Here's to our little Irish blessing." Zander clinked his glass to Elsie's and everyone cheered, taking a sip of the crisp, cool, bubbly liquid.

Orlando wrapped Elsie in a huge hug, lifting her off the ground. "Pregnancy looks good on you, El. You're glowing. I can't wait to meet the little bundle."

"Can I bless the baby in the way of Khoth?" Nate asked. The male may not have been Angus, certainly wasn't efficient at running the house, but he fit in and had worked his way firmly into the family.

"Aye, all blessings are accepted. I have a feeling our little *bairn* is going to need them." Zander said and Gerrick didn't miss the lines of worry that were already showing.

Nate lifted his head, inhaling and exhaling in a slow rhythm until dragon smoke swirled above his head. Partially shifting to his dragon, he scribed a rune into the smoke and Gerrick saw the flash of blue light when the spell snapped into place.

"What does that do?" Elsie inquired, admiring the beautiful creation.

"It's a blessing of health. It offers protection for the mother and child during the pregnancy."

Elsie put down her champagne glass and threw her arms around Nate's neck. "Thank you so much, Nate. This little one has the best protectors on the planet and I'm grateful for each and every one of you," she choked out through overwhelming emotion and went to pick up her glass of bubbly. Seconds later she seemed to deflate. "I guess this means I can't have any more Monsteritas or energy drinks for a while. By the way, how long will this pregnancy last?"

"Supernaturals' gestation is much faster than humans, about half to be exact. We need to assume that you will follow our timeline, but we really don't know," Jace explained.

Elsie laid a hand over her lower stomach. "That's so fast. I could already be over a third of the way there. There's so much to do and so little time. And, Breslin, yes, I would love your help with the nursery."

"Do you have everything you need to monitor the pregnancy?" Zander asked Jace, picking up the sandwich Elsie had set down earlier and took a bite. He grimaced and set it back down.

"No. I'm going to need to order an ultrasound machine unless you want her coming to the hospital for check-ups."

"Nay, she willna be leaving Zeum. 'Tis too dangerous."

"You can't keep me locked up here, Mr. Bossy Pants," Elsie taunted, finishing the sandwich that only seemed to suit her pregnant taste buds.

"Watch me. Kadir has done unspeakable things and I willna allow you, or our stripling, to be placed in danger. Jace, Gerrick, I want you checking and resetting the protections every hour." Gerrick wasn't shocked by Zander's orders. He would do the same thing with Shae and protect her and their child in every way he could.

Shae shifted from foot to foot and clutched her glass to her chest. "Won't that weaken them? It won't help any of us if Gerrick isn't at the top of his game."

Gerrick kissed her temple, loving that she wanted to protect him. No one ever had. "It's ok. I don't mind. This stripling must be protected at all costs. He or she will be next in line for the throne and the target of too many. Besides, Elsie is right. She's well into the pregnancy and it will be over before we know it."

"We also need to station Jax and Thane or Cade and Caelle here permanently. With so many distractions and several of us mated now, I want more Dark Warriors on hand here," Zander explained, taking a seat on one of the couches by the fireplace and picking up the book Elsie had abandoned earlier, his smile never wavering, despite the serious conversation. Gerrick understood his happiness and didn't think there was a more deserving male. Zander had devoted his entire life to not just vampires, but the entire Tehrex Realm and even the Goddess herself.

Kyran replaced his champagne with a finger of scotch and took a sip. "I'll call Nikko and tell him to rearrange assignments and transfer Cade and Caelle."

"Perfect. In the meantime, we need to finish this research. There has to be something in one of these books that will give us a clue," Zander instructed, getting everyone back to work.

Gerrick sat at the desk with Shae in his lap while the others milled about the library. Suddenly, Breslin gathered an armful of books off the table. "I'll take these to my room and look through them tomorrow. I have to get ready for a date." Gerrick had to grit his teeth. Now was not the time to play and he was surprised because Breslin was normally the first one to help with whatever needed to be done.

Rhett leaned across the table and narrowed his eyes at Breslin. "What do you mean you're going on a date?" He seemed irritated and Gerrick wondered what was up with the easy-going fire demon.

"Och, I knew you were dense. A date, you know, when a male and female spend some time together. Surely, you've been on dates."

"I know the concept. This male must be something special for you to leave when your family is in the middle of a crisis."

"Newsflash, demon, my family is always in a crisis. I would never leave if I thought it was dire. I'll be home later, and I promise you, I'll get twice as much information as you within an hour." With that, Breslin turned on her heel and walked out the door before Rhett could say anything more. Zander and his brothers laughed while a stunned Rhett watched her retreating backside.

"Doona bother trying to understand that one. She will be here when we need her. Besides, she needs to let off some steam. 'Tis easy for me to forget now that I've found Elsie that the others need time for their physical demands. Why doona you all take the night off and we can resume in the afternoon?"

Zander didn't need to tell them twice as the group simultaneously jumped to their feet. There had been a lot of stress with Angelica and then the incident with Shae. A night of relaxation would do them all some good. Orlando slapped Rhys on the back, asking the male to go to Confetti Too with him.

Gerrick quickly walked over and interrupted Santiago and Orlando. "Can I have a word with you, brother?"

"Sure." Santiago stood and Gerrick waited until everyone had left the room before speaking. "What's up?" the bald-headed warrior asked.

"I took Shae to the fight club the other night." The

male's face paled at the mention of the underground activity.

"I didn't see you there. Did you not want to fight?" he asked, turning to Gerrick's mate.

Shae shook her head at Santi. "That's the problem. I want it too much. Gerrick is right, that's not the answer for me."

"Let's get one thing clear, my mate will never be in one of those rings, but this isn't about her. This is about you and what you are doing. Have you lost your fucking mind?"

Santiago stepped into Gerrick's space and instinct had him shoving Shae behind his back to keep her out of reach. "What I do on my free time is my business. I don't follow you around judging your actions."

"Your actions affect us all. That tattoo on your arm tells everyone that a Dark Warrior is in the ring. What you do in that ring goes against everything we stand for, Santi. You are stronger and better trained than anyone in that place and you know it. When you step into the ring you are taking an unfair advantage over innocent males. I saw the money changing hands. Surely, you aren't doing this for money."

Santi balled his hands into fists and Gerrick heard the cracking of his jaw. "You know nothing about me and you sure as shit aren't my mother, so I suggest you get the fuck out of my business...or else." Santi flicked his fingers out and his claws sprouted from the tips, drops of blood on the ends from the force behind the partial shift.

Gerrick heard Shae's gasp, but he wasn't shocked by Santi's threat. They were warriors, not nannies and they lived with violence. But their violence had a code and Santi was crossing it. "We don't hit innocent people for sport, Santi. We aren't beings ruled by our inner animals. We have better control than that. What would Zander, or Hayden, think?"

Gerrick grabbed Shae's hand and left Santiago with those parting words. He hoped the threat of Zander or Hayden was enough to stop him, but he had a sinking feeling whatever nightmare was chasing Santi wasn't done with him yet.

CHAPTER 22

Shae knocked on the doorjamb of the open suit of rooms and stuck her head around the corner. Elsie and Cailyn's were in deep conversation inside the room. Shae tried to settle her nerves over being summoned by the Queen. The Dark Warriors and their females had embraced her from the moment they'd rescued her and the others, but she couldn't get rid of her fear that she'd be asked to leave the compound. A lot of bad things had happened involving her and the demons and she wouldn't blame Elsie if her presence was too high a risk, but she had grown to love it at Zeum and really wanted to stay.

At least she'd finally found the correct wing and the right room. She had insisted that she could find her own way to the Queen, asking Gerrick for his trust and faith. Of course, he'd given it to her without hesitation, but unfortunately, she hadn't considered the fact that she didn't know the house and had promptly become lost. She'd nearly called Gerrick on her cell phone to come rescue her when a maid walked by and led her to the east wing where the King's quarters were.

It was the first time she had been allowed to roam freely through Zeum and part of the reason she'd gotten lost was because Kadir had been pressing her mind to search for the amulet. It disconcerted Shae to think the archdemons were able to read her thoughts. She had to assume that they reacted to any increase in her fear and used to their advantage. Right now, she was working on remaining calm and controlling her fear which was not an easy task at the moment.

It didn't matter how many times she told herself that neither Kadir, nor Azazel, could hurt her again, the terror refused to abate. To make matters worse, the injection Jace had given her seemed to strengthen her connection to the archdemons. The last thing she wanted to do was turn on her own kind. She might not have known them long, but she would have laid down her life for any one of them.

It was one of the distinguishing factors between the humans and the Tehrex Realm. Supernaturals didn't need to be drafted into service to the government. Any civilian would do everything in their power to protect their leaders.

"Hey, Shae. Come on in." The Queen's voice echoed from inside the room.

Shae entered a room with a similar layout to Gerrick's. Each suite had a small kitchenette and living room, along with, a bedroom and bathroom. She had been surprised at the amount of space provided to each warrior. Shae half-expected to see the same dark leather furniture, but was surprised that the entire place was empty.

"If you knocked down this wall, you'd have direct access to the baby. Although, my guess is, that baby will be in bed with you for a while." Cailyn was holding paint swatches to the wall as she spoke. They sure worked fast, Shae thought, wondering if they kept paint samples on hand. She'd bet with a house that big, they did.

"I'm not sure how I will feel after I have her, but I don't want my time with Zander interrupted by the baby. And, I'm trying to convince Zander to take out this wall rather than the one he wants to take out in the kitchen. "Shae, thank you so much for coming."

Shae genuflected to the petite queen. "Highness."

Elsie crossed to Shae and pushed gently on her shoulder in a friendly gesture. "Stop that, you're one of us now. And, call me Elsie. I don't think I will ever be comfortable with others bowing to me."

"No one in the realm would dare speak to you without the proper address...Elsie. The Tarakesh family has led the vampires for as long as we have existed and it's inbred in us. You'll have to be tolerant." She lowered her head, hoping she hadn't overstepped her place. Elsie had indicated she was one of them, but it was still hard to see her as a friend rather than her Queen. Shae turned to the wall in question and changed the subject. "So, why doesn't Zander want this wall taken out?"

The queen rubbed her chest in a peculiar manner, making Shae wonder what, if any, side effects she was having with her pregnancy. She was, after all, the first human-turned-vampire so they had no idea what to expect with this pregnancy. "Apparently, not only is it a load bearing wall, but they install a special insulation that completely mutes sound."

"That makes sense. With so many living here, privacy is important. Hey, are you okay?" Shae asked, noting the Elsie looked a little green around the gills.

Elsie lowered her hand. "Yeah, I guess. I can't tell if what I'm feeling is related to the pregnancy or my ability."

Immediately concerned, Cailyn rushed to Elsie's side. "Have you had a vision?"

"Nothing exact. In fact, I didn't even sense anything about Angelica attacking during Winter Solstice. Could be the pregnancy is affecting my ability. Who knows? But, I don't feel quite right. I'll ask Zander about it since we share abilities now. Anyway, what do you think about this wall?"

Elsie's sister didn't seem completely appeased, but returned to the samples and lifted a different color. "You tell Jace if this continues. He's your doctor and needs to know everything. The load-bearing issue definitely changes the plan. We can have the kitchen wall taken out completely and have an open flow between the two suites. The open area out there can be the baby's playroom."

Cailyn had a point and it made Shae realize how much needed to be considered when having a baby. "That's a great idea and this space is big enough to place the nanny in here with the baby," Shae added.

Elsie chuckled. "She won't be taken care of by a nanny. She has enough aunts and uncles in this house that we won't need any help."

"You keep saying she. Have you learned it's a girl already?" Shae asked, unsure how soon the sex could be determined.

"You'd think with this expedited pregnancy that Jace would be able to tell by now, but no, it's just mother's intuition. Unless her aunt Cailyn can hear her thoughts?"

Shae looked from Elsie to Cailyn, wondering what she was talking about. "No, nothing's changed since the last time you asked me about an hour ago. But, you will be the first to know if it does. Hey, what if you have twins? Breslin said they run in their family."

"Don't even joke about that." Shae laughed at Elsie's

groan. "Zander will be bad enough with one baby. If I have two he won't even let me walk to the bathroom on my own."

Shae laughed, Zander seemed like he would do exactly what Elsie said. Surely, they didn't bring her here to discuss the nursery. "What did you want to see me about?"

"I wanted to talk to you about your job, actually. Has Dante called you about going back to the bank?"

Shae hadn't even given thought to going back to work. She couldn't while she was being influenced by the archdemons. Gerrick told her it would do her good to find some semblance of normalcy again, but she didn't agree where work was concerned. In her opinion, she was still a danger.

"No, he hasn't called me. After what happened with my family, I'm not comfortable around the public, yet."

Elsie waved her hands. "Nonsense. I know the demons talk to you and try to force you to do their bidding, but you never will. But, that's not why I'm asking. I don't want you to go back to the bank. I want you to go to work for me at Elsie's Hope."

Shae's jaw fell open. "What do you mean you want me to work for you?"

"Zander doesn't want me leaving the house until after the baby is born. And, as much as it annoys me, this is a battle that's not worth fighting him on. Plus, like you, I have been a victim of the demons and I will never place my child in unnecessary risk."

"Is that how you were turned? We were told you were a turned vampire, but now I can't help but wonder if you're actually more like me." Shae wanted to take the words back as soon as they slipped past her lips. "I'm sorry, I shouldn't have asked that. It's none of my business," she sputtered.

"It's ok. No, the demons didn't bite me. I became a

vampire when Jace and Zander saved me. Kadir kidnapped me and took me to a cave where a traitor nearly killed me, which is why I need your help."

"I would do anything for you, but I'm not so sure about this idea. I don't know anything about your charity."

"You are exactly what I need. The biggest hole I need filled is someone to award victim's grant money. Jessie is going to help by doing intake assessments, but she can't manage the money aspect of it, as well. You were a loan officer for the bank. This is basically the same thing. Rather than doing credit checks, I need you to investigate validity of claims and award money accordingly."

This is exactly what Gerrick would want her to do. He believed she needed a purpose and she wanted to be a female he was proud of. Still, she wasn't sure this was a good idea given her unpredictable rage. "How soon do you need someone? And, will I have to meet with the applicants?" Crossing and uncrossing her arms, she swallowed hard through a mouth that was suddenly dry. She imagined being in the office and Kadir entering her mind and demanding she take the lives of innocents.

"I won't be going into the office and we need someone right away. We're backlogged and Jessie is on vacation in San Francisco right now. I can only do so much from here. Cailyn has agreed to pick up some of the slack, but we need you. And, yes, you will meet with the people. It helps give you a feel for their needs and how we can best help them."

Shae fidgeted with the hem of her shirt while her stomach churned with nausea. "I need to think about this. I want to help, but I'm still not sure I'm right for the job."

Gerrick knocking on the door cut off Elsie's reply. Now, her stomach fluttered with butterflies for reasons other than nervousness. "I'm here to steal Shae."

Her body flooded with warmth and she ached for him as he came into view. He never failed to captivate all of her attention when he entered a room. She nearly forgot the conversation with Elsie as his lips quirked up in that way they did. Her tongue darted out to lick lips that wanted to taste him.

Elsie laughed as she took one of the paint squares from Cailyn. "I'm surprised you stayed away as long as you did."

Gerrick grunted and crossed to Shae's side. "You're lucky you got forty-five minutes."

"Do us all a favor and convince Shae that she is perfect for a position at Elsie's Hope. She's resistant, and, it's not that I don't understand why, but she's underestimating herself and I refuse to have any of my family short-change themselves." Elsie turned to Shae and met her gaze. The female meant every word she said and the intensity in her tone made it impossible to deny she saw Shae as one of them. "I mean it Shae, you're perfect for the position."

Shae felt Gerrick perk up and stand tall at her back. He placed his hands over the tops of her shoulders in blatant ownership. "I couldn't agree more. I can't promise anything, my mate is a stubborn female." Shae heard the humor in his voice and wanted to smile at his obvious teasing. "But, I will use every skill I have to convince her."

SHAE SHIFTED her head in defiance, the sleek line of her throat on display. Gerrick ran a finger down the column, enjoying her involuntary shiver. "You can try, Gerrick, but you know what a danger I am and you know that we can't take that risk."

Gerrick kissed her temple and slid his hand into hers.

The hair on his arms stood on end and his breathing increased. Fighting and killing the demons and skirm over the years had been never been dull, but he'd never felt more alive or aware as he did when he was with Shae. Every nerve ending tingled and the mere brush of her hair across his face was an exquisite torture. "We can talk about that later. I want to show you something."

She blinked and her eyebrows shot up. "What do you want to show me?" The husky tone told him where her mind had gone and he wouldn't object to what she had in mind. The pleasure he experienced with her was explosive and addictive. "That's not what I had in mind, but later," he promised, leading her from the room.

"Yeah, take that to your room. People complain if you get naked anywhere else," Elsie teased, making Gerrick smile and Shae turn a bright shade of red.

"You'd think that after living with my parents and grand-parents a statement like that wouldn't bother me, but I never expected to have the royal family harass me about my sex life. My brother, yes, but not anyone outside my family."

Gerrick hadn't given the idea much thought. His grand-parents had been killed in the Great War and his parents shortly after Evanna. He had an aunt and uncle and a few cousins, but he'd chosen to become a Dark Warrior and live at Zeum, rather than remain with his family. "At least you're used to living with extended family. Elsie and her sister lived alone before they mated with Zander and Jace. Imagine the shock for them when they first met all of us."

Shae smiled and swung their hands between their bodies as they descended the stairs. "I don't know how humans survive such solitary existences. It would have killed me to come home to an empty house every day. Where are we going anyway?"

"I was helping Nikko train the new recruits and couldn't concentrate. All I could think about was what we did in there the other day." His body hardened as he recalled her lithe body surging above him. He brought their clasped hands to his mouth and kissed the back of hers, his heart beating hard against his ribcage.

She tilted her head to the side and regarded him. "Are you blaming me for your lack of discipline?"

He chuckled, "I would never, but let's just say that Nikko is ready to throttle the Goddess for all the distractions in this house. He doesn't live here all the time, but he does rely on us to train the recruits and lately we haven't done a good job with it."

"Please tell me you aren't volunteering me to help with the warriors." He smoothed his thumb over the crease between her eyes.

"Don't worry, I won't allow another male that close to you." He pulled her into the underground room and led her to the punching bags in the corner. "I got you a pair of your own gloves so you don't hurt your hands when you come down here."

Her lips parted and she glanced from him to the shelf. He cursed as he realized he should have wrapped them and been more romantic in his presentation. "That was very thoughtful of you, but I'm not sure why you went to the trouble. I can manage without."

"It's my job to take care of you."

Her eyes flashed and she snatched her hand out of his grasp. Her chest was heaving as she took two steps then stopped. He had no idea what he'd done this time to make her angry. "What did I do now?"

Her back straightened and she stood there rigidly. "It's not what you've done, Gerrick. Just because we are mates doesn't make you obligated. I want you one hundred percent, not halfway, or, I'd rather not have you at all."

His chest twisted and his stomach dropped to his feet. He curled his arms over his head as he stared at her back. The thought of losing Shae was like being ripped n half. He could never survive without her. The mission against skirm wouldn't be enough to keep him alive this time. He was in far too deep with her, further than he had ever been with Evanna. "I don't understand. You can't walk away from me. We're Fated Mates."

She spun around and thrust her hands onto her hips, her eyes narrowed at him. "You may give me your body, but that isn't enough for me. You guard your heart and won't really let me in and I refuse to settle for that. It may kill me, but I will walk away."

His jaw dropped open. There was no waiver in her voice. He knew she was stubborn enough to follow through on her promise. "I have no idea why you say that. I may have denied you at first, but that was only because I feared the archdemons were fucking with us. I need you to explain this to me."

Shae shook her head and paced the mats, lowering her chin to her chest. He watched as she opened her mouth only to close it again. He wanted to embrace her and force her to put these crazy thoughts out of her head. He feared it was the demons messing with her again, but if he accused her of falling prey to them and found out they weren't doing anything it would backfire on him. How the hell was he supposed to combat this? He decided to wait for her to gather her thoughts and tell him what was going through that pretty head of hers.

She shook her head and stopped, turning to him. "I know about Evanna. Not the details or anything, but that she existed. And, not just that, I've had two visions of you with her."

His stomach knotted painfully and it felt as if a hot poker was being shoved through his chest. He couldn't catch his breath. He never wanted her to learn about the woman who owned his heart. His eyes widened suddenly as realization hit. She was right. He'd been holding the most important part of himself back while demanding she give him everything, but how was he supposed to give what was shattered.

CHAPTER 23

Shae wanted to rant and rave and beat the hell out of Gerrick at the same time she felt tears building behind her eyes. She heard the utter confusion and desperation in his voice, but all that changed the moment she'd spilled her guts. She hadn't meant to tell him anything, but was tired of living half a lie. There had never been any doubt that each time he staked a claim to her he was asking for everything yet unwilling to give her what she needed most.

It would be so easy to lose her heart to this gentle, scarred warrior. He was ruthless in defense of the innocent and those he loved and had given her his body and protection, but that wasn't enough. He couldn't possess her without giving to her in return. Her heart was in her throat as she waited for him to respond.

"What do you mean you know about Evanna? Where did you hear that name?"

She bit her fingernail as she resumed her pacing. It was easier to tell him if she wasn't looking at him. "The first time

I heard it was in the dungeon after we touched. I had a vision of you and her."

He leaned against the shelves and seemed to deflate, his shoulders slumping. "I don't understand. How could you have a vision? Are you psychometric? Or, are visions part of an ability you have?"

Her brow furrowed, "You mean like Elsie and the other females. No, I don't have any abilities and I've never had visions before now. Maybe it's something the demons did to me that has enabled it."

"What did you see?" He lifted his head and the torment in his eyes stopped her in her tracks. He was lost and scrambling to regain his footing. The damn mating compulsion had her barely holding back from going to him and soothing his worry. If she did that then she'd better be willing to settle for being unfulfilled the rest of her life.

"The first time I had a vision you were wearing a kilt and standing in a field of purple heather. And, you were kissing her, but it was me, only not me. I don't understand it." She shook her head trying to dispel the insecurity of knowing he would never choose her. Her throat was thick with emotion. He would always choose Evanna and it hurt.

"The next time, I saw you it was a bit more, er," she cleared her throat and swallowed through the sudden dryness, "intimate. You'd just had sex with her and were talking about when you were going to tell your parents about your mating. You were happy, Gerrick." A tear slipped past her control and rolled down her cheek.

She hung her head as the knot in her gut intensified. She didn't make him happy, not like his previous mate did. Shae wanted to shout that Evanna hadn't been perfect, but she'd seen her perfection in Gerrick's gaze. She shouldn't be jealous of a dead female and she told herself that she was far better, but that was easier said than done. That little bit of insecurity that lived in every female grew tenfold. Unfortunately, the mating compulsion made sure she couldn't focus on anything but Gerrick. She kicked an exercise ball into the wall.

Gerrick pushed off the wall and walked up to her. She pasted a fake smile on her face that threatened to crack. "That was the last time I saw her, and, you're right. I was happy, Shae. I'd never been happier in my life."

Bitterness had Shae snarling and clenching her fists at her side. "I'm sorry you lost her, Gerrick. I wish to the Goddess that you hadn't. In fact, I would trade my life with hers if I could."

Gerrick reached out and grabbed her upper arms and shook her forcefully. "Let me finish. I was aware that there had been a war going on between the demons and skirm, but nothing beyond the fact that my grandparents had been killed during the Great War. There was nothing in my life to cause me to be unhappy and then I met Evanna and it seemed as if I'd have it all. I'd never felt more blessed. But it was all ripped from me."

"I know, Breslin told me." Suddenly tired of fighting for her place in his life, Shae sat on the mat and buried her face in her hands. "Just go away, Gerrick. Leave me alone."

She didn't look up when she felt him sit down beside her. If she looked at him the mate-bond would take over and she'd be jumping into his lap.

"Did she tell you that I tried to save Evanna?" Not wanting to discourage him from talking, Shae shook her head. "I remember the day I met Evanna. I was at the lake, fishing for dinner and she came through the trees. She'd been exploring the area around her new house." She looked up at the nostalgia in his voice. His eyes went somewhere far away as he recalled the events.

"We were drawn to one another right away. For two weeks, I would sneak off and ignore my chores and responsibilities to spend time with her. My father finally caught up with me one day and made me clean the horse barn before I was able to go to her. When I finally made it to our meeting spot she wasn't there so I went looking for her. It was dark by that time and I knew she'd have headed home."

He cocked his head and finally met her gaze. "I smelled the burning flesh and death from a mile away. They were all dead. The house was on fire and Evanna was among the corpses burning inside. I rushed in heedless of my own safety and drug her out, but I was too late. She was dead. Distraught with grief, I used my powers to travel back in time and try and save her. I didn't realize who had done it until I encountered the archdemon and skirm."

"You couldn't save her." Shae felt his heartache through their bond and automatically went to him. She hesitated, kneeling before him. She didn't want to cause him more pain or remind him of what he'd lost, but she had to try and comfort him.

"No, I couldn't save her. I learned what a bitch Fate was that day. I lost my heart and soul and was scarred for life for my efforts to try and save an innocent life." She felt him lift his hand to his face and finally understood where the scar had come from. She had assumed the scar had come from some anonymous battle. Knowing it was from his attempts to save his lost love's life made it so much more painful to see.

"I can't replace her, Gerrick, and I don't want to. I am sorry for your loss, but I deserve to love and be loved by my mate in return."

He hugged her tight and she heard his ragged breathing. She swore her heart was beating as fast as his was. "I wish I still had my heart to give you, Shae, but I already gave it away. That doesn't change the fact that you belong to me. Do you hear me? You are *mine*."

She smiled, pressing her cheek against his, her heart breaking for the male in her arms. "That's not good enough, Gerrick. You use this whole situation as armor around your heart. You're so afraid of being hurt again that you haven't stopped to even consider giving me any piece of you. Forget the risk and take the fall with me, Gerrick. Learn to appreciate the rainbow after the cursing rain. Give yourself permission to feel anger, pain and resentment. You never know what else you might let in," she pulled back and captured his gaze. "I never took you for a coward."

She was stripped bare as she sat there for long seconds eyeing her mate. She'd made him think about the pain of his past and now challenged him. She wouldn't take it back. Their future was too important to leave to chance.

She meant what she'd said to him. And she knew he could do it if he would just try. Hell, he was asking the same of her. In order for them to work, she had to move beyond her past and take a chance in him. She may not have loved and lost, but she'd been through hell and it would be far safer for her heart and soul if she kept a wall between them. There was no danger of being hurt that way, but there wasn't any joy, either.

"I am not a coward, Red." His gaze traced her features and returned to her eyes. "I don't like to see the hurt in those jade eyes..." His voice trailed off as he sat up and clasped her face, bringing her close to him. His lips were a thin line and his posture was rigid.

"You said it was as if you were Evanna, only not, right?"

Sweat trickled down her back, underneath her thin t-shirt, making it stick to her skin. "Yeah," she hedged. What was he getting at?

"How did it feel exactly?"

"I believed it was a memory at first. I didn't recognize my clothing or the setting...there's no other way to explain it other than to say that I felt like I was in my own body. I could smell the flowers. I could hear the birds and the husky timber of your voice. I burned with desire when I felt your lips against mine. It was so real that I had no doubt it was me until you called me Evanna."

"Your eyes are the same color as hers...but it can't be, you're so different. Could I have missed it? There has been something from the beginning that was familiar to me."

"I'm not her, Gerrick. Please don't try to make me someone I'm not. That's worse than you walking away from me and never looking back. I may be damaged, but I'll be damned if I become someone else. I am a survivor and deserve to be cherished and loved for who I am." Her mating brand was a searing presence on her calf, reminding her that she did, in fact, belong to him.

"What if you are Evanna reincarnated?" Tears gathered in her eyes at the hope she saw in his. He wanted her to be Evanna more than anything and it was a knife straight through her heart.

"What's wrong with *me*? It doesn't matter if I'm reincarnated or not. I'm *Shae*. Evanna is dead. Nothing will ever change the fact that I'm not your perfect mate. I carry the scars of my past for all to see. I was envenomated by archdemons, I have anger issues, and I don't know if I'll ever have my mind back. Take me or leave me, Gerrick."

Gerrick kissed her then. Claimed her lips in a gentle kiss that made her bite his in return. That wasn't how he kissed her. That was how he kissed Evanna. He was still seeing her as a reincarnation. No, she wanted him wild and unhinged.

He growled at her and fisted her hair, holding her in place for his exploration. She deepened the kiss and coaxed his mouth open. She sucked his tongue into her mouth and that was all it took for him to take over. Gone was the gentleness and it its place was raw, violent need.

She crawled into his lap and felt his erection press against her aching core. "Say my name."

"I know who you are, Shae." She gasped at hearing his words and he took her lips once again.

Urgent need flowed through every limb as she remained plastered against him. She pushed, needing space from the hard line of his body, but he refused to give her an inch. He explored every nook and cranny of her mouth, branding her as thoroughly as his mate mark had.

Straddling his waist, she reached back to caress his brand, knowing the torment it would cause. He cried out against her mouth and bit her lip in reprisal. It was a fight for dominance that she refused to give up. Too much was on the line.

Holding onto his leg, she broke the kiss and ran her mouth across his scar and to the crook of his neck. Her free hand roamed his body, enjoying the way his muscles flexed under her touch.

She didn't know who she was tormenting more...him or her. Finally, his hands left her hair to grab onto her backside then trailed up the sides of her body. His thumb brushed the outside of her breasts and she moaned against his ear.

"That's it, Red. You're mine and your body knows it." His eyes glittered like ice, melting her. She needed more. She wanted to feel his skin beneath her palms as she rode him.

Fumbling with the bottom of his black shirt, it was over his head and tossed to the floor in the next instance.

Her palms traced a path down his chest and paused over his flat, male nipples. They beaded under her touch and beckoned her. She kissed her way down his neck and to the hollow of his throat before moving to his nipples. She ran her tongue around one, making him growl and pull her hair. She looked up at him and murmured, "You're mine, too, Gerrick."

Gerrick claimed her lips again and drove all other thoughts from her head. Her shirt and jeans were gone before she could blink and she lay there in her black bra and panties. He was a gorgeous sight, poised above her, heaving with promise in his eyes that made her skin simmer as her blood boiled in her veins.

She was bold in her exploration, slipping her hand beneath the waist of his pants and underwear. His ass clenched under her palm. It was the firmest ass she'd ever felt and she squeezed hard, claiming him with all she had.

She pushed his chest and he relented, rolling over. She slowly unbuttoned his pants, teasing him with light touches and flicks of her fingers. He tried to kick off his boot, but gave up after a couple tries, clearly not wanting to break contact with her.

His hands were everywhere, distracting her from her goal of getting him naked. She shoved down his pants and boxer briefs, freeing his erection. The large rigid length pulsed and a bead of moisture dripped from the tip.

Forgetting everything else, she leaned down and tasted him. He barked out a cry of pleasure, fisting her hair with one hand while the other tore her panties from her body. She writhed on his hand while she sucked him into her mouth. She'd never felt so uninhibited and it felt so good to do this to him.

"I want to be inside you." His voice was a sensual growl that was difficult to ignore.

She shook her head, not done with her treat yet. Her skin flushed and her heart was going a million beats per minute in her chest as his fingers danced between her legs, trying to coax her.

She turned to the side and widened her knees to give him better access without losing contact with his body. "Two can play this game," he promised as he parted her feminine folds and found her throbbing center.

His cock was so big in her mouth it was difficult to breathe and she couldn't take all of him in her mouth like she wanted. Instead she cupped the soft sack beneath his shaft and wrapped her fingers around the girth of him, sucking on the soft tip and stroking the hard length. He was by far the largest male she'd ever been with and he wasn't a gentle lover. Before, that would have turned her off, but now it was exactly what she needed.

She liked him mindless in his desire and loved when he lost control. It was a heady feeling to bring this strong warrior to his knees and make him crazy with lust. She glanced up and was caught in his bright gaze. His lips were slightly parted and his upper one was pulled back from his teeth. That combined with his scar made him look feral and she almost orgasmed from the sight alone.

He grabbed her breast as he continued to play with her core. His fingers teased her opening and clit, bringing her close to orgasm. She sucked him harder bucked against his hand trying to reach that peak with him. His fingers were relentless in their pursuit of her pleasure.

She hummed around his cock and squeezed his shaft

while he tempted her hotter and higher. Her body tensed when he pinched her nipple with one hand and twisted her clit with the other. When he released his magic, she cried out as she was fully engulfed by searing flames and her body exploded into climax. The orgasm barreled from her core outward and she felt it all the way to her toes.

He took over thrusting into her mouth while he played her flesh, extending her pleasure to the point of exquisite pain. The part of her brain still able to function realized he was seeking his own climax. On a whim, she let go of his sac and ignored his protests as she slipped her fingers under the end of his pants and traced over his mating brand. His body went rigid and he gave a hoarse shout as his seed shot into her mouth. She gladly took what he had to offer and continued sucking until the throbbing stopped.

Afterwards, they flopped onto the mats, panting. He wiped the sweat from her forehead and kissed her gently, reverently. "People are going to be afraid to come to the training room now."

She went up on her elbows and gazed at him. "Good, I'm beginning to understand the benefits of working out. Just sayin'," she teased, winking at him.

He gave her that half-smile that twisted her heart. "Your workout has just begun. Time to get completely naked." She laughed realizing she still had her bra on and he still had his pants around his ankles and boots on.

CHAPTER 24

Shae glared at Gerrick through narrowed eyes as they stood in their room. They'd made love in the training room before going upstairs for rounds three and four. "There was no need to ask for a meeting," she snapped at him.

When Shae had gone to take a shower he'd texted Evzen and Zander and asked to meet with the males about the possibility of Shae being the reincarnation of Evanna. Shae may not want to know, but Gerrick sure as hell did. He was well aware that she was nothing like the female he'd loved so long ago and that was actually what he loved about Shae, but his logical mind needed to understand how this new mating had happened.

That longing to have Evanna back had been replaced with a burning desire for Shae, and wasn't that a punch to the gut. When Shae's hurt reverberated through their bond he knew he should tell her, but he'd always had a problem finding the right words. "Red, this isn't about me wanting you to be Evanna. I simply need to know if it's possible. Don't you want to know why you have her memories?"

Shae evaded his reach and stormed out the door. "You want to know because you want *her* back. I told you, you either love *me* or I'm leaving."

He had no doubt that she would do it, too. "Look, I can't forget about her because she meant something to me, but trust me when I say I have no confusion about the difference between the two of you. I would never want you to be anything but the strong, stubborn, female who challenges me at every turn. What we share is explosive and something I've never experienced. And, look at me, I'm hard for *you* even as we stand here arguing."

He felt some of the hurt bleed from her before she threw him a wry smile over her shoulder. "Explosive is one way to look at it. Will you feel differently if you find out I'm not her?"

He understood she was worried about him rejecting her, but that was impossible. "Regardless of what we find out, you are my Fated Mate. Shae, I love you. I didn't know it before. Hell, I wouldn't even consider it, but I don't ever want you to doubt the way I feel about you. I want you to hear this now before we talk to Zander and Evzen so you know the voracity of my feelings for *you*."

He stopped her at the foot of the stairs and grabbed her face between his palms. "Did you hear me?"

"Yeah, but you said you couldn't love me. You only love me because you think I could be her."

He'd inadvertently hurt her in his attempt to shield himself and wanted to kick his own ass. "Feel it through our bond and know that I love you, Shae Mitchell. Not because you may be the reincarnation of Evanna, but because you are you. Your words woke me up and you were right. I was placing a wall between us and I'm not going to lose you to my own stupidity. There is enough there with the demons, we don't need me adding to it."

"There's too much in my head with the demons and Evanna's memories and our mating bond. It feels like a circus." She was trusting him with her vulnerability and looking to him for help. The tables had turned on him, he thought, as he waited for her to tell him how she felt about him. He wasn't able to tell much beyond her hurt and confusion, and yet, he needed to hear her say those three little words. Had never needed them like he did at that moment.

He opened his mouth to demand she tell him then closed it. He wrapped her in his arms and pulled her flush to his body, claiming her lips in a brief kiss. "Don't worry about sorting everything right now. We have eternity to get it figured out," he murmured, hoping to reassure her that he wanted her for the long haul. "They're waiting for us. Let's go."

Tugging her alongside him, her reticence was evident as they entered the war room where Zander and Evzen were waiting. "Liege, Guild Master. Thanks for coming on such short notice."

"I have to say I was shocked to get your request so soon after you and Shae left the training room. Och, I expected you to be busy for several days, yet." Shae's neck and cheeks flushed red at Zander's teasing.

"I would have been if the situation wasn't so dire. Evzen, this is my Fated Mate, Shae. Shae this is my Guild Master, Evzen Raziel."

"It's nice to meet you," Shae returned, shaking the male's hand.

"You as well," Evzen acknowledged then flipped open the Mystik Grimoire which had been on the table in front of him. "Your text mentioned the reincarnation of Fated Mates. Why are you asking if reincarnation is possible?"

As briefly as possible he related everything Shae had told him about her memories with her filling in some of the gaps. "The only explanation that makes any sense is that she is the reincarnation of Evanna. It's either that or the demons are responsible and I don't have to tell you how frightening that prospect is."

Zander ran his hand through his hair and blew out a breath. "Shite. It would be catastrophic and the worst kind of violation if the archdemon can steal memory and implant it in others."

Shae sat down in her seat and crossed her arms over her chest. "I've been violated enough in one lifetime, thank you very much. I don't need any more."

Gerrick glanced over at hearing the fear behind her words. She was trying to hide the tremble in her limbs. He wrapped his arm around the back of her chair and tucked a long strand of hair behind her ear. Lips that had only hours ago been red and kiss-swollen were pale and thinned and her jade green eyes were pained. When her leg began to bounce under the table he lowered his arm and touched her thigh, stilling her movements. Squeezing her flesh, he hoped she understood that he was trying to tell her that they were in this together.

Evzen looked up from the book with furrowed brows. "Kadir and Azazel will die for what they have done, evil like that never wins. But, I found the answer to your question. Surprisingly, there is an entire chapter in the Grimoire that deals with the issue."

Shae sat forward eagerly. "Is it possible? Am I Evanna's reincarnation?"

Evzen glanced from Shae to Gerrick and smiled.

"Simple answer, yes. Having her memories is one indication that you are the reincarnation of her soul. It's not just having the memories though. A reincarnation would experience the memory and feel the emotions and connection to them as well."

Shae fiddled with his fingers on her leg and he sent a flood of warmth through their bond. He was determined to rectify the hurt he had inadvertently caused her. It galled him that he was the cause of her biggest pain. He wanted to bring her passion and happiness, never anguish. "I felt everything. In fact, I didn't realize it wasn't *me* until Gerrick called me by her name. For a second I thought I'd forgotten the experience...it was that real to me."

Evzen sat forward, his eyes bright as he nodded at Shae's response. "You also have her eye color. There is no test we can perform, but I'd say that's evidence enough to conclude that you are Evanna's reincarnation. But, that doesn't mean you are her. You were born to a different family and have lived a different life and could no more be her than I could be Gerrick." Evzen captured Gerrick's gaze and delivered the warning directly to him. Gerrick understood why the male was so stern, even if it galled him to be told.

"Of course she's not Evanna," Gerrick snapped. "I would never confuse the two. Does the Mystik Grimoire talk about this happening before? I'm afraid that she will suffer Evanna's fate. I will not lose her, too."

Evzen shook his head, his face pinched in concentration. "It mentions the occurrence and discusses the signs, but it doesn't give reasons why. Nor does it provide cautionary tales."

Zander placed his hands on top of his head and crossed an ankle over one knee and Gerrick could see his concern. "Och, the Goddess designs Fated Mates and I have no doubt that she has a plan for everyone. Gerrick, you cursed fate for a verra long time for what was taken from you, and rightly so. Take this second chance and embrace it. Doona you realize how lucky you are to have been blessed a second time?"

Gerrick scowled at Zander's words. "I know exactly what I've been given and I love Shae with everything that I am. Just don't expect me to sit by and watch her suffer or risk losing her."

Shae placed her palm over his thudding heart and he met her eyes. "Gerrick, I can't truly be yours until I'm free from the demons." She turned her head and looked to Zander. "Liege, I want to use my connection to try and locate the lair again and I'm hoping you will help me."

Gerrick stood so rapidly his chair fell over. Chest heaving, heart racing and eyes black with rage, he shouted, "No! You will not open that connection any further. We will find another way to locate the bastards."

Shae hung her head for several minutes and the room fell silent. When she lifted it he saw tears shining in her eyes. "I want the idyllic life you've described, but I can't have it as long as they are in my head. I'm not even free to love you, let alone have a happy life with you. It doesn't matter what I do, they are always there insinuating their will. You have no idea what it's like to fight for your sanity every second of every day. I can never let my guard down or they will take over and use me as a weapon. And, I'm tired, Gerrick. I want this over."

Gerrick's heart broke over her suffering and he fell to his knees at her feet. He gathered her hands into his and reigned in his fury over what she was being put through. He was a warrior. A male used to taking action and battling the enemy, yet he couldn't do a fucking thing at the moment to keep the female he loved safe from the demons. There was no way to stop the bastards from entering her mind and tormenting her and it tore him up. "I'm not gonna lie, I don't like it, but I promise, I'll be by your side every step of the way. Tell me what I can do to help you."

She smiled through her tears and leaned forward to kiss him. He held her to him and deepened the kiss, pouring all of his love through their bond. He broke away and pressed his forehead to hers. "You kept me grounded after that injection and I need you to do that again. The only way I know to open the link is through the serum. I have no intention of giving into Kadir, or Azazel, but I can't do this without you," she reassured, obviously feeling his turmoil through their bond.

Gerrick swallowed thickly and nodded, "Whatever you need," he promised and pulled her into his lap. It was a matter of minutes before Jace came in the room and gave her another injection. Instantly, Shae was writhing in his arms. He felt how much pain was wracking her body, yet she didn't say a word. He didn't think he would have been able to silently bear the agony as bravely as she did and he lost the rest of his battered heart to the strong female.

Gerrick gritted his teeth and latched onto the gold thread connecting him to her. He murmured reassurances in her ear, silently begging the Goddess for her torment to end.

SHAE DIDN'T KNOW what she'd been thinking when she insisted she open the connection again. The fight had been even more brutal this time and she would have lost if Gerrick hadn't been there to keep her tethered. Kadir had been determined to win the war and used every tactic at his disposal. If she'd known the archdemon was able to project the sensation of razors shredding her insides she wouldn't have suggested this course of action. It was a good thing she'd spent all those months in Kadir's tender-loving care or she wouldn't have been able to deal with it.

Her body twitched with the remnants of the venom and she sagged into Gerrick's hold. She was depleted and didn't think she could move. It had been ten times worse than the last time she'd been given the shot. Her muscles burned, her head felt as if someone was beating her brain with a hammer, her throat felt like a desert and she wanted nothing more than to go to sleep for a year.

"Shae, baby. Open your beautiful eyes for me." Gerrick's voice was an enticement she couldn't refuse. And, she liked him calling her baby almost as much as she liked him calling her Red.

She blinked slowly and squinted at the bright overhead lights. "Hey," she croaked.

He held a cup with a straw to her lips. "Here's some water for you. How do you feel?"

"Like a house landed on me." She drank the water and glanced around the crowded room. There hadn't been this many people present when Jace had given her the shot. All of the Dark Warriors and their females were there along with several males she didn't recognize. If she had to guess, she'd say they were the members of the Dark Alliance council. They were too formidable to be the trainees. She flushed with embarrassment, uncomfortable that these strangers had seen her at her weakest.

"Actually, a two-ton Behemoth demon landed on you," Mack teased from her perch next to Kyran.

Shae couldn't help but laugh at the sarcastic female. She

really liked Mack. "Yes he did, but now I know where the bastard is hiding." She smiled and sat up, suddenly ready to see this through.

She felt Gerrick's muscles tense beneath her. "Thank fuck it worked this time. I can't watch you go through that again."

"I have no plans to *ever* go through that again," she reassured Gerrick.

The Vampire Prince, Bhric, chuckled, drawing her attention. "Kadir assed out when he messed with you, Shae. You've got grit, female. I like you."

She couldn't help but smile at the prince. Zander stepped next to her and placed his hand on her shoulder. "Please tell me they are close. Although, I'll cross oceans to get to the motherfuckers."

"They are very close, Liege. Across the lake in Carnation, actually. At an old farm." She'd initially been surprised by their proximity, but then realized they wouldn't go far from the amulet.

"Och, that's less than an hour away. Shae, if you think you're up to it, I'd like to leave now. The longer we wait, the greater the risk they will move," Zander suggested.

The buzz of expectation was invigorating. "I'm more than ready to finish this. I'd ask you to save the archdemons for me, but I want them dead more than I need revenge."

"Good," Gerrick growled, the sound vibrating against her back, "because they're mine."

Plans were quickly made with minimum fuss. It was obvious they were accustomed to fighting together and didn't need to discuss a detailed approach. They were ready to leave within the hour, their efficiency amazing Shae.

Elsie touched the small bump in her stomach. "I wish I could go with you guys. It's not going to be easy staying behind when I have my own vengeance to collect. And, be extra careful guys, I still don't feel right and I don't know if it's because of the morning sickness or something else."

Zander kissed her temple and placed his hand over hers. "Jace said you and the *bairn* are healthy. And, doona forget that you've got the tougher job carrying our *mac*."

Elsie chuckled, "You know, *she* is going to take exception to being called a boy."

Zander kissed her on the forehead and held her close for a minute. "Alright, let's suit up and head oot. Someone find Rhett. We need him on this mission. Nate, you're staying to protect my mate."

Gerrick's breath ghosted across Shae's ear as he whispered, "When this is done, I am going to make you mine. I hope you know what you want for our mating ceremony because I refuse to wait." The husky promise in his words made her shiver with anticipation.

"I don't care as long as I'm with you, but I'm sure my mom and Nana will have an opinion on the matter." She silently prayed to the Goddess that what she'd seen was accurate. She wanted freedom. Not only freedom from their hold, but freedom to be with Gerrick.

CHAPTER 25

A buzzing had started in Shae's head a few miles back, telling her they were on the right track. Hoping to hide that they were on their way to the demons, Shae imagined that they were in Zeum's kitchen. If she could feel them, she worried they could feel her too and she didn't want to give them any clues about what they were up to.

Glancing out the tinted window at the scenery, Shae watched the trees give way to cow farms and open fields. They'd left the city and suburbs behind and were in the country. Not that Carnation was completely isolated, but there was more farmland than not and the houses were spread apart by acres along with clusters of small communities.

"Hey," Gerrick tugged on her ponytail for the fifth time. She'd put it up to keep it out of her face and was coming to realize that he enjoyed playing with the tail.

"I'm good," she reassured him. "I know to stay by your side. Look, there it is," she pointed to the white house in the distance. It was bigger than she expected. The front façade had at least ten windows that were covered by blue shutters. The two-story home had a wraparound porch and the wooden rocking chairs on it swayed in the wind. The scene was serene and there was nothing to indicate it was any different from the others they'd passed, yet, she could sense the evil seeping out of the structure.

Bhric pulled over behind another SUV and they climbed out into the chilly night air. Gerrick zipped up her jacket and cupped her face in his hands. "I love you with every inch of my shattered heart, Shae. Don't get hurt in there."

"I won't, I promise."

"Here, I have something for you." He reached into his jacket pocket and pulled out a silver necklace that had a charm hanging from it. The charm was a miniature tree of life. "I had this made for my Fated Mate centuries ago to represent harmony and balance in our mating. And, before you go there, I never gave it to Evanna. I had it made to symbolize my desire for my mating and want you to have it for the same reasons."

She held the delicate jewelry in her hand and waited for jealousy to hit, but it never did. This necklace wasn't about Evanna, but about Gerrick. She was touched to be given something with so much meaning. "I'm going to take this as a good omen for the outcome of tonight." She shoved her fear and doubt aside.

"Put it on me?" He took it from her and fastened it around her neck before kissing her jaw.

"Come on, everyone's waiting," he replied and led her to the larger crowd where Zander split them into two with her and Gerrick in his group.

"Kyran, you take the back and I'll go in the front. I can smell the lesser demons from here, so be careful. Our goal is to get Kadir and Azazel, but doona risk yourself to get to them. I want everyone going home alive."

Shae crouched behind Gerrick and picked her way over tree limbs and other debris. The closer they got, the more details became obvious. There were skirm and lesser demons on both floors of the house with Kadir and Azazel on the lower floor. They paused near a huge evergreen that towered fifty feet and Shae withdrew the knives Gerrick had given her before they left the house. The fading blue door looked intact and was shut.

A causal glance at the house would give the impression that a family lived there with the porch lights on and the tricycle and other toys scattered around the yard. Nausea churned in Shae's gut as she prayed they hadn't slaughtered the family that lived there.

Adrenaline raced through her veins as Zander and two others ambushed the door. Before she knew it, she was inside and facing chaos that only came with a battle. She'd seen it when she was rescued, but didn't really appreciate how the warriors actually fought under such circumstances until that moment. Silver glinted as blades were swung and black blood collided with red blood as weapons found their mark.

She caught sight of a pus demon about to launch at Mack and without hesitation she rushed to the female's side. Kicking out, she felt the familiar give of the slimy body while she thrust one of her knives into an eye socket. Mack, whose back had been to the pus demon, plunged her blade into a skirm's chest and swiveled, ready for action. "Damn, Shae, you're fast. Thanks for the save," the female said when she eyed the creature.

Shae nodded and looked for Gerrick. He was across the room, fighting to get to her side. Azazel was in the corner and the beast inside her wanted loose. She snuck around from the other side, intending to make him pay for every second of torture he'd heaped on her, but was hit from the side by a hellhound. She hit the floor, force knocking the wind out of her. She rolled over ready to attack, but Mack beat her to it and stabbed the beast through its chest.

"Take that, you piece of shit," Mack quipped, flashing a triumphant smile before taking off towards a group of skirm. Damn, she was a badass.

Panting, on her hands and knees, Shae spotted Azazel in the same location taunting the warriors. Enraged, she was on her feet and running in the next second. This demon would not live beyond tonight.

"Shae, my pet. Good of you to make it to the party," Azazel purred, his beautiful face appearing genuine as he sauntered around her, the picture of ease. She would never fall for that again. No, she wanted to claw his eyes, especially, when she knew what he wanted to do to her. She knew him well enough after her ordeal to predict where he would begin with her and each move after. There was no way in hell she was allowing that.

"I've told you," she grunted slashing out at him. "I'm not your anything. I'm here to kill you." She remembered the first time she had seen him. He'd rushed into the room where she was held and told her that he'd been running from the devil and he knew the way out. She was too frightened at the time and fell readily into his arms. He was a twisted demon that had enjoyed playing her.

"You can try, Shae, but you are my creature and in the end you will do what I bid. Do you think you found us by accident?" He rubbed his chin with a wry smile on his face.

Her blood turned to ice with his words. Had this been a trap? Had they set her up so she could lead Zander and the warriors to this house? Frantic, she turned searching for Gerrick or Zander. It was difficult to see beyond the fighting. "Trap!" she yelled. "It's a tr..." her voice was cut off when a clawed hand covered her mouth.

"Not so fast. I'm not done playing, yet." He ran a claw down the side of her face and throat, opening an old wound. She felt the blood trickle out in a hot stream. He lapped it up and moaned, "I've missed your sweet blood, pet." Her stomach revolted and knotted into a ball.

"Stop," she whimpered, not wanting this to happen. He had proven to her time and again that he was stronger than she was and she had no way to fight him.

"That's my good, Shae. I knew you missed our time together. I promise this time will be far better than anything that came before."

She was frozen by the fear of being in his grip. Her mind flashed back on the humility of being stripped bare then bitten and raped by the demon at her back. He had torn into her flesh while he decimated her mind and he was going to do it again, only this time she would die. And, Gerrick would never survive losing another mate. That thought was enough to snap her out of her stupor.

There was no way she was sacrificing her mate to this fate. She would go down fighting with everything she had.

Her hands still held the knives and in a swift move she swung back with all her might and buried the titanium into Azazel's stomach. His curse was satisfying as she managed to twist the weapons before he shoved her away. She stumbled and caught herself on the window. She left a bloody, black palm print and swiveled to engage the injured demon.

Intestines and organs were exposed, preventing a teleportation. She sneered at him, searching for a better weapon. The small blades wouldn't do much against an archdemon, but a couple feet away she noticed a claymore that had been discarded by someone. Without giving herself away, she inched her way to the sword. "How did you know we were coming?" she asked, drawing his attention.

"You thought your little stunt to track us would work?" he tsked her and shook his head in disappointment. "You should have known better than that, Shae. Once I discovered what you were going to do, I made sure the way was clear. It was positively orgasmic to have you so deep in my mind," he purred.

She choked on bile and glared at the vile creature. Only something of pure evil would be aroused by the suffering and control of another. "So, Kadir let you come here and take the fall for him? How gallant of him."

"Oh, no, he wouldn't have missed this. You are his favorite, Shae, so blood-thirsty." She didn't bother giving him the pleasure of getting riled over the obvious provocation.

She'd made her way to the weapon, but now she needed to perfectly time her retrieval. Azazel may be injured, but that didn't mean he was helpless. For all she knew, he was faking the severity to lull her into complacency.

"I don't see him coming to your aid. You do realize he will throw you to Lucifer at the first opportunity," she said, swooping down in a rapid move and bounced on the balls of her feet, emboldened by her small victory.

Tossing the sword from hand to hand, she walked towards Azazel. "I've waited a long time for this. I just wish I could make you suffer the way you made me suffer. Sadly, I'll have to settle for killing you."

"You aren't strong enough to take out the likes of me." She clutched her head when he blasted into her mind and tried to command her to turn her weapon on Zander. Fuck that, she was done being messed with.

Dropping her hand, she gripped the sword and swung in a wide arch. The metal whistled through the air and sliced clean through skin, muscle and bone. Azazel's shocked face rolled from his body and his headless form collapsed seconds later. "Looks like you were wrong. Just sayin'," she growled in satisfaction.

GERRICK PULLED the fury demon close, careful to keep a lid on his anger. The last thing any of them wanted to do was feed the furies. He wrapped his arm around its neck and glanced around frantically for Shae. They'd been separated as soon as they'd entered the house.

Teeth sank into his forearm and he twisted, breaking vertebrae until he felt the fury go limp. It wasn't dead yet and Gerrick kept twisting until the head popped off like a grape. Tossing it away, he searched for Shae.

Zander was facing of a pus demon and a hellhound and Kyran was helping Mack with a half dozen skirm, but Shae wasn't with them. Suddenly, he saw Shae go flying toward the window. He pushed his way through the crowd, keeping his eyes trained on her as she approached Azazel. He howled when she stopped suddenly and clutched her head. The bastard was trying to control her. A skirm stepped into his path and he ashed him without a thought. He made it to Shae just as she relieved Azazel of his head.

He watched as she stared down at one of her personal demons. "Shae," he called out, yanking her into an embrace.

"Duck," she snapped and he didn't hesitate to follow her

command. Burning liquid landed on the back of his neck and Gerrick knew she'd killed whatever snuck up on him.

"Stay close this time." He didn't have time to wait for her answer as he engaged a hellhound that was slavering for them. Strong jaws clamped around his leg. He stabbed his *sgian dubh* into the animal's skull repeatedly until it went limp and Shae used her Claymore to cleave the skull.

They fought back to back and took out demon after demon, but more kept coming, making Gerrick wonder if there was an open portal to the hell realm with how many there were.

"It was a trap," Shae explained as if she'd heard his thoughts. "The trap backfired on the asshole though, didn't it?"

Gerrick chuckled at the pride in her tone. "He should know better than to fuck with my female. She's ferocious and sexy as hell."

By that point, the floor was slick with blood and it was becoming difficult to fight. The yellow walls were splattered with black and red and he wondered how his fellow warriors were faring.

Fatigued, his arm was shaking as he lifted his hand to take out a skirm. With how tired he was, he couldn't understand how Shae was continuing to fight with such vigor. She was a thing of beauty in action, but he wasn't like Kyran. He never wanted to see her fight like this ever again.

Out of the blue, an ice missile flew past his head and he heard Bhric cursing, "Feel the freeze motherfuckers." He turned and saw Bhric and Breslin fighting together with Rhett at their back. He opened his mouth to warn them, but Breslin had seen the pus demon trying to sneak up on Rhett. Gerrick grimaced when the green, slimy flesh exploded from Breslin's firebomb. A second later the stench of burning pus reached his nose and almost made him hurl.

He grabbed two swords and ran up a couple stairs then paused taking in the scene. "Come get me," he taunted those nearby who could hear him. When several had noticed him and broke off from the pack, he launched himself into the air and held his arms akimbo. He managed to remove the tops of a couple skulls and cut one demon in half during his descent down the stairs.

Sweat was pouring into his eyes and he had to use his forearm to clear his vision. When he looked up, his heart stopped. Kadir was standing beside Shae and held a knife to her throat. And Gerrick was too far away to get to her in time.

"Did you bring the amulet? That's the only thing that will save your Shae now."

Gerrick threw up his hands in surrender and tried to reason with the archdemon. "I don't have that kind of access. Trade me for Shae."

Shae's eyes went wide. "No, Gerrick. He'll kill you."

"You have bigger problems than me killing him right now, Shae. One twist and I liberate your head from your shoulders. It's a shame really. I had such big hopes for you," Kadir hissed as his razor-sharp black claws ran over her cheek.

"Sorry to disappoint you," Shae sneered while Gerrick tried to signal Zander to come up behind Kadir and attack.

"Like you disappointed Azazel? I must say your temerity is surprising, but not altogether unpleasant. Now, warrior, get me the Triskele Amulet and I may let her go."

"Zander will never trade the amulet for me, Kadir," Shae spat. "You don't hold the bargaining chip you'd hoped. Your trap backfired and now Azazel is home telling Lucifer how you've failed."

Kadir shrugged one large grey shoulder, his red hair lifting with the action. "Seems I have no more use for you then," he murmured, plunging his fist through Shae's throat, pulling her head from her shoulders.

Gerrick's entire world stopped and his heart shattered into a million pieces. One tear escaped from Shae's eye as Kadir tossed her head into the melee. Kadir was barking orders before he disappeared, but it was lost on Gerrick as he caught Shae's body before it hit the floor.

CHAPTER 26

E verything in the room seemed to stop the second Rhys heard his fellow warrior roar in anguish. It was Gerrick and the agony he heard in the howl sent him to his knees. He looked to his friend who was holding the lifeless body of his Fated Mate. Rhys' heart stopped as he saw the scene. Gerrick had lost a mate before and didn't deserve to suffer like this again. Rhys' heart ached for the male. One thing was certain, Gerrick was about to lose his shit and Rhys needed to help him.

Stumbling to his feet, Rhys grabbed onto the banister to steady himself. Instantly, white light surrounded him before three familiar figures appeared around him. The melee around him continued, but no one reacted to the newcomers. It was then that he glanced around and recognized the signs of the spell the angels had cast last time they'd cornered him.

"In case you hadn't noticed, now's not a really good time. Either pick up a sword and start fighting these demons, like a real angel should, or get the fuck out of here," Rhys snarled.

The black-haired angel's eyes widened as he got his first full glimpse of the battle. "We felt death surround you and feared it was Illianna. What is going on here?"

Rhys stiffened when the angel mentioned Illianna's death. The idea bothered Rhys more than it should at the moment. "Let me the fuck out of this bubble of bull-shit, my best friend just lost his Fated Mate and is one second from losing his shit. He needs me."

The blond-haired angel glanced at him curiously, "Why are you fighting your own kind, demon?"

"I am *not* a demon, asshole. I'm a cambion and my allegiance is to the Dark Warriors and the Goddess, I told you fuckers that already. Damn, not too many brains in those feathers. Now let me out of here. You may be okay with demons killing innocent beings, but I'm not."

"You dare impugn a warrior angel?" the brown-haired angel roared. "We were born to fight demons, just like you."

"Not now, Abraxos. This demon is right. We are needed to help in this fight," the black-haired angel chastised.

"We're going to fight beside a demon, Ayil?" Abraxos asked, incredulous.

"Of course we are. Gabriel would have our heads if we ignore our duty. We didn't kill this scourge before because we didn't sense evil in him. That hasn't changed," the blond added, placing his palm on Abraxos' shoulder.

Abraxos lowered his head and glanced askance at his blond brother. Rhys watched the exchange raptly. It made sense to him that they were warriors. Their demeanor reminded him of Zander and the Dark Warriors. "Thank you Araton. I lose my head when it comes to Illianna," Abraxos said then turned to Rhys, "We know you're involved with our missing sister somehow and we won't stop until we know."

"I'm not involved with your sister, but I respect your sense of loyalty and my offer of help finding her stands once I've dealt with this fiasco. Speaking of, can you save Shae? Gerrick is one of our best warriors and has the purest heart of anyone I've known. He deserves to have a lifetime with his mate."

Ayil stepped toward Rhys and looked at where Gerrick sat holding Shae's body. "I'm truly sorry. You're right about his heart being pure. We may not be able to save the female, but we will help clear the hoard of demons that are waiting outside. We can't allow your fellow warriors to see us." With that they disappeared along with the white light and Rhys was suddenly hit from behind by a skirm. Bastards could have warned him, Rhys thought, summoning the *sgian dubh* on the floor to his hand.

GERRICK THREW BACK his head and roared his anguish to the heavens, hoping the Goddess heard him. He was living another nightmare, only this was so much worse. It was his fault. He never should have allowed Shae to come on this mission. He should have listened to that feral part of him that wanted to lock her in the room, keeping her safe. He hadn't heeded the warning and now she was dead.

He held her close to his chest, unable to reconcile the events with reality. He didn't want to believe she was gone. There was no way he could go one minute without seeing her smile and hearing her laugh. He'd been trapped in a dark torment of his own making until she came into his life. Goddess, but he needed her more than he needed air to breathe.

He heard Zander talking to him, but he wasn't listening.

Shae had sacrificed herself and now his chest was being ripped wide open as the portion of her soul he carried vanished. He felt her death in every cell of his body. His mate mark that had been a hot blaze on his leg disappeared. He knew from experience it was because the mate mark was gone, leaving no trace of her existence. The agony of her loss was unbearable and there was no relief. It would be more pleasant to take a bath in acid.

His heart stopped for several beats in objection. Shae couldn't be gone. He was nothing without her. No fucking way was he sitting by and allowing this to happen.

Zander grabbed his shoulders and shook him. "We need to get out of here. They've set the house on fire."

Gerrick glanced down and bile rose in his throat. He saw Shae's pink sweater peeking out the top of her jacket. The necklace he'd given her had fallen off her neck and was on the ground. He picked it up and clutched it in his hand. "I'm not going anywhere," he declared, a plan formulating in his mind.

Zander gripped his upper arms and pulled. "Did you hear me? The house is on fire and we need to go, now. I'm no' letting you kill yourself, Gerrick."

"You don't have a fucking choice, Zander. I can't live without her." He wouldn't live without her.

"Gerrick, doona do this. Shae wouldna want you to kill yourself."

"I know. I don't plan on killing myself. I'm going back to try and save her. I've got a ten-minute window. That will be enough."

Zander gaped at him wide-eyed and his jaw dropped open. He snapped to attention a second later. "Och, what can I do to help?"

Gerrick forced himself to calm and replay the events

that led up to Shae's death. He replayed every move he made and pinpointed the location of everyone in the room. He nearly got lost in the crushing grief of the moment Kadir took everything from him, but the urgency to save her kept him going.

"Where are Bhric and Rhett?" he asked, glancing around.

"Right here," Bhric replied, coming into view with Rhett next to him.

"Right before Kadir killed Shae you two were the closest to them. I'm going back in time to save her, but I won't be able to do that without help from you guys. I was too far away to reach her, but you were right there. I need you to turn around and throw whatever power you have at Kadir the moment he appears. Kyran, I need you to sift to Shae and get her out of there the second they attack Kadir."

The plan was risky, but if they worked together, they might be successful. The plan had to work. If not, he didn't plan on leaving the burning building. He couldn't go through a single day without Shae in his life.

Zander stood up. "How does this work?"

"You're going to have to watch and learn. There's no time." Gerrick was grateful that he had gone through this before or he would not have been able to time-trace under the circumstances. He was also thankful that Evanna had come into his life because she was the one that helped hone his ability.

He laid Shae's body on the floor and stood up. "Keep clear of me. I have no idea what will happen if someone is touching me after I begin."

Gerrick closed his eyes and went inside his mind. He had discovered his ability when he was a stripling and asked his mother what was in the locked box he'd discovered in his mind. Even at a young age, he knew it wasn't something everyone possessed. Thankfully, the trait ran in his family and she was able to explain that he was a time-tracer and he should never open the box unless it was a dire emergency because using the gift carried severe consequences. He reached mental fingers to the lock, not giving a second thought to what the consequences might be of going back to save Shae.

In his opinion, the Goddess could pay it for him. He cursed her for putting him through this not once, but twice. There was only so much one male could go through. Ultimately, he knew he would be the one that suffered, but he didn't give a shit. He would gladly pay any price to have her back.

He unlocked the box and flipped the top open. A burst of white light filled the room and when it subsided, the room was moving in slow motion and it was almost as if Zander and the others were ghosts. A heartbeat later, everything was going in reverse at a speed too fast for Gerrick to track. He closed his eyes and waited for the world to settle around him.

He blinked and found himself standing on the stairs right before he jumped and took out several demons. He quickly closed the box and locked down his power. He looked up and saw Shae was alone, but that wouldn't last long. Bhric and Rhett were in the middle of the fury demons, but weren't moving to help Shae.

Kadir appeared in the next instant and Gerrick jumped, calling out to Shae. She turned to him, but wasn't able to avoid Kadir. Still Bhric and Rhett didn't react. What the fuck? A sickening thought struck Gerrick. What if they didn't remember his orders? After all, he was the only one who traveled back in time.

Kadir asked him about the amulet and Gerrick knew his time was running out. If he didn't save Shae this time, he wouldn't be given another chance. He dropped the sword and pulled a *sgian dubh* from the back of his pants and threw it at Bhric's back. The warrior roared his rage and Kadir was momentarily distracted.

Bhric turned, eyes black as night. Gerrick winced as a fury demon bit into Bhric's shoulder. "Get Shae from Kadir!" he yelled, seeing the moment the Vampire Prince saw Shae. Gerrick sighed in relief as Bhric surged into action. It wasn't a done deal, but he had hope of saving Shae this time.

Gerrick was running across the room, pushing skirm and fellow warriors out of his way while looking for Kyran. He needed him to sift and get Shae to safety. He spotted Kyran down a hall next to Mack. "Kyran!"

The warrior looked over and Gerrick pointed to Shae. "Get her."

Chaos ensued as Bhric lobbed ice missiles at Kadir while Rhett fought the fury demons. By that time, everyone was aware that Shae was in trouble. It was good to be part of such a loyal group, Gerrick thought, as the focus shifted to keeping the enemies at bay while he tried to reach Shae.

Kyran appeared behind the archdemon with his sword in motion before Gerrick knew what was happening. Blood bloomed across Shae's shoulder right before she fell to the floor. At first, Gerrick thought they were too late, but then he saw her crawl away from the fighting.

Disbelief stunned him. He had fucking done it. He had saved Shae!

Gerrick reached her side and pulled her into his arms at the same time Kadir disappeared, leaving behind his severed arm. "Oh my Goddess, Shae. I lost you," he sobbed into her shoulder.

Soft hands that he never thought he'd feel again cupped his face. Shae lifted onto her tiptoes and pressed her lips to his. "You haven't lost me, but we're in the middle of a battle," she quirked, flashing him the most vibrant smile he'd ever seen.

She was right, now was not the time. Just because Kadir was gone didn't meant they were out of danger. "This time, don't leave my side, Shae. Do you hear me?"

She picked up a chair leg and swung it at a hellhound. "Wouldn't dream of it."

"I love you, Red."

She stuck the makeshift weapon through the hound's ear and grimaced. "I love you, too, Gerrick. Just sayin'."

Gerrick handed her his knife, his heart swelling at hearing her declaration. He kicked and punched, disabling enemies for Shae to finish off. His side ached and his strength was waning. He had used up his reserves time-tracing and was going to be useless in a minute.

He pulled her behind him and they made their way to Zander's side. "I want that arm for a souvenir," Shae told Bhric as he used Kadir's severed limb to club a fury demon to death.

Bhric chuckled. "I knew there was a reason I liked you."

The floor looked like a toddler's finger painting with all the black and red blood. There were so many bodies strewn about that it made being efficient nearly impossible. Shae jumped onto the carcass of a hellhound and fought from that position. Gerrick was going to lose an arm himself if he didn't pay attention, but he couldn't keep his eyes from straying back to make sure she was still there.

They were down to the last few lesser demons and all the skirm had been killed. A pus demon and a hellhound tried to run out the front door, but Bhric froze them in place.

Frozen drool was hanging from the hound's jowls, making Gerrick chuckle. It was such a different culmination to the battle than before where the house was burning around him while he cradled his dead mate.

Somehow he didn't think it was a good sign that things were going so smoothly and he wondered when he would pay for using his ability. He decided not to worry about that at the moment. They made quick work of the remaining enemies and Gerrick had Shae in his arms in the next instant.

He took her mouth in a rough kiss. He was crushing her to his chest, where he realized her soul had returned. He kissed her with all the anger and elation that was tearing him up inside. She ran her hands up his back in calming strokes. He felt tears behind his closed eyes and welcomed the persistent burn of his mate mark. The bond was there and stronger than ever.

He broke the kiss and buried his face in her hair. Cold sweat covered his skin with the remembered loss. He listened to her heart thud strong and sure beneath his ear. She was warm and lush and alive in his arms. He would never forget the feel of her cold, lifeless body. It would haunt his dreams for centuries to come and made his heart pound so hard he thought it was going to explode. He held her tighter, not able to let go.

"Shh. It's ok. I'm okay. It's over, although we still didn't get Kadir. I really wish he were lying in this heap of bodies," Shae observed as she looked around the house.

Gerrick lifted his head, his blood boiling in his veins at the thought of the archdemon. "Kadir will pay for what he did. Do you still feel him in your head?"

Shae tilted her head to the side and went silent. She blinked several times and then a huge smile broke over her face. "No. I don't feel them at all! Gerrick, they're gone." She jumped into his arms and peppered his face with kisses.

"Do you think it's because I killed Azazel?" she asked, wrapping her arms around his neck.

"I'm not sure. Let's get out of here. I want to take you home and make love to you."

"Hmmm," she hummed. "I like the sound of that. But, what about this mess?"

Gerrick shrugged his shoulders and started walking out the front door. "I say we burn the motherfucker."

Bhric clapped him on the shoulder. "I like how you think."

All of the Dark Warriors gathered on the front lawn and Gerrick was glad to see that none of them had been injured too badly. Rhett and Breslin had just set the house on fire when Shae touched her throat and gasped. "Wait, we have to stop the fire. Gerrick, my necklace is gone."

He set her down and reached into his front pocket and pulled it out, dangling it from his finger. "It fell off when Kadir took your head." Turning her around, he placed it back where it belonged around her neck.

She had gone pale and was gazing up at him in disbelief. In fact, the entire group fell silent, only the crackle of the fire could be heard. "What are you talking about?" she whispered, clearly confused.

Zander was aware of his ability and had crossed to their sides the moment he heard Gerrick's comment. Gerrick cleared his throat, finding it impossible to speak past the lump. After several tries, Gerrick was finally able to tell them about her being killed and his time-tracing.

"I can't believe I was dead," she mumbled, looking lost. He pulled her to him and cradled her head against his chest.

Zander ran his hand through his hair and lowered his

head. "Bluidy hell. There aren't words for what you went through, Gerrick. I canna believe Kadir slipped away once again. That fucker is worse than a case of black mold. We can't seem to get rid of him. I'm just glad you saved Shae."

Gerrick wrapped his hand around the back of Shae's neck, reassuring himself she was okay. He'd be doing that the rest of his life. There was no erasing the trauma. "I wouldn't be standing here right now if I hadn't. In time, my heart may go back to a normal rhythm, but for right now, I just want to take my mate to bed."

Zander held his gaze and Gerrick saw his friend's worry and relief over his well-being. "You once told me there was a cost for using your power. What was it this time?"

Gerrick grabbed Shae's hand and blew out a breath. "Well, nothing as obvious as a scarred face. I'm sure the Goddess is working on it."

Shae smacked his chest. "Don't you ever put yourself at risk like that again! And, if I ever hear you talking about ending your life, I will do it for you. Do you know what it would do to me to lose you?"

He began walking to the car, pulling her along, ready to reaffirm in the most primal way possible, that she was alive and well. "Yes, I do know, Shae, and I never want to feel that pain again. I would trade my life for yours in a heartbeat, Red. That's what mate's do, so get over it. We have a mating ceremony to plan and I need you naked in my bed. Just sayin'," he teased and Shae burst into laughter.

CHAPTER 27

E very one of Shae's muscles hurt, the night had taken its toll on her physically, as well as, emotionally. She wondered how much of what she was feeling was due to dying and coming back to life. The events Gerrick had described were unbelievable. She kept feeling her throat. It boggled her mind that a few hours ago she didn't have a head. She knew Gerrick wasn't lying with the way he had clung to her.

The desperation in the clasp he had on her hand told her he was afraid she was going to disappear. She patted his chest, letting him know she understood. If he had died, she would have lost her mind completely and she would have had no way to save him.

He unlocked their door and stopped her before she got too far inside the room. He cupped her cheek and glowing ice-blue eyes gazed down at her from a face that had come to be her entire world. "I keep expecting this to be a dream. My heart hasn't stopped racing from the fear that I will wake and find you gone. I need to make love to you."

She turned to face him fully and wrapped her hands

around the back of his neck. "I'm not going anywhere without you, Gerrick. I want to make love to you, too, but I really need a shower. Or, better yet, a long soak in the bathtub."

He leaned down and pressed his lips to hers. His flesh was warm and soft as it meshed with hers and it ignited her arousal. "Give me ten minutes," he whispered.

He nudged her onto the sofa and knelt before her to take her boots off. He massaged one foot and then the other before her caressed her cheek. "Don't move." He hurried out of the room before she could respond. She stared at the open door wondering what he was up to. She nearly got up to check on him, but stopped herself, deciding to wait and see what he had planned.

She laid her head back on the sofa and closed her eyes, enjoying the peace and quiet. It hadn't been quiet in her head for months. The demons had been in the back of her mind urging her to take action for so long that she didn't remember what it was like to be alone in her mind. The relief of not having the constant pressure and chatter in the background was unbelievable.

It was so quiet and she was so tired that she nearly fell asleep, until she heard him come back into the room. She cracked open an eye and watched as he continued walking through to the bedroom without saying a word. What was he up to and what was a warrior's idea of a surprise?

"Don't go to sleep on me." The husky voice had her snapping her eyes open. Gerrick was barefoot in nothing but his low-slung black jeans. She couldn't help but admire the God before her. His muscular chest tapered to wash-board abs. She smirked at the slight tension that entered his body.

She lifted her gaze and noticed he was holding his hand

out to her with a sexy grin on his face. "Where are you taking me?" She climbed to her feet and slid her hand into his, letting him lead her into the bedroom.

Figuring his intention, her blood began to hum with anticipation. Sure, she wanted to be clean, but that was fast coming in second to her need for him. Her brows furrowed when he took them past the bed and toward the bathroom. She perked up at the thought of taking a shower with him.

He pushed open the door and stood aside for her to enter. Tears misted in her eyes as she saw the scene he had prepared. The room was dark except for the light given off by the dozen, lit candles scattered around. Red rose petals covered the floor and there was a bubble bath in the giant Jacuzzi tub. The steam rising off the water was an enticing sight.

"Gerrick, this is the sweetest thing anyone has ever done for me. I've never been spoiled like this before. You'd better watch it or I might get used to it," she teased, stepping so close she felt the heat from his body. In fact, there was more steam coming off of him than the hot water.

Reaching out, he tugged the hem of her sweater over her head, tossing it in the corner and placed a kiss on her shoulder. "I hope you do get used to this. I plan to do this for you every chance I get."

He rubbed her back lightly, placing kisses across her shoulder to her neck and throat. She was lost to his mouth when she felt her bra pop open. She gasped at the unexpected sensation of his hand covering the middle of her back. She'd been thinking about how his lips were leaving a burning trail of desire in their wake. She'd never realized her shoulder was an erogenous zone until Gerrick placed his soft lips there, igniting arousal with one kiss.

She dropped her arms, letting her bra fall to the floor.

"You won't get any complaints out of me. Just sayin'," she whispered, lost to his touch. He took a step back and his eyes drank her in, pausing over her naked breasts. His gaze felt like a caress across her sensitive flesh.

"You are an exquisite creature. And, you're all mine." He claimed her mouth once again and took his time kissing her. He was such an intense male and he kissed with the same intensity he did everything else. He mastered her mouth and demanded entry.

Already a puddle in his arms, she willingly gave him everything. He took full advantage, sliding his tongue into the hot cavern of her mouth, cradling her head in his hands as he tasted every corner. He claimed everything, even her very breath. By the time he eased back from the kiss, she was breathless and lightheaded, drunk on him.

His masculine groan sounded against the column of her bared neck and she felt it all the way to her toes and she noted that he was just as out of breath and aroused. The bulge pressing against his zipper looked painful and she reached out to give him some relief.

He stopped her hands and brought them to his chest. "Don't move. For every moment of pain you've suffered, I plan to give you hours of pleasure. And, by my calculations I will never be done. Zander will be lucky if we ever leave this room." His dominance and command made her core weep with desire.

That sounded perfect to her. "We could stay naked. It would save a lot of money on clothes. I imagine you go through a fair amount of leathers with what you do."

He chuckled and led her to the edge of the tub. "I don't want you ever fighting again, Red. I know some of the other females fight in the battles, but I can't handle you being in harm's way like that again."

He trailed a finger down her chest and paused at the snap to her jeans. He unbuttoned the top and then pushed down the zipper. More of her arousal seeped from her body and her insides were quivering. She needed him desperately.

"You have given me a reason to live, Gerrick. For so long, I wanted nothing more than to return to the Goddess and now she has given me my own little piece of *Annwyn*. I will guard you and us ferociously; otherwise, I have no desire to fight. Elsie asked me to be part of Elsie's Hope and I am going to accept her offer. I don't need anything else, but you."

Through their bond she felt his joy and relief over her response. He gave her that smile of his, "I love you, Red. With all my heart."

"I love you, too."

With the lightest of touches, she felt his hands push down her pants, taking her panties with them. He pushed her down onto the edge of the tub. "Sit."

He crouched in front of her and spread her thighs apart with gentle hands. She nearly came unglued when he lowered his head and his tongue slid through her slick folds. Hands flew to his hair and she fisted handfuls of the silky blonde strands. His tongue was relentless as he licked and nibbled her. Gone was the gentle lover and in its place was the raw animal she'd become addicted to.

He grabbed her legs and threw them over his shoulders, forcing her to let go of his hair and grip the side of the tub. He looked up at her, his face bare inches from her aching core. "You smell like lavender and taste sweet like nectar. I could feast on you for centuries and never get enough. If I resigned my post as a warrior, would you forever let me stay right where I am?"

"Goddess, yes. And, please stop teasing me. I need you inside me."

"All in good time, Red." His mouth glistened with her arousal as he perched between her thighs. The sight of him made her pant. "Goddess, I love your fangs. I haven't had a chance to explore them, yet. I want them buried in my neck while I fuck you."

The image had her at the edge of climax. His tongue continued its erotic torment. One hand pulled and plucked one of her nipples while the other went between her legs. As he sucked her clit into his mouth, he inserted two fingers into her core, scissoring his fingers. Blue light danced along his digits and into her body while she felt the vibration from his magic against her clit. The slight pain was just what she needed to splinter into a million pieces.

"I want your pants off." With shaking hands, she fumbled with his waistband. She could love him with her whole heart now and that changed things between them. They had always been explosive together, but now it was so much more.

She finally managed to get his pants undone and shoved them to his ankles. He kicked them off as she came to her feet. His cock stood thick and strong between them. He picked her up and stepped into the hot bath. The water played at her skin as he sat down with her on his lap, adding another layer of sensation to the experience.

His hands were splayed across her back in a blatant possession. He was claiming his territory. She settled on her knees and purposefully rubbed against his erection.

"You are perfect," he told her as he placed a kiss to her scarred throat. He made sure she knew he loved every inch of her. She'd hated her appearance after her ordeal and thought she would be a social outcast the rest of her life, but Gerrick made her feel feminine and attractive, sexy even.

She came alive in his arms. "You're too good to me." She undulated her hips, teasing her slick feminine flesh around his throbbing shaft.

He surged forward, causing ripples in the water and closed his hot mouth around one of her distended nipples. He sucked on her deeply, grabbed onto her hips and took control, encouraging a faster pace. She cried out, needing more.

She pulled his head up and cupped his scarred cheek. She kissed him as she lost herself in his rhythm. Breaking away to catch her breath, she thought of his comment about her fangs and ran them over his pulse.

"Do it. Bite me," he ordered.

"You want my fangs?"

"You know I do."

"Have you ever been bitten?"

He shuddered beneath her. "Never. Never even wanted to before you."

She smiled, thinking this was something she could give him that neither of them had ever experienced. She'd fed countless times throughout her life, but had never bitten anyone during sex.

She sank her fangs into his neck and he jerked in her hold. "Holy shit," he breathed. Her mate mark was soothed the instant his blood hit her tongue and electricity sizzled in her veins.

"I'm going to fuck you," he declared, positioning his cock at her opening. Inch by inch he stretched her, pushing inside. She'd feared she would never enjoy sex again after her months in the hands of the demons, but Gerrick had proved she could experience so much more.

He promised her hours of pleasure to make up for her suffering, but it took only a minute with him and it was all forgotten. Unable to allow his leisurely pace, she impaled herself onto him and he cried out. "Fuck, Shae."

She removed her fangs from his flesh and watched the blood trickle out of the punctures before she licked the area, sealing them. "That's the point and you were going too slow."

"I'll show you slow." He lifted her up and bent her over the side of the tub.

He knelt behind her, placed his legs between her body, spreading her as wide as he could and reentered in one long thrust. He felt even bigger from this angle. He hit a part of her that had her toes curling and close to orgasm. Gripping her hips, he thrust back into her and pounded her hard and fast. He grabbed onto a breast and played with her sensitive nipple.

He leaned over her and his other hand slid around her hip to tunnel in her thatch of curls. "You okay, Red?" Unable to speak, she nodded her head and he leaned down and bit her neck without breaking the skin. The sound of flesh slapping flesh echoed throughout the room, adding to the eroticism.

Her body short-circuited the second he pinched her clit and she detonated again. Every move made him pull on the distended nub. He increased his pace and she felt the swelling at the middle of his shaft that indicated he was close.

She reached back and grabbed a fistful of his hair while her other hand went between their legs. She found the taut skin of his scrotum and squeezed gently. Every muscle at her back went tense and he threw back his head, roaring his release. He ejaculated in hot streams into her convulsing womb. Someday she would become pregnant with their child and she found that she liked the idea.

Panting, he collapsed onto her back. He lifted his head and kissed the back of her shoulder.

She looked around and laughed. "We got water all over the floor."

"I don't care," he said, separating their bodies. He stood and picked her up, carrying her with him. "I'm taking you to our bed now."

"And, I'm never letting you go."

"Never," he echoed dropping her onto the mattress. She bounced a couple times and laughed, her heart light and free for the first time in what seemed like forever.

He crawled nude onto the bed and settled next to her. He lay on his side, supporting his head on his hand. He traced lazy patterns across her stomach and ribcage. "How does one week from today sound for the mating ceremony?" He walked his fingers between her bare breasts and toyed with the necklace he'd given her.

"I think I can pull it together that quick. My mom and Nana have probably already planned the damned thing since you told them I belonged to you." She smiled at the thought of him telling her family the news. It had taken a bit for her to get over the anger of him sharing the news without her, but she didn't blame him. A supernatural in the throes of the mating compulsion was a protective, possessive being, driven by primal instincts. "Where are we going to have it?"

She shivered and snuggled closer to his side. She preferred the heat coming off his body to a blanket. "The only mating ceremonies we've had have been held here at Zeum, in the enclosed patio. Zander and the Dark Warriors are the only family I have and I'd like to have it here, if that's ok. There's enough room here to invite whoever you'd like."

"Having it here sounds wonderful. My parents and grandparents will be beside themselves to be in the presence of the royal family."

"Good, because I want to shout to the whole world that you belong to me. I should let you get some rest," he murmured, climbing on top of her. His big body blocked the entire world out as his weight settled on her and his erection prodded her inner thigh. "But, I can't get enough of you and I'm going to fuck you again." Her toes curled in anticipation, all of her fatigue vanishing in an instant.

CHAPTER 28

A million butterflies swarmed in Shae's stomach as she followed her mother and Nana down the hall. She was about to be mated to Gerrick and become an official member of Zeum. Her Nana stopped her in the large kitchen where the staff was busy preparing food for the party that would follow the ceremony.

"I want you to have this," Nana said, placing a brooch on her dress above her left breast. It was a beautiful platinum spray with pearls and diamonds that Shae remembered playing dress-up with many times when she was a young stripling. "My mother gave it to me many centuries ago and I know you love it."

For the hundredth time that day, Shae felt tears fill her eyes and emotion clog her throat. "Oh, Nana. Thank you, this means the world to me. I promise to take good care of it."

Her mother touched the jeweled comb that was holding Shae's hair off her neck. Her mother had given it to her earlier that day. "You look beautiful, sweetheart." Shae reached up and touched her neck. She hadn't wanted to put her hair up because it left her scarred neck on clear display for everyone to see. But, her mom and Nana, along with the females in the compound had insisted, saying it was a beautiful part of who she was. In the end, it was the way Gerrick always made sure to kiss the marks in a display of his affection that made her decision.

"Stop that. Wear them proudly," her mother insisted, pushing her hand aside. "Now, come on, your mate is waiting."

Shae nodded and smoothed her hands down the front of her dress. It may have been incredibly old-fashioned, but she'd chosen to continue family tradition and was wearing the silk and lace gown her Nana and mother had worn at their mating ceremonies. The dress was still a crisp white silk with off-the-shoulder lace sleeves. She hadn't ever dreamed of wearing it because no one had believed the mating curse would ever be lifted, but here she was, about to be mated.

Her Nana stopped in the entryway and placed a hand to her bosom. "Oh, my, look at how handsome the King and his brothers are in their traditional, Scottish wear. It has been many centuries since I've seen men in kilts."

She laughed at her Nana and gave her a one-armed hug. "Don't let Papa hear you say that. He might start an inter-species war by attacking the Vampire King."

Her mother rolled her eyes and waved her hand dismissively. "Come on, mother. They're waiting for us."

Shae didn't see them walk away from her because the sight of Gerrick caught her. He stood next to Zander and although the Vampire King was a good-looking male, he paled in comparison to Gerrick. Gerrick's blonde hair was in careless disarray and he was wearing a black tuxedo with a silver vest and tie.

He turned, catching her eyeing him hungrily and gave her that smile of his that always had her in a puddle. She was moving and at his side before she knew she was in motion. Shae noticed that they were standing on the tiled image of the Triskele Amulet. Gerrick grabbed her hand and brought it to his lips and placed a kiss on her flesh.

She shivered in anticipated of the blood exchange that would occur after the party. Her fangs erupted into her mouth as she watched the pulse in his throat. The butterflies in her stomach turned to lava, heating her insides. The blood exchange would complete the bond between them, linking them together forever. Only then would the pain in her mate mark stop and the brand transform into a tattoo.

"Friends and family please form a circle around the couple," Zander instructed, removing the amulet from around his neck. The King met Elsie's eyes across the circle, clearly sharing a private moment. Shae wondered if they were thinking about their own mating ceremony or perhaps the life that was growing inside Elsie.

"We have gathered here in this beautiful place, under the eye of the Sun and the glow of the Moon. Let the circle be blessed and consecrated with Fire and Water," Zander recited in a clear, deep voice.

Bhric and Breslin stepped forward and with a flourish, fire shot forth from Breslin's outstretched palm to flow around the outskirts of the circle. The fire rose from the earth to the heavens, like shooting stars. Bhric raised his hands and water cascaded down in a sheer waterfall, from heaven back to the earth, extinguishing the fire. The sight took Shae's breath away. She'd never seen such a spectacular display.

Zander lifted the amulet in one hand and held out their stone in the other. "We call to the Goddess Morrigan, and invoke her to bless this mating." Zander smiled broadly at her and Gerrick, placing their mating stone into Gerrick's hand. Shae gasped at the electrical pulses that crawled up her arm when Zander grabbed her hand and placed it, palm down, over Gerrick's and the stone.

As he chanted, Shae noticed that Zander's power was tangible throughout the room. "We call upon the spirits of the East, of Air, Spring and new beginnings. We call upon the spirits of the South and the inner Fire of the Sun, Summer and personal will. We call upon the spirits of the West, of Water, Autumn, and healing and dreaming. We call upon the spirits of the North, of Earth, Winter, and the time of cleansing and renewal. Join us to bless this couple with your guidance and inspiration," Zander recited. Magic cocooned Shae and Gerrick and emotion choked her while she watched her mate. This male carried the missing piece of her soul and did more to make her feel whole then he would ever know.

Zander lifted his hand from where he had joined theirs, leaving theirs clasped together, surrounding the stone. Gerrick grabbed her other hand and placed it on his chest, over his heart, then placed his free hand over hers. His heart pounded so hard, she swore it was trying to jump out of his chest and into hers.

"I bless this mating under the Sun and the Moon. This circle of love and honour is open and never broken, so may it be," Zander's voice resonated with the blessing.

Heat built in the stone as she felt both souls leave her body to enter the stone. She had lived for so long with the comfort of Gerrick's soul and she was going to miss it. That was the case for all supernaturals, but it was more for her given how Gerrick's soul had helped her survive those months of torture. A small, selfish part of her prayed to the

Goddess, asking that she be allowed to keep Gerrick's soul with her always.

A brilliant light flashed between their fingers and her skin tingled with the magic of the mating. The connection she felt to Gerrick fortified, and she could now see the bond between them, plain as day. A thick, golden ribbon wrapped around her heart and ran to his, entwining them. Her soul surged back into her body at that moment, causing her to gasp. Looking up, she saw the elation and wonder she felt mirrored in Gerrick's eyes.

Shae watched the emotions cross Gerrick's face and saw when he realized he wasn't going to lose her. His eyes narrowed with intent and his body unconsciously leaned toward her. Reaching up, he cupped the scarred side of her throat and mouthed the word *mine* to her. She nodded and willed her tears away. The last thing she wanted was to lose sight of Gerrick's gorgeous face.

The warmth in her chest quickly became an inferno as her new soul settled into place. Immediately, she felt echoes of Gerrick and knew that she still carried a piece of him. In fact, their souls were so intertwined that she couldn't tell where he ended and she began. Whether the Goddess designed matings this way or in answer to her prayer, Shae didn't care. She was simply grateful beyond measure.

Her eyes widened and her nerves tingled as she realized she was aware of what Gerrick was feeling. And, what he was feeling wasn't appropriate for mixed company, but when they were alone...she didn't plan to let him leave the room for at least a month.

A feeling of tranquility passed over her right before ancient power suffused the air. The entire gathering glanced around expectantly. A second later she heard a delicate feminine laugh just before a musical voice whispered in her head. *"No power, not even death, can sever this bond. You have lived two lifetimes and managed to find your mate both times. You are a strong one, Shae, one of my most beloved subjects. Mating stones protect and bless different aspects for different couples. Yours blesses and protects your Gerrick. You will never live without one another again."*

She raised one of her fingers and looked into their palms. She gasped and lifted her palm. The ordinary, granite rock was now the biggest, most alluring, aquamarine she had ever seen. And, the best part was that it matched her sorcerer's eyes.

She glanced up and bright, ice-blue eyes captivated her. Shae blinked and in the next instant the ancient power in the room dissipated. Her fierce warrior pulled her close to the line of his body. She'd been aching for him all day and now her need for him was excruciating.

GERRICK FINALLY RELEASED the breath he'd been holding and let go of some of the anxiety he'd been carrying around for the past week. He hadn't slept, had hardly eaten anything and hadn't left Shae's side since he'd time-traced and saved her life.

So far the Goddess hadn't called in her due for using his power. It always carried a high price and he was afraid that Shae would be taken from him at any moment. He'd spent hours in prayer, pleading that she be spared any more pain or suffering.

He'd felt the Goddess' power a few minutes ago and had reacted on instinct, pulling Shae into his body. He had no idea what the Goddess had done, but she was gone now.

He gentled the hold he had around Shae and glanced

around the room. Their family and friends were clapping and shouting their congratulations and Shae was staring at their mating stone. He never expected to be blessed with this experience after he'd lost Evanna and now he had so much more than he could possibly imagine.

Gripping Shae's chin between his thumb and forefinger, he tilted her head back and claimed her lips. She always brought him to his knees with her kiss. Her tongue tangled with his in an age-old dance, reflecting what their bodies were straining to achieve.

He placed their mating stone in his pocket and placed his hands on her shoulders. Breaking the kiss, he turned her and presented her to the group of family and friends waiting to congratulate them.

He found himself enveloped in her Nana's warm embrace. "Welcome to the family, Gerrick. Treat our Shae right or her Papa will beat you senseless."

He couldn't help but smile at the threat from the female. Unlike humans, supernaturals never aged beyond the age of twenty-five so she didn't have grey hair and a wrinkled face. No, only Philomena's eyes carried evidence of her many centuries.

"I wouldn't dream of it...Nana."

Nana patted his cheek with a smile. "You're a smart male, Gerrick. Just sayin'."

Gerrick burst into laughter. So that's where Shae got it. He should've known.

Zander cleared his throat and cupped his hands around his mouth to be heard over the noise of the crowd. "There's food, drinks and music in the ballroom for those who are interested."

Elsie approached Zander and tugged on his arm. Gerrick heard her mention not feeling well. Poor female was having a rough pregnancy so far, suffering from morning sickness. Better Zander than him, Gerrick wanted at least a decade with Shae before they had children.

Gerrick ran his finger over the apple of Shae's cheek, watching it flush under his touch. "Are you hungry?"

Her pupils dilated and her eyes glowed green. She licked her slightly parted lips. "Very hungry," she husked, leaning to place a kiss to the pulse thudding at the base of his neck. He turned his head and pressed his lips to her in a brief but passionate kiss that had him panting when he finally broke away.

Glass breaking shattered the moment. Gerrick looked up in time to see Bhric and Kyran bolt into action, leading guests away from the patio. Skirm and lesser demons were pouring through the broken windows. How the hell had they gotten on the property? The area should be sealed against any intruders. He and Jace had cast countless spells with the addition of the Rowan sisters' power.

Was this the Goddess' way of making him pay for saving Shae? As long as Shae wasn't injured, he'd take it as fair punishment.

"Go with them," Gerrick ordered, motioning to the retreating guests. He didn't want her anywhere near this trouble.

"I can't leave you. Besides, this could be a diversion. The real attack could be taking place in the ball room like before."

"Shite," Zander barked next to them. "Bhric, Kyran, and Mack stay with the guests and take Evzen and Hayden with you for extra protection. Orlando, you stay next to my mate and doona let her oot of your sight. Shift if you must, but protect her with your life." Orlando shifted in a burst of white light and took on his massive snow leopard form, standing guard over Elsie.

Elsie gasped and placed her hands over her mouth. "My sickness has been premonitions all along. I thought it was morning sickness." Hell of a time to lose the ability to see details of the future, Gerrick thought.

He couldn't think about it anymore as *sgian dubhs* were out and every Dark Warrior in attendance was in motion a second later. The new recruits, as well as, several other supernaturals also sprang into action.

Gerrick had dusted several skirm and was fighting off a hellhound when the air next to Orlando and Elsie shimmered with the black light he associated with Kadir's Dark magic. Before he could shout a warning, Kadir had appeared and thrust a sword through Orlando's feline chest. The male let out an awful roar of agony before he collapsed to the ground.

In a flash of movement, Kadir had his fully healed arm wrapped around Elsie's stomach while he held a knife to her throat. Gerrick stopped in his tracks as he realized Kadir's knife-sized claws were poised right over her pregnant belly. Zander lunged for the pair, only to be brought up short. "You don't want to do that, Vampire King. You have something I want and your little mate and unborn child will be dead before I take my next breath unless you give it to me. And, if you try to use the amulet to kill me, I will take them to hell with me."

Zander kept eye contact with Elsie, who was remarkably calm. "What do you want?"

Kadir tsked Zander. "Your mate cannot sift out of my hold so don't waste anymore of my time." Gerrick cursed and drove his knife into the skull of the hellhound wrapped around his leg. This demon was far stronger than they had anticipated. Not only was he fully healed in only a week, he'd figured a way around their protections and knew about Elsie's pregnancy.

Zander looked down at the amulet he had clutched in his hand. Gerrick saw the battle cross Zander's features and understood the dilemma he currently faced. Gerrick wouldn't blame him for giving over the amulet, no one would. Your mate and child were far more important than an amulet.

Zander nodded at Elsie a second before he tossed the necklace into the air yelling, "Catch." Kadir was forced to release Elsie who sifted to safety on the other side of the room.

Kadir laughed, swiping the platinum charm out of the air. The Triskele Amulet had Celtic knots around the outer circle and a spiral triquetra and bloodstone in the center. It represented the Goddess and had given the Tehrex Realm a way of communicating with her. It was vital to all their rituals and had the ability to destroy a demon's soul, but it paled in comparison to the value of Elsie and her baby. Gerrick only wished Zander had had a chance to use it against Kadir.

"I'll see you soon and I'm bringing hell with me," Kadir taunted then disappeared.

Gerrick looked back to see Shae kill a skirm. Her beautiful dress had a rip in the side and was covered in ash and demon blood, but she looked unharmed. It was too much to hope that the skirm and lesser demons would go with Kadir.

Several staff and guests were huddled by the side of the room where Mack fought to protect them. Gerrick and Shae made their way to Mack's side. He had no doubt it was his fault the amulet was stolen, and knew it was the cost of him saving Shae, but even knowing this outcome, he wouldn't have changed his decision.

"Cover me," Mack suddenly called out as she dashed to a small round ball that was sitting under a window. Gerrick had no idea what it was. It was black metal and about the size of a small orange.

A skirm stumbled into his line of sight and Gerrick smiled broadly, plunging his blade into the skirm's heart, turning it to ash. When the dust settled, Gerrick watched as Mack ran her finger over the ball.

Suddenly, magic filled the room and the skirm and lesser demons were being sucked into the metal ball Mack was holding. Gerrick gaped when the last enemy disappeared into the black light that emanated from the object. Gerrick felt the reinstatement of their spells and breathed a sigh of relief. Somehow that object was responsible for allowing the demons onto their property. The question was how did it get into this room and who activated it.

"What the fuck?" Kyran barked, grabbing onto his mate's arms.

"It's okay. I'm okay. I saw this and thought it was a bomb, but felt the magic when I picked it up. I followed my instinct, focusing on the intent to save everyone. That's twice, ya know. I'm like a superhero, or something. All I need is a cape," she joked.

Kyran crushed her to his chest. "Damn, female, you never learn. Doona pick up what you think is a bomb. You could have been killed," Kyran chastised.

Gerrick glanced around the room. Jace was busy tending Orlando as Zander and Elsie hovered beside them. Gerrick turned at the sound of whispering behind him. Sheila, one of the household staff was sitting in a ball, rocking back and forth muttering to herself. Gerrick crossed to her. "It's okay.

They're gone and the protections are back in place. They can't get back in." Well, he hoped not.

"He told me he could bring her back, but he lied. I did what he asked, but he didn't give her back to me."

Gerrick laid a hand on her shoulder, making her pause in her motion. "What do you mean, Sheila? Who promised you what and what did he ask you to do?"

Tears filled eyes looked up at Gerrick. "Kadir. He approached me at the market and told me he could bring Shannon back to me and all he needed was for me to put that ball thing in the room during your mating ceremony." She sat up suddenly, clutching Gerrick's arm. "I had no idea it allowed him to come in here. Please, you have to believe me when I say that I didn't know. I just wanted Shannon back. She's my twin and I don't think I can live without her."

Sheila burst into tears and Shae gathered her into her arms. Gerrick sat back on his heels stunned. He understood profound loss and the pain that came with it. It was difficult to fault Sheila for grabbing that option. Hell, Gerrick would have done anything to get Shae back. Still, Sheila's decision had cost them the amulet.

"Every choice we make has a consequence and we must live with the results. The people most eager to influence what choice you make are usually the ones least likely to be around in the end. You made a deal with the devil and where is he now? He has left you to deal with the fallout," Gerrick told the female.

Gerrick looked up and noticed Zander and the rest of the Dark Warriors had been listening to them. The look on Zander's face told him that Sheila's life was forfeit. He wanted to defend and protect her, but he meant what he said. She had to accept the consequences, just like he did.

"Put her in the dungeons. I'll deal with her later. We

have bigger issues at the moment. This is no' how I saw this night going," Zander exclaimed, drawing Elsie into his side.

Rhys walked up and handed a drink to Bhric, taking a sip of his own. "I guess that means our next trip is going to be to hell and not Tahiti," Rhys sighed. "I could have lived my entire life without visiting dear-old-dad again." Gerrick knew there was bad blood between him and his father, but he had no idea what had happened between the two. Rhys had been preoccupied and acting different for a couple weeks, but this situation made his attitude even worse.

"Let's take this to the war room. We need to assume that by now Lucifer has been set free. The plan now is no' only to get the amulet back, but more importantly, to stop Armageddon. If Lucifer is allowed to bring his demon horde to earth, all life will cease to exist."

Gerrick wrapped his arm around Shae who was shaken from the experience. He placed their mating stone in her palm as a silent reminder. Gerrick knew what lay ahead of them wasn't going to be easy and he wasn't sure of the outcome, but he was taking this moment with her. He had his Fated Mate and she was alive and well.

They followed everyone to the war room, but Gerrick's mind wasn't on the conversation around him. The night wasn't going to end like this for him and Shae. He was going to take her upstairs, make love to her and have the blood exchange to complete their mating. The rest was going to have to wait.

"Thank you for saving me...again. I love you, Gerrick, with my whole heart." He looked into jade green eyes that shone with the depth of her feelings.

"I'll always save you, Red. Just sayin'."

EPILOGUE

Rhys needed a drink, or ten. What had started as a promising day had turned into his worst night-mare. Demons and skirm had once again turned one of their own against them and that had to chap Zander's ass. The male had been betrayed twice now by one of his subjects. At least Sheila wasn't a former lover like Lena had been.

Rhys had planned on bedding one, maybe two, females after the mating celebration in hopes of banishing the angels from his mind. They hadn't appeared again, but their visits had haunted him, making it difficult to get the sexual relief he needed. He couldn't rid thoughts of Illianna or why her brothers were so adamant that he was connected to this angel. Truth be told, he was more connected to the demons he despised rather than a bunch of holy creatures.

And, fuck if he didn't loathe the demons that had ruined his best friend's mating ceremony. He felt terrible for Gerrick. The poor male led his Fated Mate into what was supposed to be their Eve of Eternal Union and it had been marred by that asshole, Kadir. Of all of them, Rhys thought, Gerrick deserved to have love and happiness. But, there was no rest for the wicked this night. There was an incursion into the Hell Realm to plan and Rhys knew what that meant for him. Lemuel. Yup, alcohol was in order.

The large conference room had a well-stocked bar in one corner and a bank of computers along the back wall. He headed straight for the bar and grabbed a bottle of scotch. He grabbed a tumbler and took a seat at the large wood as the Dark Warriors and council members piled into the room.

"Alright, what do we know aboot Hell? How do we even get there? And, do we have to use the Cave of Cruachan or can we open a portal directly to the inner circle of hell?" Zander asked as he took a seat at the head of the table.

Rhys took a deep gulp of his scotch and turned to Zander. "No, Liege, we don't open a portal directly into one of the circles. There is only one way into hell and it's through the entrance. We have to travel through each of the outer circles to reach Lucifer."

"Shite, there's really no way to portal directly to Lake Crocytus?" Zander asked.

The talk about that infernal place pulled Rhys into memories he would rather never think about. Rhys refused to recall his last time in hell and focused on the reality of their situation. "No, and it wouldn't be wise even if we could. For one, Lucifer surrounds himself by a hundred thousand Behemoth demons like Kadir, as well as, having untold powers in his home realm. He has a court there where they entertain him by torturing souls in ways you can't begin to imagine. But, the point is moot since we can't open a portal directly into any of the nine circles."

"We use the cave then," Zander said. "I suspect it's not going to be as easy as sending a thousand warriors through to track down Kadir."

Evzen cleared his throat and lifted his head from the Mystik Grimoire. "I'm afraid it's far more complicated than that. When we are able to locate the Cave of Cruachan, according to the Grimoire, we can only send those who carry the blood of a demon. Oh, and the Gates of Hell are guarded by Cerberus, the three-headed hellhound. It says here that he's the size of a small skyscraper and his main role is to keep the dead from leaving, but also to keep creatures of the Gods and Goddesses out."

"Shite," Zander cursed. "Dante, select a handful of your best men. If I can't send a strike force, I'll send operatives they will never suspect. Choose individuals who know at least some of the realms they will be asked to traverse. Does the Grimoire tell us anything aboot what they will encounter?"

Rhys' blood iced over because he was going to have to go back to a place he swore he would never return to. It was too dangerous to send individuals who had no experience with at least some of the trials of Hell.

Evzen flipped through several pages before shaking his head. "It doesn't tell us much. Just that each circle has its own way of punishing you. One passage indicates you will not only face the lesser demons, but also inner ones, as well."

They could send the entire population of the Tehrex Realm and it wouldn't matter if they couldn't survive the inner battles that would occur. Rhys listened to them discuss how to select the task force for several minutes before he spoke up. "It's not the number we send that will matter. It's their integrity and perseverance that count. They will face unspeakable obstacles. We need a spell, or a plan, on how we are going to either re-imprison Lucifer, or restrict his movement, or the whole mission is for naught."

Dante sat down next to Rhys and grabbed the bottle of Scotch from him. "Rhys is right. I've heard stories about there being a way to close portal access between Hell and earth, as well as, tying Lucifer to the realm. The way I remember it, if we are able to cast the spell and he leaves Hell then he loses all of his power."

Rhys tossed back a swallow of the alcohol, enjoying the burn. "I've heard about that, too. Perhaps there is something in the Mystik Grimoire about these spells. We don't want Lucifer free to roam this world at full power. He will make Kadir look like a toddler throwing a tantrum."

"Fuck," Zander cursed. "How was Lucifer imprisoned in the first place? Was it really by an angry God that he committed treachery against?"

Dante took a drink and sat back in his chair. For all appearances, he was the picture of ease and nonchalance, but Rhys saw the tension bracketing his mouth. Rhys wondered if he was in need of sex, or if he, too, had spent time in Hell. It was dangerous territory if a cambion was in desperate need of sex. "Yes. The lore handed down indicates that it was indeed a God and that the lake is made up of Lucifer's tears over his treachery and imprisonment and it's kept frozen by the beating of his wings. It's all part of the curse of the God. Our best bet is to do as Rhys suggested and find a way to restrict him to hell. That's not to say he won't still be able to wreak havoc on earth, but it will be secondhand through his weaker minions."

"This is a bluidy fucking mess," Zander cursed, running his hand over Elsie's shoulders. The Queen was visibly shaken, but it seemed her illness had passed. Rhys guessed she was right about the cause of her sickness being the premonitions and not her pregnancy. "I will try to reach the Goddess, but withoot the amulet, I doubt I will get anywhere. Everyone needs to start combing through every book we have aboot Lucifer and how to contain him."

EXCERPT HELLBOUND WARRIOR, DARK
WARRIOR ALLIANCE BOOK 8

"This is your last chance to back oot," the Vampire King offered Rhys. Rhys was no an idiot and backing out wasn't an option. The Triskele Amulet had been stolen by that piece of shit, Kadir, and Lucifer was on the verge of being released from his frozen prison in the Ninth Circle of Hell. So, unless Rhys wanted his home to be turned into the devil's playground, he was going.

"This is more dangerous than anything you've ever done. Shite, I doona think anyone in the history of the Tehrex Realm has had a more treacherous mission," Zander continued, locking eyes with Rhys. The concern was clear in Zander's blue gaze, but it wasn't because the leader of the Dark Warriors didn't believe in Rhys. It was because he didn't want to lose a member of their family.

The Vampire King had recruited Rhys to join the Dark Warriors a little over a century ago, after Rhys had escaped his father's clutches. Rhys had never wanted to go back to the Underworld where his father had tried to rear him like a proper cambion.

Rhys' father supported the idea of releasing the inner beast, giving it free rein. When Rhys had defied his father, he was cast into the dungeons, forcing his demon to the surface. And, that wasn't the worst part. Instead of throwing willing, or unwilling, females as his victims, his father had thrown males in the dungeon as his bedfellows.

Many cambions enjoyed sex with both species, but Rhys wasn't sexually attracted to men. It disgusted him to have sex with the males, but he had to do what was necessary. Otherwise, his rational mind would've been lost to him forever. Ultimately, he had forced himself on the males countless times and the memories still had bile rising in his throat.

Eventually, he had escaped, leaving that world behind, but he loathed his father and didn't know what might happen if he saw him again. He could only hope to slip through his father's realm and avoid that confrontation.

Shoving those darkest memories back into his steel-lined box, Rhys wondered what Zander had seen in him all those years ago to give him a place in his most trusted circle. When they first met, Rhys was had been a wreck. He had never been at a lower point in his life. Zander was the only being that knew about Rhys' suffering when he had been with dear-old-dad and still the male had believed in him. No way was he going to fail when so much was riding on his success.

Rhys found a home and family within Zeum's walls and would do anything to protect those he loved, even if it meant returning to the one place he swore to never go again. Rhys was a Dark Warrior now, not a low-life demon and his fellow warriors and their mates accepted Rhys for who and that meant more to him than anything.

Rhys rubbed his chin and let his breath out in a long hiss before responding, "Fuck no, I'm not sure, but I'm the only one who can go." He wished they could send a legion of warriors on the mission, it would certainly make Rhys feel better about their chances, but the fact was that only those with demon blood could pass through the veil.

"I would never send Dante alone. After the Rowan sisters locate the cave, we need to find out if there is another warrior in the area that would be willing to go, as well. Preferably a female that can keep our demons fed," Rhys finished. Rhys liked Dante, but he had no desire to have sex with the Lord of all cambions. The thought alone had the locks on his steel-lined box rattling in the back of his mind.

He supposed he could go to some of the females he had spent time with when he lived there in order to feed his demon. Surely, there were still some that held enough affection for him to keep his presence secret from his father. He couldn't go without sex for long so when they passed through his father's territory, this would become a much bigger issue. Without sex to calm and placate his inner beast, their mission would become secondary to seeking sexual gratification. His stomach turned. He hated the lengths to which his inner beast would go in order to have his carnal needs met.

Zander ran a hand through his shoulder-length black hair. "Shite, I hadna thought of your demon's needs. That complicates matters. I still think we need to send every cambion warrior who's ever been to Hell. Three seems like an insignificant number when faced with the multitudes you will encounter." Zander was wearing a path in the rug with his pacing.

The Vampire King continued, "You will be on Lucifer's turf, and more than likely he already has the amulet. We should operate under the assumption that he has been freed from Lake Crocytus and is searching for a way to get to earth." Zander's Scottish accent became thicker when he was agitated and right now he was on the brink of violence. His Fated Mate, Elsie, was pregnant, and, if worrying about them wasn't enough, he also had an entire realm relying on him to keep them safe.

Rhys smiled wryly at Zander. He dreaded the idea of doing this without having his closest friends at his back, especially Gerrick. Fuck, the more he considered it, the more he realized that it was going to be odd not having him there now. He and Gerrick had been patrolling and fighting together for nearly a century. He knew what to expect from Gerrick and they fought seamlessly together. Gerrick was newly mated and Rhys could see how mating had softened the male, but he was still the most ruthless warrior ever born.

He scanned the media room and looked at each of the Dark Warriors.

Even if it were possible for them to get through the portal, Rhys wouldn't want any of them to go. They were his only family and he would die to protect them.

"We have no way of knowing where Lucifer currently is, but the last thing we need is to send a bunch of pissed off cambions into Hell. Not only will it do nothing to help us face and pass the trials of each circle, but it will also paint a target on our backs. Traveling in small numbers means that we can slip through virtually unnoticed," Rhys added.

Zander sighed and shook his head. Yeah, Rhys could relate, he was already exhausted and he hadn't even started yet. He was so over the shit with the demons and skirm. They'd been fighting to protect the humans and realm for centuries, but lately it seemed as if things had compounded with them on the losing side of this war.

Ever since Elsie's first husband had been murdered the demons had been taking more and more chances. They had been turning skirm without care, kidnapping human and supernatural females, and bringing lesser demons through the veil to earth in droves.

Never before had the archdemons taken such chances. In the past, they hadn't wanted to add the humans to their list of enemies. The supernatural population was miniscule compared to the human one. The demons couldn't take the risk of the humans hunting and eradicating them. At least, not until Lucifer was able to obliterate the veil and lead his countless hoards through.

It chapped Rhys' ass that Lucifer's efforts had finally paid off, and the archdemons had been able to confiscate the Triskele Amulet. Zander and his family had kept the amulet safe for eons until Kadir's claws had literally been held to Elsie's pregnant belly, threatening the heir to the Vampire throne, and Zander had been forced to give up the amulet to save them both.

Now, it fell to Rhys and Dante to retrieve the necklace before Lucifer put it to use. Nothing like having the fate of the world on your shoulders, Rhys mused, refusing to contemplate their chances of success. The odds were against them, but they had to try. Rhys grabbed his collar and tugged, the pressure of the task at hand suffocating him.

Rolling his shoulders to dissipate some of the tension, he realized he'd been on edge for weeks, and it had only gotten worse. Not only was he facing the impossible, he was unable to stop thinking about the angry angels who'd cornered him weeks before, accusing him of kidnapping their sister.

The idea was fucking ridiculous. Rhys loved females and enjoyed their soft bodies as often as possible, but he'd never resort to holding one captive just to meet his base needs. He wasn't a total bastard. And, it infuriated him that those haughty angels had asserted that she was connected to him.

No, he hadn't been able to get Illianna off his mind. He hadn't ever met the female and her brothers had never described her to him, but in his mind, the image of a tall, voluptuous female with flowing blond hair, gold wings and striking silver eyes haunted him.

His inner beast shifted restlessly, reminding him that it had been two days since he'd had sex. Too much had been going on. Not that that excused his oversight. He knew better than to go so long. If he wasn't with a female soon, he'd become a creature of nightmares, using his ability to create illusion and manipulate minds to lull prey into having sex with him, or worse, he'd rape anyone, or anything.

He would need to feed his beast before he left or there would be nothing he could do to stop his demon nature from taking over when he crossed into Hell. He recalled all too well how much more power his beast had in that realm. Most days he didn't give it a second thought and pursued females and sex freely, but he was about to venture into Hell and would face unending temptation, so it weighed heavily on him.

He had his father to thank for passing on the incubus demon genes that never let him rest. He loved sex and adored females, but Rhys had always been different than most cambions, thanks to his mother's human genes.

A small hand on his forearm brought him out of his thoughts. Shaking himself, he hadn't realized he'd completely checked out of the conversation until Elsie touched him, a sad smile on her lovely face. "Here, take this key...for luck. Something tells me that you're going to need it." He accepted the key and looked down to see he was holding a car key. How was this going to help him?

Suddenly, she hugged him tight, a wet sheen to her eyes. She had hugged him many times before, but this felt very different. It struck him that she believed this was the last time she'd see him. The thought nearly felled him. He liked his life at Zeum, and wasn't ready to give it up.

No words could express how much he hated leaving, knowing he might not return. Choking on emotion, he returned her embrace and fell back on his humor. It was his way of dealing with everything in life. Somehow, everything was better when you were laughing or smiling.

"Thanks, sweetcheeks. I'll be cruising the streets of Dys in style. Now, we need to find a way to get the Jag through the portal," he announced to the room. "There are a few female djinn that I could impress with this ride," he chuckled.

Elsie pulled out of his arms and smacked his shoulder. "This isn't a laughing matter. I *saw* that you will need it."

Everyone in the room snapped to attention. Rhys glanced around and noticed that each of the Dark Warrior's, as well as, their mates and several council members had all frozen at the Vampire Queen's words, concern clear on their faces.

Elsie's premonitions were usually attached to death and destruction. He couldn't recall a premonition of hers that hadn't involved doom and gloom, and suddenly, Rhys wanted to leave the room. He didn't want the details of his demise. It would only make it harder to do what he needed to do.

Before he could tell her to keep the information to herself, Zander interrupted, "What did you see? I canna believe I havena seen anything aboot this. For months now, we've been sharing the visions."

Elsie crossed to her mate and placed her palm on his chest, rubbing circles over his heart. "Relax, I didn't see much and it was so different from other visions I've had. I saw Rhys standing in front of a huge black door and no way to get through. It was nighttime and some creature was screeching in the background and then the key to my car was hovering in the vision and I knew that he needed it."

Rhys rubbed his chin and contemplated what she'd said. He wasn't familiar with a black door in the Underworld, but then he had never traveled to the inner circles of Hell, either. Pocketing the key, he knew better than to question Elsie's logic or premonitions. "Now that that's settled, all that's left is to locate the cave and get that binding spell so we keep Lucifer in his prison world. You ready, witches?" Rhys quipped, turning to the Rowan sisters.

Pema, the oldest of the triplets, smiled widely. He'd shared many passionate nights with the sisters, and had even been disciplined for his time with them. On one particular occasion, he missed several nights of patrolling because the triplets had his undivided attention and Zander had been furious. He had gladly paid the price of a month in the dungeons for the pleasure they'd brought him. They were fantastic females and his demon had enjoyed their company. It was too bad that they were all mated now, because he could take one, or all, of them to his room and feed.

The Rowan sisters hadn't been immune to the changes that had been sweeping through the Tehrex Realm the past year. If anything, they'd been through the most drastic changes. At only twenty-eight years old, they were newly mated and had recently been crowned the High Priestesses, overseeing all witches.

"We're ready to begin. I think it's best if you remain in the far corner, Elsie. We have no idea what accessing this kind of power will unleash or tap into and we don't want to risk the baby. And, we need the sofas moved out of the way, please" Pema began, motioning across the room.

The instant Pema mentioned a possible risk to the baby, Zander quickly grasped his mate's arm, pulling her out of range. Elsie objected as Zander led her to the far corner and took a stance in front of her while Gerrick and Jace moved one sofa and Bhric and Kyran moved another.

Rhys loved the feisty vampire queen. She'd been the best thing to happen to the compound. And, it was obvious how much she meant to every Dark Warrior as they all crossed to Rhys' side. Together, they created a layered barrier of flesh between the witches and Elsie and Zander. No one would take any risks with the female or the miracle she carried.

"Oh, for Christ's sake. Get out of the way, you guys. I highly doubt anything will happen to me all the way over here with Zander in front of me. I want to see what's going on," the queen demanded, trying to look around walls of muscle.

"'Tis no' happening, *a ghra*. No one's moving. You're lucky I doona drag you oot of the room altogether," Zander countered, no compromise in his tone.

"I see Mr. Bossy Pants is back. Good thing supernatural

pregnancies are faster, otherwise, this could become a prob-lem," Elsie teased, standing on her tiptoes and placing a gentle kiss to his lips. Rhys noticed the way some of the tension left Zander's shoulders. This was how it was between Fated Mates, a profound connection that inflamed and centered all at once.

"Place your candles to north and east, Suvi, and put yours to the south and west, Isis," Pema instructed, ignoring the byplay between the King and Queen and focusing on their task.

While her sisters did as instructed, Pema placed a large, silver bowl of water on the coffee table that acted as their makeshift altar. The room went completely silent as the witches quickly set the stage for their spell.

"You guys doing this sky-clad?" Rhys asked on a chuckle.

"Fucking Rhys," the room erupted collectively.

"What?" Everyone was always saying that and he didn't understand why. He was only asking if they were going to perform their ceremony accessing the most power possible. Not to mention, he had no problem seeing three beautiful females naked.

Shaking their heads, the witches proceeded to pull incense from their bag. Rhys detected hints of lotus, jasmine and hyacinth. Thinking back, he thought his mother had told him the flowers were connected to water, which was the one medium that was used in location spells.

For the first time since the attack during Gerrick's mating ceremony, hope surged through him. This could work. His anticipation rose as the sisters joined hands and their mates placed their hands on their shoulders. He could feel the energy from their collective magic fill the room. Their power staggered him, making him grateful the sisters were on the side of the Goddess. The power those females wielded would be a devastating weapon in evil's hands.

"*Doiteain*," they chanted together. The candles and incense ignited and the witches knelt before the altar. Suvi and Isis grabbed Pema's waist as she reached into the bowl of water and invoked the element of water.

Relaxing into a meditative state, Pema plunged two fingers into the water and swirled in a clockwise motion. Repeating this four times, the sisters began chanting in unison, "Let the water reveal to me the location of the Cave of Cruachan. Let the water show me where it is. So mote it be."

On completion of the fourth time, the lights in the room flickered and the water clouded over then cleared to reveal a small cement tunnel in a creepy-looking forest. The cement had brightly-painted graffiti and the trees and groundcover were barren. Rhys had seen some evil shit in his life, and the vision of the tunnel screamed sinister to him. He shuddered as a dark sense of foreboding filled the room. The image disappeared and the word Sensabaugh took its place.

The triplets raised their heads and Rhys saw the confusion and unease that he was feeling reflected on their expressions. They swiped their hands over the water and it returned to the placid clear liquid it had been. Thankfully, the malignant atmosphere disappeared alongside it.

At that moment, Rhys' stomach dropped to his feet, his previous hope diminishing. They had a location, all that was left was a spell to trap Lucifer and he was going to have to leave for wherever Sensabaugh was.

"Thank you for getting the location. I know that was taxing, but we have more work to do and doona have time to waste. This has suddenly become verra fucking real. Every second Lucifer has the Goddess' necklace is one too many.

Cade, look up Sensabaugh and get the information we need while the Rowans set up for the binding spell," Zander ordered, wrapping Elsie in his arms as she eased her way from behind him.

The sound of typing echoed as the witches cleared the altar and set up for the next step. The energy in the room was even grimmer, making his heart and mind race, trying to remember everything he'd forced out over a hundred years before. He needed to recall every detail he could about the Nine Circles of Hell.

It was ironic that the worst moments of his life now held the key to saving the world.

"The portal to the Cave of Cruachan is in Tennessee," Cade called out as he eyed the laptop in front of him. Rhys had come to appreciate having Cade and his twin, Caell, around.

The two vampires had been transferred from New Orleans to Seattle recently. With all the new matings in the compound and the fact that Seattle had been targeted heavily by the archdemons, they had needed the extra help, and the new Dark Warriors had proven to be invaluable.

What was in Tennessee that attracted such evil energy to the area, Rhys wondered. Whatever was there, Rhys could guarantee that it had to be a vile place for the portal to choose the site.

"The lore behind the place is horrendous. Rumor has it that it's been the sight of grisly murders, deaths and satanic rituals. And, get this, demonic apparitions have been sighted in and around the tunnel," Cade continued as he leaned back in his chair.

Pema sat forward and placed a black candle where the bowl had been. Suvi held two vials and Isis had a rope in her hand. "Turn off the lights, please. Breslin, can you light the candles in the room? And, be prepared to extinguish them when I signal you." Pema asked. The Vampire Princess had the ability to control fire and her twin brother, Bhric, manipulated water.

In an instant, the lights were out and the candles were flickering. Isis placed the rope behind the lit candle while Suvi poured the contents of both vials into Pema's outstretched hands. Rhys noticed that one of the vials held water and the other dirt. Pema mixed the contents of her palm together with her free fingers and then held it before the candle. She closed her eyes before pulling in a breath and blowing the combined mixture through the flame, extinguishing it. There had to be an element of magic used to propel the mud that far.

The mud flew onto candle and rope as Pema and her sisters chanted, "*Per elementum ego tardus vos.*"

Suvi picked up a flashlight and turned it on, pointing it at the rope and then the trio continued their chant, "*Per lux lucis ego caecus vos.*"

The light went out and Pema called out, "Now Breslin." And with those words, the room plunged into darkness. Rhys' eyes quickly adjusted and he noticed that Pema was tying a small piece of twine to the rope and then the chanting resumed. "*Per obscurum ego redimio vos.*"

"It's done," Pema announced and the lights came back on. "Cover the rope in the soil of Hell as soon as you cross into the realm and then all you need to do is make this rope touch Lucifer and say the word, *ceangailteach*. That should keep him bound to Hell. Of course, we can't guarantee anything. Usually the spell we just performed is done with a personal belonging or a photograph, but since that isn't possible, we spelled the rope to act as a conduit for the magic."

"This is the one time I can tell you to go to Hell and you have to do it," Dante teased Rhys. The Cambion Lord's nervousness was obvious.

Rhys chuckled, "Grab your gasoline underwear, bro. You're riding shotgun."

AUTHOR'S NOTE

Authors' Note

With new digital download trends, authors rely on readers to spread the word more than ever. Here are some ways to help us.

Leave a review! Every author asks their readers to take five minutes and let others know how much you enjoyed their work. Here's the reason why. Reviews help your favorite authors to become visible. It's simple and easy to do. If you are a Kindle user turn to the last page and leave a review before you close your book. For other retailers, just visit their online site and leave a brief review.

Don't forget to visit our website: www.trimandjulka.com and sign up for our newsletter, which is jam-packed with exciting news and monthly giveaways. Also, be sure to visit and like our Facebook page https://www.facebook.com/TrimAndJulka to see our daily themes, including hot guys, drink recipes and book teasers.

Trust your journey and remember that the future is yours and it's filled with endless possibilities!

DREAM BIG!
XOXO,
Brenda & Tami

OTHER WORKS BY TRIM AND JULKA

The Dark Warrior Alliance

Dream Warrior (Dark Warrior Alliance, Book One)

Mystik Warrior (Dark Warrior Alliance, Book Two)

Pema's Storm (Dark Warrior Alliance, Book Three)

Deviant Warrior (Dark Warrior Alliance, Book Four)

Isis' Betrayal (Dark Warrior Alliance, Book Five)

Suvi's Revenge (Dark Warrior Alliance, Book Six)

Mistletoe & Mayhem (Dark Warrior Alliance, Book 6.5)

Scarred Warrior (Dark Warrior Alliance, Book Seven)

Heat in the Bayou (Dark Warrior Alliance, Novella, Book 7.5)

Hellbound Warrior (Dark Warrior Alliance, Book Eight)

Isobel (Dark Warrior Alliance, Book Nine)

Rogue Warrior (Dark Warrior Alliance, Book Ten)

Tinsel & Temptation (Dark Warrior Alliance, Book 10.5)

Shattered Warrior (Dark Warrior Alliance, Book Eleven)

King of Khoth (Dark Warrior Alliance, Book Twelve)

The Rowan Sisters' Trilogy

<u>The Rowan Sisters' Trilogy Boxset (Books 1-3)</u>

NEWSLETTER SIGN UP

Don't miss out!
Click the button below and you can sign up to receive
emails from Trim and Julka about new releases, fantastic
giveaways, and their latest hand made jewelry. There's no
charge and no obligation.

Printed in Great Britain
by Amazon